MARIGOLD AND THE *Marquess*

MEARA PLATT

CHAPTER 1

Chipping Way, London
April 1825

LEONIDES POOLE, MARQUESS of Muir, had been warned about moving onto Chipping Way, one of the loveliest streets in Mayfair, for it had become known as a parson's trap for the unwary bachelor. He had dismissed the notion as preposterous until this very moment when a breathless and utterly stunning young lady ran into the garden of his townhouse at Number 2 Chipping Way on what was a crisp and pleasant spring day.

He watched from his study window as the little whirlwind in blue muslin lunged and leaped amid his shrubbery attempting to catch a swiftly moving...was that a skull she was chasing? "Sterling, who is that odd young lady?"

His usually staid butler peered out the window and immediately chuckled. "That would be Miss Marigold Farthingale, my lord. I believe her father is cousin to your neighbor at Number 3, Mr. John Farthingale. He and his wife are sponsoring her come-out."

"Well, she is certainly *out there*, isn't she? What in heaven's name is she doing?"

A twinkle sprang into his stoic butler's eyes. "I have no idea. Shall I assist her?"

"No, I'll go to her." Leo buttoned his waistcoat in order to make himself moderately presentable, and then walked out of his study. He had purchased the townhouse only a month ago and the house was still sparsely furnished, although the rooms he had attended to were handsomely decorated, but not overly elegant since he had no wish to live in a museum.

A man ought to be comfortable in his own home.

Was he not desperate for that elusive comfort?

There were no dark curtains shutting off light to his rooms and no windowless rooms to remind him of a prison cell.

He strode through his parlor and out the matching glass doors leading onto his terrace, scanning the professionally landscaped garden in search of Miss Farthingale. A moment's disappointment washed over him when he did not see her, nor did he catch sight of her when he stepped onto the grass and began to peer through the flower beds.

Had she run back home?

Suddenly, the skull tore past him.

Chasing after it was the angel in blue who was so intent on her mission, she did not watch where she was going and ran straight into him. "*Oof!* Goodness, where did you come from? I did not see you there."

How could she miss him? He was built like a block of stone.

Blue eyes the color of a tropical sea and framed by velvet-black lashes stared up at Leo as he wrapped his arms around her to keep her from losing her balance and tumbling into one of the thornier flower beds. "What are you—"

"I shall explain later," she said, pushing out of his grasp and now attempting to dive into a nearby patch of rhododendron.

"Oh, no, you don't. You'll tell me now." He caught her by the waist before she disappeared within the greenery, turning her to face him.

He now managed a good look at the girl.

Blessed saints.

He suddenly forgot to breathe.

Gad, she was exquisite.

Not a sophisticated, *ton* beauty at all, but beautiful in an ethereal, faeries-dancing-amid-the-bluebells way.

He smothered the urge to grin, for her features could only be described as part angel and part imp.

Mostly imp because of her big eyes and slightly pointy ears.

"Who are you, and why is your skull running circles around my garden?" In his entire life, Leo did not think to ever ask anyone this question. It was absurd but also wonderful because he was in desperate need of just this ridiculous intrusion in his life to make him feel alive again.

"Sir, I do apologize," she said, with a lick of her cherry lips, the gesture immediately putting his heart in palpitations. A light breeze blew a few dark curls across her brow, but she merely shook them off while he still held her. "I am your neighbor at Number 3, Miss Marigold Farthingale. A pleasure to meet you...er, may we dispense with the introductions for the moment? Please let me go. I must stop Mallow before he buries my treasure."

"Treasure?" Since when were skulls prized as such by anyone other than ghouls who crept into cemeteries at night to steal them?

The skull darted out of the rhododendron and leaped into his forsythia.

The lovely Miss Farthingale moaned, squirmed out of his grasp again, and was about to plunge head first into the forsythia when he stopped her by wrapping an arm around her waist and drawing her solidly up against him. "I forbid you to destroy my flower beds."

She turned to face him, frowning up at him. "Sir, I shall never catch him if you insist on holding me back."

He was no coxcomb, but women usually enjoyed being in his arms. This young woman was paying absolutely no attention to this fact, nor did she seem to care he was a marquess. Instead, she cast him a look of irritation before peering over his shoulder to shout at the now barking skull. "Bad dog! Oh, you are a very bad dog, Mallow!"

Leo sighed and waited for her dog – a little fellow who could be no bigger than the size of a squirrel – to dart past them again. "Mallow, sit!" he commanded in his most authoritative voice.

The skull immediately came to a halt on the grass beside them.

"Well done," Marigold said, now casting him the softest smile before kneeling beside this *thing* that appeared to be a head but not of any creature Leo recognized. She popped it off Mallow and then sank down on the lawn and tucked her legs beneath her shapely bottom.

She took both her dog and that bizarre oddity onto her lap.

Mallow turned out to be a little spaniel with a big attitude.

He growled as Leo knelt beside him and his mistress.

Leo shot him a look of caution to establish that he was the dominant male in this relation. Fortunately, the dog quickly acquiesced. "We shall become good friends, you little knave," he said, giving Mallow a gentle rub to his belly before turning his attention to the exquisite girl. "Would you mind explaining what that was all about?"

She graced him with another soft smile. "Have you heard of the Huntsford Academy?"

"Yes, Huntsford is a friend of mine."

"His wife, Duchess Adela, is a very good friend of mine, and this is one of the relics from her Devonshire dig. I helped unearth it. In fact, I just returned from there this morning with a crateful of bones I must deliver to the academy as soon as my aunt and uncle return from visiting their daughter, Dillie. Thursdays are her 'at home' days. Well, she is Duchess Dillie, the Duke of Edgeware's wife. Do you know them?"

He nodded. "Edgeware and I are quite well acquainted."

"Is it not odd?" She absently petted Mallow who was now licking himself obscenely while sprawled on her lap.

Leo stifled a grin. "What do you mean?"

The sun shone down upon both of them and a light breeze carried the scent of lilac in the air. The girl cast him another smile, and he realized this was her naturally cheerful repose when she was not chattering or thinking of pressing thoughts.

It did not surprise him that Marigold was a happy soul. Yet, she did not appear to be the empty-headed sort to prattle incessantly.

That was a point in her favor.

Leo could not abide people who would not stop talking simply because they liked to hear the sound of their voice. Hers was quite pleasant, not that it should matter to him.

So was the lovely shape of her lips, not that this should matter, either.

Mallow paused in his preening to growl at him again.

Oh, that little hound knew what he was thinking.

Marigold was obviously too innocent to understand the surprising need she stirred in him, and had not a clue how tempting she looked.

Her hair was dark, the color of black satin.

And those eyes, that deep azure of the sea.

She smiled up at him yet again. "We know several people in common but have never met each other until this very moment. Do you not find it curious?"

"No, I have not been in London for a while."

"Are you back now to stay? Since you mentioned this was your home, I assume you are the Marquess of Muir, Leonides Poole."

He nodded. "That I am."

"A pleasure to meet you, Lord Muir. Forgive my intrusion."

"No harm done." It was early afternoon and Leo was ready to take a break from his work, anyway. "Would you care to join me? I was about to have refreshments on the terrace."

"I should like that very much, but I had better not. I hope you will invite me again soon, however."

"Yes, I will." One in his position could not afford to let a ray of sunshine like Marigold slip away.

She glanced at Mallow. "He is restless and will not behave for long. He can be a very naughty fellow, at times."

Leo smothered another grin, for so could he be naughty.

Men were men, no matter what breed, and this girl was lovely.

He would never misbehave with Marigold, of course.

The girl was luscious, but far too innocent.

He lifted the skull from her lap and reached out a hand. "Let me help you up, Miss Farthingale."

She plunked Mallow in his outstretched hand instead and gracefully rose on her own.

"Behave," she warned the tiny spaniel when he barked as she

took him back in her arms. She was trying to come across as stern, but her voice was too soft and lilting to scare that impudent beast.

Since she had her hands full with the squirming spaniel, Leo offered to carry the skull for her as he escorted her across the street. "You are frowning, Miss Farthingale."

She shook her satin mane of hair. "The hour is growing late and I must get that crate of bones to the Huntsford Academy before it closes. But Aunt Sophie and Uncle John are not back yet. Well, they are not truly my aunt and uncle but it seems quite cumbersome to constantly refer to John as my first cousin once removed. He and my father are cousins."

He merely nodded, for Sterling had confirmed this to him earlier. "I can take you to Huntsford's museum. Most of my work is done for the day and it will do me good to get out. Bring your maid along for the sake of propriety."

Her eyes sparkled as they widened in surprise. "Are you certain you do not mind?"

"It will be my pleasure." He opened the gate to the Farthingale townhouse and escorted her up the walk. "Give me a few minutes to have my carriage readied and I'll come by to collect you shortly."

She cast him a radiant smile. "I shall be waiting with the crate, but without Mallow. He may be little, but he can cause big mischief. It would not do to bring him with us only to have him chew the prized exhibits. However, I had better ask my cousin Violet to join us. She is more appropriate a chaperone than my maid. She and her husband reside at Number 1 Chipping Way. Do you know Captain Brayden?"

"Yes, Romulus? I also know his brother, James, Earl of Exmoor."

She shook her head. "You really know everyone, don't you?"

He shrugged. "Our elite circles are small. We go to the same schools, fight the same wars, belong to the same clubs, go to the same parties. I've been away from England for a while and haven't seen any of them in several years."

"And now you are rekindling your acquaintances?"

"You might say that."

"Then shall I see you at the round of balls, soirees, and teas? This is my first year on the marriage mart, however I have been in London for quite a few months now…well, traveling back and forth to Devonshire and those ancient caves. Thank goodness for my friends and family. I would otherwise find this matchmaking marketplace quite daunting."

"You won't be in it for long, I'm sure. Some gentleman will come along and quickly claim you."

She laughed. "I hope not. I am in no hurry to wed. Eighteen years is a little too young to be married, don't you think? Twenty is a much better age. I wish I were twenty, already. Most of my friends are, but they think of me as a child and do not take me very seriously."

"Because you are charmingly innocent and obviously have little experience in the world. That is a good thing. The world can be harsh."

He had walked her to the door and now waited for Pruitt, the Farthingale butler, to open it and allow her in before he left Marigold's side to call for his carriage.

"My time in the Devonshire caves with the duke and duchess, and the Huntsford archeological staff was a marvelous experience. But you are right. Other than that, I've done nothing of note."

"I was not criticizing your inexperience, Miss Farthingale. All I meant is that you have time to achieve your dreams. There is no need for you to rush through life." He caressed her cheek, annoyed with himself for doing so. But she was such a bright, little thing and he had been in a dark pit far too long.

A literal dark pit, imprisoned overseas as he was for years until the Crown negotiated his recent release.

Perhaps this is why Marigold and her sunshine disposition fascinated him.

This girl was the *Elysian Fields* to him, the paradise where heroes went upon their death. He was still living and breathing, of course. But his soul had died while he was locked away in that enemy dungeon without hope of ever finding freedom again.

Perhaps this is why he felt a sudden ache to kiss her.

Why had he warned her against rushing her life experiences?

Was his own life not a perfect example of why one must seize every moment offered? Four years lost in that purgatory and never to be reclaimed.

He felt the loss acutely.

Pruitt opened the door, bringing an end to their conversation.

Marigold cast him that soft look again. "I shall see you in a few minutes."

He nodded, surprised by how much he was looking forward to it.

Whether the Chipping Way curse held true and he would inevitably marry this girl was another matter entirely, for he was not fit yet to undertake a serious courtship.

Perhaps he would be ready by the time Marigold turned twenty.

He dismissed the notion as he strode across the street to return to his home. The girl was a diamond of the first water and would be taken well before the end of this Season.

The possibility hit him like a punch in the gut.

To his dismay, he wanted her.

His idiotically possessive instincts were taking over and he could not see himself with anyone but this girl.

By all that was sainted.

Had he lost his mind?

It was too soon for him to think seriously about commitment when he could not even trust himself with as simple a chore as getting back into circulation among the *ton* elite.

Besides, he had unfinished business here in London and dared not drag that innocent girl into his life should matters turn ugly.

No, he was not under any circumstances going to court that ebullient bit of froth by the name of Marigold Farthingale.

But would his heart listen?

CHAPTER 2

MARIGOLD ASKED THE Farthingale butler for assistance in carrying her crate to the Marquess of Muir's carriage as it drew up in front of their townhouse. "I shall have the footmen attend to it immediately," Pruitt said, his manner kindly toward her and endlessly patient. Perhaps it was the lilt of his Scottish accent and the way he spoke to her with fatherly care that always put her at ease. He never seemed to mind or cut her off whenever she spoke to him about her skulls. "I shall also advise Bessie to collect your reticule and accompany you, Miss Marigold."

"Thank you. I do wish Violet was home, but apparently she is visiting Dillie as well." She sighed as she donned her pelisse. "Bessie will do nicely."

She hurried outside to greet the Marquess of Muir who was now standing in front of his carriage, looking warrior-big and quite formidable. His carriage was incredibly elegant, a sleek black coach emblazoned with his family crest on the door. The crest was straightforward in design, two lions rampant upon a bed of thistles to designate the Scottish origins of his title. The background on the crest was a deep blue, and if one looked closely in that bed of thistles, one could make out the bloodied form of a hare that was obviously dead. Well, that was a bit violent, wasn't it? But such was life back then, for feudal lords had to constantly fight to hold onto what they owned. "I must thank you again, my lord."

"Not at all. In fact, you are doing me the favor of getting me out of the house. I am in danger of becoming too reclusive."

She doubted that would ever happen, for he was exceedingly handsome and must have received invitations aplenty that were piling up on his desk. Marigold knew London's most renowned hostesses would be eager to have him attend their balls and soirees in the hope a daughter or other young female relation caught his eye.

His name appeared in the London gossip rags quite often of late, for there was much speculation about his marital intentions. He appeared to have no intention of marrying, which only stoked the fires of speculation. She had read about him in those London scandal sheets delivered daily to Devonshire where she had been working in the caves recently.

She now understood why he was all the rage.

His facial structure was magnificent.

In truth, so was his body.

She itched to run her hands over his solid musculature, but he would misunderstand and consider her too forward.

Marigold smiled as the footmen toted the crate and lifted it into his carriage since it could not properly be perched atop the roof nor would it fit in the rear of the carriage without being laid on its side. That would force the contents to shift and cause the carefully placed bones to tumble one atop the other in disarray.

No, it had to be laid flat.

However, now that it was in place inside the carriage, Marigold realized with much dismay that it took up almost all the space. There was only the tiniest corner available on each bench for them to sit. "Your maid will have to ride with my driver," the marquess said, coming to the same conclusion. He gave Bessie a hand up onto the seat beside his coachman.

"Oh, but that will leave you and me alone in your carriage," Marigold remarked, although the prospect secretly pleased her. Riding alone with this big, muscled, and utterly stunning man was rather exciting in itself.

He did not have to work hard at looking handsome. His chestnut brown hair had a natural wave to it and a lustrous fullness despite it being cut short at the back and sides. The style, which struck her as a little military, accentuated the strikingly beautiful angles of his face. His firm jaw, fine cheekbones, and aquiline nose were all in perfect proportion.

His eyes were deep set and darkest green, seemingly able to pierce souls. Warmth flooded through her whenever he looked at her.

She could not tell what he was thinking, but his eyes were fascinating and were the sort that held dark secrets.

His mouth had a decidedly sensual curve to it.

A perfect mouth for delivering a first kiss.

Namely hers, since she had not yet been kissed.

The marquess would be the perfect candidate for this endeavor, but she did not know how to go about enticing him. She dared not overtly suggest such a thing or attempt to initiate something so intimate. She was not brazen by nature, and it would give him the wrong impression.

"*Eep*," she squeaked, caught by surprise when he wrapped his hands around her waist and lifted her into his carriage. He settled her in the tiny space available on the forward facing bench, and then climbed in next, squeezing his broad-shouldered frame into the tiny space left for him on the opposite facing bench.

He tapped on the roof. "Huntsford Academy, Collins."

"Aye, my lord."

The team, a beautiful pair of matched bays, took off at a lively clip, leaving the serene confines of Chipping Way and turning onto the busier thoroughfares that were filled with carriages, tradesmen's carts, and wagons loaded with wares. They slowed along Regent Street, not that they had much choice, for how else were they to avoid the ladies and gentlemen darting and dashing across the much traveled roadway?

The liveliness of London still fascinated Marigold, for life in her quieter Lancashire village of Little Mutton moved at a much slower pace. She watched those walking along this busy shopping street, the fashionably dressed elite strolling leisurely while the more humbly attired working men and women bustled with a determined step toward their destinations.

It was all a marvelously mad scramble, and now more

carriages and carts converged onto the already crowded lanes to slow them down further. Marigold worried this ride would take much longer than either of them considered. "My lord, I apologize for the inconvenience and hope our delay is not creating a problem for you. Did you have plans for the evening?"

"None at all. In fact, I was much in need for an adventure just like this one." His voice had a deep, resonant quality to it that was cultured and at the same time a little daunting. He was polite with her, yet she did not sense he was a polite man by nature. He was also being extremely kind and tolerant, yet he did not strike her as someone who suffered fools gladly. She did not think he enjoyed taking his time about anything.

He looked like a man of action.

Decisive. Get the job done. Impatient to move on to the next bit of business.

However, his smile was sincerely warm and he appeared relaxed in her company.

She would not call him an amiable man, for there was an aura of danger about him. It was unmistakable. This marquess was a man of contradictions, she decided. She could not quite make him out, but he was very much a gentleman with her and she liked being with him.

Oh, dear.

He would not like her very much once he realized the crate had scratched his exquisite, leather seat benches. She nibbled her lip, now worried what he might say or do when he noticed the damage.

There was no help for it. She would have to offer to repair the seats, never mind that she did not have the funds to do so.

"Miss Farthingale, you appear to be fretting." His keen gaze fixed on her lips.

She nodded. "I am, my lord."

His own twitched ever so slightly at the corners, as though he found her comment amusing. "May I ask why?"

She had to be truthful with him. "The seats of your coach are of the finest black leather, but they have been quite scuffed by the rough wood of my crate. It is all my fault. I should have thought to lay a blanket atop the seats first. I would gladly repay you for the damage...but, I do not have the funds at my disposal at the moment. In fact, I am not likely ever to have the funds available at any future moment either."

He cast her a soft smile.

Why was he not angry?

"Um, I shall apply to the Duke of Huntsford since one could say this damage is a legitimate cost of delivering these artifacts to his museum. In fact, I shall write to him as soon as we return to Chipping Way. However, if he refuses, which I do not think he will do because he is exceedingly kind and generous, I shall endeavor to pay you back even if it takes me a lifetime. You will not charge interest, will you? That might be a problem because I–"

"Don't."

"Don't?" She stared at him, not certain she had heard right.

"I do not need you to involve Huntsford nor do I require repayment from you. The cost is mine alone." He frowned lightly when she opened her mouth to protest. "Do you hear me, Miss Farthingale?"

Oh, there really was nothing soft about this man.

"I do hear you quite clearly. I merely disagreed with your conclusion. You needn't bark at me."

He sighed. "I did not mean to come across as harsh. You are putting all the blame on yourself when it is as much mine. I saw at once the condition of your crate and suspected this might happen."

"But if you knew, then why did you permit me to load it into your beautiful carriage?"

He arched an eyebrow and cast her a gentle smile that melted her insides. "Is this not the risk one takes when one is on an adventure? Besides, I can easily afford the expense of any repairs. Many of the scuffs were there already. At worst, your crate added one or two more. You are not to concern yourself. All right?"

"All right." However, it did not sit well with her. Should she not accept some of the blame?

"Tell me about the contents we are delivering to the Huntsford Academy. Is it an entire shipment of skulls?"

"This is exceptionally kind of you, my lord." She emitted a breath of relief. "No, not only skulls. In truth, it is mostly bones. The Duke of Huntsford and his wife, Adela, think this trove is one of their most important discoveries ever. This is why it is imperative to get the crate securely under guard as soon as possible."

He leaned forward in his seat. "Seems I missed a lot while I was away. I would like to see what is in the crate. Am I permitted?"

"Yes, of course," she said with an eager smile. "I'll have it opened as soon as we arrive. It shouldn't be long now. The contents will all have to be entered into the inventory immediately. We cannot risk a single bone being lost or misplaced, or worse…stolen."

"Who would want to steal bones?"

Her eyes widened. "Relic hunters, of course. I would not be surprised if they were lurking nearby just for the purpose of grabbing this crate and looting its contents."

"I see."

"Lord Muir, I do not think you believe me. But do keep alert, for they are scoundrels and cannot be trusted. This is why it is so important for me to inventory the contents immediately upon arrival. Do you mind? I will work as fast as possible."

"Do whatever you must, Miss Farthingale. As I said, I do not have any commitments this evening. I am entirely at your service."

"Oh, that is excellent." She tried not to sound too pleased to have him all to herself for the next few hours. Butterflies began to dance in her stomach, but she ignored them. "I mean, this will also give me the chance to give you a tour of the museum displays, the library, and lecture halls. You will be amazed, not only by the contents of this crate, but by the entire museum itself. That skull you saw tearing across your garden earlier happens to belong to an ancient, flying lizard-like bird. It will be added to the Hall of Dragons displays. I am the one who found this skull and dug it up. Well, I dug up some of it. Professionals took over once we realized what we had."

He smiled once again with genuine warmth. "That must have been quite thrilling for you."

"It was the most exciting moment of my life. Tingles shot through me." To emphasize her point, she lightly rubbed her hands up and down her arms. "My heart raced wildly so that I could hardly catch my breath. But I expect others must have felt the same exquisite pleasure in a first discovery."

"A first time is always special." He seemed to catch on to her excitement, for his eyes glittered. Yet, he managed to look dangerous even though he was being quite pleasant. His smile was one of the most appealing ever bestowed on her.

She was glad he understood her rapture, the heightened pleasure of it all.

She smiled back at him.

"You are quite passionate about your skull," he remarked.

"Yes, I am." More tingles shot through her, for there was something exquisite in the way he was looking at her. "Is it possible to be too passionate about a thing, my lord? Or am I hopelessly eccentric because this is what I felt as I began to unearth this giant lizard head and realized what it was?"

He grinned. "I would call you charming rather than eccentric. You do appear to be expressive in your feelings, not that I find fault with that either."

"I know I am," she said with a nod. "At times, I wish I were a bit more stoic and better able to hide my feelings. But not about these cave discoveries. I hope you will not be bored watching me and the curators sort through the contents. I cannot lay claim to finding anything beyond this skull and a few of the bones. We work as a team and most of the finds belong to Duchess Adela and the members of her Devonshire explorer's club."

"You will not bore me, Miss Farthingale. I do not believe there is the slightest chance of it."

"Thank you, Lord Muir. Most people would disagree with you, especially the young men I am introduced to at these elegant *ton* affairs." She cast him a wincing smile. "I have gotten quite good at chasing them away. Not on purpose, mind you. But honestly, what else are we to talk about if not these extraordinary finds? The weather?" She rolled her eyes. "Their latest horse purchases? These gentlemen all seem to spend their lives at the Tattersalls auctions looking for the next horse they will race at Newmarket."

"Well, it is an interesting pastime. Better than gambling, although I expect some hefty wagers are placed on those horses."

"I did find these conversations interesting, at first. But every one of my dance partners would speak of nothing else."

"So, it quickly became tiresome for you?"

"Yes." She sighed and shook her head. "And then they had the gall to find my bones and skulls tedious. Some gentlemen even yawned as I spoke of them. Can you imagine? If I were less polite, I would have yawned right back at them when they began to prattle about their horse auctions."

His eyes glittered with mirth. "It is their loss, Miss Farthingale."

"That is very kind of you to say, my lord. Please call me Marigold. All my friends do. Or is this request too forward of me?"

"Do you consider me a friend?" He must have found the notion amusing, if one judged by the growing smile on his nicely formed lips.

"I do." She nodded. "Helping me out with this unwieldy crate was very kind of you. And you haven't yawned once as I spoke of skulls and bones. Or are you merely being polite? Do you find me as deadly dull as those other gentlemen do?

"You are not dull at all." His expression had that dangerous look again, but his smile was exquisite. "Nor am I a polite person. You would know if I were not enjoying myself. I can be quite abrasive, at times."

"I sensed you were not quite a gentleman, but thought it rude to say so. Especially since you have been very kind to me. I truly appreciate it, even more so because this is not in your nature and must feel quite odd to you."

He laughed. "I do try to be polite most of the time. It isn't really a chore. However, if I found you dull, I would have made an excuse to be rid of you by now."

"And avoid me in the future?"

"Yes, although it is not so easily done since we are neighbors. But I find you most agreeable. You need not worry about the impression you are making on me. Still, it is best that we do not consider each other friends. People will make too much of it."

"How so?"

"You are fresh and innocent, and new to the marriage mart. It is a cutthroat place. Some of these young ladies can be as dangerous as your relic hunters. They are your competition. Do not ever consider them as friends. They will look for any reason to have you ruined. Even something as innocent as your calling me Leo or my calling you Marigold could be sufficient to cause scandal."

"Because we would then appear to be *too* friendly with each other?"

"Quite so. I am not considered harmless. I have a rakish reputation. It is highly exaggerated, I assure you. Still, it is for your sake that we must keep to formality at all times."

"I see, or else we might slip when in company and that would be disastrous for me?"

"Yes. You are, and must always be, Miss Farthingale to me, and nothing more."

She tried not to appear dejected, but his words had crushed her. "And you are always to be Lord Muir? I shall try my best to remember, but Leonides suits you so well. It is a lovely name."

"Marigold is a charming name and suits you, too. But we have only just met. You know nothing about me. I am not certain you will want to consider me a friend once you learn more."

"Oh. Do you have many scandals attached to you?"

"Yes, and I do not intend to add flirtation with one Miss Marigold Farthingale to the extensive list."

"I appreciate your consideration. However, I am a bit puzzled."

He arched an eyebrow. "How so?"

"You are constantly mentioned in the gossip rags, but I have not read of any specific wrongdoing on your part. Does it not bother you that you are innocent and yet so often accused?"

That dangerous glint sprang into his eyes again. "Miss

Farthingale, I am not innocent. Do not be so foolish as to put it to the test."

Heat rose in her cheeks, for she had been too forward and inadvertently prodded this gorgeous, dark-maned lion of a man. She took his words, although spoken gently and rather protectively, as an admonishment. "I do apologize again. I thought we might be kindred spirits, considering our mutual love of ancient artifacts. Well, you have been most helpful and seemed genuinely interested. I thought you were an explorer too, or had an interest in becoming one."

His gaze fixed on her, a rather hot gaze as he cast her an enigmatic smile. "I do not think we are of the same mind in the things we wish to explore."

She was not certain what he meant, so she moved on...well, she tried. But it hurt not to be considered his friend, and hurt that he would not allow her to consider him as one of hers. "Am I to understand you are not interested in ancient bones?"

"That's right. My preference is for living bodies. I like to know the person I am with is actually breathing."

"Oh, you are mocking me."

"No, Miss Farthingale. Forgive me if I gave that impression. I am sincerely enjoying my time with you."

"As I am with you. Are you quite certain I am not permitted to call you by your given name? Leonides...Leo. You resemble a lion, for there is something quite magnificently predatory in your aspect. Perhaps in the darkness of your eyes and the powerful build of your body. Forgive me, is that also too forward of me? I mean nothing by it. I am fascinated by your bone structure. It is quite exceptional."

He arched his eyebrow again. "Is that so?"

"Yes, quite. Should I be afraid of you?"

"Because I remind you of a lion and you are now worried I might eat you?" His regard softened, which was a relief because he had been looking at her quite dangerously a moment ago. "I hope not, Miss Farthingale."

She pursed her lips as she studied him. "Good, because I feel we have taken two steps backward after we started our acquaintance with such promise. Despite your warnings, I find it very hard to be wary of you. In fact, I like you and do not even mind that you have no fascination for my skulls and bones."

He leaned forward. "Miss Farthingale, I hope you will never fear me or have cause to be wary of me. I would never hurt you. More than that, do not ever hesitate to come to me if any of your suitors make you feel at all uncomfortable. I will always protect you."

He may as well have lit a match to her, for her insides turned fiery. This big, glorious man watching over her? She cast him her brightest smile. "I was sure you would never hurt me. But I do appreciate your confirming it. This proves you are truly your namesake, does it not? If a lion takes you into his pride, then he will protect you to the death. This is the other side of being a predator, you protect what you deem yours."

He groaned, obviously exasperated with her.

Still, he laughed softly and shook his head. "Miss Farthingale, being my neighbor hardly makes you mine. But as I said, come to me if ever you feel the need for protection. It is an offer that is always open to you."

"I will, my lord." She regarded him warmly. "Lions are territorial animals and it could be said that you have marked Chipping Way as your territory. My cousin, Lily, is an authority on the topic of dominant behavior in the male animal. Her research was primarily on baboons. Did you know men and male baboons are remarkably similar? Both are aggressively territorial. Of course, the Royal Society was in an uproar when she presented her findings."

"Good gracious, I can understand why." But he chuckled heartily. "I wish I had been at that lecture."

"Me, too. A riot almost broke out. What fun that must have been. Lord Muir, I am glad we met today, even if you won't permit me to acknowledge it. Do you mind if I ask you questions about yourself?"

He glanced out the carriage window, saw they were still some distance away from the Huntsford Academy, and shrugged. "It depends on the questions."

"Well, you can refuse to answer any you deem too personal. I will not take offense. I know I have an inquisitive nature." She laughed lightly. "That is a polite way of saying I am an incorrigible snoop."

"Miss Farthingale," he said, his manner suddenly serious, "I cannot impress on you enough to be careful where you choose to nose about. Many people have secrets they will kill to keep quiet."

"Do you?"

"Yes." His eyes grew dark for a moment, then he sighed and eased back against the squabs. "I did not mean to frighten you, but you must be careful what you say and to whom you say it, especially while in London."

She nodded. "My family advised the same."

"Well, you must take their advice to heart." He regarded her sternly a while longer before letting go of his admonition. "I know you enjoy digging up fossils. What else do you like to dig up?"

"As in dirt…gossip…secrets? Oh, nothing wicked or sordid. I do not skulk behind draperies to spy on others. I would never wish to hurt anyone, despite what you obviously think. I keep my snooping mostly to harmless matters, to new fossil finds or advances in medical science. I would never repeat something I was not meant to overhear, unless it involved harm to someone else and they needed to be warned. Then I would report it straight to one of my uncles."

She emitted a sight and continued. "Mostly, I enjoy gossip of a romantic nature. As I said, nothing sordid or humiliating. You know, figuring out who might hold a *tendre* for a certain gentleman? Or which young lady would be a good match for one of the eligible lords? It is a harmless occupation, merely a game of romantic attachments."

"And this satisfies your curiosity?"

"Yes. It is fun trying to spot who will make a love match and who won't. The game is not always enjoyable, however. It pains me to see a gentleman and lady thrown together when they are clearly mismatched. Sometimes the parties do not care, both quite content to marry for purposes of advancement and will not shed a tear over what the other one does so long as they are discreet about it."

He nodded. "That is usually the way of things."

"It breaks my heart when one party is clearly in love with the other and that affection is not reciprocated. A marriage should be a thing of happiness, but with such couples, one is doomed to misery."

"Miss Farthingale, the world on the whole is not a happy place. Sometimes, people must lower their expectations and be grateful they have a roof over their head and food on the table. When one is in fear of starving, it will not matter very much to them if the one providing the food and a warming fire has a wandering eye."

"I know. You must think me quite foolish for holding onto the hope of love for myself or wishing it for others. By the way, I was raised in comfort but not in wealth. In fact, I come from the poorer side of the Farthingale family. I was orphaned young and raised primarily by my mother's family in Little Mutton, Lancashire. Do you know it?"

He shook his head. "No."

"Well, it is a quiet village. It is only due to the generosity of Uncle John and Aunt Sophie that I am in London at all. They have provided me with new clothes and introduced me to a wonderful circle of family and friends that includes Duchess Adela, the Duke of Huntsford's wife."

She had also met Adela's friends, Lady Sydney Harcourt and Lady Gregoria Easton who were considered bluestockings. This is what she wished to be. But other than her accidental find of that dragon-lizard skull, she had no real bluestocking credentials.

Her looks and young age were also an impediment to anyone taking her seriously.

"May I ask how old you are, my lord?"

He grinned. "Much older than you, my pet."

She sighed. "I really do wish I was twenty already."

"I am a cynical and sarcastic man of twenty-eight years. I have seen too much of the world and done too much in those years to ever restore my faith in mankind. In fact, my experiences have completely destroyed my faith in everyone and everything. You probably thought I was older."

"Yes, in fact I did. It isn't that you look older...you are very handsome and quite vigorous-looking. But it is your attitude toward life that hardens you. Still, there is much to like about you. I would refer to my cousin Lily's monographs on baboon colonies again and say that you would clearly be the dominant male in any gathering, be it picking berries on a rocky, equatorial outcropping, or attending a *ton* party, or fighting on a battlefield."

"Some of those *ton* parties can be battlefields," he remarked. "The tables are turned on the dominant males and we become the prey for the highly skilled, marriage-minded mamas and their eager daughters."

"Oh, I think you are too clever for them. You have managed to elude their schemes so far."

"Only because I have been away from London for quite a while."

"Yes, you mentioned it earlier. May I ask what kept you away?"

"No, Miss Farthingale. You may not." He sighed, no doubt realizing his abrupt tone had startled her. "It is not anything I wish to discuss."

"I'm sorry. Of course. I did not realize it was a sensitive matter for you." She now felt awful about stirring up the bad feelings he obviously struggled to suppress. "Look, we have arrived at the Huntsford Academy. Give me a moment to summon the staff. They'll assist us with the crate."

"All right." He stepped out of the carriage ahead of her and took her hands to help her down.

Standing as close as they were for the moment, he looked quite splendid. In fact, as sleek and powerful as a lion. "I won't be long," she said quietly. "I do apologize if I made our ride uncomfortable for you. If you wish to deposit me and my crate here and leave, I–"

"I have enjoyed our time together." He gave her hand a light caress before releasing it. "Having brought you here, I am now responsible for getting you safely back home. Besides, I do wish to see your treasured finds, and would not mind a tour of Huntsford's museum. I owe you the apology for being abrupt with you. Shall I escort you inside?"

"No, my lord. I would rather you remained here to protect the crate. As I've warned, these relic hunters are a dastardly lot and cannot be trusted. They will stoop to any means, even thievery, to get their hands on these prized fossils. I have seen them in action firsthand."

He frowned. "Someone stole from you?"

"Not from me, but villains from the Royal Society attempted to steal from Duchess Adela and her friends. Is it not shocking and a sad commentary on the narrow minds of our scientific community that knaves such as these are permitted into the ranks of the Royal Society and women as worthy as my cousin Lily and Duchess Adela are denied?"

"Indeed."

"Oh, you must think I am ranting now. It is just a comment on the deplorable state of our scientific societies. Well, I had better summon the staff before the museum closes and we are locked out. Watch that crate closely. Ruthless villains may be lurking close even now." She hurried inside and went in search of the head curator, Mr. Smythe-Owens.

He noticed her first and rushed toward her. "Miss Farthingale, I have been expecting you. His Grace's letter reached me yesterday about your find. Is this not the most exciting news?"

"Yes, indeed. I am still breathless over it. However, much as I would love to discuss this trove in greater detail, I cannot right now. The Marquess of Muir escorted me here and is now waiting beside his carriage with our crate of treasures. He has been very kind and most helpful. I dare not leave him alone for too long considering the value of this property. Have you had any trouble with those relic-hunting knaves lately?"

"Yes. They are getting more brazen by the day," he said quite seriously. "Word has gotten around and we must not underestimate the jealousy rampant over these astounding fossil discoveries." He motioned to two of the Huntsford guards. "Mr. Carver. Mr. Finn. Follow me and Miss Farthingale. We must be quick about it."

They marched out just as the marquess was set upon by three

unpleasant looking men.

Before Marigold had the chance to cry out a warning, she heard the marquess bellow swift orders for his coachman to drive away.

She gasped. "No! Wait! Come back!"

"Miss Marigoooollllddd!" Bessie, her poor maid, was still perched on the driver's bench, quite terrified and screaming as she held on for dear life.

Marigold could only watch helplessly as the carriage careened around the corner and out of sight.

No! No!

But she could not forget the marquess was in danger.

She ran toward him.

Dear heaven!

She had to rescue him, of course.

But her crate!

Would she ever see her precious skull again?

CHAPTER 3

LEO COULD NOT believe what was happening.

Marigold had not been exaggerating when she commented on the treachery of these relic hunters. They were explorers and naturalists, supposed pillars of scientific learning. He would have thought these men coming at him were mere ruffians hired out of a dockside tavern were it not for their reference to some incomprehensible Latin name given to this unique skull he had first seen skittering across his garden.

Sending his carriage off had enraged these men and they now came at him with knives and fists. There were three of them, quite big and brawny, but clearly not disciplined fighters. He kicked the first one in his privates knowing it would incapacitate him for some time, then spun around and smashed his fist into the face of the second man with enough force to drop the villain to his knees.

He managed to dodge the third man's attempt to slash him with a rather long knife. It had nothing to do with his prowess and all to do with Marigold hurling her reticule at the fiend with remarkable precision and striking him squarely in the face.

Lord, he should be angry with her.

Was she now running toward him?

Bloody blazes, did she think to rescue him?

Hurling her reticule at the bounder gave Leo those precious few seconds he needed to subdue this bounder. Having taken down the first two men, he now whirled behind the third, grabbed him by the throat, and slammed him to the ground. He then placed his booted foot atop the man's hand, crushing it until he heard a crunch of bone.

The man screamed in pain.

Leo bent to take the knife out of his now useless hand.

His companions were still writhing on the ground.

"Oh, thank goodness!" Marigold retrieved her reticule and warned back the men who had run out of the museum behind her. No doubt, she wanted to make certain Leo knew they were friendly and would not harm him.

She was right to be cautious, for he was in a rage and still up for a fight.

He took several deep breaths, knowing he needed to calm down.

Marigold had remarked upon his name…Leonides, going on about animal societies and their dominant predators. Apparently, he reminded her of a lion. Well, he felt like a wild beast at the moment, a seething, angry beast with a frighteningly lethal look in his eyes. "I won't hurt you, Marigold. But you should not have run forward to help me. You might have been injured in the fray."

She cast him a stubborn look. "You were the one in danger. That despicable fiend was about to stab you. I could not just stand there and do nothing. My aim was straight on, wasn't it?" she remarked proudly. "I got him squarely in the face. Of course, you were quite brilliant. Did they injure you?"

"No. I am unscathed." It wasn't quite the truth. His right hand throbbed since it was the one he had used to punch his attackers. But he expected it was merely bruised and no bones were broken.

As a precaution, he switched hold of the knife to his left hand.

Despite assurances he would never harm her, Marigold approached him cautiously. "Um, may I introduce you to the museum's head curator, Mr. Smythe-Owens? And these gentlemen standing over these fiends are part of the museum's security, Mr. Carver and Mr. Finn."

"My lord," each of them mumbled in turn.

Leo nodded to acknowledge them. "These curs need to be bound and held for the magistrate. Send someone off to fetch his constables. I fully intend to see them charged with assault on a marquess."

More guards came running out of the museum to assist in securing them. At Mr. Smythe-Owens' instruction, one of the guards ran off to the magistrate's office.

"My lord," Marigold said softly, looking up at him with worry.

"I am fine, Miss Farthingale. You needn't be concerned about me."

She took the knife gently out of his hand and gave it over to the man she had introduced as the head curator. He was a little fellow, but quite efficient as he issued brisk instructions to the guards. "Bind their hands behind their back. Yes, that's it. Now bind the three of them together so they will trip over each other if they think to run."

Marigold cradled Leo's hand in both of hers. "You've bruised your knuckles. They are swelling noticeably."

He cast her a lopsided grin. "All worth it. I enjoyed that fight, perhaps a little too much. Those knaves got the worst of it."

"No doubt of that." She nibbled her fleshy, lower lip. "Um, my lord…where has your driver taken my crate? And my maid?"

He was too busy watching the soft nip of her teeth to her lower lip to respond. Lord, she had a mouth as sweet as cherries, and he liked the pouting way it pursed whenever she was worried.

She also had the deepest, blue eyes, perhaps seeming bluer because of the long, black lashes surrounding those magnificent orbs.

He bent his head toward hers, aching to touch his lips to hers. "Not far. He will return your skull, bones, and maidservant to you shortly. Just wait here with me and he ought to be circling around at any moment."

"All right, but as soon as he is back, Mr. Smythe-Owens will have the crate brought inside. Then I must treat your hand."

"It isn't broken," he assured Marigold.

What a lovely thing she was.

She regarded him thoughtfully. "I suppose you know best. Where did you learn to fight like that? You were fierce as a lion, but I knew you would be. You could not have been named Leonides for nothing. Those men did not stand a chance of winning, even though they had you outnumbered."

"I had the better odds. Their only weapons were knives and fists. Although they were big men and looked rough, I quickly saw they were undisciplined fighters. The odds would have shifted in their favor had one of them drawn a pistol."

Her eyes widened. "They would have to be mad to shoot a marquess."

"Is it not just as mad to attack a marquess with knives and fists? They must have noticed the crest on my carriage door when we drew up."

"We had the door open. They might not have realized. Still, your carriage is quite magnificent. They had to know you were someone important. And yet, they did not care. I warned you, some of these relic hunters are unabashed villains. I recognize these three as Fellows in the Royal Society. They are the lowest creatures you shall ever meet."

He glanced around. "Marigold, are they always lurking around here? How did they know to expect your crate? They also seemed to know exactly what was in it."

"Someone could have mentioned it," she said, looking up at him with her eyes wide. "A news reporter. Or someone working in the Devonshire caves. Do not make too much of it. We do not have a traitor in our midst. This delivery was never meant to be a secret, although after this incident, we ought to consider moving precious cargo about with more discretion. Our cave finds have been getting a lot of public notice for quite some time now. People are fascinated with the myth of dragons, and the museum staff has been touting the "new" dragons about to arrive. I'm sure it was reported in all the papers."

She rubbed her thumbs gently over his fisted hand as she spoke. "We really ought to get you treated. Your entire hand is dangerously swelling. My uncle, George Farthingale, is a highly respected doctor and his infirmary is not far from here. Do you mind if we unload the crate first? Then I'll assist Mr. Smythe-Owens in taking quick inventory. Immediately afterward, we'll go off to see Uncle George. How does that sound?"

"It isn't necessary."

"What? The inventory? Or your visit to the doctor? I think both are quite necessary. However, I will put off most of the cataloguing work until tomorrow. You are welcome to join me here tomorrow, as well. That is, if you feel up to it. My work won't take very long and then I can show you around the museum. That is, if Uncle George says you are fit to go out."

"Marigold," he said with a chuckle, "it is just a bruised hand. By the way, I know your uncle quite well." He was not going to reveal to this delightful girl how many months it took for George to treat his injuries after he had come out of that devil's hole of a foreign prison on the verge of death.

In truth, he probably owed his life to Marigold's Uncle George. The man was a brilliant doctor. As for his rescue, he owed that to some very brave agents of the Crown operating abroad. He did not know how he would ever repay these men for their valorous acts.

And yet, he had been the one bestowed with England's highest medal of honor, a medal he had placed in his bureau drawer and did not care to see again. He wanted to forget about his ordeal, not be reminded of it every time he pinned that medal on.

Well, this was not a discussion he wished to have with this tender girl.

"Oh, thank goodness! Here comes your carriage! Poor Bessie. She is pale as a ghost. Oh, drat. Now she is going to report what happened to John and Sophie, and they might never let me out of their home again. But they must let me go. I have to help organize this exhibit. Mr. Smythe-Owens and his team cannot manage without me."

Leo cast her a wry smile. "Cannot? Or is it that you do not want them to work on it without you?"

She blushed. "I would be devastated if I could not participate. I know it is terribly wrong of me, but I would sneak out of the house if I were forbidden. There is a lovely oak tree with branches that lean close to my bedroom window. It would not be so hard to climb down and–"

"Marigold! It is bad enough you would defy John and Sophie, but to then think you can make your way here on your own? How do you intend to do it? Steal money for a hackney?"

She gasped. "I would never steal!"

"Then you would walk the entire way? A girl like you? All alone? Do you have any idea how dangerous that is? Has this incident not made clear the depravity of your fossil hunters? They would not hesitate to abduct you if it served their purpose. You are as much a prize to them as these skulls and bones. No, you must always come to me. I must insist on it."

"How does this help me? Would you not stop me if you disapproved?"

"No, I would protect you even though I disagreed wholeheartedly with what you were doing. It is more important that you trust me and know you can always rely on me to keep you safe. I would not lecture you. I am not your father."

She blushed, gave a small cough, and then smiled up at him. "I am quite aware. Do you think I have not noticed?"

He sighed. "You are still holding my hand."

"Because it is hurt. You are too stubborn to admit it."

"It isn't very sore. I hardly feel any discomfort." She had no idea just how badly he had been injured while locked away in that black hole and regularly beaten. "Mr. Smythe-Owens and more guards are here to carry the crate inside. Let us keep out of their way."

"All right."

They stepped aside, but Marigold was still stubbornly holding onto his hand. Well, perhaps it was not so much to soothe him as it was to calm herself down. If she needed to hold onto him, use him as her anchor, he was not going to complain.

"You have called me Marigold a time or two. Does this mean I may now call you Leo?"

Drat, he had slipped and used her given name. That was a mistake, for he was already feeling too drawn to this girl. "No, you may not. I apologize for the familiarity. It should not have happened."

"I did not mind."

"That is all the more reason for us to keep to formality, Miss Farthingale."

She let go of his hand after easing it to his side. "I understand."
In truth, she did not understand at all.

She thought he was rejecting her when, in fact, he was feeling far too strongly attracted to her. "Come, Miss Farthingale. Let's go inside."

The guards had carried the crate in, so they followed.

Marigold then instructed the men to carry it up to the duke's office. "Mr. Smythe-Owens, we ought to start immediately entering each artifact into the logbook."

"If you wish. The book is here on His Grace's desk." He motioned to it.

"Once we are done, we ought to keep the crate and its contents locked in His Grace's office. I think it is safer than anywhere else for now."

"I agree, Miss Farthingale."

The hour was getting late and Leo expected the Huntsford staff wished to go home. "It will not take us long to get through this inventory," Marigold assured him when he mentioned it. "Besides, we should remain at least until the constables arrive. They'll have questions for us. By your expression, I do not think you like to answer questions."

"I don't," he said tersely. He still had the scars from his last interrogations while held prisoner, so this was not a preferred pastime of his by any means. "I am not in the habit of answering to anyone."

"Lord Muir," the curator said in a helpful tone, "I saw the whole thing and can tell the constables anything they wish to know."

"That would be most appreciated," Leo acknowledged. "Thank you, Mr. Smythe-Owens."

Having resolved this matter, the curator and Marigold now set about opening the crate. "Watch your fingers, Miss Farthingale. The wood is a bit splintered."

Leo sank into the imposing leather chair behind the duke's desk and watched the curator and Marigold begin to methodically sort through the crate. They took note of each artifact and assigned to it a specific series of letters and numbers. "The letter represents the animal to which the bone or skull belongs," Marigold explained as she worked. "We also assign two sets of numbers to the particular fragment. The first indicates its exact position on the animal and the next simply indicates the number it corresponds to in our logbook."

She then returned to her work.

Leo did not think he would get anything done if she were his colleague and they were assigned a project together.

She was utterly delicious and he could stare at her all day.

Fortunately, they did not have much reason to be thrown together going forward. She would be caught up in the whirlwind of her debut and the excitement of putting together a new museum exhibit.

Either one of those duties would keep her fully occupied.

He doubted she would have a moment to catch her breath.

It was for the best.

He had no time for Marigold while on the hunt for the traitor who had ambushed his royal delegation and put him into enemy hands.

This traitor to England probably thought him long since dead.

He was not.

Indeed, he was very much alive and thirsting for revenge.

Things were about to get nasty.

"Miss Farthingale, are we done? Shall I close up the crate?" the curator asked, awaiting her direction.

Leo decided he liked this little man because he treated Marigold with respect. It was no small thing because she was young and beautiful. Few men would ever take her seriously. Even he had spent much of the time gawking at her.

How could he not?

She was so lovely.

Leo rose from the duke's chair. "It is getting late, Miss Farthingale. I had better get you and your maid home."

"But what about the constables?"

Mr. Smythe-Owens jumped in to respond. "I'm sure Mr. Carver and Mr. Finn are at this moment telling them everything they need to know. I'll add my statement to theirs. I expect the magistrate himself will come around to see Lord Muir at his home within the next day or two. Do not worry for your safety, Miss Farthingale. Those men will never be released."

"Thank you, Mr. Smythe-Owens," Marigold said with a nod. "I'm sure they will remain locked up, but I would like to know their names. I intend to report them to the Duke of Lotheil. He is chairman of the Royal Society and must be made aware. These academic societies have lowered their standards to a shocking degree."

Leo frowned.

This innocent was on a crusade to make the world a better place, which meant she was bound to run into trouble. He fully intended to protect her, but he had other matters on his mind and did not need to be constantly pulling her out of scrapes. "Miss Farthingale, I suggest you concentrate on your skull and bones. Mr. Smythe-Owens will report their names to me and I will speak to Lotheil about them."

She did not look pleased. "Why you and not me?"

"Because I am a marquess and you are not."

A blush he recognized as the heat of anger ran up her cheeks.

He knew he was being highhanded, but these were not nice men. It was possible they had friends who would take revenge. If so, he did not want her name mentioned anywhere. Not on an affidavit, not on a Royal Society report, and certainly not anywhere in the magistrate's records.

If she chose to remain angry, so be it.

"I thought you were better than the others," she grumbled. "But you are just as bad as they are, dismissing me because I am a woman."

"I assure you, Miss Farthingale, I am not dismissing you at all. Time to take you home. Good evening, Mr. Smythe-Owens."

"Good evening, my lord. Miss Farthingale."

She had set aside her pelisse and reticule as she worked. Leo now grabbed them off the chair for her, then took her by the elbow and led her out.

The air had turned cooler as the hour grew late.

Bessie was seated beside his driver, a blanket covering her legs.

The pair seemed quite cozy with each other. Leo noticed his driver had his hands beneath the blanket doing Leo dared not think what to the girl.

When Marigold, completely oblivious to the goings on, suggested Bessie ride in the carriage with them, the girl made up an excuse about her stomach not being right, blaming it on the scare they'd all had.

Marigold believed the girl's fib. "Oh, dear. Yes, stay where you are. Keep that blanket tucked about you. I'll have Mrs. Mayhew prepare something to calm your stomach once we return home."

While Leo did not usually condone liars, he was glad to have Marigold all to himself. He placed his hands around her slender waist and helped her into the carriage. He then climbed in and took the seat opposite hers.

They rode in silence for a while, but she was still peeved about his insistence on handling the matter of those villains. He did not want things to end on a sour note between them, even though she looked quite beautiful while angry. Her eyes were ablaze and her lips were in a kissable pout.

She was incensed and passionate.

He liked that spark of fire in her.

A little too much.

He was going to pull her onto his lap and ravage her if she kept this up, so he cleared his throat and got her talking instead. "Tell me about these fossil hunters, Miss Farthingale. You seem to have encountered bounders like these three before."

Her anger melted away and her eyes lit up. "I have had dealings with their sort, although I was not directly involved in the brawls that—"

"Brawls?" He leaned forward and frowned. "How? Where?"

She quickly told him about the fossil hunter who had stolen Duchess Adela's research notes on the significance of ancient cave drawings. "He took a valuable book from the Duke of Huntsford's private collection along with her research notes. Adela had been working with those materials and blamed herself when the fiend took that priceless book. He only stole it accidentally, for his true goal was to abscond with all of Adela's work."

"Did he return the book afterward?"

"No, which only proves how depraved these relic hunters are. Adela felt compelled to retrieve that book for Huntsford. Matters got quite physical. I missed most of the excitement, but Adela and her friends, Syd and Gory, along with the Duke of Huntsford's brothers were drawn into the melee. A tavern brawl erupted as Syd and Gory attempted to question some of the serving maids."

He frowned. "When was this?"

"Last year."

"But you were only seventeen."

She nodded. "And because of this, they would not allow me to participate in their investigation. I missed out on most of the excitement."

"Blessed saints, I'm glad they showed some sense even if you did not. You could have been hurt."

She frowned at him again. "I am not a child, nor am I a porcelain doll. Plenty of girls marry at seventeen and plenty have children by the time they are eighteen. And plenty struggle through hard times and manage to survive on their own. Not that I ever will have to struggle. My family is quite large and exceedingly generous. They are treating me like a princess."

"You make it sound as though it is a bad thing."

"And now you are certain I am an ungrateful peahen." She turned to stare out the window again. "I appreciate all they are doing. I am thankful every day for having kind relatives. My mother's family took me in and raised me in Lancashire. My father's side of the family was always attentive and have now brought me to London for my debut. I am forever in their debt. But how am I ever to gain experience if I am kept locked away?"

"It is to protect you."

"Did I or did I not save you from being stabbed?" She turned to face him with furrowed brow.

He smiled. "Will you stop scowling at me if I admit that you did?"

She nodded and managed a small smile. "I do not mean to sound petty. You've been wonderful and have done so much for me today. I am just frustrated. It feels as though I am held back at every turn, as though no one trusts me because they believe I am an incompetent child."

"You are certainly not a child," he remarked, trying not to be too obvious as his gaze raked over her body. "Nor are you incompetent. In fact, you are inquisitive and clever."

"I hope to be a bluestocking, just like Adela, Syd, and Gory. Being on the marriage mart does not mean I should stop improving my mind."

"I heartily agree, but it still does not mean you should run into taverns and start brawls. Ah, we are turning onto Chipping Way. What time do you intend to leave for the Huntsford Academy tomorrow?"

"Around ten o'clock in the morning."

"I'll take you. Be ready with your maid…perhaps another maid." His driver had been a little too friendly with Bessie. He did not need the tearful maid announcing she was with child. He would have a word with Collins. "Will you give me a personal tour of the exhibits? We did not have the chance today."

"Truly? I was sure you found me tiresome by now."

He cast her an affectionate smile. "No, Miss Farthingale. You have not bored me yet. My answer will be the same should you ask this same question an hour from now. As for my insistence on speaking to the Duke of Lotheil in your stead, it is for your safety. These Fellows already resent women in their presence. If it is found out you were the one to report those three, others may not take it too kindly and seek retribution. That you were in the right and they were in the wrong will not matter to such men."

"I see." She cast him a thoughtful look. "Thank you, Lord Muir. Sincerely, thank you for thinking of me when I was clearly not considering the potential consequences."

It struck him suddenly just how special Marigold was. Thoughtful. Gracious. To his dismay, he did not think she would ever bore him. He liked her more than he dared admit.

Of course, he would have to keep the little sprite at arm's length since he had returned to London to put his revenge plan into effect. He was not looking to find a wife. In fact, he was intent on dissuading anyone who thought him eligible.

Marigold would be safe enough with him in the meanwhile, but he could not have her anywhere near him once his plan began to unfold.

She was frothy and delightful, pure sunlight.

He was ominous shadows, vengeance, and pain.

It was safest for both of them not to feel any attraction toward each other.

However, it was easier said than done.

In truth, he was in danger of forming a serious attachment to Marigold.

Blast.

He could not afford any entanglements.

Why her?

And why now?

CHAPTER 4

LEO WAS NOT one for sleeping at night. He rarely managed more than two or three hours rest before he jerked awake with a pounding heart and a struggle for air. There was nothing wrong with his breathing, for he never had this difficulty in daylight. It was the silence and the darkness within enclosed surroundings that did this to him.

He emitted a ragged sigh as he strode to the window and noticed the first cracks of light on the horizon. Since he always kept his windows open except on the coldest nights, he now stood before it and allowed the cool air to wrap around his skin. He took a deep breath and inhaled the scent of lilacs from his garden, smiling as the memory of Marigold chasing her little dog and that hideous skull amid his shrubbery came to mind.

He would see her again in a few hours.

The notion pleased him more than he cared to admit. It worried him, too. He was determined to carry out his plans for revenge and could not let anything distract him, especially not a girl with satin-black hair and eyes of vivid blue.

Marigold would not like him very much once she learned why he had returned to London.

It had nothing to do with finding himself a wife.

Perhaps this is something he would do after discovering the identity of the man who had betrayed him. He wanted to kill him slowly, make him suffer as much as he had endured while imprisoned in that pit.

Then again, a quick killing would also satisfy him.

The point of his plan was to see justice done. That he was judge, jury of his peers, and executioner was beside the point. He could not move on with his life until achieving the satisfaction of a revenge completed.

He shook out of his dark thoughts.

Think of Marigold.

She would never have him if she knew he was a cold-blooded killer.

What did it matter? He'd only known the girl a few hours. He would take whatever innocent enjoyment he could and simply pass the day with her.

Tomorrow was Lady Balfour's ball. This is when he would start reacquainting himself with the men, diplomats and fellow officers, assigned to the delegation he had been leading into foreign lands when captured and tossed into that dark pit.

He would start asking all the questions that should have been asked four years ago.

Feeling too restless to return to his bed, he dressed and took his powerful gray stallion, Archimedes, for an early morning run in the park. Afterward, he returned to his townhouse, wishing he could wash the demons out of his soul as easily as he could wash the sweat off his body.

After washing and dressing, he sorted through the pile of Muir estate matters that were atop his desk awaiting his attention. He dealt with the most pressing, and as the ten o'clock hour approached, he ordered his carriage readied. "Have Collins draw it up in front of the Farthingale residence."

"At once, my lord," Sterling said, attending to it with the same quiet efficiency as he attended to all of his requests.

Leo walked over to the Farthingale home.

He knew John and Sophie would question his motives in escorting Marigold. A few minutes in idle chatter with them might allay their concerns. Perhaps Sophie herself would chaperone them, for neither she nor John would ever allow Marigold to ride alone with him. He was an unmarried man with a reputation for seducing ladies.

The reputation was unearned.

He was not a hound by nature.

But what was a man to do when ladies approached offering wild nights of pleasure? He usually made polite excuses and declined. But sometimes, he accepted the invitation. He was not a eunuch, after all. "Good morning, Pruitt," he said as the butler opened the door to let him in. "Is Mr. Farthingale at home?"

The old Scot's lips twitched in the semblance of a smile. "All three brothers happen to be at home and waiting for ye, my lord."

"Three?" He chuckled. "Lead the way."

He knew George Farthingale quite well since he was the man who had worked the miracle on his ailing body. He had met and chatted with John more than a time or two since acquiring his home across the street, and now allowed himself to be introduced to Rupert Farthingale, the brother who did most of the traveling for the family business.

Leo noticed at once where Marigold got her looks, for it was known that many of these Farthingales had dark hair and blue eyes. These three brothers were no exception, although they were all graying at the temples now. "I assume you will provide a proper chaperone for Marigold," he said, staring at the three stern faces studying him.

John was the eldest and obviously the patriarch of the family, but it was George who answered for them. "Oh, yes. You will have the pleasure of meeting Aunt Hortensia. She will keep eagle eyes on Marigold," George said, his grin wide.

Gad, they were setting the old battleaxe on him.

All for the best, he supposed. Not even he trusted himself to behave around Marigold. She was too delicious and he already ached to have her in his arms. "I look forward to it."

Now all three brothers were grinning, but it was only brief humor at his expense before they turned serious. "Marigold told us what happened yesterday," George said. "Let me have a look at your hand."

Leo sighed as he held it out. "It is nothing. The swelling has already subsided."

George pressed carefully on the bones of his hand then flexed his fingers one by one. "Yes, nothing damaged. Now let's get down to the important business. What are your intentions toward Marigold?"

"I have no intentions toward her. Yesterday was just happenstance. No one was available when she returned home with her valuable artifacts. I offered to assist her in delivering them to Huntsford's museum. It was a good thing, too. Do you have any idea how dangerous this archeology business can be?"

"Yes, we do," John said, "but Marigold will not be talked out of this hobby of hers, especially not now that she has made this extraordinary find."

"We're hoping Sophie and the other ladies in the family will make her see reason," Rupert added.

Leo frowned. "You are not thinking to deny her, are you? I've only known her for a few hours and already understand how important these discoveries are to her. You cannot deprive her of this thing she loves. It is more than a mere hobby for her."

"We know," Rupert said. "But neither can we ignore the men who attacked you. Or the attack on Huntsford and Adela last year."

Leo turned to George. "All the more reason why I should be allowed to escort Marigold while her treasure trove is being set up for display. You know I am not going to let anyone hurt her."

"Why step forward if you have no interest in her?" John asked.

George grunted. "I can answer that. May I speak of your situation, my lord? What you endured will not go beyond these walls. My brothers know how to keep a confidence."

Leo gave a curt nod, grateful George would speak for him because he could not talk about his ordeal without turning into a wild beast...a lion, as Marigold had called him. To his relief, George was brief and related only the most pertinent details. "Having been trapped, I expect Lord Muir feels Marigold's frustration acutely. Of course, she is not imprisoned by us. But if we barred her from the museum, we would certainly be depriving her of her own sense of worth and all confidence in her abilities."

John sighed. "My brother vouches highly for you, so I will not refuse your offer to assist Marigold. But be careful with her, Lord

Muir. She is young and impressionable. She may not appeal to you, for I expect your tastes run toward the more elegant and sophisticated *ton* diamonds. But Marigold may find you very much to her liking."

"I have already made clear to her that I am merely escorting her and there will be nothing more beyond a neighborly interest. I am certain the formidable Hortensia will make certain it stays this way."

Marigold was standing in the hall, her hands clasped in worry, as he and the Farthingale elders emerged from John's study. Leo's heart gave a lurch, noting the strain on Marigold's lovely face. These archeological artifacts were not mere pieces of bone and mineral to her. They represented respect, accomplishment, and pride in achievement.

He smiled and gave her a nod.

Her entire being lit up and she shone as brightly as a little star. "You are allowing me to go?" She gave each uncle a quick hug and ran up the stairs excitedly calling for Hortensia. "We must hurry, Hortensia! The museum has already opened its doors!"

Mixed in with her joyful cries were Mallow's excited barks.

Leo suddenly heard the scamper of paws on the stairs, and in the next moment, the little beast gave another excited bark and launched himself into Leo's arms.

Leo laughed and cradled the spaniel as he now attempted to lick Leo's face.

"Oh, Mallow! Bad dog!" Marigold called down from the top of the stairs. "I am so sorry, Lord Muir. He must have heard your voice and tore out of my bedchamber as soon as I opened the door to retrieve my reticule."

She hurried down and took the excited spaniel from his arms. "He certainly likes you. He is quite finicky usually. In fact, he never approves of anyone. But he adores you." She glanced upstairs and grinned. "He won't go near Hortensia," she said in a merry whisper. "He thinks she is scarier than any of my dragon finds."

Marigold's maid, Bessie, rushed down a moment later with Marigold's reticule and pelisse in hand. The two of them traded,

Marigold taking her belongings and Bessie scooping Mallow into her arms. "Bessie, please let Aunt Hortensia know we are waiting for her."

The maid scurried upstairs.

It was not long before the daunting figure of a gray-haired, bombazine clad, older woman sauntered down the stairs. She was tall and held herself quite proudly. One might easily mistake her for the royal consort of a Russian prince by her stern expression and the severe style of her clothes. She wore gray from head to toe, and the lace trim of her gown was as gray as the crisp fabric of her gown. An emerald brooch was the only hint of color to be found on her. "You are Muir?"

"Yes," he said with a nod, bowing over Hortensia's hand as she approached. "A pleasure to meet you, Miss Farthingale."

She merely grumbled. "We'll see about that."

George chuckled. "Take it easy on him, Hortensia. He's one of the good ones."

"Is he?" She did not appear at all impressed.

Marigold was now hopping with excitement just as Mallow had been only a moment ago. "Let's be off."

Leaving the Farthingale residence took forever, or so it seemed to Leo, for every member of the family needed to be kissed farewell by Marigold who also held a little conversation with each of them out of an abundance of politeness. Finally, the three of them were in his carriage and on their way. Hortensia and Marigold took seats opposite his, leaving him plenty of room to stretch out on his own bench.

"Your leather is scuffed," Hortensia remarked, obviously intending to give him a hard time despite the fact he had saved Marigold's skull from villains yesterday and was doing her the favor of escorting her today.

"That is all my fault," Marigold interjected before he managed to fashion a response, one that might not have been all that polite. "Lord Muir has refused my offer of repayment, but perhaps you can convince him to allow me to contribute in some small way. It feels wrong to–"

"Marigold," she intoned, "I shall do no such thing. If he has refused, then leave it be."

A blush stained Marigold's cheeks. "But was this not generous of him?"

Hortensia frowned and did not respond beyond a harrumph.

Marigold sighed. "Aunt Hortensia, he will think you are a dragon if you do not stop scowling at him. I assure you, Lord Muir, she can be quite pleasant when she wants to be. Kindly assure her that you are not romantically interested in me. She is under the mistaken impression that you like me and therefore must be put in your place. She believes all young men have one thing in mind when it comes to–"

"Marigold! Confine your comments to the weather and your museum trove. Honestly, child. You are far too trusting of this man."

This man?

In this, Leo supposed the harridan was right.

It took all his restraint not to stare at Marigold.

She looked beautiful in her gown of blue muslin that matched the color of her eyes. The gown was modestly cut, but Marigold had a spectacular body – pert, full breasts, slender waist and hips, and a long, silky neck. Her features were delicate, but at the same time ripe and tempting.

He had been dreaming hot dreams of her last night.

They were a pleasant reprieve from the dreams usually overwhelming his sleep. Of course, those bad dreams always came on. They arose from a dark place and left him gasping for air. He always awoke feeling as though he were buried alive in an underground tomb.

Hortensia was right to be mindful of him.

He was beginning to think of Marigold as his oasis in the desert, a well of cool water from which he might drink and drink, and then drink some more. "Ah, we have arrived."

Mr. Smythe-Owens hurried out to greet them.

Leo stepped down first to assist Hortensia in descending from the carriage. The little curator immediately offered his arm to escort the harridan inside. He gushed and chattered as he led her away.

This gave Leo a moment alone with the bubble of froth that was Marigold.

She cast him a gloriously soft smile as she poked her head out of the carriage. "I'm so glad Uncle John gave his permission to have you escort us. We are going to have such an exciting day."

He could think of many more exciting things to do with this girl than dig through crates of old bones, but he was determined to behave himself around her.

All he had to do was stop undressing her in his thoughts.

But that only made him think of it all the more.

There was already too much of a charge in the air between them, that sizzle palpable.

"Let me help you down." He put his hands around her waist and lifted her out of the carriage. "You look very pretty today."

She wore a stylish cap that matched her gown. The cap had a small feather sticking up from it. Leo far preferred it to the frilly bonnets women often wore. Those were such hideous things, designed to cover everything interesting on a woman's head. But Marigold's pert cap was slightly angled to accentuate her big eyes and the gentle line of her jaw, as well as show off her dark satin hair.

"Thank you," she said, casting him another of her sunshine smiles as she held onto his shoulders to steady herself. "You look very handsome yourself."

He chuckled and released her. "Men do not need to be complimented on their appearance, but thank you."

They walked inside, her hand lightly resting in the crook of his arm. This girl fired his blood, singed him from head to toe with her casual touch.

Bollocks.

He raked a hand through his hair as he walked her inside, knowing he needed to stop this ridiculous surge of desire that came on every time he looked at her. Even her scent was arousing, a light cinnamon or some other similar spice that evoked memories of warm winter nights beside the fire and a cup of eggnog in one's hand...which probably explained why he had the sudden urge to lick her warm skin.

What he ought to do was get out more often, go to the sort of clubs where a man with lustful urges could satisfy himself on women who were experienced in bed. He could afford to frequent the more exclusive clubs or find a few widows who hosted scandalous salons. How hard could it be to find himself a courtesan or two, or perhaps seek out an unhappily married countess to relieve his agony? Women such as these were rife in the *ton* and made themselves easily available. They would not put claims on his heart or threaten his bachelorhood if scandal broke out.

He dismissed the idea immediately because none of them would be Marigold. He shook his head over the frustration of it, but his father and grandfather had been faithful to one woman all their lives, and it seemed he was no exception.

He would have to brace himself for an agonizing Season.

Marigold was too innocent to seduce.

But he wanted no one other than Marigold.

To add to his stupid misery, he had no intention of courting Marigold.

Were he capable of thinking with the brain in his head instead of the brainless organ between his legs, he would have avoided Marigold as one might avoid a fatal disease.

Why risk the distraction?

This was her Season to find a husband.

But this was his Season for revenge.

Finding out who had set him up for ambush and left him to rot in an enemy prison was his priority.

Killing this man was at the top of his list of things to do.

Falling in love was never contemplated and not on his list at all.

Marigold released his arm and hurried to her crate the moment they entered the Duke of Huntsford's office. It already lay open, her precious skull perched on top. "There you are, my beauty," she crooned. "Aunt Hortensia, come have a look."

"Not on your life. Mr. Smythe-Owens, ring for tea. I shall settle myself here and read my book while you and Marigold do whatever ghoulish thing you do with those bones."

"At once, Madam," he said, bowing and scraping as though Hortensia was indeed a royal consort gracing the museum with a visit. He called to a young man walking along the hall. "Send up a tea cart for our guests, Mr. Wilson. Cups and plates for four."

Hortensia now turned to Leo. "And what shall you be doing while they work?"

"Helping them out, if they will allow me."

Marigold nodded. "That is most generous of you, my lord. Yes, I think we shall need your help as we begin to set up this new exhibit display. Neither Mr. Smythe-Owens nor I have the height required or the brawn. There will be climbing and lifting involved."

"Ever at your service." He gave a slight bow, and then folded his arms across his chest while waiting for the work to begin.

To Marigold's credit, she was an engaging tutor and surprisingly knowledgeable about these artifacts. She had an eager lilt to her voice as she explained the significance of each item lifted from the crate. Next, she set them out upon the floor of the duke's large office in what appeared to be some sort of pattern. "Miss Farthingale, the duke has a large table in the corner," he said, motioning to what was an elegant conference table. "Why do you not use that?"

She laughed lightly. "It is far too small."

He shook his head. "But it easily fits ten men around it."

"This flying creature is five times the size of the table. You'll see, won't he Mr. Smythe-Owens?"

The curator chuckled. "Indeed, Miss Farthingale."

Leo was not convinced. Since these bones had easily fit into the crate, how could they now dwarf the long table? However, as each piece was placed in its position on the floor, he realized these bones did not comprise a complete set but were merely remnants of a giant creature. Marigold and the curator were kneeling on the floor, as though figuring out pieces of a puzzle that would form a portrait of this ancient animal.

The skull was easiest to place since it was obviously the animal's head.

As they began to lay out more bones, Leo saw these fragments actually begin to take the form of enormous wings that spanned the entire width of the room. Some of the bones were part of its legs and talons. Each talon alone was the length of Leo's forearm.

Good grief.

Was it possible such an animal had once existed?

This explained why they had not bothered to set up on the table.

He rested on his haunches beside Marigold, genuinely intrigued. "How can you tell what fits where?"

"I was not adept, at first. But Duchess Adela's friends, Lady Sydney Harcourt and Lady Gregoria Easton have specialized medical knowledge and taught me all they could while with us at the Devonshire caves. Their anatomical expertise is invaluable." She tried not to rake her gaze over his body, but he caught her blush as her eyes darted up and down the length of him.

He grinned, knowing the little minx wanted to examine his anatomical structure in thorough detail.

Well, why not?

He certainly wished to do the same with hers.

She cleared her throat. "Some of these placements are just educated guesses. We have an idea of what this creature looked like from the cave drawings Adela found. A few of these bones," she said, motioning to those still in the crate, "belong to another animal, one who does not fly. You will notice those bones are quite dense while the ones on this flying lizard are much lighter in comparison. But we don't have enough pieces of this other creature to guess what it might be. That's why Huntsford and Adela are still at the dig site. They are hoping to deliver more bones and an artist's rendering or two, so that we might see the possibilities."

Leo watched and listened, his admiration genuine for Marigold.

She was not yet twenty, but did not allow her age or considerable beauty to define her. It would have been so easy for her to preen for hours in front of a mirror, or expend her energy shopping for new gowns.

These idle pastimes were not for Marigold. She had no interest in using her looks to land a rich, possibly titled husband.

Well, he was rich and titled.

Marigold did not seem to care about that.

She had removed her pert hat and now had two pencils poking out of her silky hair.

She was on her knees, crawling carefully over the outline of a massive bird.

"The wings of this flying lizard are something like a kite," Marigold said, her excitement obvious. "Or should I say, our kites are fashioned after these wings. A firm skeletal structure to support the skin – or cloth in the case of a kite – stretched over it to catch the air and lift it off the ground."

"Have you heard of Leonardo Da Vinci?" he asked Marigold.

She nodded enthusiastically. "The Duke of Huntsford has several of his original drawings regarding this very thing on display in his private library. I'll show them to you as soon as we are finished here. Leonardo was convinced man could fly, if only we could get the wing structure right." She smiled at him. "He was a Leo, too."

Leo emitted a short burst of laughter.

After taking precise measurements, Marigold and Mr. Smythe-Owens then put the pieces back in the crate, and Leo hammered in the nails to seal it.

He did not mind providing the necessary brawn.

Once done, the three of them went downstairs to the recently opened Hall of Dragons, leaving the Farthingale dragon, Hortensia, comfortably ensconced in the duke's office. "I am too old to be running up and down stairs," she remarked. "Marigold, I want your word that you shall not allow yourself to be alone with Lord Muir."

"I hardly think we shall be alone, Aunt Hortensia. The museum is full of visitors and we are going to inspect its most popular exhibit. It is more likely we shall lose each other in the crowd."

Leo was surprised Hortensia did not demand his promise. Then again, she did not trust him, so his word of honor held no value to her. In truth, it was insulting. However, he would get over this slight since this now left him free to do whatever he wished to do if he and Marigold ever did find themselves alone.

He would need no more than ten seconds to properly ravish those gorgeous lips of hers.

Bollocks.

He was doing it again, thinking of her when he should not.

He followed Marigold and the curator downstairs, marveling at the relics on display. Huntsford had done a magnificent job, obviously knowing what he was doing in putting together these exhibits. He brought these ancient worlds to life and fascinated the visitors who crowded through here.

Leo stopped suddenly at the entrance to the Hall of Dragons.

Why was it so dark in there?

Well, it wasn't completely dark.

The so-called dragons were lit up from below, illuminating these creatures to make them appear larger and more frightening than they might be in bright light. Visitors were led along designated walking paths which remained in relative darkness, but there were ropes to guide them. Those ropes also served the purpose of keeping the onlookers from getting too close to the exhibits.

The effect of all this was to heighten the imagination of each visitor and make them feel the dangers of the past.

This was a little too successfully done, as far as Leo was concerned.

The walls suddenly seemed to close in around him.

He froze.

Others pushed past him.

Marigold had been walking ahead with the curator, and now motioned for the man to walk on while she hurried back to Leo's side. "Lord Muir, is something wrong?"

Leo could not find his voice.

The Hall of Dragons was a windowless room.

In his mind's eye, it resembled a tomb…or a dark, dank prison.

This exhibit sucked the breath from him.

Marigold took his hand.

Lord, he was shaking.

How utterly humiliating.

She led him back into the main hall that had tall windows to allow in plenty of light. "Is it the darkness, Leo?"

"No." He finally let out a breath. "It is the lack of windows. The closed-in walls."

"I see."

No, she could not possibly understand.

"Please stay right here," she said, her voice quite gentle. "I'll ask Mr. Smythe-Owens to summon his assistants. They only need to measure the available exhibit space within that room. I'll let him know you are pressed for time and I promised you a tour of the museum."

She took off into that darkened hall.

He stood there like an idiot, sweating and his heart racing.

She was back a moment later, and immediately placed her hand in the crook of his arm to lead him past rows of glass cases and take him back upstairs. "I'll walk you through the exhibits later. Let me show you the duke's private library first. Only scholars are permitted inside. Security is very tight because the library holds too many priceless manuscripts to allow regular visitors in."

She did not stop chattering the entire way upstairs, but the gentle tone of her voice soothed him. He realized she was talking to him on purpose, giving him the chance to calm down. She handled him beautifully, he had to allow. Not fussing over him, which would have added to his embarrassment. Not ridiculing him, which would have angered him.

This girl did not have a wicked bone in her body. The thought of mocking him had not even entered her mind.

He had mostly calmed down by the time they entered the private library. "Thank you, Miss Farthingale."

Big, blue eyes stared back at him. "May I ask, what happened back there?"

"You may ask, but I have no answer for you." He noticed books piled up on several tables along with some notebooks and satchels to indicate at least two scholars were using the library. Since it was past noon, he expected they had left their belongings in place in this secure area while they went off to have a meal.

Obviously, Huntsford would never allow drink or food near these valuable texts.

At the thought, Leo realized his throat was parched.

Marigold seemed to read his mind. "There's a private dining room for use of the duke and any visiting scholars. Poor Aunt Hortensia is probably starving by now. Let me show you quickly around the bookshelves and then we shall fetch her. How does that sound?"

"Enticing," he said with a short laugh. "My throat is rather dry, and I do find I am famished."

But his hunger was mostly for Marigold.

He wanted to wrap her in his arms and savor her beautiful lips.

She had handled him expertly and with an inordinate amount of compassion.

He was impressed.

One thing for certain, he would not underestimate this girl again. She had saved him yesterday from a knife-wielding villain, and now again today had saved him from himself.

She was far more intelligent than he or others gave her credit for.

There were two guards at the entrance to the private library whose job it was to check everyone coming in and those going out to make certain nothing of value was removed. But those guards remained at the entrance and no one was actually in the library at present except for him and Marigold.

She pointed out the Da Vinci drawings and several of his original texts.

She pointed out some writings on papyrus and one or two illuminated manuscripts prepared by monks in some alpine monastery over five hundred years ago.

She next took him along a row of shelves filled with magnificently bound volumes. They were mostly works of archeological or botanical significance. "Well, that's about everything to see in here," Marigold remarked. "I'm sure the duke would not mind your returning at your leisure if you wish to explore further. Shall we go?"

He held her back.

She looked up at him. "Would you like another moment? We can stay here as long as you need. Are you sure you cannot tell me what happened to you downstairs, Leo?"

"It was nothing, just a bit of my past catching up to me." He kissed her on the forehead. "Do not ask me to talk about it."

"I won't. You'll tell me whenever you are ready."

He would never be ready to talk about those lost years. The anger and bitterness were still too raw and would always fester in his mind until he had his revenge. Even if he could talk about those years of captivity, he did not wish to shove that horror onto Marigold. The world needed innocent rays of sunshine like her.

"A man could drown in the fathomless pools of your eyes," he whispered raggedly.

Surprise flickered in her gorgeous orbs. "Leo, are you flirting with me?"

He laughed. "No, the thought just popped into my head. I did not mean to say it aloud."

Men like him did not flirt.

They simply took what they wanted, and he seemed to be desperately wanting Marigold at the moment. She was nothing like most women of his acquaintance, and he was not certain if this was good or bad. He usually engaged with women who were experienced sexually, had done a bit of traveling thereby gaining a bit of sophistication, and who might be considered more classically beautiful than this girl.

Marigold even had dimples when she smiled.

And those damn adorable elf ears.

"Leo, I–"

Did she have to be so temptingly sweet? "Stop calling me Leo."

"I will not. And do not growl at me. Admit it, you like me." She leaned smugly against the bookshelves, showing no fear as he took another step closer.

"Marigold, don't you know it is dangerous to prod a lion?" He placed his hands on either side of her body to hold her against the bookshelves. He meant to intimidate her, but only a little. He kept his hold loose because he wanted her to know she could move away if she wished.

To his dismay, she did not attempt to move away. Instead, she wrapped her delicate fingers around his lapels and nudged him closer, taking too much delight in his nearness. "How dangerous, Leo?"

He emitted another soft growl and moved closer, pinning her against his body so that she could not escape unless she pushed him away.

To his frustration, she did not seem inclined to do so. A shudder ran through him as his chest was now pressed against her lusciously soft bosom.

Blessed saints.

What was he doing?

This was not at all in his plans.

Well, he could forget those blasted plans for the moment.

He kissed her softly on the neck, inhaling the cinnamon scent of her or whatever that evocative mix was, perhaps nutmeg, raisins, plum pudding, warming fire, sweet memories he'd lost during his ordeal and she was now bringing back to him. "Push me away, Marigold," he said in a raw whisper.

She emitted a breathy sigh. "That felt nice. I have no intention of pushing you away. Are you going to give me a proper kiss or not?"

"Not," he said, silently cursing his inability to draw away.

What was it about this girl?

He could not get enough of her.

"Are you sure? Because this is the perfect moment for my first kiss, and you do not strike me as the sort to pass up such an obvious opportunity. I certainly have no wish to pass it up. I have never been held in a man's arms before."

"I am not holding you, I am pinning you against the books. It is not at all the same thing. And quite inappropriate, I might add."

"Well, I am not complaining. It feels nice. *You* feel nice. Are you sure you will not kiss me until I am breathless?"

He did not know whether to laugh or groan, so he did a little of both. "Yes, I am sure. It is not wise for me to kiss you."

She closed her eyes. "I hope you will reconsider."

"Why?" he asked, unable to resist placing a gentle kiss on her eyes now that they had fluttered shut. She had the prettiest dark eyelashes.

"Because I shall die an unhappy and frustrated spinster if you do not."

"Marigold, that is the last thing you will ever be." He laughed softly, forgetting formality since he was practically atop her and already burning because of the light press of her bosom to his chest. Why would she not push him away? Did she have to make things so difficult for him? Of course, none of this could be blamed on her since he was the one pressing himself against her. Lightly, but still pressing. "You will have a line of men out the door of your townhouse, all of them aching to court you. I expect that will entail kisses, as well."

Of course, the possessive part of him wanted to be the first man ever to touch his lips to hers.

That dominant, baboonish part of him wanted to be the first and *only* man to ever kiss her.

Lord, this was not good.

"Marigold, you do not need me to be the first."

"Yes, I do," she said with a hopeful ache that touched his heart. "It has to be you, Leo. I would not trust anyone else to do it so perfectly and with caring."

Her exquisite first kiss?

And she trusted him?

He wanted to lecture her on the folly of it and admonish her for misbehaving.

However, he reminded himself again, since he was the big oaf with his body pressed to hers, it could be said he was the one misbehaving.

He was a grown man.

Usually clever and sensible.

Why could he not behave like a gentleman?

But he had no intention of doing so.

He desperately needed to hold this sparkling light that was Marigold and taste the sweetness of her lips.

"You must never trust me, Marigold." That said, he closed his mouth over hers and devoured her with a barely controlled animal hunger. She was delectable and he had a voracious appetite for this girl.

He plundered her deliciously soft lips. Yet, despite the savage power of his desire, he had not lost all vestige of common sense. He forced his heart to stop pounding through his ears, and made certain to keep their kiss gentle...mostly gentle. But he had built up quite a bit of raw need for Marigold and could not hold all of it back.

Hence the devouring grind of his mouth upon hers.

He hoped to excite her but not scare her.

After all, there was an etiquette to a first kiss. It should not be too bland or she would be disappointed. Nor should it be too rough and ravaging or it would frighten her. It had to be deep, possessive, and just intense enough to sweep her off her feet. His pride would not permit anything less than her complete surrender and wholehearted satisfaction.

He meant to give her a first kiss that was all she had ever dreamed of receiving.

As for him, he would remember it, too.

Every blessed detail.

The sweet taste of mint and cocoa on her lips.

The swan-like arch of her body as she melted against him.

The perfect pleasure of her breasts molding to his chest.

Why did it feel as though their bodies were meant to be one?

This was very bad.

He could let nothing interfere with his plans.

Not even this delectable morsel.

Instead of withdrawing and ending the kiss, he deepened it, pouring his soul into the cavern of her mouth because this would be the first and last time he ever touched her.

He meant to make it count.

Which probably explained why he needed to run his hands along her body and memorize her every curve.

It also explained why he felt a crushing ache in his heart when he finally drew away.

Perhaps he would rethink this matter of this first kiss being their last.

Having tasted her once, he needed more.

But he could not have revenge *and* happiness.

Marigold would never forgive him if she knew he meant to kill his nemesis. She could not talk him out of it, either. No matter how much she pleaded, he would never give up his vengeful quest.

What possible future could they have together then?

Nothing beyond this one, glorious kiss.

Marigold brought him to his senses with a soft cry of dismay. "Leo, did you hate it? Why are you looking at me like that?"

"How am I looking at you?"

"As though you have just made the worst mistake of your life."

This was his chance to end their attraction right now.

"I have, Marigold."

"You have? Are you sure it was a mistake? Our kiss was the best ever for me."

"It is not possible. How can you judge whether it was your best ever when it was your first and only kiss?"

She cast him a stubborn look. "Kindly do not minimize the splendor of it. Why should I not appreciate when something is wonderful? And it was wonderful. How can I kiss any other man after this?"

"And there's the tragedy of it."

"What do you mean?"

"It was a good kiss," he admitted, unable to completely shatter this important moment in her life. "In truth, it was a spectacular kiss. I will not lie to you."

"Then why are you looking at me with such a forlorn expression?"

"Because no matter how exquisite it was—"

"Which it was," she insisted with a stubborn frown and the prettiest, pouty lips.

"Yes, it was." He sighed and continued. "Because no matter how exquisite, there can never be anything between us. Marigold, I will never marry you."

CHAPTER 5

MARIGOLD FELT AS though a block of stone had just fallen on her heart and crushed it. What was wrong with this man? By his own admission, he had just given her the best kiss either of them had ever received in their lives. With that perfect kiss, he had thoroughly ruined her for anyone else, and he thought not to marry her?

Why was he even mentioning marriage when they had only just met?

Of course, she had already fallen in love with him.

She had known it since setting eyes on him yesterday.

Even she understood she was rushing things a bit. After all, last year she had thought herself attracted to Lord Julius Thorne, the Duke of Huntsford's youngest brother. But she had never felt anything like this about him. Also, she had sensed her friend Gregoria liked him and months ago decided to step aside so they were not in competition. With that decision, she thought there would be some tug to her heart at the loss, but there hadn't been so much as a twinge.

But with Leo, even now she could feel her heart ripping to shreds.

Still, there was no mistaking *his* desire or the pleasure he had felt. She was inexperienced, but not completely ignorant. He had put his heart and soul into that kiss. One did not put one's soul into anything with that depth of feeling and then dismiss its importance.

Were there not rules about this sort of thing?

"Marigold, I'm sorry."

She met his gaze squarely and did not shirk. "I'm not."

He shook his head. "You're not?"

"No."

"Would you care to elaborate?"

"No, I would not." He deserved no explanations after making his ridiculous statement. He was a bachelor and free to marry, so why would he not choose her? Not that he had to, but could he not give it a little more thought?

They returned to pick up Hortensia and dine in Huntsford's private dining room. The steward attending them offered a choice of rack of lamb or smoked haddock. Leo chose the lamb while she and Hortensia selected the haddock.

Afterward, Marigold assisted Mr. Smythe-Owens in sketching out the design of their new dragon display. Hortensia returned to the duke's office to await her while Leo muttered something about stopping by the magistrate's office to give his statement relating to yesterday's attempt to steal her artifacts.

She did not mind his leaving.

In truth, she needed to put a little distance between them after that indescribably wonderful kiss. Perhaps he had been scared off by his own desires and the fact he had acted upon them within a day of meeting her. She knew he was a gentleman at heart. It must have been quite upsetting for him to realize how innocent she was. Of course, it did not stop him from running his big, rough hands all over her body.

Obviously, he was feeling badly about it now.

However, not badly enough to have kept his hands to himself in the first place.

Dear heaven.

This man knew how to scorch a woman.

Mentioning this to him would only upset him further.

He returned shortly after four o'clock. Marigold was beginning to worry he had forgotten about her and gone off in his carriage, leaving her and Hortensia to make their own way home. But he strode in with apologies for his tardiness. "After giving my statement to the magistrate, I dashed off to the Royal Society to speak to Lotheil about those villains. He was furious, especially after last year's incident between Huntsford's wife and one of their Fellows. To have three more caught attempting to steal, this time your bones, put him in an apoplectic fit. He called an immediate meeting of the board and wanted me to remain there to address them. I hurried back as soon as I was done giving them a piece of my mind."

"I wish I could have seen you excoriate those bounders. I certainly have a lot to say about their intolerable standards and the scoundrels they are admitting into their member ranks over serious scholars who happen to be women."

"If it is any consolation, I said much the same to them."

She smiled up at him. "Well, thank you for that."

He gave a small nod. "I think it is time I took you home. I did not mean to be so delayed. How is Hortensia doing?"

"She is fine. Probably took a nap after we ate. I wanted to take her on a tour of the museum but she had no interest in it."

"You sound disappointed."

She nodded. "I am."

"Don't be," he said, trying to mollify her. "At Hortensia's age, merely walking might be too stressful for her. Having to navigate amid a crowd would be impossible."

"She walks just fine. I don't think she cares about old fossils."

Leo grinned. "Because she is one. Hits too close to home."

Marigold laughed. "That is a mean thing to say, but accurate."

She placed her arm in his as they climbed the stairs to retrieve Hortensia. The instinct to hold onto him was so natural, Marigold did not realize she was doing it until they reached the landing. Even then, she found it hard to let go of him. "Oh."

"Did you forget something?"

She shook her head. "No, it is nothing."

They rode back to Chipping Way, keeping their conversation to the museum artifacts and the design she and Mr. Smythe-Owens had decided upon for the display of her strange skull and the creature to which it belonged.

Marigold was a little saddened Hortensia had shown no

interest, but Leo more than made up for it by asking detailed and intelligent questions that went a long way toward cheering her up. The carriage drew up in front of the Farthingale townhouse and he helped both of them down. Hortensia hurried inside, but as Marigold was about to follow, he held her back.

Marigold sighed as she watched Hortensia scamper inside with the agility of a gazelle. "She is glad this day is finally over."

"Don't fret over her," Leo said, his voice a deep, gentle rumble. "I am very proud of you, Marigold. Proud of all the work you are doing at the museum. Not everyone will appreciate your efforts, but I want you to know that I do."

His kind words almost reduced her to tears.

How could he be so genuinely thoughtful and not intend to marry her?

Well, it would take months of getting to know each other better before he would ever seriously consider offering for her hand. As to *never* marrying her? That was too ridiculous to contemplate. "Thank you, Leo."

"What matters most is that you love what you are doing. I'm sorry for what happened today."

She placed her hand lightly on his arm. "Don't be. It was the best day ever for me."

He nodded. "It was nice for me, too."

"Only nice? Leo, admit it. The day was splendid."

"All right. Yes, it was splendid. Best ever."

She knew he was only saying this to be polite. He had enjoyed some of it, particularly their kiss. Yet, neither of them could forget what happened in the Hall of Dragons. Why had he become physically ill at the mere thought of entering that exhibit?

In time, she hoped to learn the answer.

For now, she would hold onto the magic of their kiss.

Dream of it.

But never push him to kiss her again.

He was a wealthy, bachelor marquess just returned to town and not looking to form any attachments right now. "I had better see to Mallow. I'm sure he missed me."

She had no sooner uttered the words than the little spaniel

came tearing out of the house and leaped straight into Leo's arms. "Traitor!" she said with a laugh, wanting to spank the impertinent dog. She had bent down and stretched out her arms to pick him up, but he had run straight past her, finding a new favorite in Leo.

The laughter caught in her throat when she turned to Leo, for he had such a raw expression on his face.

Traitor.

That word had stirred something inside of him.

What was it?

Obviously something to do with lies, betrayal...dishonor. Was he the one betrayed? Or had he done the betraying?

"Mallow, I cannot play with you today," he mumbled, handing the spaniel into Marigold's arms. He bid her a hasty farewell and strode across the street to his home.

His driver flicked the reins to return the carriage to the mews.

Marigold sighed. "Mallow, we are going to have to talk to the family about the marquess. Something is going on with him."

She walked back into the house, determined to do some investigating about this man who had been fearless when taking on three attackers but could not walk into a windowless room. He had kissed her with glorious heat and gentle possession. Yet, the look in his eyes after she had blurted the word 'traitor' had been icy and filled with murderous rage.

Then that lethal look was gone in the blink of an eye, leaving her wondering whether she had imagined his response.

The man was considered a hero, which meant he was unlikely to be the traitor.

But had someone betrayed him?

Mallow barked to shake her out of her thoughts. "You are right, you little scamp. I had better not get involved. In fact, I think we need to put a little distance between ourselves and the marquess. He will come to us when he is ready."

But Marigold did not see him for a full week afterward.

She occupied her days by helping Mr. Smythe-Owens set up the elaborate dragon display. It would take weeks to finish. She even allowed Mallow to escape into the marquess's garden a time or two so she could pretend to be searching for him. But the marquess never came out. Instead, he sent his butler to see to her and Mallow each time. "I'm sorry, Miss Farthingale," Sterling would say. "The marquess is busy at the moment and cannot come out to greet you."

Each time, she responded equally disingenuously. "Thank you, Sterling. Please convey my regards. I did not intend to intrude, but Mallow escaped. He misses Lord Muir. I'll do my best to keep us from irritating him."

Sterling would then smile kindly because he truly was a kind man. "It is always a delight to see you, Miss Farthingale."

Each time, she would walk back across the street, trying not to appear dejected. She had tried again today and received the same crushing response. It was time to forget Leo and his scorching kisses. Well, she'd had only the one kiss.

There was a soiree to attend this evening at her cousin Dillie's house. Marigold returned to her bedchamber to prepare for it. She had attended one ball and two musicales this week, acquiring three suitors over the course of these affairs.

Her family was pleased.

She was heartbroken.

Leo had gone to those as well, but took pains to ignore her.

In truth, he ignored almost everyone while taking a turn about the room before heading off to do whatever handsome, wealthy bachelors did on their own in an evening.

Not that she cared.

That he had not deigned to acknowledge her just proved what an oaf he was. She was invisible to him, but other gentlemen liked her. One had even declared her to be a diamond. However, she did not feel very bright or lustrous.

Her three suitors kept her entertained. They flirted with her outrageously and fought for her attention. Unfortunately, they did not interest her. How could they compare to Leo? She always found them lacking.

Leo was in attendance at her cousin's soiree.

To her surprise, he did not simply take a turn about the room and then dash off. He seemed resolved to remain the entire evening. Perhaps it was not all that surprising. Her cousin Dillie happened to be the Duchess of Edgeware. Her husband, Ian, was one of the most powerful men in England, second in rank at the Home Office only to the Duke of Wooton.

She'd heard the Duke of Wooton was also known as the Duke of Ice. But Ian and Leo were also quite icy and fierce when they wanted to be.

Leo had the power to freeze her with his cold stare.

She turned away, refusing to torment herself by looking at him.

There were plenty of people at Dillie and Ian's party, many of them happy to talk to her. More young men surrounded her and tossed empty compliments at her.

Had Leo noticed?

Leo and Ian were off in a corner speaking rather seriously, if the tension in their bearing and their frowns were any indication. Their conversation did not last long since Ian had hosting duties that required his attention. As soon as Ian left him to return to his wife's side, Leo strode outdoors.

Marigold wished to follow him, but she was now in conversation with Dillie and some of their other cousins, so she could not simply dart away. As Ian joined them, his frown evaporated, for Dillie was smiling up at him. Marigold could see this duke was madly in love with his wife and she found this a most commendable trait.

In fact, all her cousins had made love matches.

She had no intention of being the first Farthingale to settle for a marriage of convenience. While she debated whether to follow Leo out, one of her suitors approached. "Miss Farthingale, you are a vision in rose silk. Indeed, radiant."

"Thank you, Lord Beldon." She smiled politely, but was not keen on the man. He fawned and flattered, but there was something about him that put her off. His attentions seemed forced, as though courting her was a chore. Then why waste his time on her?

Perhaps she was not being fair.

She knew little about him and may have been judging him too harshly.

Nor did she know anything about men in general.

Leo had kissed her with heat and passion, as though crashing headlong into love with her. Then the next words out of his mouth were a glib declaration that he would never marry her.

After this, he had immediately cut off their friendship.

He could not make it any more clear he had abandoned all intention of courting her. Still, his kiss had felt real. She suspected his reason for abruptly ending their friendship was because he liked her more than he was ready to handle.

Yes, she would hold onto that hope.

She shook her head, knowing her instincts were all in a jumble.

Leo claimed he wanted nothing to do with her, but sparks ignited whenever their gazes met. Lord Beldon claimed to be enraptured with her, but there was a big, vast nothing between them. He did not like her very much, she was certain of it. Yet, he spouted insipid poetry and fawned over her to the point she wanted to scream and run away.

It all felt fake.

So why flirt with her?

She was not an heiress.

The best that could be said of her is that she was well connected. All her cousins had married important men, although some of them at the time were considered reprehensible cads. But she understood why her cousins refused to marry anyone else. One had a sense of who was right for them and who was not.

Lord Beldon's affection for her simply did not ring true.

She listened politely as he continued to fawn over her. Then he spoke of his true passion, his newly acquired racehorse. "Got him last week at Tattersalls. Outbid Muir for him."

That caught Marigold's attention. "Oh, you both wanted the horse?"

"To tell you the truth, I hadn't thought to purchase him until Muir started bidding on him. We all know he has an excellent eye for ladies and horses. If he wanted that beast, then I was going to grab him first."

And if Leo wanted Marigold? Was this the reason Lord Beldon was paying attention to her? She dismissed the notion since Leo had not paid her the slightest attention this entire week.

Lord Beldon's chuckle, large and springing from deep within his belly, reclaimed her attention. "We've always had a bit of competition going, Muir and I. Ever since our school days."

Was she wrong?

Had Beldon noticed Leo eyeing her and decided to make his play for her?

She would find the right moment to disabuse the dolt of the notion Leo might be holding a *tendre* for her. Were her other two suitors also in competition with Leo? Is this why she suddenly found herself surrounded by eager, young men?

Where was Leo?

She meant to give him a piece of her mind, for his behavior simply would not do…not that she understood what he was doing to make these men think he cared for her.

He hadn't come back inside yet.

Drat.

She wished so much to follow him out onto the terrace, but too many people were watching her.

The dinner bell rang and conversation came to a momentary end. Lord Beldon offered his arm to escort her in. "Well, look at that. Miss Farthingale, I am seated beside you."

"How nice." She forced a smile, hoping it came across as genuine.

Where was Leo seated?

He strolled in late, the last to take his seat which happened to be directly across the table from her. But it was a large table and there was an ornate epergne between them that partially blocked her view of him. Of all the bad luck. Her view of the ladies seated on either side of him was completely clear. Her cousin Daisy, wife of Gabriel Dayne, first Earl of Blackthorne, was to his right. A beautiful young lady she did not recognize was to his left and tossing Leo flirtatious glances.

The young lady's flirtation carried on throughout the meal.

Marigold lost her appetite.

Digging up skulls in those Devonshire caves was a much easier proposition than entering the marriage mart.

She hardly paid attention to Lord Beldon as he bloviated about the horse he had stolen out from under Leo at auction, nor could she eat a bite of her quail or the buttered potatoes that now lay in a glop on her plate.

When the meal was over, the ladies rose to retire to the drawing room for coffee and sherry. The lady seated beside Leo swept her hand along his shoulder as she rose, an intimate gesture that could not be mistaken for anything other than solicitation of an assignation or confirmation of one they had already arranged.

This was too much for Marigold to bear.

She took the opportunity to sneak off to the Edgeware library and have a good cry. It was completely childish of her, but that little scene had utterly destroyed her. Yes, it was foolish to cry over a man she had known merely a week, especially since he had spent most of that time avoiding her.

She decided he had been extremely cruel and selfish to kiss her.

If all he meant to do was assuage his curiosity, then he should have restrained himself and left her alone. His actions were unpardonable. One kiss. Done. Shake off the little nuisance and find himself a real woman.

If this is all he thought of her, then he was a wretched scoundrel and she refused to shed another tear over him after she cried her heart out tonight. Feeling her tears coming on, she hastened down the elegant hallway and ran into the library. A lamp had been left burning atop the desk. A soft, golden light now filled the room. "Good," she muttered, since she did not wish to trip over something in the dark and break her ankle.

She did not need anything more to add to her misery.

After taking out her handkerchief, she waited for her anguished tears to fall. However, she managed no more than a sniffle before she heard voices outside the door. At least three or four male voices by her count. "Oh!"

She started to panic, realizing she could not be found in here alone. She would be ruined if seen, for everyone would believe she had come in here to meet a man. The fact that there was no man with her was irrelevant.

As the door slowly opened, she dove behind one of the massive window curtains and prayed fervently these gentlemen would not stay in here long. But this explained why a lamp had been left lit. Their meeting was planned.

She held her breath.

Her heart sank as they closed the door and settled in for a chat.

Her face turned to flame when the first thing she heard was a string of curses emanating from Leo's lips. "Do not ask me again to be patient. I am going to find that traitor and kill him. You cannot stop me."

"Cool that hot head of yours, Leo. And rest assured, we are going to stop you if you attempt to hunt for him on your own. This is for your own good. Your anger is out of control. Will you kill us too?" She recognized the voice of Daisy's husband, Gabriel. He had been awarded the earldom of Blackthorne for his wartime valor.

She knew Leo had tremendous respect for him.

Still, the tension was so thick, one could cut it with a knife.

Ian spoke up next. "We are on the task, Leo. Now that you have given us your report and told us what you believe happened, we have opened a covert investigation. But you have to give us time to—"

"Time?" Leo said, his anger barely leashed. "I spent four years in a dark pit because of that traitorous bastard. Starved, beaten, left to freeze in the winter. Not a glimpse of sunshine. Put through hell. Four years of my life destroyed. Gone. I gave you three names. The traitor has to be one of them."

"And we are retracing each of their steps," said Graelem Dayne, her cousin Laurel's husband, who held the title of Baron Moray. She easily recognized him by his Scottish brogue. "We are working as fast as we can. Ye canno' expect results in a month when the traitor has had four years to cover his tracks."

John and Sophie Farthingale had five daughters, Rose, Laurel, Daisy, and the twins, Lily and Daffodil who everyone called Dillie. Had they all married agents of the Crown? Or was ferreting out traitors something all peers took on as their duty?

What she had overheard now explained Leo's reaction in the

Hall of Dragons. *Dear heaven.* He had spent four years in a dungeon.

Starved, beaten, and left to die.

No wonder he needed windows and light.

"Include me in the investigation," Leo said. "It will move along faster. I led that royal delegation. I ought to be the one to question the men who were with me when we were ambushed in the Carpathian mountains. I'll know immediately if any of them are lying."

Ian crossed to a cabinet, which must be where he stocked his port and brandy, for she heard the clink of glasses as he asked, "Anyone care for a drink?"

No. No. No.

Marigold knew she would never get out of here if they settled in for a round of drinks. How was she to escape? They would notice immediately if she opened a window and attempted to climb out of it.

"We've given you their original reports, Leo," Ian said. "Read through those again. Read them as many times as necessary. That will be immensely helpful."

"Don't patronize me, Ian."

"I am not at all. Only you would know if anything in their statements did not ring true. But as for dealing with these men face to face? You are a lit fuse heading toward a powder keg. Any of us would feel the same had we gone through what you endured. I understand what you are feeling. But it changes nothing. We cannot let you near any of these men yet. You are too angry, and I will not have you beating the truth out of them. First of all, the real villain is not likely to give over the information you seek."

"And," Graelem added, "it is more likely one of the innocent men will confess just to make ye stop beating him."

"Not that I blame you for wanting to go at the traitor," Ian continued. "As I said, I would feel the same were I in your situation. But we must play this with finesse. No one can know we are investigating anything. We cannot risk tipping off the guilty party when we have no idea which one of the three he is."

"Assuming he is any of those three," Graelem added. "None of these men strike me as masterminds. Someone else could be pulling the strings. Perhaps there is something larger going on that we are not aware. Who knows what else this traitor has managed to sabotage? Or what government secrets he has revealed to his foreign contacts."

Gabriel sank into one of the leather chairs and took the drink offered by Ian. "Right now, we are contacting all of those who rode with you on the pretext of gathering commemorative stories on behalf of His Majesty for the ceremony investing you as a Knight of the Order of the Thistle."

Leo snorted. "Do you really believe any of them will fall for that ruse?"

"Yes," Ian said, handing Leo his glass. "First of all, it is no ruse that you are being given the knighthood. The king has announced it himself. It is the highest honor a man can receive and you have earned it. Putting together a commemorative tribute is routine and should not raise any eyebrows. So leave Beldon, Cummings, and Denby to us."

Beldon?

Marigold's heart leaped into her throat.

As in the Lord Beldon who was presently wooing her? No wonder his professions of admiration had felt fake. He wasn't really interested in her. But could he possibly be pretending because Leo was her neighbor? Courting her would provide the perfect cover for his spending time on Chipping Way.

She would mention it to Ian.

He would probably be furious with her for listening in on their conversation, but how was she to blame? If the conversation was so sensitive, should they not have given the library a cursory search before blabbing about this traitor?

She debated whether to pop her head out right now, but decided against it because Leo was there and already agitated. He would be furious and perhaps never forgive her if she showed herself.

It was best to simply wait it out.

She would say nothing to Leo afterward.

Approaching Ian, Gabriel, or Graelem tomorrow and confessing she had heard everything was the prudent thing to do. They might be angry, but they would blame and curse themselves instead of her. Besides, their wives would never allow any of them to punish her or even raise a voice to her.

But Leo?

He would hate that she had snooped and learned his secrets.

Fortunately, the foursome did not remain long afterward. They rose from their chairs still trying to convince Leo to give them more than a month's time to figure out who was the traitor. "One month is all I will agree to give you."

"But Leo, it–"

"I give you my word of honor. I will not interfere in your investigation for the next thirty days. But do not ask me to hold off a minute longer," Leo insisted as they began to walk out of the room.

Marigold sighed in relief as she heard the door close behind them.

She sagged against the window pane and silently counted to thirty before daring to draw the curtain aside. But her relief immediately turned to panic when she stepped out from behind the curtain.

Standing there, as stone-faced as a gargoyle, was Leo. "Care to explain what you are doing in here, Marigold?"

CHAPTER 6

MARIGOLD SWALLOWED HARD to ease her fear. "No, I would not care to explain."

Leo folded his arms across his chest. "You are mistaken if you believe I am giving you a choice in the matter. Explain yourself."

Had he been a tea kettle, steam would now be pouring out of his ears.

Marigold knew better than to rile him further. "How did you know I was in here?"

"My companions are not in the habit of wearing feminine-scented cologne. I did not pick up on it right away, only as we were about to leave. Something had felt *off* in here, and then I realized what it was. You forget, I breathed you in," he said, his voice turning husky. "I would know your scent anywhere, my pet. Even the lightest trace of it. Now, your turn to answer. Why were you in here?"

"If you must know, I needed to find a quiet place to cry."

His manner instantly gentled. "Why, Marigold? Who hurt you enough to make you cry?"

"You did."

His brow furrowed in confusion. "Me?"

She nodded. "You were so cozy with your dinner companion and I could not bear to watch her flirt with you and see you flirt back."

"I did not flirt back," he insisted, looking quite surprised.

Well, she hadn't actually seen him because of that enormous

epergne blocking her view. But he must have done something to encourage her because she had flirted outrageously throughout their meal and then swept her hand over his shoulder with obvious intimacy when she left his side. "You needn't deny it. I saw the way she touched you. Now you are going to meet her somewhere dark and secret."

He laughed. "Dark and secret?"

"I believe they call these assignations. Clothes fly off because this is what one does when engaged in this sort of tryst."

"Is that so?"

"Yes, I have been told it is so from reliable sources. Well, if you like that sort of woman, then enjoy yourself. She did not look at all innocent to me. In truth, she looked lean and hungry, and it was not for the food on her plate."

"Lean and hungry? Are you quoting Shakespeare now?"

"I have read most of his works. I am not illiterate." She tipped her chin up in defiance. "I may not ever have experienced a passionate liaison, but I do understand the significance of her looks and how she touched you."

She wanted to remain defiant, but her tears suddenly began to flow and she could not hold them back. "You broke my heart, Leo. There, are you satisfied? I would appreciate your leaving me alone so I may now indulge in my well-deserved pity fest."

He groaned. "Marigold, why do you have to be so...*you*? I have no interest in Lady Barrington. I know what she wanted and I am not going to provide it to her now or later or ever."

"Am I supposed to believe you? If you are going to indulge in sordid affairs, pray be more discreet about it. I do not wish to have your paramours shoved in my face."

"Sordid affairs? Paramours?" He shook his head and stared at her in disbelief. "I was minding my own business and eating my meal. Women come on to me all the time. What am I supposed to do? Lecture them on the sins of the flesh? Frankly, Marigold, why is it any of your business what I do?"

"None. This is not your fault at all. You have not led me on. Good grief, I hardly know you. Do you think I am happy that my heart feels ripped apart?" Her tears now fell onto her cheeks and wet them. "I was completely caught by surprise by my feelings for you. I had no idea of the power in a kiss."

She had not let go of her handkerchief in all this time and now used it to dry her tears. "Oh, Leo. I thought I could satisfy my curiosity and it would be enough. A first kiss. With you. I know I am making too much of it. Fool that I am, I truly believed it meant something special to you. Then seeing you with Lady Barrington...I knew you had already forgotten me."

"I will never forget you," he said in a raspy whisper, cupping her face in his hands as he stared at her with dark, hot eyes. "Our kiss was special. It was genuine."

"Oh, yes, for my part. But I am nothing more than a witless innocent to you. You have been avoiding me ever since that kiss, and this is what hurts most. I thought you understood me, saw me as something more than a little ball of fluff. But this is all anyone thinks of me. No one takes me seriously." She tried to shove him away when he wrapped his arms around her to draw her up against him. "Release me or I shall scream."

"And have yourself ruined as everyone rushes in here to find us together? Oh, I will probably have no choice but to marry you then. However, since you overheard everything, you now understand the reason why I cannot marry you. I am going to kill that traitor, shoot him down in cold blood if this is what it takes to have my revenge. And if my friends cannot figure out which of those three is the traitor, then I will kill all three men because this is how tortured I feel inside. Is this what you wish for yourself? To be married to a murderer?"

She stared at him in horror. "You cannot be serious. You would kill two innocent men?"

His eyes were crystals of ice. "To still the demons in my soul? Without hesitation."

"No...no. You are not thinking straight."

"Forgive me, my pet. But four years in a hellish hole has a way of skewing a man's sense of honor."

"Leo, I will not allow you to do this."

He kissed her softly on the mouth. "My sweet ray of sunshine, you cannot stop me. So have your cry, although I am not worth it." He kissed her again, another achingly soft kiss. "If it is any consolation, I am also in agony. I know what my dinner companion was hoping for, but I ignored the obvious proposition because…"

"Because you cannot be distracted from your murderous designs?"

"No, that meaningless romp would never distract me. The reason I declined is that I have no desire to be with anyone but you. Is this not the grandest jest? I am to be a monk because I will have no one but you. And yet, you are the last person I want anywhere near me as I destroy myself along with that traitor. You are too precious to me and I never want to hurt you. Run away from me, Marigold. Run before you are also damaged by this doomed affair."

"Our kiss really meant something to you?"

"It meant *everything*."

His lips crushed down on hers to prove his point, although his words conveyed the feeling quite eloquently. She loved his kisses, the warmth of his mouth on hers, the possessive heat as his lips ground on hers with just enough force to reveal his desire and also his promise never to hurt her.

Well, this was a coil.

How was she to dismiss her feelings for him now?

More important, how was she to save him when he was determined to push her away? She would have to give it thought and come up with a plan. But any sensible thinking would have to wait until tomorrow because his kiss had her mindless and craving more of him.

"Leo," she whispered against his mouth, probably unintelligibly because their mouths were like two hot metals fused together by fire.

She wrapped her arms around his neck and held onto his hard, muscled frame as shudders tore through her.

He groaned and lifted her up against him, his mouth never leaving hers.

She was still lost in his kiss when he suddenly froze.

Before she knew what was happening, he set her down,

nudged her behind him, and whirled to face the door, pistol in hand. Where had that weapon come from? And who were all those people standing in the doorway? Oh, dear.

She recognized most of these witnesses.

How much had they seen?

"Uncle John...*erm*. And you are here too, Uncle George. Ah, and Uncle Rupert is with you. Um, what is that *thucking* sound?"

Thuck, thuck, thuck.

Lady Withnall, London's most notorious gossip, marched in with her cane in hand. "Good evening, Lady Withnall. I can explain. It was all a silly misunderstanding, you see."

She knew the woman fairly well and liked her, for Lady Withnall and her bosom companion, Lady Eloise Dayne, had sponsored her friend Adela's come-out and took credit for Adela's love match with the Duke of Huntsford when they wed. There was no escaping either of those Society grand dames, for two of Eloise's grandsons had married two of John's daughters, and Eloise lived next door to them at Number 5 Chipping Way.

As for Lady Withnall, one could not shake her once she was on the scent. By the twitch of her ferret nose, she was decidedly on the scent.

Marigold groaned, for she and Leo were about to be roasted. They had been caught, he with his tongue plundering her mouth and his hands in places they should never have been on her body.

All this in full view of the elders when they had walked in.

Leo glared at her.

She frowned back. "You should have walked out with the others and left me to cry. Do not try to pin this disaster solely on me."

"He made you cry?" her Uncle Rupert said with a growl.

She shook her head furiously. "No...well, yes...but not in the way you think. He was trying to push me away, supposedly for my own good."

Lady Withnall cleared her throat. "You were twisted around each other like two clinging vines. I do not think your definition and ours of *push me away* are quite the same."

"Lady Withnall, I assure you, he wants nothing to do with me.

We were bidding farewell to each other." Her protestations were ignored, for Lady Barrington now walked in and Marigold knew there would be no turning back.

The others, as angry as they were, could be convinced to remain silent.

But Lady Barrington?

She was a woman scorned and out for Leo's blood. "You deserve that little nobody," she said, spitting the words at Leo. "I will not be silenced."

She hurried off to do her worst.

John, patriarch of the Farthingale family, stepped forward. "Lord Muir, need I involve my sons-in-law to convince you to do the right thing?"

After their conversation with Leo, she knew marrying her was the last thing Ian, Gabriel, or Graelem would ever recommend. "Yes," she blurted, "bring them into the discussion. It is an excellent idea."

Leo threw his hands up in exasperation. "Yes, why do we not hold a street fair and invite all of London to walk through? It is unnecessary to bring anyone else into this…this situation. I shall obtain the license first thing tomorrow morning. I assume you have authority to give your consent, Mr. Farthingale?"

"Why must he consent to anything?" Marigold's eyes narrowed. "Uncle John, please believe me when I say it is entirely unnecess–"

Leo emitted a low growl to silence her. "Marigold, do you think I am going to allow Lady Barrington to destroy your reputation? We are getting married. That is an end to it."

His eyes were a fiery blaze, as though he was a demon just emerged from the underworld.

"But–"

"The matter is resolved," he said with another deep growl that had her insides fluttering. "We are getting married."

She opened her mouth to continue her protest, then snapped it shut because she suddenly realized why Leo dared not make a scene. If Ian, Gabriel, or Graelem were summoned, there would be further discussion about his quest for vengeance.

He was concerned word would spread about that. He could not risk his quarry being put on alert as to his plans. To Leo, this was the true danger. He did not care about being caught in a minor scandal over his kissing a virginal debutante. He did not care if news of their kiss appeared in the gossip rags. *Was a certain Marquess M caught in the Duke of Edgeware's library ruining an innocent debutante rumored to be a certain Miss F?*

Their scandal could appear on the front page of every newspaper in London and he would not care because he was going to make it right. But his quest for revenge? That needed to be kept secret. "Did you hear me, Marigold? There is no way out of this. We are getting married."

Was he awaiting her nod? "Yes, Leo."

She fully comprehended the necessity of it and felt terrible she had led him to this end. However, he was as much to blame for not leaving her to her bout of sobbing.

Lady Barrington was now back with a group of her friends, all of them determined to make a circus of her being caught in an indiscretion.

Marigold sighed.

He hadn't proposed.

She hadn't accepted.

But they would be husband and wife by the end of the week.

"Happy?" Leo grumbled, as though the blame was entirely hers when it clearly was not. She did not beg him to stay behind in the library, nor did she plead for his scorching kisses that left her breathless.

Actually, she was happy.

This unexpected crisis of their forced marriage would give her a real chance to change his mind about his bloodthirsty quest. Did he not have a responsibility to his wife?

Well, he might not feel this same duty.

She would have to convince him.

However, she kept her mouth shut for now. She knew better than to respond to his loaded question.

Lord Beldon did not take it well when Marigold told him of her betrothal. She thought it only polite to give him the news personally. "You accepted that beast?"

She tilted her chin up, mildly indignant that he would question her decision. "I do not appreciate your calling my betrothed a beast."

Lord Beldon stood there looking as fiery as Leo had looked when they were caught. "I dare because he is one. Do you have any idea how those four years in captivity have twisted his mind?"

She was surprised Lord Beldon spoke with such familiarity about Leo's ordeal. Should she have said anything to Lord Beldon about their farce of a betrothal? It did not feel right to lead him on when he was under the impression they were courting. Besides, he had been named as one of three potential traitors. Did it not make sense to ask him questions under the pretext of defending the man she was to marry? "How do you know what he went through?"

A waltz was starting up.

He grabbed her hand and led her onto the dance floor, holding tightly onto her as he began to twirl her around the room in time with the other couples. He had no need to restrain her since she wanted to talk to him. "How do you know?" she repeated.

"Because I was there when the ambush occurred."

She almost stumbled in surprise, somehow not putting together that Lord Beldon had actually been there and was not orchestrating the ambush from the safety of London...assuming he was at all involved. "You were? What happened? You seem to have escaped without injury."

"What are you suggesting, Miss Farthingale?"

She frowned at him as he led her in another twirl around the dance floor. "I am suggesting nothing, only trying to determine why you are tossing these insulting accusations at Lord Muir. Who else was harmed?"

"All of us received minor injuries, but we managed to escape."

"And you left Lord Muir behind?" This did not sound right to her. "Is there not some code of honor that requires you to recover all your men before retreating?"

"This is what we tried to do, but it was impossible once our assailants had taken him captive. We were out of food and ammunition. Even so, we pressed on in our search but could not pick up their trail. It was as though the enemy had vanished into thin air. And the air was quite thin in those mountains. We spent days chasing shadows. I was second in command, and then assumed command after Lord Muir was taken. I made the decision to abandon the search before we all died from exposure, starvation, or further attack. We had to make a tactical retreat. After that, it became an affair for the diplomats."

"And they took four years to get him out?"

Beldon hand tensed at her waist. "I cannot say what mistakes were made once the government emissaries took over. All I can attest to is that I reported it promptly and we all gave whatever information we could in the hope they would act quickly and find him. From what I gather, the problem was that no one came forward to claim responsibility for capturing him. How can the Crown negotiate the release of one of their envoys when no one will admit they have him? Once the Crown agents finally tracked down his captors, it was a quick negotiation to free him."

"Yet it took four years? How could it not be obvious who had him?"

"We were traveling on Crown business in the Carpathian mountains, an area rife with rebellion. There were too many tribal factions fighting in the area, not to mention the government forces could not be trusted either. His abduction was obviously meant to disrupt certain mineral rights negotiations. We were not sent there as soldiers but as government representatives. All of us who were on that mission expected Muir would be released within a few days. But those days turned into weeks and then months."

"And then years passed. Why do you think he was held all this time?"

"Miss Farthingale, I have no idea. It is possible he was transferred from one rebel faction to another as power shifted in this lawless area. He was probably considered a useful pawn. Only Lord Muir can confirm this. Some captors might have treated him better than others. I hope they were not all brutal animals. He and I are not friends, but I would never wish his fate on anyone."

The waltz ended and he led her back to her Uncle John and Aunt Sophie who were standing at the opposite side of the dance floor. "Well," he said, shouldering his way through the crowd, "this was probably our last dance, Miss Farthingale. I'm sorry you chose to wed Lord Muir. I hope for your sake it will be a happy union. But I must express my grave doubts."

"Duly noted, Lord Beldon," she remarked, just wanting to reach her aunt and uncle in order to be left alone with her thoughts. Of course, her aunt and uncle might have a few choice words for her.

She noticed they had almost reached the other side of the dance floor when Lord Beldon held her back a moment. "Miss Farthingale, send word to me if you realize you have made a mistake and need to escape."

She regarded him in stunned disbelief. "Are you suggesting you would help me run away? And what then? How would running off with you help my situation?"

He took her hand, obviously wishing to raise it to his lips, but he merely bowed over it. "I would elope with you. Just say the word and we'll flee north to Scotland in my carriage."

This was all too much for one night. "Lord Beldon, thank you for the offer. But I do not require your assistance."

"It is offered anyway. I'll be waiting."

"Kindly do not."

"I will be waiting, Miss Farthingale," he said with greater insistence.

Just perfect.

She had Leo, an avenging angel more resembling an angry demon, who did not wish to marry her, and Lord Beldon, a possible traitor to the Crown, who supposedly did.

Aunt Sophie must have been alerted about her betrothal, for she shook her head and sighed at Marigold the moment she was left in her care. "For pity's sake, what is it with you girls?"

"Girls? How many of us in the family have been ruined by scandal?"

She rolled her eyes. "Oh, I think just about all of you."

Marigold wanted to laugh, but dared not. The elders did not view this as a joking matter. However, it was a relief to know she wasn't the only Farthingale debutante to stumble down that path to ruin.

"I have become quite adept at these hasty weddings since none of my daughters or their cousins seem capable of getting through a Season without landing on the front page of the gossip sheets," Sophie muttered. "Lady Withnall told me what happened in the library. Honestly, Marigold. I expected better from you."

"So did I," she admitted. "I did not wish to marry before I reached the age of twenty. This was not at all in my plans."

"Well, prepare yourself to become the wife of a marquess. That elevation in status will come with responsibilities. I'm sure Dillie will guide you. She's done marvelously stepping into the role of Ian's duchess. Her twin Lily, on the other hand, remains completely oblivious to the obligations of her station. She is more than happy to conduct her research in Scotland and ignore these Society affairs. She claims the marriage mart is a jungle and her baboons have better manners than some of these young men on the hunt for a wife. Ewan indulges her far too much. But what can we say? He loves her and wishes to see her happy."

"Is that not better than an unhappy match?"

Sophie nodded. "Yes, it is. On the whole, I am very proud of all my girls. They have often shown more common sense and made better choices for themselves than their elders have desired for them. However, could not one of you have had a traditional courtship? Dull. Uneventful. Stretched out to a full year. The gossip rag editors salivate whenever they hear a Farthingale is about to make her debut. We never seem to disappoint."

Marigold winced. "I am happy for my match, even though it all happened so fast. Lord Muir is not happy about it, however."

Sophie arched an eyebrow. "If he was kissing you with the fervor Lady Withnall described, I expect he will come around in time and be a model husband."

"I hope you are right, Aunt Sophie."

But Marigold knew he wouldn't.

Leo was a haunted and damaged man.

Her aunt patted her hand. "I am right, Marigold. It took Ian a while into their marriage before he came around and declared he loved Dillie. Of course, we all knew he did. I think he loved her from the first moment he met her. But men are often quite stubborn and he was a very hard nut to crack."

"I think Lord Muir will also be difficult."

"You are only moving across the street from us," Sophie pointed out. "Just walk over if ever you wish to talk."

She nodded. "Thank you, I will."

Not only did she have Sophie – never mind that Aunt Hortensia lived with her, for she was a curmudgeon and resolute spinster who would not be helpful in the least – but Marigold also had her cousin Violet and Lady Eloise residing on Chipping Way. It would take nothing to call a family meeting if she needed advice.

This was something to keep in mind if Leo proved difficult.

The following morning, Marigold decided to walk over to Leo's townhouse with Mallow. After all, was it not right and proper that his staff should become acquainted with the incoming residents? "Good morning," she said with cheer as Leo's kindly butler opened the door.

Mallow squirmed out of her grasp and tore into the house. He ran down the hall before she could stop him. "Oh, dear. I do apologize to you, Sterling. As you can see, Mallow requires a little more training."

The butler smiled. "He is a delightful, little fellow. I expect we shall find him scratching at his lordship's study door. That is where Lord Muir happens to be at the moment."

Marigold sighed. "Mallow does adore him."

"He is a most worthy master and is respected by all of us."

"Sterling, what do you know about his..." She did not know how much to say about Leo's four years in captivity. What if his staff knew nothing? Well, that was unlikely. But who could say what they had been told? "Never mind. May I see Lord Muir?"

He led her into the parlor and had her wait there.

Marigold was not offended since Leo's staff might not even be aware they were betrothed. If Leo had not told them, she certainly was not going to blurt the news.

It did not take long for Leo to enter the parlor and greet her, Mallow trotting in beside him.

Leo looked strikingly handsome in dark breeches, polished Hessians, a white lawn shirt, and silk cravat in a pinecone design of dark green and gray that was also shot through with threads of silver. The cravat was tied in an impeccably elegant and understated knot. His waistcoat was of green brocade that matched the green of his cravat. "Good morning, Miss Farthingale. I did not expect to see you this bright and early."

Was he admonishing her?

Should she have awaited an invitation?

She blushed. "Forgive me, I did not think."

"Neither of us was thinking too clearly last night, were we?" he said softly, as he leaned in and surprised her with a genuinely tender kiss on the cheek.

He then straightened to his impressive height and turned to his butler. "Sterling, kindly gather the staff in the hall. Miss Farthingale and I have an announcement to make."

The man's eyes popped wide and his smile stretched from ear to ear. "At once, my lord."

He bustled out.

"I'll be meeting your uncle at the bishop's office this afternoon to obtain the license."

Her heart did a little flip within her chest, for this marriage business was suddenly feeling very real. "Am I permitted to join you?"

He frowned as he shook his head. "I doubt your uncle will allow it. I'm sure he also intends to discuss the terms of our marriage contract and will not want you around while we negotiate."

"I see. Leo, my parents and I lived modestly. We were not paupers, mind you. But when they died, I was left with very little. My mother's family took me in and had me settle in with them. They were kind and I was comfortable. Their house was just down the street from ours as I was growing up."

He nodded. "In the village of Little Mutton?"

"Yes. So, I do not require elaborate arrangements. Whatever I have now is due to the generosity of my father's side of the family…the Farthingale side. My needs are not extravagant."

He kissed her on the forehead. "And this is why your uncle does not want you with us while we discuss the terms. You are far too reasonable, as I knew you would be. However, you are to be my wife, Marigold. Whether I like it or not, you and I will soon be bound. I take care of what's mine. You shall never be left wanting."

She cast him a sincere smile. "Spoken like a true lion, Leo."

His eyes lit up and he laughed. "Come on, I hear my staff gathering in the hall. Time to introduce them to my future marchioness."

"When do you expect we'll be married?"

"Now that the damage has been done?" He arched an eyebrow. "The sooner, the better."

He did not appear overset by the fact.

In truth, he seemed to be taking this disaster quite well.

As he introduced her to the butlers, maids, and his cook and her scullery girls, Marigold realized he did not have a housekeeper or a valet. Since he was only one person and did not seem the sort to rely on anyone but himself, she supposed his household functioned smoothly. But once they were married, they would be expected to host parties and in general do more entertaining than he had ever done.

She did not think he had done any entertaining at all, unless it was to bring a paramour up to his bedchamber. Yet, she did not think he would ever permit a woman other than his wife into that sanctuary. It was likely he did no entertaining whatsoever in his home. But she hoped to host her local explorer's club which at the moment consisted only of bluestockings Adela, Syd, Gory, and her. As they got the word out about their finds in the Devonshire caves, Marigold was certain the club's popularity would grow. She also wished to take a turn hosting her Farthingale cousins meetings.

Those engagements could be sorted out at a later time.

She also dared not ask about their sleeping arrangements.

Having forced this wedding on him, she did not think he wished to share a bedchamber with her. She would not press him on the matter. Perhaps it was something to consider in the future, once they got to know each other better.

However, she would ask permission to hire a lady's maid to attend to her personally since this could not be put off. One of the maids on staff might do, so long as she could style hair and knew how to properly maintain her clothes.

"Miss Farthingale and I are betrothed," Leo said, addressing his staff. "We shall marry within the week. Sir Mallow will be moving in, as well."

Mallow barked his approval.

Marigold smiled at all of them, told them how pleased she was to meet them, and then returned to the parlor with Leo. "Your lips are pursed, Marigold. What is the matter?"

"Nothing, really. It's just that...would you mind very much if I hired a housekeeper for us once we are married?" She hurriedly explained her reasoning. "And I will need a maid to help me with my hair and dressing. Um, I think you will also require a valet. But we can manage if you prefer not to engage one."

She was waiting for him to pass a remark, but he merely nodded as he closed the door to the parlor to give them privacy. Mallow had trotted in with them and was now shadowing Leo as he walked back to her side and took the seat next to her. "I'll leave it up to you to do whatever you think best in the running of the house."

She stared at him. "Really?"

He grinned. "Yes, Marigold. Really. Just let me know how much of an allowance you'll require for your weekly needs and I will make certain sufficient funds are put at your disposal. However, I would like to interview the candidate you select as my valet before you offer him the position."

"Of course. I'll speak to Aunt Sophie before I interview anyone. Pruitt and Sterling might also offer helpful suggestions. Perhaps you ought to be the one to actually interview these valet candidates since you are the one who must get along with the man."

He nodded again. "All right, I will. That settles it. Is there anything else you wish to discuss?"

"No, not at present. How about you? Is there anything you wish to ask of me?"

"No, my pet. Nothing about the household. What are your plans for today?"

"I had hoped to spend time at the Huntsford Academy overseeing the new exhibit, but I think the ladies in my family have other ideas. I fear I will be caught up in wedding preparations for most of the day. You know my cousins Dillie, Daisy, and Laurel since they are Sophie's daughters, and you were arguing with their husbands in the library last night. But I have another six cousins living in London, all of them married, and all of them meddlesome. They will be coming over to Sophie's today, as well as Eloise and Lady Withnall."

"That is quite a group."

"I think they are more excited about the wedding than I am. Oh, I am very pleased to be marrying you, but it is all quite hurried and I am saddened that it has been forced upon you."

"Don't be. I was to blame. So, no Hall of Dragons for you today?"

She sighed. "No, not a single dragon skull in the offing. I will be immersed in talk of flowers, cakes, wedding gowns, and invitations. Oh, Leo, I'm so sorry. We'll have at least sixty guests for the ceremony and wedding breakfast afterward...and those are solely on my side of the family and my explorer's club friends. Is there anyone you wish to invite?"

"No, I have no siblings. The nearest relation is a cousin who resides in Exeter. I haven't seen him above three times in my entire life. He would never make it in time, not to mention he is among my list of suspects. As for my friends, I haven't seen most in over four years, and more than half of them are related to you anyway. I am well acquainted with Ian, Gabriel, and Graelem, as well as Julian Emory who is married to your cousin, Rose. I owe all of them a debt of gratitude, for they looked after my estate while I was...well, they were appointed by the Crown as my conservators during my absence. Good thing, too. That cousin of mine is a weasel and would have squandered all my assets had he been put in charge. By the way, I hold a minority interest in Julian and Rose's pottery business."

"Oh, Rose will be there today without question. As eldest of Sophie's daughters, she is bound to take charge...or at least attempt it. They are all going to have opinions and will not hesitate to express them. I might sneak off to the Huntsford Academy if it all gets too much for me."

He took her hands in his. "I think you will manage your family quite well, Marigold. You seem to manage me with little difficulty."

She looked at him, surprised. "I? Manage you?"

"Yes, though it is mostly because I don't mind your intrusion."

She rose. "It was not my intention to intrude on your day. I merely wanted to see how you were faring. I thought you would be livid about what happened last night and I came over in the hope of calming you down. But you are not angry at all. Or are you seething and merely hiding it very well?"

He rose along with her. "I am not angry, nor am I seething. I plan to enjoy our wedded bliss for as long as it lasts."

"Should it not last forever?" Marigold's heart tightened. "Leo, what do you mean by that remark?"

"What do you think I mean?"

"Will...that is...are you going to take on a mistress? Or have other casual affairs? If this is what you intend, then please tell me the truth right now. I will never marry you if you choose to be unfaithful. I cannot. I would rather face the scandal."

He took her in his arms. "I am going to be faithful, Marigold. That will never be our problem. I give you my sacred oath on it."

She threw her arms around him. "Thank you, Leo. I knew you were too honorable ever to hurt me."

"Don't thank me. And how can you think of me as honorable? You know very well what I mean to do, and it is likely going to ruin our marriage."

"That vengeful quest of yours. Yes, I know. I give you fair warning that I will do all in my power to keep you from succeeding. I don't want you to become a murderer."

"Marigold, keep out of this." He frowned at her. "Going after a traitor is not murder."

"If you've got the right man, perhaps not. But you are far too casual about determining guilt or innocence. You simply wish to be rid of them all, thinking that one of them must be the culprit. But what if you are wrong and none of them had anything to do with your capture?"

"Marigold, stop. You are to keep out of this."

"I cannot. It is too late to stop me. I have already started gathering information. Why did you not tell me Lord Beldon was your second in command?"

She had been in his arms, but in the blink of an eye he had his hands on her shoulders and was now shaking her lightly. "How did you find this out?"

"He told me last night while he and I were waltzing. It was easy to gather bits of information from him. Men love to talk about themselves, especially when they are with a woman they wish to impress. It was not hard to get him talking. All it took was a slight nudge from me, a few pointed remarks, and you were all he spoke about."

"Marigold," he said, his expression darkening, "you are not to meddle. Beldon could be the traitor. I will not allow you to put yourself in danger."

"But I am already in it. Why else was he supposedly courting me but to rile you? In truth, his courtship felt odd, as though he was merely tossing me compliments by rote. You know, following a script he had written out and memorized because he did not really care about me. If you wish to know what I think–"

Leo groaned, but then nodded. "Fine. Of course, I do."

"Lord Beldon was only ever after me because he thought you were interested in me. Well, it is all over with now that you are going to marry me."

"So you believe there's an end to his ploy?" Leo's expression turned grim. "The pleasure will be all the greater because he will now work on seducing my wife. It is far better sport than pretending to court a young lady I was hoping to court. Not that I ever meant to wage a campaign to woo you, for I had no intention of bringing you into this mess."

"Have you and Beldon always had this competitive animosity between you?"

"Yes, but he's been the competitive one. I couldn't give a rat's arse what he does or who he likes. But he's always felt this perverse need to grab whatever is mine. Horses, women, it does not matter. If he thinks I desire something, he will go after it."

She pursed her lips. "He caught on very quickly to your liking me, did he not? I wasn't even aware of it, but he was."

"He's known me much longer than you have and always studies me closely. Which is why he is at the top of my list of suspected traitors."

"Does this not seem a drastic escalation? Being competitive does not mean he wishes to destroy you. In fact, he seems to enjoy the game. Why would he end it?"

"He may have grown bored with it."

"If that were so, he could have merely stopped playing the game. What reason would he have to attempt to destroy you?"

"I don't know. That is not my concern. He is among my suspects and I will have my revenge. How am I not within my rights to shoot him if attempts to seduce you once we are husband and wife?"

"Leo, you are not really going to do anything to harm him, are you? First of all, I do not like him, and more to the point, I am not going to break my marriage vows. Second, you gave Ian your word that you would hold off and allow him time to investigate. I heard you give your word. You cannot renege. Tell me you will hold to this pledge." This mattered to her because she needed to confide in Leo, be able to tell him all she had learned so they might solve this mystery together. How could she confide in him if she could not trust him to keep a cool head?

She did not think it wise to tell him everything just yet. Revealing Beldon's offer to elope with her would set him off.

She did not need that powder keg exploding.

He clenched his jaw. "I am not going to renege on my word. I said I would give him and the Crown agents a month, and this is what I will do. A month, but not a minute beyond. Do not look at me that way, Marigold. I am not going to agree to give them more time."

She understood his impatience and most certainly the pain and deprivation he'd suffered. But he needed to be reined in for his own good. "Nor should you," she retorted, staring up at him with a frown to match his own. "By all means, go after those three men, Leo. Never mind that two of them will be innocent. Or perhaps all three of them are innocent. After all, getting revenge is more important than anything in the world. I applaud your determination. I think you should go right ahead and destroy the lives of those innocent men along with your own life and our marriage. Not to mention the devastation it will wreak on their families. It makes entirely good sense. I aspire to becoming a widow before I turn nineteen."

She thought he would become angry and put an end to their wedding plans, but he merely cast her a wry smile. "For a sweet thing, you certainly know how to be sarcastic."

"I am going to fight for our marriage, Leo. I give you fair warning. If you wish to back out of marrying me, now is your chance."

He gave a curt, bitter laugh. "Back out? I have no intention of it."

She shook her head in confusion. "Why go to the bother if you are going to destroy everything in thirty days' time?"

He sank back in his chair and cast her a piercing look. "Because I shall be married to you and those are going to be the best thirty days of my life."

Best? How can he possibly be serious?

And now, how can she not rise to the challenge? He believed marriage to her would be bliss? Well, it could be if he would leave the hunt for the traitor to the Crown agents. But he was too stubborn and impatient to let the investigation play out. "Lord Cummings is the name of your cousin, is it not?"

He nodded.

"Who is Lord Denby?"

"Why do you wish to know?"

"Because I intend to conduct my own investigation. If you are determined to keep up this foolishness, then I will have to find a way to stop you."

His expression once more turned darker than a looming storm as he shot up from his chair. "You are to stay away from those three men."

She stared up at him. "I will promise to do so only if you give me the same promise."

"You know I will not."

"Then I will not, either."

He raked a hand through his hair. "Whoever did this to me is ruthless, Marigold. There is a very good chance he will come after you simply because you are my wife. I do not mean in any harmless way, as in flirting with you or attempting to seduce you. I mean really come after you with the intention of hurting you. Drawing blood. Killing you if he thought this would hurt me worse. Rest assured, I will do whatever I must to keep you safe. If that means locking you in your bedchamber and chaining you to your bed, then I will do so."

"An idle threat. You will have every Farthingale son-in-law at your throat within a day if you attempt it. You will not be able to fight them all. So, be reasonable. Work with me or not, the choice is yours. However, if you refuse to work with me, then I will hold you to your duty. You are Leo, my lion. You had better protect what is yours. That means me, for I truly belong to you with all my heart and every scintilla of my soul." She scooped up Mallow, who immediately whined when he realized they were leaving. "Well, Leo? What do you say? Will you protect me?"

"Of course, I will. Is that not part of the marriage pledge?"

"It is."

"Good, then rest assured of my protection, even if it means locking you up until I am through with those men. If you think you will have your family on your side, then think again. Every one of your male relatives will side with me once I tell them the reason why I had to take drastic measures."

"They will likely lock us both up," she retorted, sticking her chin in the air. "Rest assured, I will insist on it."

She wanted to hit him over the head in the hope of knocking

sense into him, but she could never use physical force against him, not after the violence he had endured. Anyway, she could not hurt a butterfly.

Brutality was not in her nature.

He grinned. "You are going to be a formidable force when you are older."

"If it saves your life, then I do not care if you think of me as a crazed Harpy."

"Marigold, do not push me."

"I am only trying to make you see reason."

"You are interfering in matters of which you know nothing. I may have agreed too swiftly to doing what seemed like the honorable thing last night. If you are also having doubts, then–"

"Doubts? I haven't a one. You are the only man for me, Leo. Oh, I know you think I am too young to know my own mind, but it is not so. I am clever and sensible. I am also not afraid of facing challenges."

"So be it. However, until the matter of the traitor is settled, I want you able to get out of this marriage if you ever do have second thoughts."

"What do you mean?"

"You and I will maintain separate quarters. We shall not share a bed."

"We won't?" She tried to hide her disappointment, but she was never very good at hiding her feelings.

"No," he said, his manner gentling. "It will be much easier for you to obtain an annulment on the grounds of my madness and inability to consummate our marriage if we maintain this arrangement."

"Are you saying you will not properly make me your wife?"

"Not quite. I am not that much of a monk. There are ways to pleasure you in bed short of coupling. I will come to your bed, just not share it with you all night long."

"I have no idea what you are talking about. Why can we not simply be married like any other couple? I am not going to seek an annulment, so you may as well set that plan aside."

"No. And do not frown at me, Marigold. I promise, you will

not be disappointed in our arrangement."

"Our thirty days of bliss?" She blushed. "If you say so. However, I shall reserve judgement."

He cast her a conquering sort of look, as though confident of his abilities.

Well, he had only to look at her and she melted, so perhaps she would enjoy whatever he had planned. But she would never agree to an annulment, so this objective of his was a complete waste of time. "Leo, what if it turns out none of those men are guilty? What if you are looking completely in the wrong direction? Have you ever considered this?"

"I am not wrong about them."

"Can you say this with a moral certainty?"

"It has to be one of them."

"Why? Is this your anger speaking because you do not like those men and want them to be guilty? You chose Beldon because he is a little rat always trying to steal what is yours. You chose Cummings because he is next in line to your title and he's probably also a little rat. He would not be on your list if you thought he had any honor in him. Next is Denby."

"Are you going to tell me what I feel about him?"

She nibbled her lip. "I would like to, but you haven't told me anything about him yet. Who is Denby? Why are you so set on seeking vengeance on him?"

CHAPTER 7

LEO HAD THOUGHT Marigold would be more biddable because this was her first year out and she was inexperienced. Not only was she inexperienced, but she had a genuinely sweet disposition and was not inclined to hurt anyone's feelings. So it irritated the hell out of him that she was determined to kick his arse into shape.

He had spent four years in a dark pit sustained by thoughts of revenge, and not even Marigold, this little ray of sunshine his soul seemed to crave, was going to change his mind.

Had he made a mistake in stepping forward to do the honorable thing when they were caught in the library?

Were he not so desperate for this taste of bliss, he would have found a way to quietly avoid marrying her and also make their scandal disappear. He did not know if Lady Barrington could be paid off to retract her story, but it would have been worth a try.

As for Marigold, she scorched his soul.

Now that he was betrothed to her, it would take every last drop of his strength to let her go. He would do it, if this became necessary to protect her.

She was stubborn, opinionated, and far more self-assured than he had expected. In truth, these qualities made him like her more.

She thought he was a lion, but she was just as fierce in her determination to have their marriage succeed.

No one had ever fought for him as she was willing to fight, not even his parents who were not often around but had always shown him affection when they did deign to spent time with him.

They had grown fairly close by the time he was old enough to go to university.

They would have grown closer had his parents not died soon after. First his mother, then a few months later his father.

Upon his father's passing, Leo had suddenly felt completely alone.

Of course, Cummings, his little rat of a cousin, wasted no time in coming around to sniff out the situation, using his father's funeral as a pretext to glean whatever information he could about the extensive Muir holdings and the state of Leo's health. No doubt Cummings was hoping the next influenza outbreak would do him in, as the recent outbreak had done in his parents.

Well, Leo was tough as old boots and not departing this earth anytime soon.

Now, he was about to take Marigold as his wife.

A wife in name only for now since he needed to protect her whether she liked it or not.

Failing to consummate the marriage was a first step in giving her a way out of what could turn out to be a dangerous proposition. If necessary, he could also feign madness in addition to supposed impotence. Surely, a court would grant her an annulment if he were declared to be so afflicted.

Not that he wanted to end this marriage.

In truth, he yearned for it to be a happy and successful one filled with children who had Marigold's enthusiasm for life.

However, he could not have it both ways.

He had to make a choice.

A successful marriage?

Or revenge?

Right now, he wanted revenge.

Those four years had destroyed him.

Perhaps things would change once the traitor was caught.

He would not dwell too much on it now. Time would reveal the paths he and Marigold were destined to take.

He also knew Marigold had been right about his giving Ian and the Crown agents more than thirty days to discover the identity of the traitor. However, he was not going to admit this to

Marigold, for she would be even more impossible to dissuade if circumstances forced him to change his mind again and act immediately.

She was determined to heal his ravaged soul.

He was just as determined to keep her safe and would do everything possible to accomplish this.

As for him, he was beyond caring about his safety.

In fact, he was eager for a confrontation with the traitor and did not care if they both drowned in a pool of blood. All that mattered was taking this man down before he harmed anyone else, especially Marigold.

This traitor had singled him out for a reason, but how did one turn back the clock four years to discover what it could be?

Was this man mad or simply cruel? And what had the wretch hoped to gain by getting him out of the way? Why single him out specifically when there had been others in the delegation? Yet, no one else had been taken or even more than slightly injured.

What set him apart?

He had asked himself these questions over and over again ever since his capture and not come up with any solid answers.

Perhaps marrying Marigold would rile this villain into acting again.

But would the man go after him? Or Marigold?

Leo knew he had to make himself the target. To accomplish this, he had to show no affection toward Marigold whenever they were out in public. More than this, he had to make everyone believe he was angry to be trapped in an unwanted marriage and eager for a way out. The task would be much easier if he actually felt nothing for her.

Not that he loved her yet, but he was more than halfway there. He had to be, for he had never burned for any woman as he burned for Marigold. Ironically, she was clueless about seductive wiles and had no idea how desperately he craved her.

How was he to keep up the illusion of this union being forced on him?

He had better hone his acting skills.

TWO DAYS LATER, Leo stood beside Marigold as they were about to exchange wedding vows.

Marigold smiled up at him, her gaze hopeful and her eyes shining brightly. They stood side by side beside the altar of St. Mary's Church, a quaint but beautifully appointed edifice tucked in a quiet corner of Mayfair not far from Chipping Way. She looked stunning in a gown of palest pink silk and wore a small circlet of roses in a matching shade of pink pinned in her ebony hair.

He wished they could have had a moment alone, for he wanted to tell her how lovely she looked. But it was not to be, for their guests were streaming in from all doors. Final certificates needed to be signed by John Farthingale as Marigold's guardian and their witnesses, Ian and Gabriel, who had agreed to serve in that capacity.

In all, they wound up with seventy guests filling the pews for the ceremony. Most were Marigold's family members. Marigold also pointed out her friends, Lady Sydney Harcourt and Lady Gregoria Easton. Syd and Gory, as Marigold referred to them. Seated beside these two ladies were Huntsford's brothers, Captain Octavian Thorne and Lord Julius Thorne. "Your skull and bones club," Leo remarked with a grin at Marigold.

"Yes, and I am quite proud of them. Octavian and Julius would officially join our club if they could, but their duties keep them too occupied. However, they are quite supportive of us."

Leo was not surprised Huntsford's brothers were enthusiasts. In addition to the obvious reason of supporting their brother's academy, it did not escape anyone's notice that Syd and Gory were very pretty, young ladies.

But his thoughts now turned to his own match.

As a marquess, Leo knew his wedding was small by society standards, a fact that helped substantiate the rumor this affair had been hastily cobbled together because of scandal.

No doubt Lady Barrington, still angry over being spurned, had kept herself busy fanning those flames. His and Marigold's indiscretion continued to appear in the gossip rags. All the better. Marigold was safest if the traitor believed that woman's lies and thought Leo had been trapped into marrying this glorious girl.

As the vicar droned on, Leo silently mapped out his next steps.

No outward show of affection when in public.

But in private? It was all about keeping Marigold happy in the marriage.

But no consummation.

Everything short of that was permitted.

This way, he could pleasure her and also give her the grounds to dissolve their union if she needed to seek an annulment.

This could work.

After all, how long did he have to keep up this ruse? With the Crown's best agents on the task, it was quite possible the traitor would soon be caught. Leo could then end the abhorrent deception and truly claim Marigold as his wife.

In the meantime, he would not deprive himself or Marigold of the pleasures of the bedchamber. There was nothing to stop him from visiting her each night, spending the hours showing her the intimacy that could exist between husband and wife.

Nothing was forbidden as far as he was concerned, except for the actual act of coupling.

"Do you, Leonides Poole, Marquess of Muir, Earl of Allenby…" Leo shook out of his thoughts and concentrated on the wedding ceremony as the vicar read off a string of his titles. "Do you take Marigold Farthingale to be your lawful wife…"

"I do."

Marigold had already pledged herself to him while he listened with half an ear, so lost was he in his thoughts.

"I now pronounce you husband and wife…"

Dear heaven.

He was married.

Marigold cast him one of her sunshine smiles. "We will figure it out, Leo. I don't want to lose you."

"Nor I you." He kissed her lightly on the cheek before leading her down the aisle to be congratulated by their guests.

Was there anyone in the crowd who did not belong?

He scanned the small church with eagle eyes, leaving not a niche unchecked. To his relief, he noticed Ian, Gabriel, and Graelem doing the same. Perhaps he was not alone in considering this ceremony a likely time for the traitor to appear. While all the crowd hovered around them and distracted his attention, the traitor could easily take the measure of his new wife.

Not only were these three friends on the task, but he realized Marigold's connections also extended by way of marriage to the Brayden clan. These Braydens were military men, even the peers among them having extensive battle experience.

Had Ian quietly brought any of them into this investigation?

Good grief.

It was also likely Marigold had done the same with their wives, bringing them into *her* investigation. These Farthingales were a very close family unit. Well, perhaps it was not a bad idea to keep as many eyes as possible on their street.

Violet Farthingale had married Romulus Brayden and they resided at Number 1 Chipping Way. Romulus was a much decorated captain in the Royal Navy and presently home on leave. It could not hurt to have him watching who rode in and out of their quiet street.

He glanced at Violet and Romulus.

They had been seated in one of the third row pews and were now on their feet making their way toward him and Marigold. It struck him that Violet and Marigold could pass as sisters. They looked very much alike, but same could be said of most of these Farthingale females. Same delicate frame, same dark hair and big, ensorcelling eyes.

No wonder Chipping Way had become a parson's trap, and he had fallen straight into it. No, not just fallen. He had leaped in with both feet.

Leo dismissed the thought as more guests came forward to congratulate them. Then everyone returned to John and Sophie's townhouse where the wedding breakfast was to take place.

Leo did not need to pretend to be overwhelmed, for he was used to solitude and isolation. Those words were not in the

Farthingale vocabulary.

Romulus patted him on the back. "You will get used to this crush eventually."

Leo shook his head and grinned. "I was an only child and never close to the few cousins I could claim as family. Then to be tossed in an enemy prison and left staring into the dark, dank walls for what felt like an eternity. The last thing I ever expected was to have this chaos in my life. I'm not sure I am ready for it."

"You won't be given the choice. For the most part, you will find these family connections helpful rather than a nuisance. Besides, these Farthingale women are a force of nature. You will never win if you try to fight against their current. They may look small and delicate, but do not be fooled. Strength is bred in them."

"I already see it in Marigold. I was afraid I might overwhelm her, but she knows how to hold her ground. It is quite possible I will never win an argument with her." He raked a hand through his hair. "Should I worry?"

Romulus laughed. "No. She has a good heart and is as sweet as Violet. If she argues with you, it is likely because you are being unreasonable. I think I fell in love with Violet at first sight. Ours was also a forced marriage. I'm sure you will soon hear of the beehive incident, if you haven't already. It was all completely innocent...but appeared terribly scandalous."

"Did you not resent it?"

Romulus grinned. "No, not even I would have believed me. I knew I was done for. There would be no way of talking my way out of a hasty marriage while her gown was unlaced and she was half spilling out of it. What was everyone to think? It did look as though I had thoroughly compromised her. Then again, my thoughts were not all that innocent. I would never have acted upon them, of course. But no one believed me. I did not bother to argue. One look at Violet and I knew we were meant to be together. My greatest concern was how to be a proper husband to her, one who could provide her the happiness she deserved."

"Seems you've figured it out."

"I suppose, but she makes it easy. Leo, she is amazing. I feel as though I walk into paradise whenever I come home. Having her

102 | MEARA PLATT

reside next door to John and Sophie also gives me comfort. That is always my greatest worry, leaving Violet and my daughter alone for months at a time while I am at sea. But her family is right there, and mine is also close by. It works out, I suppose. Violet and I are committed to making it work."

"Marigold is certainly determined, I will give her that."

Romulus arched an eyebrow. "And you?"

"She is the perfect cure for the darkness in my soul. However, whether we succeed or not is yet to be determined."

They had no chance to speak further before Leo was dragged back into the center of activity. Family members and friends made speeches. Glasses of champagne were passed around and refilled. He and Marigold chatted with every guest.

Lord, would this never end?

Leo had more to discuss with Romulus. He needed to be certain Romulus was aware that Beldon, Cummings, and Denby were the specific men under suspicion as traitors. Romulus ought to have the choice of moving his wife and baby daughter out of harm's way if he thought it was necessary. Violet's sister, Poppy, had married the Earl of Welles whose estate was in the Cotswolds. Violet and her daughter, little Hyacinth, could remain there for the month, out of the path of potential danger if Leo's unknown nemesis chose to strike close to home.

He finally found a moment to warn him.

Romulus frowned. "I cannot leave London. If I am here, Violet will never leave either. But we shall make certain to remain alert at all times."

"I plan to engage Bow Street runners," Leo said. "It cannot hurt to have professional watchdogs guarding Chipping Way. It is a small street and they will easily spot anyone lurking in the bushes."

He asked Ian for recommendations when they had a moment to talk.

"Homer Barrow. He's the best Bow Street runner around, Leo. It is a good idea. Engage him immediately."

Leo nodded. "I'll send word to him first thing in the morning."

Ian grimaced. "Not an ideal way to spend your honeymoon,

but it is a priority and must be done."

When the wedding breakfast ended late into the evening, Leo escorted Marigold across the street to their home. Her belongings had been moved over by the Farthingale staff earlier in the day and his staff had her quarters in readiness. "That is quite some family you have," he remarked as they walked the short distance.

"Aren't they wonderful? A bit much at times, I expect. I'll do my best to ease you in."

Leo shook his head. "Don't fill our calendar up too soon with commitments, Marigold."

"I won't. I know you are distracted. Let tonight be just for us, free from our cares. We'll get to the business of our investigation in the morning."

Leo groaned. "*Our* investigation?"

She nodded. "We are in this together whether you like it or not. And you still haven't told me who Denby is."

He supposed it was best she knew all the facts. He did not want her going off on her own to snoop while ignorant of the dangers.

Perhaps he ought not dismiss her assistance since four years of his thinking about this situation had yielded him nothing beyond these three suspects. "Denby is the diplomat I was charged with escorting on that fateful mission. I have started looking into his business affairs. On His Majesty's orders, he was sent to negotiate mineral and precious metal rights agreements with the Carpathian representatives. But I understand nothing came of it after I was captured. Relations fell apart and the Crown pursued other resources."

Marigold pursed her lips as she took in this information. "So Denby had no more contact with the Carpathian government after your ambush?"

"They are more tribal units than one unified government, but that was his claim in the original statement he made four years ago. Ian showed all of them to me several days ago. Beldon's, Denby's, and those of the other officers on this mission."

"You do not appear convinced Denby had no contact with any of the Carpathian factions."

"I'm not. This is what he claims. However, it is reputed his wealth has increased substantially in the four years since the incident. It feels suspicious to me. How did he suddenly come into all this bounty?"

"Assuming the rumors are true."

He nodded. "It is something easily checked out. Ian is looking into it and ought to have something for me by the end of the week. I suspect Denby made his own private agreement with the Carpathians and, in turn, has secretly been selling their mined minerals through some middleman to conceal his identity while the English government purchases them at exorbitant prices."

"That seems more promising than a schoolmate's petty jealousy or a cousin's desire to inherit your title. Not that I am dismissing Beldon or Cummings. But Cummings would have needed you dead, so the fact that you have returned alive when it would have been so easy to dispose of you, leads me to believe he is not your traitor. And as I've said, if Beldon had tired of his games of jealousy, he could have simply stopped playing them."

"But if he is deranged and hides it well, he could be plotting something sinister right now."

Marigold said nothing.

"Marigold?" He shook his head and emitted a curt laugh. "Gad, I know you are keeping something from me. Tell me now or I shall hunt Beldon down and beat it out of him."

"Leo! You wouldn't dare."

He cast her a look that warned he would.

She sighed as they entered his townhouse and stepped into the entry hall. "All right, I will tell you. But not before we are alone upstairs."

"Why wait? Are you stalling for time?"

"No, I promise. I will tell you all in the privacy of our bedchamber."

He grunted in approval, for he did not want Marigold keeping anything from him. It had nothing to do with his being demanding or possessive and all to do with keeping her safe.

Candles were lit in the wall sconces in the entry hall and along the stairs in preparation for their return. Leo also knew Sterling had done the same in the upper hallway since this was a hard and fast rule in his household. All the main access halls were to be illuminated so he would never have to walk in darkness.

"Good evening, my lord," Sterling said in greeting, then bowed to Marigold. "My lady."

She cast him a glowing smile. "Good evening, Sterling. We had a lovely day. I hope yours was just as pleasant."

Leo stifled his laughter, for Marigold was much like her little pup, Mallow, in her enthusiasm and the purity of her joy. What a pair of opposites he and Marigold were. However, she was good for him. He was too cynical for his own good. He trusted few people and always looked at the world through doubting eyes.

She grabbed life with boundless exuberance and optimism. Her smiles had a way of touching his heart. There would be no descending into a dark pit of despair for him while she was close by to draw him back.

She truly was a ray of sunshine.

Leo escorted Marigold into her bedchamber which was next to his. The rooms had a private interior door between them so they could come and go as they pleased, and in whatever state of undress, without need to use the hallway and risk being seen by others.

Her lamp was also lit and her draperies had been left open at his direction. Their chambers overlooked the private garden in the rear of his house which had a high wall surrounding it and trees that loomed above that wall so that no one could see into their rooms.

Of course, Marigold could close her drapes if she wished for complete privacy.

She was modest and probably slept in a prim nightgown that buttoned to her throat. He saw one just like it laid out on the bed for her.

She noticed the direction of his gaze. "My cousins wanted to get me something silky and scandalous to wear," she said, her voice light and melodic, "but I refused. Do you mind, Leo? Was it something I ought to have done?"

"To tempt me?" He chuckled. "No, my pet. You are already

more temptation than I can handle."

The comment delighted her and she cast him another of her radiant smiles.

As for him, he had no modesty whatsoever.

He preferred to sleep naked. Nor did he care who saw him in the altogether since he needed sunshine and soft breezes upon his skin in order to nourish his soul more than he needed privacy.

He was not afraid of the darkness.

But he simply could not bear to be *enclosed* in it.

However, he now had Marigold to lie beside him and bring her soft warmth to nestle against his body. He longed to have her in his bed, share it with her, and share a lifetime together, although he had no idea how long his life was meant to last.

Well, he would concern himself with this tomorrow.

Tonight would be about Marigold and the pleasures they were to share. He looked forward to teaching her about intimacy and had no intention of getting any sleep tonight.

Nor would Marigold, for that matter.

"Let me help you out of your gown," he said, betraying no sense of urgency on his part since he did not wish to rush her as she explored sensations that were new to her.

"Thank you, yes," she said with a shaky laugh. "I'll never be able to manage on my own."

Since Leo had yet to engage a lady's maid for her or a valet for himself, they would have to assist each other for the next few days until those positions were filled. Leo preferred this forced nearness since it would allow them to get to know each other better and also put Marigold more at ease before tumbling into bed with him.

However, Leo had not forgotten the matter of Beldon that now teased in a recess of his restless brain. Whatever Marigold had held back about the man was going to bother him all night unless he cleared the air now. "Marigold, what did Beldon say to you that you are so reluctant to share with me?"

She frowned lightly.

Yes, he was an obsessive idiot who could not seem to forget his need for revenge even on his wedding night. This obsession had taken years to lodge in his soul while this need to marry Marigold had come upon him mere days ago.

"Promise you won't run off after him if I tell you." Marigold tried to look serious, but she was just too lovely and gentle to put anyone in fear. He was the first to admit he deserved a good scolding, so he listened patiently while she turned prim schoolmistress on him. "I will not have you prowling the London streets on our wedding night, Leo."

"I am not going to prowl anywhere but straight to your bed. Just tell me, will you?" He turned her so that her back was to him as he unfastened her buttons and lacings.

"All right, but do not make me regret my trust in you." She glanced back at him, tossing another stern look for good measure.

Gad, he wanted to kiss those sweet, puckered lips of hers. Had any of his tutors ever been this enticing? "You can always trust me, Marigold. If I give you my word, I shall keep to it."

She gave a little huff when he kissed her softly on the neck, but she was soon sighing and leaning against him. "Lord Beldon suggested," she said with a lick of her lips, "um…he suggested that if I had a change of heart and did not wish to marry you, that he would marry me."

Leo's fingers stiffened on her lacings, but she did not seem to notice his tension and just kept talking. "He gave the impression of our eloping to Gretna Green. Honestly, Leo, I wasn't paying any attention to him because the notion is simply ridiculous. Beyond ridiculous. Imagine, that I should choose him over you? Never in a thousand years. Nor a million years. In truth, why even put a time limit on my feelings for you when everyone knows love has no bounds? It is timeless and eternal."

Leo meant to be irritated, but Marigold had a way of delivering the news in such a way that his heart swelled with delight. "What a bloody arse he is. All these years and he still covets what I have."

"Well, I told him in no uncertain terms that I was marrying you. He seemed to take it rather well. Not pleased, but not enraged. What are you thinking Leo?"

First, that he did not deserve Marigold.

She was a little star fallen from heaven to shine just for him.

Second, that he wanted to give Beldon a beating long overdue because he was a sniveling, conniving, and backstabbing weasel.

But most of all, he wanted to be rid of all three men who were nothing but liars, cheats, and scoundrels. They contributed nothing to society. No one would miss them if they suddenly disappeared and were never seen again. "You don't want to know."

Marigold would not see the efficiency of his vengeance in quite the same way.

He helped her take the flowers out of her hair, unpinning her curls so that they tumbled in smooth waves over her shoulders. "Black silk," he murmured, running his fingers through the beautiful strands.

As her hair gently fell over her shoulders, he eased the luscious mane aside and began kissing her neck, at first suckling lightly at the spots he knew would be the most sensitive. Just beneath her earlobe. At the junction of her neck and shoulder. Feather-soft kisses along her throat.

She sighed and turned to him. "Leo, that was nice."

He had managed to undo the lacings of her gown in the meanwhile so that it now slipped off her shoulders. He held his breath as the delicate silk slid to the floor and pooled at her feet. He helped her step out of it, and then set the elegant gown aside.

Turning back to her, he drew in another breath.

Lovely.

Marigold wore only a sheer chemise.

His body responded with arousing heat.

He needed to be doused in a vat of cold water if he was going to make it through the night without claiming her fully.

Or he could just turn away, but that was never going to happen. Instead of looking away, he stared.

Her breasts were naturally firm and round.

So was her delightful derriere.

This girl did not need a corset, nor had she worn one today. Well, he knew Marigold was beautiful.

She made his heart thrum and his every pulse throb. In fact, all of him was throbbing, including his privates which had to be kept in check because he could not, and would not, make her his own yet.

He left her in the chemise even though that gossamer fabric hid little, and began to undress himself. Jacket, cravat, waistcoat, shirt. Boots. All flew off as he wasted no time on himself.

Marigold neatly folded each item over a chair as he tossed them off. "We are hiring a valet for you tomorrow," she muttered.

"Sterling usually attends to it, but I suppose he'll be kept too busy now that I have gained a wife." He smiled. "I'm usually more methodical. However, I feel particularly urgent tonight."

She looked at him and blushed. "What happens next?"

"I remove your chemise and then kiss you with all the passion you deserve along the entire length of your body."

A hot, pink blush stained her cheeks. "Oh, and what am I to do while you are doing that?"

He lifted her into his arms. "You are simply to enjoy the experience, my pet."

She glanced at the nightgown at the foot of the bed. "Um…"

"We'll leave that for another night." He set her down in the center of the large bed and then placed her nightgown atop the pile of her clothes on the nearby chair. When he returned, he nudged her down so that she lay on her back, her hair naturally fanning out across their pillows.

He stretched out beside her, his big body sinking into the mattress.

When he turned to Marigold, she was frowning. "Leo, why did you not tell me?"

"Tell you what?"

She sat up and nudged him to sit up as well so that she could look at his back.

Blast.

His scars.

He should have warned her about those.

Now she was struggling to hold back her tears. "Is this what they did to you?"

"In captivity? Yes." Perhaps she would now understand why

he wanted to kill those men. His back was not going to heal any more than it already had, and would always bear the marks of those beatings. Sometimes his captors had beaten him with a stick, sometimes with a whip. Each lash was burned into his skin and his memory. But this is not what he wanted to think about tonight or ever again for the rest of his life.

He wanted the memory of Marigold's soft kisses on his body and her scent that reminded him of crisp autumn days, cinnamon, and chestnuts roasting on a crackling fire lingering on his skin. He rolled her back down and settled over her, determined to give them both a memorable night.

The *best* night of their lives would have to wait until he claimed her fully, for only then would he truly make her his own.

This was not going to happen tonight, no matter how desperately each of them wished for it. He intended to make up for the lack by sending her soaring in every other way possible. "Ready, love? Hold onto me."

"All right. What are you about to do?"

He kissed her softly on the mouth. "Send you on a journey to the stars."

Her laughter was light and melodic. "No, really Leo. What are we going to do?"

CHAPTER 8

MARIGOLD HAD NO idea what to expect on her wedding night, but lying in Leo's arms while he made her body hum like the soft strains of a harp plucked by a master was exquisite beyond anything she could have imagined.

Sweet salvation!

This man knew what he was doing.

But everything contributed to the magic of the night, the large bed and clean sheets that felt cool beneath their bodies, and the windows left open to allow in the scent of flowers from Leo's magnificent garden. A refreshing breeze washed over their heated bodies, while a big, silver moon glowed majestically and filled the window's frame. Moonlight slanted across their bed, wrapping them in silvery beams of light.

Mostly, there was Leo.

Big and muscled, his body beautifully taut as he settled over her.

Leo with all his pain and anguish momentarily forgotten while he kissed her as though she was the breath of life to him. He suckled her breasts, teasing them lightly with his tongue and lips, smiling as fire shot through her veins and she moaned in response. "This is just the beginning, love."

Tingles skittered along her dampening skin whenever he referred to her as his love. "Oh, Leo."

She wanted to believe him, to pretend it was possible for this man who had survived the bowels of hell to love her. How could he when she was inexperienced, not well-traveled, not sophisticated or beautiful in a traditional way, and was probably far too cheerful for someone as tormented as him to tolerate?

"Close your eyes, sweetheart. Feel the flames sweep through you."

She was feeling the fire, for certain.

Just when she thought her body could not get hotter, he slid his hand between her legs and gently parted them. *Dear heaven.* What was he doing?

The answer came in a trice as he touched her intimately, his fingers finding her core and stroking her *there*, coaxing the wildest sensations out of her.

Her body turned molten.

She was lost to him, lost in the splendor of the moment.

He had a way of touching her, looking at her, kissing her. Making her believe he cherished her.

He could not have lost his heart to her as quickly as she had lost hers to him. She knew it could not be, for there was still too much anger inside of him, the cold sort of anger that turned one's heart to ice.

But he allowed her to pretend she meant everything to him because he made her feel as though she did.

Any worries about this night not turning out well just melted away. He had been resolute in his determination not to claim her as a husband ought to claim his wife, but how was she missing out on anything?

Dear heaven.

Was this intimacy not complete enough?

Molten lava poured through her limbs and flowed throughout her body, the heat so intense, she felt like a volcano about to erupt. "Marigold, don't hold back. Let whatever you are feeling come out."

Come out?

She was a fire raging out of control.

This intense power he held over her was thrilling and also alarming.

Was this supposed to happen?

She trusted Leo to protect her if something went awry, for he took care of what was his as any lion would.

This knowledge and Leo's soft words of encouragement allowed her to follow the path along which he guided her. She sighed and moaned, squirmed and arched. Held onto his big, muscled shoulders.

He was so beautifully built.

As sleek and powerful as a predator.

"Leo...I..." She was suddenly completely liquid, caught up in molten waves. Giant waves that carried her upward as high as the soaring birds. These cresting waves came one after another, each one stronger and sending her somewhere she had never been before.

Higher and higher they took her.

She no longer recognized her body.

"That's it, love," Leo whispered and kissed her as these sensations ripped through her and she shattered. "Leo!"

"I have you, love. My sweet, sweet love."

She shattered again, crying out his name as more fiery waves ripped through her.

Then Leo drew her into his arms and wrapped those big muscles around her. She collapsed against him, trying to calm her racing heart and cool the flames still smoldering within her body.

He caressed her all the while, telling her how beautiful she was. He kissed her lips, and then kissed her closed eyes. He kissed her throat. The swell of her breast.

She opened her eyes and stared up at him with all the love she felt in her heart.

He was grinning at her like a conquering hero.

"Oh, Leo." She put her hands to her face to cover her embarrassment, but he gently drew them off so he could look at her.

"Marigold, you are my wife," he said with a note of wonder. "I wanted you to experience the pleasure that can exist between us."

"But my response, Leo. Oh, was it not too wanton?"

"No such thing as too wanton in bed, certainly not between a husband and wife. Marigold, you are sweet as honey. This is just the beginning, love. Next time, I hope to have you wildly crying out as you claw my back."

She gasped. "Claw you? I could never hurt you!"

"You are thinking of my scars, aren't you? They have long since healed, my pet. Even if they hadn't, your delicate hands could never do me harm."

She appeared genuinely distressed. He ought to have realized she would always think of him first.

"Are you sure, Leo?"

"Gad, you're a gentle thing, aren't you? Marigold, I won't ever force you to do something you are not willing to do. But I promise, you will enjoy everything we do tonight and you are incapable of hurting me...even if you claw at me like a cat in heat."

Her blush returned.

She felt it spread up her neck and into her face. Even the tips of her ears burned. "What do you have in mind for us to do next?"

"Something quite wicked that I think you are going to enjoy immensely."

He spoke with such certainty, she was intrigued. "Are you sure, Leo?"

"Yes, love. Trust me."

"I do." She nestled against his chest, her cheek resting against the light dusting of hair along his finely sculpted torso.

She was soothed by the steady beat of his heart and the warmth of his deep, resonant voice. "Ah, I see I have worried you now."

She nodded. "Only a little."

"There is nothing to worry about, love." He cast her an affectionate, but entirely wicked grin. "Are you still in heartache over my scars? I've told you they do not hurt me, but you needn't clutch my back if this troubles you."

"What shall I hold onto?"

He laughed. "Hold onto the headboard once we get started because I am going to send you to the stars."

"You've sent me there already," she admitted, blushing again.

"Ah, love. That pleases me greatly. But there's more for you to experience." He rolled her onto her back and leaned over her, propping on his elbows to keep from crushing her with his big body. Their gazes met, his tender and devouring. "We can stop if you do not feel ready."

Not ready?

Her insides were already enveloped in fire and her heart was beating too rapidly. She would expire if she did not have more of him. "I am ready."

Judging by his sensual grin, this next round of 'pleasuring' was going to be something naughty.

Dear heaven.

How could it be better than her first time?

Oh, that wicked smile of his.

"Leo, what are you going to do to me?"

"Trust me, my pet," he said, settling himself between her legs. "You are going to like this immensely."

She wasn't sure.

He had positioned his shoulders between her legs and was still smiling like a conquering hero. "Are you holding onto the headboard, Marigold?"

"No. You are jesting, aren't you? Why should I–"

He lowered his mouth to her intimate core and gave a soft lick.

If her bed had a canopy, she would have exploded like fireworks straight through the overhanging fabric. "Leeeooo!"

She tried to hold out, but it was an impossible feat. She shattered soon after, unable to control those soaring waves that swept over her body and engulfed her in a rippling, quivering mass of liquid fire. She cried his name over and over, and gripped his shoulders when he rose to cover her and gather her in his arms. "Hush, my beautiful love. I have you."

She needed to hold onto him for fear of disappearing into sea foam, something so light and ephemeral that he could no longer see or touch her.

He kissed her and caressed her, stroked his fingers gently through her hair to calm her. He spoke softly to her, his voice deep and soothing as she struggled to regain her composure. "Oh, Leo, I cannot seem to resist you. A single touch and I come undone."

"There is nothing wrong with that, sweetheart. In fact, it is entirely the point."

"Are you sure, Leo? You would tell me if I am doing something wrong, wouldn't you?"

"Yes, love. I would. Do you hear me voicing a complaint?"

"No," she admitted, snuggling against him as settled onto his back and drew her into his embrace.

Come morning, Marigold awoke still held in Leo's arms.

She had wrapped herself around his body like a vine clinging to a tree.

Oh, heavens.

How could she ever face him and not blush after what they did last night?

"Good morning, my pet," he said with a smug grin. His light growth of beard scratched her cheek as he leaned forward to nuzzle her neck. "How do you feel?"

"Oh, Leo." She buried her head against his chest, trying to avoid his gaze. "I cannot look at you."

His chuckle was tender and indulgent. "Why not, love?"

"I know what you said about you and me in bed, but I am certain I was unforgivably...*expressive.* Are there not rules about this sort of thing?" She had also taken up three-quarters of the bed and was still squeezed against him because she loved the scent of his skin and the warmth of his body.

He shifted his position to roll her under him while he settled over her with elbows propped to carry most of his weight.

He was big and all solid muscle.

"The only rule that counts is the one that says we must please each other. You were delightfully responsive." He kissed her deeply. "Marigold, you were perfect. You are perfect. I would keep you in my bed for a full month if I could." He moaned and touched his forehead to hers. "But I hear a scratching at our door. Since Sterling usually knocks before entering, I would guess it is Mallow who is begging to come in. The little fellow is not one to be ignored and now requires our attention."

Marigold smiled. "He has given us the night to ourselves and is at the limit of his indulgence. I think we must pay homage to him. Do you mind if we play with him a little?"

Leo shook his head and rolled onto his back with a playful growl. "After last night, I don't mind a blessed thing. I am happy to have both of you with me. Especially you. This is your home now, just as much as it is mine. Ours to share."

"Oh, is that right? Yours and mine? Is that what you think?" She laughed softly. "Mallow believes it is *his* house and he is kindly allowing *us* to reside with him. Of course, he will toss us out unless we agree to feed him on schedule and walk him whenever he barks. He will allow us to sleep in this bed, which he will now claim as his, on the condition that we pet him and pamper him whenever he demands it."

"I had no idea Mallow was such a tyrannical, little fellow." Leo emitted another soft growl as he slowly stretched his arms over his head. He resembled a sleek, jungle cat about to rouse after a night of sleep.

Goodness, she could not stop staring at his big, naked body.

They heard more scratches and an impatient bark.

"The master calls," Leo joked, rolling out of bed and striding to the door.

He was about to open it to let Mallow in, when Marigold's gasp stopped him. "Wait! I need to find my robe."

"You are dressing for a dog?" He cast her a lazy smile. "All right, I'll find it for you. Here it is, love." He bent to scoop it off the carpet where it must have fallen sometime in the night.

"Thank you, Leo. Aren't you going to put on clothes?"

"Do you think Mallow will care if my privates are showing? He'll probably compare his to mine. Besides, it is hardly daybreak. We are in no hurry to get out of bed, although I will need to get a little work done at some point today."

"Work?"

"Yes, love. First, I intend to pay a call on a Mr. Homer Barrow who is reputed to be London's finest Bow Street runner."

"I know of him. Are you going to seek his help in investigating those three men?" Marigold hastily wrapped the robe around herself and scrambled out of bed. "I'll go with you."

Leo groaned. "Marigold–"

"I'm going with you, Leo. We are safer together than apart. Besides, we have not been married even a full day yet. Do I not get at least one day with you before I return to the Huntsford Academy and you do whatever takes up a marquess's time in the conduct of his business affairs?"

"All right, you win. It is a good thing I am still in your thrall from last night's exertions. Seems I cannot summon up the will to protest. But to be precise, the Crown agents are running the investigation. This Bow Street man is to be hired to protect you. Yes, I'll also have him send men into the seedier parts of town on the chance they'll dig up something the Crown agents will find helpful. But mostly, he is to keep close watch over you." He donned his breeches while she opened the door.

Mallow trotted in and immediately hopped onto Marigold's bed, settling comfortably in the center of it.

Leo laughed as he nudged Mallow to the foot of the bed. "Oh, no. You will not get away with claiming the entire bed, you little imp. I'll be sneezing dog hairs all night if you lie down on these sheets."

Mallow accepted the demotion without protest, seeming to recognize Leo as the dominant male in their relationship. He rolled onto his back and allowed Leo to scratch his belly.

Marigold curled up beside Leo, resting her head against his shoulder because she felt such a compelling need to touch him.

When Mallow began to whine, they quietly made their way downstairs. Leo opened the parlor doors that led onto his terrace. Mallow shot past them and disappeared into the garden, running behind some yew bushes to attend to nature's call.

Leo wrapped his arms around Marigold while they stood in silence and waited for Mallow to finish his necessities.

Marigold's gaze wandered over his garden. It was remarkably beautiful in its design. More of a country garden with its wild sweeps of color, of yellows and whites, and a few pinks that were common this early in the season. These spring blooms attracted butterflies and bees that were already actively flitting about.

Morning dew glistened on the grass.

The gazebo off in the far corner was shrouded in a light mist that would burn off as the sun rose.

Birdsong filled the air.

"Are you happy, Marigold?" Leo asked.

"Yes, can you doubt it?" She looked up at him, her heart aching because she was so filled with love for this man and he was so desperately tormented. He seemed at peace in this moment, but she knew it would not last. "What about you, Leo? I think this question is more pertinent to you."

He nodded.

This was all the response she got, but she did not press him. He had endured evils that would break most men. If he was happy for the moment, it would be enough for now.

"Come, love. Let's go back inside. The staff will soon rise and we are barefoot and half dressed. Hardly presentable." He gave a soft whistle and Mallow scampered back to him.

Leo knelt and gave Mallow a good scratch behind the ears, then rose and motioned for the now happy spaniel to follow them inside.

Marigold paused in the doorway, enjoying this early morning hour when the world seemed peaceful and silent.

There was a refreshing chill to the air.

Their resident birds now tweeted noisily in the treetops.

"Leo…" She wanted to tell him how perfect last night had been for her and the same for this moment, as well. But she did not know where to start, and could not get the words out while her heart was in a jumble.

"I know, love." He wrapped his hand around hers and led her upstairs.

Mallow's little paws clicked on the marble floor as he pattered across the entry hall ahead of them and then started up the stairs. His breath came in soft pants and his tail wagged as he beat them onto the landing.

Leo was still holding her hand.

He had said nothing as they returned to her bedchamber. But the moment they were inside, he shut the door, lifted her into his arms, and then had them both naked and tumbling onto the mattress while he kissed her with enough heat to scorch the entire city of London.

Mallow barked to regain their attention.

Leo nudged him aside. "Get your own girl, Mallow. Marigold is mine."

Marigold's heart hitched.

Yes, she was Leo's.

But for how long?

CHAPTER 9

"GOOD OF YOU to see us on such short notice, Mr. Barrow," Leo said as he and Marigold were escorted into the Bow Street runner's office later that morning. The chairs beside the man's desk were solidly built and comfortable, but his office on the whole was a working man's space. His desk was piled high with folders while bookshelves and cabinets lined the walls.

Mr. Barrow himself was a portly man with a red, bulbous nose, prominent jowls, and keen eyes that overlooked nothing. "How may I help you, my lord? Lady Muir, would you care for a cup of tea?"

"Thank you for the offer, but I am fine for now." She sat and smiled at the Bow Street runner. "We have heard wonderful reports about you, Mr. Barrow. In fact, I am already quite familiar with your good work since you helped dear friends of mine recently, the Duke of Huntsford and his wife, Duchess Adela. I hope you can help my husband as you did my friends."

Leo took her hand and gave it a light squeeze, but his attention remained fixed on Mr. Barrow. "What I need are two good men to protect my wife." He quickly recounted his story and mentioned the three men of particular concern. He was quite thorough and Marigold struggled several times in the retelling to hold back her tears.

"So I need watch kept on Chipping Way," Leo said, finishing his tale. "Specifically to make note of anyone lurking near our house. My wife will have footmen to accompany her whenever she leaves home, but they are not trained as your men are. Do you have experienced investigators who can be discreet when following her around?"

"Or following my husband," Marigold added, shooting Leo a frown. "Honestly, Leo. You are in more dire need of protection now that you are determined to turn over every rock to uncover the snake who betrayed you. You will stir him again and he will come after you once he learns you intend to go after him."

Mr. Barrow shook his head. "My lady, I have heard all that you and his lordship have told me. I do not wish to frighten you, but you must not dismiss the danger to yourself. The greatest pain this villain can inflict on your husband is to hurt you. Rest assured, we shall keep diligent watch over you. At a respectful distance, of course. For us to be most effective, we will require your cooperation."

"You will have it," Marigold assured him. "I shall make a list of my daily engagements so you will always know ahead of time where I plan to be."

He nodded and then turned to Leo. "Would it be possible to put one of my men in your household as a footman, my lord? This way, he can keep an eye on your wife while inside the house and also accompany her whenever she goes out."

Leo nodded. "Quite easily done. My wife insists we have a dire shortage of staff. Apparently, I cannot possibly do without a valet. Nor can she manage without a lady's maid. Or housekeeper. We had planned to hire more staff in every capacity."

Mr. Barrow pursed his lips. "Keep in mind this also gives your nemesis the opportunity to plant one of his people inside your household."

Marigold's eyes widened. "Oh, how wicked."

"He can try but he will not succeed," Leo said. "We shall not rush to fill all the positions, and I will insist that our immediate hires be known or personally related to those long-time retainers on staff with our neighbors."

Marigold nodded. "The Mayhew family has worked for my Aunt Sophie and Uncle John for decades. I had planned on seeking their recommendations first. The Mayhews always have a niece or nephew newly arrived in town and seeking employment. This will not be a problem."

"Good. You need to surround yourself with people you can trust. I'll have my best men on the task of protecting you. If you have no objections, I will assign two of my experienced runners to start, Henry as footman and Arthur as gardener. One to work inside and one outside. I'll also do a little digging along the docks and elsewhere I might learn more about these three men who concern you, my lord."

"You'll need a retainer, of course. I'll make funds readily available to you today. I'd like you to get started as soon as possible. Just be discreet and keep out of the way of the Crown's investigation."

"Won't be a problem. I know most of their agents and they know me."

Having now finished their business, they rose to leave. Marigold, in her true ray of sunshine fashion, smiled at Mr. Barrow. "Thank you, sir. You have no idea how relieved I am to know we shall now be in your capable hands. To be as successful as you are requires true caring and devotion to saving lives. Please know we are grateful to you and your men. We shall not do anything foolish to put you or them in danger."

Mr. Barrow was obviously taken by surprise. "You are most gracious, Lady Muir."

Leo laughed. "It is her subtle way of warning me to let you and the Crown agents do their job and not go off on my own to murder these suspects."

"Well, my lord. She has a point."

Leo raked a hand through his hair. "I know, but it is still very hard to let the days go by without seeing the culprit punished."

They left Mr. Barrow's office, then stopped by Leo's bank.

The bank manager attended to them personally, bowing and fussing over Leo so obsequiously, he wanted to throttle the man just to shut him up. Of course, he was not going to do or say anything impolite. Marigold was already worried he was in a blind rage and would act like a madman at the slightest provocation. He did not need to add this toady manager to the list of men he wished to see dead.

He made arrangements for Homer Barrow to be paid, then opened up an account for Marigold. She shot out of her chair when he mentioned the amount he wished to transfer into her account. "Leo, that is too much!"

He gently nudged her back in her chair. "It is not nearly enough."

Leo waited for the manager to leave his office to attend to the transfers before he turned to Marigold again. "There is more to come, the bulk of which will be left in trust with the Duke of Edgeware to head a committee of trustees, all of whom will not hesitate to grind my worm of a cousin to dust if he dares attempt to wrest so much as a shilling away from you. I can do nothing about the entailed properties. But whatever is mine alone shall be left to you."

Marigold frowned.

"Why are you making that face?" he asked.

"We have only been married a day, Leo. *A day.* And you have not even...*you know.*"

He sighed. "Yes, I know. Believe me, keeping you chaste is killing me."

"Should you not hold off with this transfer of funds to my account until you are certain you want this marriage to continue?"

"No. I mean to protect you no matter what happens in the future. Whether we stay together or not."

She gasped. "We are most definitely staying together. I will kick you if you dare suggest otherwise."

He sighed. "Marigold, are you going to cry? Don't you dare cry while we are in the bank."

"I am not going to cry, but I will not deny your comments are upsetting me. Nor am I going to leave you. We pledged to remain true to each other for better or for worse. I will fight any attempt of yours to annul our marriage unless you truly do not want me. Only your heart can chase me away. But how can you kiss me the way you do, or hold me in your arms so tenderly all night, if you do not care for me a little?"

"The act of sex is not the same as being in love."

She put her hands to her temples and rubbed them gently. "Was it all fake then?"

He groaned. "No, none of it was fake. It was more real than I wished it to be."

"And you still believe our feelings don't count? That you or I will not be devastated to part ways merely because we haven't performed the act of...*you know*."

"Coupling. You can refer to it as coupling."

She harrumped.

"Nor will we ever consummate this marriage until I am certain the danger to you has passed. But for the record, sex can be enjoyed in many ways other than just coupling. Did I not prove that to you last night?"

She glanced toward the door in panic. "Leo," she said in a whisper, "let's please speak of something else. All right?"

"All right." But as delicious as she was, and as desperately as he wanted her, he intended to end this marriage if this was the only way to keep her safe.

After finishing at the bank, they rode to the Huntsford Academy since it was close by. Leo knew Marigold was eager to see how the new dragon display was coming along. He thought they could take a quick look and then be on their way, but her friends Syd and Gory were there as well as the Duke of Huntsford's brothers, Octavian and Julius.

After getting a tour of the museum, and a quick peek at the display under construction, which Leo was able to walk through without the ground eating him up because that part of the hall was now bathed in light while the workers built what would ultimately be a mammoth beast, the six of them then sat down to a meal in the duke's private dining room. Mr. Smythe-Owens, the head curator who had led them on the quick tour, was invited to join them but he declined since he had other exhibits requiring his attention.

"My brother and Adela return to London at the end of the week," Octavian remarked as they enjoyed main courses of roast duck and fish pie along with a mash of leeks, onions, and potatoes. "From Ambrose's latest letter, I gather they'll be bringing back more impressive finds."

"How did they manage with the little duke-to-be?" Marigold asked. "It could not have been easy for them to explore around the dig site with a newborn in tow."

"Well, they haven't put the little heir to work in the cave yet," Octavian teased. "I'm sure Ambrose is not allowing Adela and the baby anywhere near the site if anything remotely dangerous is going on. Nor will he allow them out of the inn if there is even a drop of rain threatening."

"If I know my brother," Julius remarked, "he has organized an efficient system of getting drawings, relic samples, fossil bones, and the like, over to Adela so she doesn't ever have to leave the inn. From the tone of his letters, there's more of interest coming, and I'm sure Miss Appleby's sketches are going to be brilliant."

Marigold, Syd, and Gory were caught up in the conversation.

"Did they say what else they have found?" Marigold asked.

Octavian shook his head. "No, it will be a surprise for all of us."

"I cannot wait to see their trove," Gory said. "I hope they found more skulls. Although I would be just as happy for cervical bones or teeth. I wonder if they will have found any human remains. It would be fascinating to study our ancestors and discover how we have developed over the millennia. I wonder if we used to have fangs? Or tails?"

Marigold laughed. "Can you imagine tails poking out from our silk gowns? I don't know if there will be any clues as to that found in these caves. So far, all we have uncovered are ancient creatures and few of them are recognizable."

"Including the creature whose skull you found. Your latest addition to the Hall of Dragons is coming along well," Julius remarked. "The wing span is astounding. I wonder what our ancestors must have thought seeing something that size swoop down on them? Our father loved to take us exploring around the caves on our Devonshire property, but we never found anything this interesting."

They enjoyed a lively lunch, then Leo had Marigold show him more of the museum for no reason other than she glowed as she spoke of these finds. He took pleasure in seeing her so happy.

They bid farewell to Marigold's friends and were about to climb into Leo's carriage when he spotted the familiar figure of Lord Beldon approaching.

Was it mere chance or had the bastard been following them?

Leo immediately tensed and drew Marigold slightly behind him, but she resisted. "Leo, he is merely walking down the street. You cannot do anything to him."

He did not believe for a moment this was a chance meeting. Beldon must have put his own men to watch them and report their whereabouts back to him. In truth, he had felt they were being watched since leaving their home this morning. "Get in the carriage, Marigold."

Leo was steaming and did not expect this encounter to end well. He had been waiting four years to confront Beldon and put an end to his vicious games.

Marigold grabbed his arm. "No, Leo. Please. You will play straight into his hands if you cause a scene. Let's go home."

"In a moment," he said.

"Now," she countered, refusing to let go of his arm. "I know you are angry because you think he has been following us. But do not forget, Crown agents are following him. They will stop him if he attempts anything."

"So long as they do not stop me," he replied, his voice raw with a building rage and his expression lethal. "It is time to stir this hornet's nest."

She gasped. "You would purposely goad him to take action against you? Leo, that is a terrible idea."

"I did not ask for you opinion. Get in the carriage. I mean it, Marigold." He gave her no choice but lifted her inside.

To his relief, she did not hop back down, merely remained watching him warily. He knew he was frightening her, but he had made no secret of his hatred for Beldon. What had started as irksome jealousy on Beldon's part had escalated into four years of humiliation and torture. It was time for repayment.

He must have frightened the wits out of Marigold, for the color had drained from her cheeks and her lips were pursed with tension. He would never harm her, but he did not want her so confident that she would ignore his wishes and blithely rush into danger.

"Beldon," he said, as the puffed up lord now approached with a smug expression on his face.

"Fancy meeting you here, Muir. Afraid your pretty wife might run off with one of the curators if you do not watch her like a hawk? Perhaps it is one of Huntsford's brothers who has you jealous." The fiend's gaze came to rest on Marigold with an intensity Leo did not like.

Leo took him by the throat. "Keep away from my wife. If I catch you anywhere near her, I shall gut you. This is the only warning you will receive."

He released Beldon and turned to walk away, then noticed Marigold – whose head was still poking out from the carriage – suddenly go from concerned to alarmed.

This is what he had hoped for, the opportunity to do Beldon in.

He whirled just as Beldon withdrew the blade hidden within his walking stick and attempted to stab Leo with it. Leo wrestled it out of his hands, kicked it away, and then landed a solid punch that dropped Beldon to his knees.

Blood spurted from Beldon's nostrils.

Leo punched him again and this time cut his lip.

It wasn't nearly enough blood, to Leo's way of thinking. He was ready to finish Beldon off, but Octavian and Julius ran forward to stop him.

Leo was strong, but Octavian was built like an ox and hauled him back. "Leo, I will break your hand if I must do it to protect you from yourself."

Marigold rushed to them. "Oh, thank goodness you stopped him. Leo, are you out of your mind?"

Perhaps he was.

All the more grounds for Marigold to pursue that annulment if it became necessary.

He tried to calm himself, for he was an enraged animal and wanted to rip Beldon apart piece by piece until the sniveling coward was dead. If Beldon was responsible for his capture and confinement all these years, then was his revenge not justice? "Get up, Beldon," he said with a growl. "Come at me again."

"I want him arrested! Hanged!" Beldon shouted, but his words were muffled while he pressed his elegant handkerchief to his mouth and nose.

Octavian rolled his eyes. "Shut up, Beldon. First of all, he is a peer. No one is going to arrest him. Second of all, it will be your word against ours. All we saw was you removing your weapon to attack a man while his back was turned. What did you intend to do? Stab him in the back? He is the one with every right to see you arrested and hanged."

Beldon turned pale. "He grabbed me by the throat and threatened me!"

"He was assisting you with your cravat," Julius said. "Dear heaven, man. Do you always walk out with it so inelegantly tied?"

"What rot! Is this how it is to be?" Beldon's pristine handkerchief was now soaked in blood as well as the front of his shirt. "I'll see all of you hanged!"

"And we'll see you dead first if you do not walk away this instant," Octavian growled. "Just walk away before I let go of Lord Muir and let him at you."

Marigold now hopped out of the carriage. Thankfully, Julius stopped her from running forward. Leo did not want her to be the last thing Beldon saw as he ran off. Beldon already had an unhealthy interest in her.

No, he wanted Beldon to be thinking of him.

To be hating *him*.

Wanting *him* dead.

Beldon cursed Leo and hurried off.

Octavian now eased his grip on him. "If I take my hands off you, I want your word that you will not chase after him. Control that rage of yours, Leo. What were you thinking, you bloody fool? To attack him while Marigold was with you."

Julius was also frowning at him, clearly furious. "What the hell was that about?"

"Nothing." Leo still had not calmed down, but all his anger was trained on Beldon who kept looking back as though Leo was going to shoot him down like the dog he was while he retreated from sight.

Leo would never do such a cowardly thing as shoot Beldon in the back. No, he wanted Beldon to see the jaws of death coming at him and know exactly who was taking his life.

Marigold's friends now rushed out of the museum to join them.

"What happened?" Gory asked.

"Nothing," Leo repeated.

Gory cast him a worried look. "That was hardly nothing, Leo."

"Indeed, it wasn't," Marigold said, her eyes narrowed as she stared at him in exasperation. "My friends can be trusted. Please tell them what this is about."

"No." He bid her friends a curt farewell and once again hurried Marigold toward their carriage. He lifted her into it as though she weighed no more than a feather, climbed in after her, and then slammed the door shut as he settled against the squabs opposite her. "Collins, home!"

The carriage took off with a jerk that sent Marigold tumbling into his arms since the jolt had popped her out of her seat, lips pursed in that prim, schoolmistress way that made him want to kiss her even as she obviously intended to berate him. He wasn't angry with her. Lord, he was desperate to hold her and keep her beautiful light shining for him. "Marigold," he said in a raw whisper and crushed his lips to hers.

But it was a short kiss, for he was still too angry and did not wish to accidentally hurt her as he ground his mouth on hers. He wanted to devour her, needed to absorb every bit of her sunlight as he tried to shed his anguish. "Sorry," he muttered, breaking it off with a suddenness that left her dazed.

He kept her on his lap, not letting her push away because he needed to hold onto this one good thing in his life before he ruined their marriage.

Had he ruined it already?

Marigold rested her hands on his chest, making no more effort to push out of his grasp. "Oh, Leo. How terribly this villain must have hurt you. Do you think Beldon was the one who ordered your ambush?"

"I don't know. I don't care. He could be the one. But he's an arse, for certain. Are you taking his side? He came after me with knife drawn while my back was turned. Any man would be within his rights to kill him. Octavian should not have stopped me."

"Are you going to blame him now?"

He sighed. "No, of course not. I would have done the same if our positions had been reversed."

She placed her hand on his cheek and must have felt the grinding tension in his jaw. Sighing, she turned her face to his and gave him a light kiss on the lips, her touch so soft and gentle while his had been hard and crushing moments ago. "Well, you have certainly stirred this hornet's nest."

"I know." He buried his head against her neck, inhaling the scent of her skin as he attempted to calm himself down.

"Dearest Leo," she said in a whisper. "How stupid of me not to fully appreciate how badly you are hurting."

But it did not hurt when he held onto her, breathed in her delicate scent, a hint of cinnamon today, and put his lips to her warm skin.

She was the balm for his torment.

"I'll be spending a lot of time at the Huntsford Academy over the next few weeks as the new exhibit is readied for display. Huntsford and Adela will return in a few days with more artifacts to be studied."

"Are you worried that I will stop you from going there? You love that place. I would never deprive you of it."

"Thank you, Leo. But my friends will ask me questions about you and what led to today's incident. Please, let me tell them something. Octavian and Julius can be of help to you."

He tensed. "And bring them down along with me? No."

"Syd and Gory will also help. My point is that they can all be trusted to keep whatever they are told in confidence."

He emitted a mirthless laugh. "No, my pet. Too many people are involved already. The bloody Crown investigation already feels like too much of a circus."

"But you confided in Homer Barrow."

"Because you need protection. And this circus will continue since His Majesty intends to have me installed as a Knight of the Thistle. Everyone views it as an honor, but do you know what I hope happens?"

She shook her head. "No."

"I'm hoping the traitor approaches me there so I can kill him in front of that crowd. I don't care who it is, Beldon, Cummings, or Denby. I just want him to make a move, and I will gut him like a fish."

She pushed off his lap and sat across from him. "Leo, are you purposely trying to upset me? Even you must realize how awful that sounds. To dream of avenging the wrong by shedding blood in front of the king and his entire court? You are too riled."

He shrugged. "I know."

"You have the best men in England on the task. Perhaps the best of all is Mr. Barrow because he seems able to get into places and talk to people no one else can. You must give them time, Leo."

"Are you through slapping my hand and telling me I should behave?"

"Now you are just being contrary."

"It is who I am, Marigold. I warned you to keep away. I did you no favor by marrying you."

"We were caught in Ian's library because neither of us wanted to pull away from the other. You kissed me first and only stopped kissing me because we were interrupted. If this is how you thought to warn me away, then you ought to rethink your approach."

"Are you through lecturing me?" He did not mean to smile, but could not help it. He loved the way Marigold stood up to him, for she did it so sweetly even as she boxed his ears.

"You will not get through your torment on your own, Leo. Let others help you. Me, of course. You caused a scene in front of Huntsford's museum and his brothers came to your rescue. Do you not think you owe them some explanation?"

"No. Nor did they come to my rescue. The notion is absurd. I had Beldon on the ground and–"

"You were about to kill him. Were you really going to do it?"
He refused to answer.

"Never mind. Your silence tells me all I need to know. They did not rescue you from Beldon but from yourself. You owe them for protecting you from your own anger and bile. If you do not care for your own safety, then think of mine. You ought to tell them what is going on so they can protect *me* whenever I am not with you. Think about it, Leo."

He groaned. "I will. Later, not now."

"No, you won't. You will dismiss it because it does not suit you to be contradicted in your plans. You think Beldon has been subdued, but what about the other suspects? None of my friends will understand the extent of the danger unless you tell them."

"Marigold, stop belaboring the point. It is enough that Huntsford's brothers know to keep Beldon away from you if they see him poking around the museum again."

"I think you frightened the life out of Beldon. I would not be surprised if he disappeared from London for a few months. What of your cousin or this Denby fellow? They might start to poke around, too. Who will know to protect me from them?"

"I'll take care of them."

"As you took care of Beldon? Leo…"

"What, Marigold?" he snapped, sounding harsher than intended. "Are you going to pass your moral judgment on me again? I've had all I can take for today."

She was fretting again as she stared at him. "Should I be afraid that you might hit me?"

"No. How can you think I ever would?" But he groaned and shook his head. "Never, my pet. No matter how enraged I am, I will never hurt you." Of course she had to be worried. He had gone after Beldon like a raging bull. "I'm sorry if I frightened you into thinking I might."

"You have always been gentle with me, Leo. But you are so badly beaten and bruised, it overwhelms you. Is it all right if I tell you something else? Or will you bite my head off?"

"You can tell me anything. Just no more about Beldon, all right?" She was probably going to ignore his wishes because

Marigold had a streak of stubbornness to match his own. "I will not apologize for what I did to him. If I am sorry for anything, it is that I was stopped before he got what he deserved. At the very least, he deserved a few more punches before I let him up."

She eyed him warily. "You would have controlled yourself?"

He shrugged. "Possibly. I might have, depending on what I saw reflected in his eyes...innocence or guilt."

"I'm glad you said that, Leo. Truly, it is very important to me."

"I'm not trying to kill anyone innocent," he said in a shaky breath. "Even if Beldon is innocent of what was done to me, he is still a craven bastard and you can never let him anywhere near you. Now, what is it you wish to tell me?"

"Promise me you will not be angry." She moved back to his side once again and took his hand in hers. "It has nothing to do with Beldon."

He raised her hand to his lips and gave it a light kiss. "I do not think I can ever be angry with you. How's that for an admission?"

"Well, it is good to know because I intend to tell you something..."

He lifted her onto his lap and wrapped his arms around her. "Just say it, Marigold. What is so awful that you dread telling me? Especially if it has nothing to do with Beldon."

She licked her lips and wrapped her arms around his neck as she curled up against him. "I did not want to tell you yet. I meant to wait until we were married a full month before I said anything."

"Marigold, stop squirming on my lap or I am going to hike up your skirts and do something quite lewd to you."

"Don't rush me, Leo. It is not an easy thing to say." She took a deep breath. "Here's my admission...I love you. It does not require a response on your part, mostly because I am afraid of what you will say, or not say. But I wanted you to know my feelings. I wanted you to know how much you matter to me and how important it is to me that you stay safe and give us the chance for a happy life."

She loved him?

This little gem loved him?

He was a wild, unmanageable ape who might have accidentally hurt her while he was out of control during his confrontation with Beldon. "Stop, Marigold."

"No, I must get this out. I do not want so much as a ha'penny from you. Calling myself a marchioness is quite a mouthful to swallow. I was content being merely a Miss Farthingale. I hope you know that marrying you was never about your wealth or title. I do not want your house or fancy carriage that I damaged with my box of bones and skulls even though you insist I didn't." She took another deep breath. "I want *you*."

Bollocks.

This girl was determined to claim his heart.

It was the last thing he wanted, especially since he was going to wreck their marriage in his quest for vengeance.

Why could she not be greedy and care nothing about him?

She puckered her lips in that priggish way that made him want to kiss her. "Leo, I am going to tell you how much I love you every day from this day forward. I shall make it a point to tell you how important you are to me and how much I value our marriage. I hope we have a *long* and happy marriage which shall last decades and not merely a month because you are so obsessed with your dark past that you refuse to see the bright future."

"Are you through boxing my ears?"

"Is that what I am doing?"

"Marigold, we hardly know each other. Our marriage was a rushed affair. The only reason you *think* you love me is because I am the only man you've known intimately or who has gained intimate knowledge of your body, which is a beautiful body, by the way."

She sat up stiffly. "Are you suggesting I do not know my own mind?"

"I am suggesting you are swayed by my introducing you to the pleasures of the bed."

She frowned at him. "I knew you thought I was too wanton."

He laughed. "Blessed saints, you are not. You are expressive and responsive. In short, you are perfect in the bedchamber and out of it. Just let us not have this conversation yet. It is early days and you have now seen I am not entirely in control of my rage. It will never be aimed at you, I give you my word of honor."

She nodded. "I believe you. I trust you."

Gad, did she have to trust him, too?

Love and trust?

How was he to combat that? "I cannot say what will happen if ever I face Cummings or Denby. I will likely rip them apart as I tried to do to Beldon. So you would be wise not to get too attached to me because I have no idea how this will all work out."

"Leo, think of *us* and not merely of yourself. If you dare rush off and get yourself killed, I will haul you out of your grave and then kill you myself."

He laughed.

"Well, I wouldn't really."

"I know."

Her eyes began to tear. "Leo, please. Don't you dare leave me."

Lord, was she going to cry?

Did she think he ever wanted to be apart from her?

She was the sunshine nourishing his bleak soul.

But he was beyond saving and so was their marriage. The incident with Beldon proved his need for revenge was stronger than her love. He'd told her that he might have stopped had he seen innocence reflected in Beldon's eyes, but he doubted he would have done so. First of all, he was rabid with rage. If Octavian hadn't held him back, Beldon would not have been left breathing. Perhaps this blind rage would change over time, but not now. He was a savage beast with massive teeth who needed to feed on death and retribution.

However, once his vengeance was complete, he could love her.

Dear heaven, how could he not love her?

Perhaps he was there already, but how could he trust his feelings?

Their meeting and marriage had happened impossibly fast.

They had been married a day and he had almost killed Beldon.

She was trying to soften him with her declaration of love, trying to make him see reason when his feelings were not driven by reason but anger, hate, and destruction.

How could she love him?

He would destroy her.

In doing so, he would forever destroy himself.

Why did she have to love him?

This ought to have elated him, even if he never admitted the feeling was reciprocated. But it did not make him feel good at all.

He had such a sense of foreboding.

Something bad was going to happen soon.

Could he protect Marigold?

Or would she be the next victim?

CHAPTER 10

TWO WEEKS HAD gone by and Leo was going out of his mind with frustration.

The gossip rags reported Beldon had taken himself off to France. This gave Homer Barrow and the Crown agents the opportunity to search his townhouse and his country estate, delve into his investments and bank records, read his journals and letters, question his friends, enemies, and neighbors, for any hint, any note, of involvement in the ambush of their delegation to Carpathia four years ago.

The Crown agents had even ripped up floorboards and broken through walls in search of evidence.

Beldon would be livid when he returned to find this mess, assuming the coward ever returned to England.

Not that Leo cared. The man was a pompous arse who never paid his bills on time, lost heavily at the gaming tables, and clearly had been envious of Leo ever since their school days. But so far there was no indication he had ordered his capture or imprisonment. In fact, it appeared Beldon had promptly reported the incident and railed at the higher ups to do something about securing his freedom, then diligently followed up for months afterward.

Leo knew Beldon had never liked him.

That diligence in having him freed was merely because the oaf wanted to resume his game of jealousy.

Unfortunately, it truly appeared to be nothing more than a

game.

One suspect reluctantly struck off the list...well, unless something new turned up.

Leo looked toward the door when he heard a light knock. It slowly opened to reveal Marigold popping her head in. "May I come in?"

She stood at the threshold of his study, her eyes bright and cheeks pink. Gad, would his heart always beat this wildly whenever she was near? She seemed to grow more beautiful by the day. Was this to be his fate? Being led by the nose by this sprite of a girl who had quietly gained complete control of his heart?

Mallow was obediently standing by her side, his little tail wagging. "Yes, of course. Come in. How was the park?"

"We had a lovely time." They had just returned from a walk along the Serpentine, spending hours there despite the weather being cooler than usual and threatening rain.

He rose and came around to the front of his desk, kneeling as Mallow scurried toward him and leaped into his arms. "Ah, wet fur. How appealing." But he gave the pup scratches behind the ears and felt the wet fur soak into his shirt which would have to be changed anyway before he and Marigold headed out for the evening.

Marigold giggled as she removed her pelisse, a pretty coat of meadow green that she wore over a matching light wool gown. She set the pelisse over the settee as she entered his study and walked toward him. "Did you miss us?"

"Ever so much. I was bereft."

"I'm sure you were," she said with a roll of her eyes, but her expression quickly softened. "I love you, Leo."

He groaned. "Come here, sweetheart."

She came closer to kiss him, ignoring Mallow's bark of indignation at momentarily being forgotten by the two of them. "How are you and your new valet getting along?" she asked after Leo reluctantly ended their kiss.

He arched an eyebrow. "We are bosom friends. He is a complete joy to have around. I have no idea how I ever managed without him."

Marigold laughed. "I shall ignore your sarcasm. Ethan Mayhew is a very nice young man and you are fortunate to have him taking care of you. Sterling is too busy to attend to his butler duties *and* you, especially now that our explorer's club is growing and the meetings are held here every Thursday afternoon."

"Which is tomorrow."

"True, but we won't be holding any until after the opening of the new Hall of Dragons exhibit. After that, they will mostly be held at Adela's house whenever she is in residence and I will hold them here whenever Adela is not in London. She and Ambrose just returned to London but they intend to head right back to Devonshire at the end of the month. In the meantime, I am in charge of getting the word out and preparing lectures to entice like-minded, amateur archeologists to join us. We are up to fifteen members now. Isn't that exciting?"

"Yes, love." He kissed her again.

Mallow became fed up and leaped out of his arms to trot back to Sterling since the Muir butler had taken to keeping treats in his pocket just for the demanding little despot.

Marigold laughed softly as her spaniel left in a huff. "What was I saying? Oh, yes. The new dragon exhibit opens next week. Leo, you must come see how beautifully it has taken shape. Adela found more bones that we are sure belonged to this flying creature. They confirm our guesses on its size and shape. The public will be amazed."

He loved her enthusiasm for these archeological discoveries.

He also loved her enthusiasm for their bedroom activities.

Were he not so wretchedly obsessed with bringing the traitor to justice, he could very well be one of the happiest married men in all of England. But he was still in the grip of this darkness. His soul still craved vengeance at any cost, not only for his sake but for protection of the royal family. They needed to know who within their intimate circle had sabotaged his delegation and their mission four years ago.

Was it Denby?

He was the most obvious suspect since he was the envoy sent

to secure those mining and mineral rights on behalf of the Crown. How many other assignments had he sabotaged?

Leo had heard the reclusive Lord Denby would attend Lady Gaston's soiree this evening. Ian had warned him not to confront the man, but Leo was not certain yet what he would do. Killing him was not ruled out.

Marigold did not know Denby was to be at tonight's soiree.

Perhaps it was cowardly of him to withhold the news and only advise her once they were in the carriage on their way to Lady Gaston's affair. Yes, it was completely cowardly of him. In his own defense, it was only because she held more sway over him than he dared admit. If he told her, she would find a way to stop him.

Her tears tore at his heart.

Her love for him humbled him.

Her anger…the girl did not know how to be truly angry. Her heart was too soft ever to properly rail at him. She did not insult or manipulate. At worst, she boxed his ears. And when she boxed his ears, her lips pursed in that prim schoolmistress way that made him want to strip the clothes off her and kiss every inch of her body starting with those plump, rosy lips, which would then lead to his kissing his way down her body to her lush, creamy breasts and the sweet dessert between her thighs.

Gad, did his every thought have to lead back to Marigold and the bed they shared?

She was more than a lovely bed partner.

She was what his heart had been missing all these years.

He had not even mentioned Denby to her and he was already in a roil.

Was it not sensible of him to avoid all these complications?

He poured himself a glass of port and drank it down fast.

Practically guzzled it.

Denby.

Revenge.

Loving Marigold.

He refused to allow himself to love her. Was his life not complicated enough? He turned away from her while he drank.

Did she have to look at him with those soft, loving eyes?

He firmed his resolve and set his glass aside. He would warn Marigold in the carriage ride to Lady Gaston's affair and not a moment sooner.

Marigold frowned as she watched him. "Leo, are you all right?"

"In the pink of health, love. Why?"

She shook her head. "You suddenly look flushed. Let me feel your forehead."

If she wanted to know what was wrong with him, she need only feel lower. However, since he had taken great pains never to consummate their union, she had no reason to think of that part of his anatomy.

"Oh, good," she said, placing her hand to his brow, "you are not burning up."

Again, she had only to look lower to figure out what was ailing him. "Indeed not. I am fine, Marigold. Truly."

"Well, if you are certain." She nibbled her fleshy, lower lip.

"I am." He circled an arm around her waist and drew her closer. "Tell me you love me and then kiss me."

She laughed and lifted onto her tiptoes to place her arms around his neck. "All right. I love you, Leo. I love you with all my heart and with every breath in me."

"Nicely said." He lowered his mouth to hers and kissed her long and hard, and with an aching depth of feeling. It must have been minutes before he finally drew his lips off hers.

She looked up at him, her eyes soft and questioning. "That was nice. *Too* nice. What is going on, Leo?"

"Can a man not kiss his wife?"

"Yes, but not you." Her eyes suddenly widened. "There *is* something going on. I knew it! Tell me."

"There is nothing going on other than a husband feeling an urgent need for his wife." He cast her a wicked smile as he lifted her in his arms and strode out of his study to march toward the stairs.

"Leo! It is the middle of the day! What will everyone think?"

"If you keep protesting, everyone will hear you."

She gasped and clamped her pretty, puckered mouth shut.

Sterling noticed them but merely cleared his throat and then poked his head out the front door as though someone had knocked, which they hadn't.

Marigold had her arms wrapped around his neck and her eyes were wide. "Really, Leo," she said in a whisper as he started up the stairs. "You cannot be serious. What are you doing?"

"Is it not obvious? I am taking you up to our bedchamber. I would think climbing the stairs was a hint." He then looked down at Mallow who was skipping up the steps beside him. "Go to Sterling, he has more treats for you. That's a good boy."

Mallow immediately turned and headed downstairs.

Marigold shook her head. "How do you make him follow your instructions? He never listens to me."

"Because you are not the dominant dog in this family. I am." He chuckled. "Although you certainly know how to control me in the bedchamber."

Her face turned scarlet.

This girl was so sweet.

He almost let slip that he loved her, but caught himself in time.

They had taken to leaving the interior door between the marquess and marchioness chambers open so that each could freely come and go between their rooms. They always slept together, usually in her bed since it was easier for him to toss on his breeches and walk back to his room when her maid and his valet, both new hires, came knocking in the morning.

Her maid, another of the Mayhew nieces who had been in the employ of John and Sophie Farthingale but was now working for them, stopped sorting out Marigold's wardrobe and bobbed a curtsy. "Out, Jenny. Come back in an hour," Leo said, hoping he did not sound as urgent as he felt. "And have a bath brought up for my wife when you do return. Have Ethan do the same for me."

Jenny nodded. "Two baths. Yes, my lord."

He wanted to tell her to make it just one bath that he and Marigold could share, but Jenny and Marigold might faint at the remark.

Leo growled low in his throat once they were alone in

Marigold's chamber and all doors securely closed. "Let me help you out of that confining gown."

She turned her back to him to give access to her lacings. "I haven't forgotten what led us up here."

"Yes, you were going to tease me with your wanton ways," he said, his voice a deep, aching rumble. "I am breathless in anticipation."

"I never said I was going to do any such thing. You are the brute who hauled me up here because you think to distract me. I will not be distracted, Leo. What is going on? I want the truth out of you."

He slipped the gown off her, then knelt to remove her walking boots and stockings, evoking soft, breathy cries as he kissed his way down her legs as her stockings came off. She was now wearing only her corset and gossamer chemise.

The corset came off with a few tugs, leaving her only in the chemise that hid almost nothing from his view. "Your turn to undress me, love."

Was that his voice? Had that tense, raspy growl emanated from his throat?

"Gladly," she said with an impudent and rather smug smile.

Blessed saints.

What was she going to do?

Did she think to seduce the truth out of him?

She tried to look sexy as she removed his cravat and then his waistcoat which had already been unbuttoned and opened so that Mallow had only managed to dampen his shirt earlier. Fortunately, Leo had not been wearing his jacket, either. His shirt sleeves were rolled up, making it easier to remove, although Marigold was insisting on undoing all the buttons instead of just letting him slip the shirt over his head.

He bit back a laugh because she looked like a big-eyed kitten and not a sultry temptress. However, he was insanely fond of big-eyed kittens and his blood was duly heating.

A chuckle escaped his lips as he watched her fumble over the shirt buttons. "This could take weeks," he teased. "Shall I help you, love?"

"All right. But do not look so smug about it."

He removed his shirt, pleased to see her eyes grow wide and hungry. She raked her tongue across her lips while studying him. "My boots next, love. You'll have to help me take them off."

She nodded and motioned for him to sit on the bed.

He did and then held out one leg.

She straddled his leg, clamping it between her thighs as she turned her back to him, wrapped her small hands around the boot, and tried to tug it off. It took her several tries to finally manage the task, but he was not complaining. While she tugged, he was watching her derriere wiggle.

What a sweet, tight thing of beauty it was.

She moved to straddle his other leg.

Same splendid thighs clamping his leg in place.

Same delightful wiggle of her pert derriere.

She turned to him after accomplishing the task, her smile triumphant although her cheeks were pink from exertion and she was breathless.

He sucked in his own breath when she reached for the buttons of his falls. "Ah, love. You had better not touch me there."

"Why not?"

Since he had not put his shaft to good use in quite a while, he did not trust himself to contain the volcanic build of desire.

This was quite embarrassing.

He was hot and hard for her.

Could he hold off?

"Leo, it is time to make me your wife in every way."

Instead of responding, he ran his hands under her chemise and lifted the garment off her shapely body. He then carried her to bed and settled her flat on her back. He stretched over her, crushing her slightly with his weight.

She did not complain, seeming to love the feel of his body on hers.

He eased downward and began to tease her breasts with his lips and tongue.

"No, you fiend!"

He stopped immediately. "Fiend?"

She nodded. "It is my turn to wickedly torment you. You need to be on your back and I shall be atop you."

He let out a breath and shifted their positions. "Ah, all right. What are you going to do?"

"Kiss you and put my tongue on you as you do to me."

Blessed saints.

He was doomed. "Are you sure?"

"Yes, Leo." She nudged him onto his back and knelt between his legs.

Her sweet mouth on...him? He was going to expire from the pleasure of it.

He cast her a wicked smile. "Have at it, Marigold. Do your worst."

In truth, he did not believe she would go through with it because she was a proper lady and he did not think most proper ladies ever would do such a thing. This activity was considered highly improper.

But Marigold was Marigold, and she had her own sense of rules.

Besides, he still had his breeches on and had not unbuttoned the falls. He could not imagine her following through on the proposition...not...*blessed saints.*

It was the best afternoon Leo had ever spent in his life or expected ever to spend. In all his years of experience...well, not all had gone exactly as planned.

In truth, he had not held out even close to five minutes.

But who could with Marigold?

Her lips.

Her tongue.

He had released fast, like a schoolboy experiencing his first carnal encounter.

Worse, he had squirted in her face because she was so damned innocent and had no idea what to look out for or that there was anything to look out for or move aside to avoid. "Leo!" she had cried out as the result of months of abstinence came spurting out of him like the legendary eruption of Mt. Vesuvius.

Afterward, he had lain there like a lump, caught up in a climax coma and trying to recover his breath while she sputtered and *eewed*, and then scrambled off the bed to wet a washcloth and vigorously scrub her face.

He finally rose to her side to assist her, then took the wet cloth to clean himself off.

Marigold was now staring at him wide-eyed. "You must think I am an idiot."

He took her into his embrace. "You are the most beautiful thing in my life. This was the best moment ever. You'll know what to look out for next time and anticipate me better."

He kissed her on the forehead, his arms folded around her as he told her how precious she was to him. "You are splendid and wonderful. If you are to accuse anyone of being an idiot, it should be me. But we are neither of us fools. Come back to bed with me, Marigold. I want to hold you in my arms. I want to kiss you and tell you how beautiful you are."

There was nothing more soothing to him than the feel of her silken skin against his rough hide.

"Then you are not laughing at me?"

"Well, just a little. But it is only that I am so delighted with you. You are fresh and innocent. Do not be angry with me, love. You've won. I am thoroughly seduced. You have me in your thrall."

"Do I? Then will you tell me what I want to know?"

He carried her back to bed and slipped in beside her. "Yes."

He tucked his arm around her so that she rested her head against his chest and her body was curled up against his. "Ask your questions."

She sighed. "I forgot what I wanted to ask you."

He could have avoided the unpleasantness and distracted her with other topics while keeping to his original cowardly plan of waiting until their carriage ride to tell her about Denby. But there was no reason to hold off, certainly not after their glorious, and admittedly bordering on the disastrous, afternoon romp in the sack.

Yes, some might call it a disaster.

He had been a hot coil of desire ready to burst at the first flick of her tongue. Well, it had taken a little more than that because she had no idea what she was doing.

And yet, she was wonderful.

He would call it the most unforgettable afternoon of sex he had ever experienced…all five minutes of it.

"Marigold, you wanted to know what was troubling me."

Her cheek grazed his chest as she looked up at him. "Oh, yes. Leo, what is wrong? You did look troubled."

"Denby will be at Lady Gaston's soiree."

"He will?" She sat up and stared at him. "What are you going to do?"

Right now, he wanted to kiss her naked body and forget about what tonight might bring. But she was not going to let him touch her now that her mind was racing over what he might do to Denby. "I don't know, my pet. That's the truth. I simply do not know."

"Dillie mentioned she and Ian will also be there. I think you must discuss this with Ian as soon as we arrive at Lady Gaston's. It is quite possible he has discovered something relevant. After all, he and the best Crown agents have been on this investigation for weeks now. So has Mr. Barrow. Has he turned up anything yet?"

"No, love. He would have contacted me if he had found anything worthwhile."

She looked around as though considering getting out of bed, then sighed and nestled against him once more. "I am going to stick to you like a barnacle to a ship. If you haul back your fist to strike a blow, you will have to strike me down first because I will be right beside you."

His stomach began to churn at the thought of her meddling, for he wanted her to remain completely out of this. "Do not interfere, Marigold. You will only put us both in danger with that foolish action."

She hugged him tightly. "Foolish would be your killing him, Leo. Do not throw away your life and our marriage. Let the authorities handle him. You don't even know if he is the guilty party."

"He is guilty. He has to be the one."

"But you still do not know for certain. You cannot convict him before all the evidence is in."

"What evidence? He's had four years to burn it."

Marigold spent the rest of the hour trembling in his arms.

He was in agony.

She wanted him to be reasonable.

He could not.

They washed and dressed in their separate bedchambers, Ethan assisting him and Jenny assisting Marigold. Their doors were closed to each other and he feared Marigold's heart would close to him now because he knew how badly he was hurting her.

And yet, he was not going to stop.

If Denby made the slightest slip, Leo meant to kill him.

They rode in silence to Lady Gaston's home, seated beside each other in his carriage. But they were miles apart. This left him in agony. "You look beautiful, Marigold."

She did look achingly lovely in a gown of blue silk that matched the vivid splendor of her eyes. "You look handsome as sin," she replied, immediately turning away before he noticed tears forming in her eyes.

"Don't you dare cry, love."

She sniffled. "Don't tell me what to do, Leo."

He sighed.

When they arrived, Leo hopped down from the carriage to assist her out of it. He shooed away the Gaston footman, suddenly feeling ridiculously possessive of this wife he was about to lose if the evening went as badly as Marigold feared it would.

As for Marigold, she would not leave his side and remained constantly underfoot. He could not walk away without almost tripping over her.

To Leo's surprise, Denby did not show up.

He was missing at the supper table, a fact that upset Lady Gaston since her table was now out of balance and everyone remarked upon the empty seat.

He did not send a note expressing his regrets, nor did he show up for the musicale or the card games afterward or the desserts served at midnight, after which there was dancing. "Leo, where are you going?" Marigold asked as the evening drew near its end.

"Something is wrong."

"Here? At Lady Gaston's?"

"Denby did not show up. The reason has to be directly related to that mission four years ago. I am going to scout the property."

She cast him a stubborn look. "I'll go with you."

"Enough, my pet. I need to do this on my own. I won't be more than a few minutes." He left Marigold in the watchful care of her friends, Syd, Gory, and the Thorne brothers, Octavian and Julius.

He searched Lady Gaston's house and garden because this unexpected turn of events had him on edge.

Where was Denby? And did this mean someone was coming after him next? He doubted they would do it here, but it was possible he was being watched.

Or was he overly thinking this? Denby may have heard he was to attend and merely feared facing him.

With good reason, Leo supposed. Four years of rage and despair had turned him savage. It had not escaped his notice that Ian had stayed close, watching him much of the evening. Well, he also had to be worried about what he would do at the first sight of Denby.

Why wasn't the man here?

Or was the miserable vermin hiding in the bushes and waiting for the opportunity to get a clear shot at him?

He returned to Marigold's side a few minutes later. "No sign of him," he muttered in response to her questioning gaze.

She released a soft breath. "Good."

He frowned at her, annoyed because she was right.

"Lord Muir," a footman said, approaching Leo as he was about to lead Marigold onto the dance floor for a waltz. It wasn't so much that he wished to dance but wanted a reason to hold her in his arms.

Leo reluctantly released Marigold and turned to the footman who was holding out a note for him. "The gentleman said it was urgent he speak to you. He looks rather common, my lord."

"Did he have a red, bulbous nose and sharp eyes?" Marigold asked. "A portly man?"

"Yes, my lady. He gave his name as Mr. Barrow and said you would know who he was. I could not permit him to enter the house. Lady Gaston would never allow the likes of him in through the front door. He asked for this message to be delivered to you, Lord Muir, and said he would wait outside by the carriages."

Leo wanted to read the note in private, but Marigold had her snoopy, little nose in a twitch and was eagerly leaning over his arm to read it as he unfurled the vellum. It did not take long for them to read the short message.

Denby is dead. H. Barrow.

"Dear heaven!" Marigold looked up at him in alarm.

He said nothing, merely folded the note and tucked it in the breast pocket of his formal jacket before turning to the footman. "Ask the Duke of Edgeware to meet me by the horse carriages. At once. It is urgent."

Marigold had a stubborn set to her slender jaw. "I'm coming with you."

He did not bother to argue, for he would never win. Nor did he mind keeping her close. If this was a trick to draw him away from her side, then she was safest beside him. "All right, but you are to stick to me like a barnacle. This could be a trap. If I push you down, you are to stay down. If I tell you to run, you are to run into the house. If I tell you to get behind me, you are to get behind me." He raked a hand through his hair. "And most important of all, if this is a trap…you are not to come to my rescue or attempt in any way to save my life."

"You would never allow me to set foot out of this ballroom if you truly thought it was a trap."

"Marigold, do not give me a hard time about this. Did you not stand before the altar and promise to honor and obey me? Even Mallow is more obedient than you."

She placed her arm in his. "I will listen to you, Leo. I promise."

"I don't need you to just listen. I need you to *obey*."

"Now you are being ridiculous. Don't you trust me?"

"About this? Not in the least."

"Leo!"

The little sprite loved him and meant to protect him. This was completely unacceptable to him. "Do I have your promise to obey me, Marigold?"

She sighed. "Yes, Leo. I will obey."

"Give me your *sacred* promise."

Her expression turned pained.

"Marigold, I need to keep you safe. Do you have any idea what I will become if I lose you? Do not be difficult about this."

She nodded. "You have my sacred promise that I will obey you."

"That you will obey me in all things and for always?" he said with a wry grin, knowing there was little humor in the situation, but he needed to do something to break the tension.

She gave a soft laugh. "Don't push it, Leo."

CHAPTER 11

THE FIRST THING to strike Marigold as Leo led her outside was how damp the air was now. Indeed, it surrounded them like a cold blanket, thick with the threat of rain, as they made their way down the street to where the carriages were being held. Homer Barrow was easily spotted standing under a street lamp while resting his shoulder against the lamp post. "My lord," he said, straightening immediately as he spotted them. "Thank goodness. I was concerned my note would not reach you."

"It was promptly delivered to me, but I wasted time attempting to convince my wife not to join us," he said with the wry arch of an eyebrow. "As you can see, I ought to have saved my breath."

Mr. Barrow smiled kindly at her. "Well, m'lord. She cares for you and wishes you safe."

Marigold responded with a genuine smile in response. "Thank you, Mr. Barrow. I'm glad you understand, even if my stubborn husband does not."

Leo frowned as he raked a hand through his mane of hair. "I've asked the Duke of Edgeware to meet us here, as well. He should be told of this development. Who else has been alerted?"

Homer cleared his throat. "Lord Denby has a very small staff, just a housekeeper and cook in residence, and they have little love for their master. He also had a butler, but we were able to buy him off and replace him for the month with one of my men. Gibson, my man, is the one who discovered the body. I am the only one he has alerted. The cook and housekeeper are asleep in their beds."

"But the activity will now rouse them, surely," Marigold said.

"No, m'lady. They are tipplers and fall nightly into a drunken sleep. Nothing will awaken them until morning. Your husband and His Grace, the Duke of Edgeware, are not likely to be disturbed by them while they investigate. In any event, Gibson is still on duty and will confine them to their quarters should they wake, at least until we have had the chance to properly search the entire scene of the crime, after which we shall interrogate them."

"Yes, best to keep them in their quarters and separated until we have a better understanding of what happened. If they are in any way involved, I do not want them collaborating on a story," Leo said.

"Aye, m'lord. Gibson and I conducted a cursory search, just to make certain the killer was not still lurking in the house. He wasn't. Nor did he leave behind any obvious clues, unfortunately. But we will go over everything with a more thorough eye once you and His Grace return with me. We have left everything as we found it."

"I see you have things well in hand, Mr. Barrow."

"I try my best, m'lord."

Marigold listened attentively and nodded as the Bow Street runner continued his report to Leo. "My man Gibson estimates the murder happened no more than an hour ago, probably less. The body was quite fresh when he stumbled upon it."

"Cause of death?" Leo asked.

"He was stabbed through the heart. The perpetrator likely came in through an open window in the study."

"No more than an hour ago?" Marigold stared at Leo, her thoughts now fixed on the time of death. Leo had been out of her sight no more than five minutes the entire evening…ten minutes at most.

What had he really been doing in that time?

No, no, no.

Her heart beat faster as she quietly panicked. Leo could not have done this. Still, she had to be sure. "How far is Lord Denby's residence from here, Mr. Barrow?"

"Oh, about ten minutes by carriage, m'lady. Assuming no delays, but there are always delays on these busy streets."

"And if one walked? Or rather, if one ran? Cut across gardens and alleyways? Or rode by horse?"

Leo inhaled sharply as he realized what she was asking and why she needed to know. He glowered at her. "You think I did this? That I secretly kept a horse at the ready to gallop there and back? Do I smell as though I have been on a horse?"

Marigold had to admit he did not. "No, Leo."

In truth, his scent was of musk and maleness, and simply divine.

"Then you believe I ran there, killed him, and sauntered back without breaking into a sweat?"

"Leo, I am not being unreasonable."

His frown said otherwise. "You were with me all night except for those ten minutes."

"M'lady," Mr. Barrow said kindly, "It would take about the same time no matter what method anyone used to get from here to Lord Denby's home and back. At fastest, ten minutes there and ten minutes return. Plus an added few minutes for committing the crime."

Marigold's mind raced.

If true, this would prove Leo's innocence beyond a doubt because he was with her the entire night, other than those five or ten minutes he was scouting the grounds. She put a hand to her heart as it fluttered in relief.

Of more importance was the fact he was in sight of every other guest attending Lady Gaston's party. She was sure they all took notice of him, for he was not someone easily overlooked. He was tall. Handsome. Commanding. Indeed, most women had not taken their eyes off him all evening. "Thank goodness," she said in a whisper.

Leo cast her a sardonic smile. "And here I was looking forward to killing him. What a disappointment."

"Leo! Do not even joke about such a thing." She did not bother to hide her irritation.

She noted the blaze in his eyes, and knew despite his attempt at a jest, that it really was no jest for him. He was angry someone had gotten to Denby first.

"What have I missed?" Ian asked, now joining them.

Leo and Mr. Barrow quickly recounted what had happened.

Ian also tossed Leo a glance. "Thank goodness you were here."

"There is nothing good about it," Leo grumbled.

Marigold shook her head in disgust. "I cannot believe you are annoyed someone interfered with your quest for vengeance. You ought to be relieved there are one hundred guests who can attest to your presence at this soiree. Otherwise, you would be at the top of everyone's list of suspects."

He arched an eyebrow. "Including yours, obviously."

She blushed. "Yes, I will not deny it."

He turned to Mr. Barrow. "Who else besides me wanted Denby dead?"

"It is an easier task to figure out who did not wish him dead," he muttered. "Not even his mother liked him."

Marigold noticed Ian flinch at that remark.

Perhaps Denby was not the only one with an unhappy family situation.

That particular torment was not one of Leo's issues. He had spoken kindly of his parents the one time they had come up in conversation, which was a good thing because Leo already had more torments than any man should bear.

Well, she had no time to muse about this now. They needed to figure out whether Denby's death was related to Leo's capture and imprisonment or completely unrelated to that horrible incident.

"I can question the cook and housekeeper," Marigold said. "Perhaps they noticed something odd or overheard something useful. The housekeeper in particular ought to be aware of visitors to the house over these past few months. These ladies might open up to me since I will appear less threatening to them than you men."

Leo shook his head and laughed. "Absolutely not. You are to go back inside right now and stay close to your friends. I'll have Octavian and Julius escort you, Syd, and Gory back to our home.

Let them all stay with you until I return."

She hated to be pushed away, especially since Leo was seething and obviously frustrated by Denby's unexpected demise.

He needed her more than ever now, didn't he?

But there was a dangerous glint in his eyes which meant he was through listening to her and not about to indulge her in any way. She was not going to win any arguments with him tonight. Still, she had to make him see reason. "When do you expect to return home?"

Leo shrugged. "I have no idea. Depends on what we find out."

"So I am to be left behind."

"Yes, Marigold. Stop riling me. Can you not see I am at the end of my patience?"

"So am I." Why did men always believe women were helpless and had to be protected from all unpleasantness? "You need me, Leo. I can help."

"Indeed, you can…by keeping out of the way." He took her by the hand and led her back inside, his hold gentle but firm. She thought to resist, but knew she would only embarrass herself since Leo was not going to relent.

She scurried along beside him, having to take two steps for his one in order to keep up as he practically dragged her across the ballroom. "Slow down, Leo. I am going to trip over the hem of my gown."

He ignored her.

She gave up protesting, for there was no reasoning with an unreasonable man.

Leo led her to her friends, and unceremoniously planted her in the wallflower corner with Syd and Gory. He then took a moment to confer with Octavian and Julius. It was truly insulting of him to keep his frowning gaze on her all the while he spoke to them, as though he did not trust her to stay put.

Well, she did consider sneaking back outside and following him to Lord Denby's residence.

Octavian and Julius turned to stare at her.

What had Leo just told them?

Drat, there would be no escaping their watch now.

"He's an ogre," Marigold said of her husband who happened to look spectacular in his black tie and tails. He melted her insides even though he was behaving like a beast to her at the moment. "Can either of you read lips?"

"No," Gory muttered.

Syd sighed. "Sorry. Not a talent of mine. What is going on?"

"A man Leo considered a lethal enemy has just been killed in his own home."

Both their eyes lit up.

Syd grasped her wrist. "Was he shot? Bludgeoned? Poisoned? Stabbed? Run down by a runaway carriage as he walked out of his home? Was there a lot of blood?"

Gory pursed her lips. "I hope his body was not too badly damaged. I wonder what they plan to do with his remains. Do you think I might–"

"Gory! They are not going hand the body over to you." Marigold wondered whether she ought to be more selective in her choice of friends. One would think she had just offered them a year's supply of ice cream at Gunter's instead of reporting a gruesome murder. "And he was stabbed through the heart, not shot, bludgeoned, poisoned, or run over."

"How long do they think he has been dead?" Syd asked. "Bodies deteriorate in very specific ways. I could be helpful in determining the time of death. Perhaps even the cause of death, although I suppose being stabbed through the heart is a dead giveaway...pardon the pun."

"I wonder if worms have formed on his body yet," Gory mused. "We really could be very helpful. I'm sure our knowledge of anatomy and body decomposition is far better than theirs. They ought to take us along. It isn't as though we are going to attract any bachelors or dance with anyone other than Octavian and Julius."

Syd nodded. "We have already danced with those two. I'm sure they only took it upon themselves to ask us as a favor to their brother and Adela. They would have looked after you, too, had you not already been married to Leo. Besides, I'll wager they would rather be investigating alongside Leo."

Gory nodded. "Maybe we can convince them to–"

Marigold groaned. "Do not get your hopes up. Leo will not allow us anywhere near the spot of the crime. In fact, he will *never* forgive me if we do not go straight to Chipping Way and dutifully await his return."

"Men," Syd said with an irritated grunt. "Lord Denby's home is along the way to your home. We have to pass his street…well, fairly close by. And does not his manner of death raise questions? If someone is stabbed through the heart, he would be facing his assailant. Did anyone hear him cry out? What if he did not expect to draw his last breath because he knew his assailant and trusted him? Or her. It could have been a woman, although I cannot imagine a woman overpowering a man so easily."

"Well, she could have lured him in close with the offer of sex," Gory mused. "Men always have their guard down when thinking with their privates instead of with their brain. Were there defensive wounds? Signs of a struggle? Did he fight back and scratch his assailant? Or perhaps manage to wound him? And how did the perpetrator get inside unobserved? Wouldn't Lord Denby's butler have had to let this guest in?"

"Not necessarily," Marigold said. "It seems he might have crept in through an unlocked door or upper floor window. Even if the house had been locked up, I cannot imagine it being too difficult to break a window or find some other means into the house."

Octavian and Julius returned to their side, noted the looks on their faces, and frowned at the three of them.

"Out of the question," Octavian said. "The answer is no. Do not even bother to ask us to take you anywhere but straight to Marigold's home. We shall sit up with her until Leo returns."

"If the assailant was injured," Gory said, ignoring Octavian's remark, "there could be a trail of blood along the street." She glanced toward Leo as he made his way through the crush of guests toward the front door. "Leo, Edgeware, and Mr. Barrow will be busy investigating *inside* the house. It is threatening rain. Any blood droplets will be washed away if we do not get there in time to look around. How can we allow such a vital clue to be lost?"

Marigold and Syd heartily agreed.

Julius groaned. "Dare I say it? They do have a point."

Octavian scowled. "Julius, we promised. Do not dare weaken. And what makes you think they will overlook this possible evidence? Edgeware and Barrow are experienced investigators, probably among the finest in England. If Gory thought of a potential blood trail, I'm sure they will, too."

"And what if they do not?" Marigold felt completely downcast.

Why had Leo shunted her aside?

During their weeks of marriage, she had opened up to him about her hopes and dreams. They'd had several conversations about all she had accomplished and what she hoped to achieve in the future. He had seemed to be supportive, but was it all a lie?

Did he regard her as a mere trinket to adorn his bed?

Perhaps she had been so clouded by love that she did not notice how easily he had been manipulating her. *Oh, yes. There's a good girl, Marigold. Come to bed and let me hold you in my arms.*

It worked every time because she was a besotted fool. All he ever needed to do was give her a gentle pat on the head and a little rub behind her ears.

He treated her much as he treated Mallow.

He even called her *my pet.*

And how many times had he warned her their marriage would be annulled if he thought it was necessary to protect her? Who made him the final arbiter? Did she not have a say in a decision of this importance?

She thought their marriage had been perfect bliss, but he merely thought of her as a commodity to be disposed of when the time was right.

He had never once said he loved her.

He had never once assured her their marriage would last forever.

She shook out of these thoughts because they would make her cry and she dared not show any weakness. "Investigators do not cry," Leo would insist and point to her behavior as confirmation he was right to keep her out of his business and perhaps even out of his life.

It was not long after Leo's departure that the five of them bid their hostess a good evening and made their way back to Chipping Way in the Thorne carriage. It was a magnificent coach, as big and impressive as Leo's. In truth, it was more impressive since the exquisite leather seating was in pristine condition, not at all scratched or scuffed.

Marigold was feeling particularly desolate as they passed by Lord Denby's street.

Suddenly, Syd opened the window and hurled her reticule out of it. "Oh, dear. I've dropped my reticule."

Octavian emitted a string of curses, not caring that the three of them were innocent females and therefore ought to have had delicate sensibilities. He barked orders for their driver to stop the carriage immediately. "You ladies stay here," he commanded, his eyes the silvery glint of steel. "I will retrieve it. Julius, do not let them climb out for any reason. I do not care if they set fire to this damn conveyance. Let them burn alive inside."

Syd feigned indignation.

Octavian growled low in his throat. "Move a muscle and I will haul you over my lap and spank your backside raw, Syd. Do not dare think I won't."

She was not intimidated so much as frustrated that he was thwarting her plans. "Julius, are you going to let your brother speak to me this way?"

Julius grinned. "Um, yes."

Syd was momentarily taken aback. "So you will let your brute of a brother hit me?"

"First of all, you know Octavian has no intention of hitting you. Nor will he ever strike a woman, any woman, no matter how vexing she might be. Syd, you must admit you are the most vexing woman my brother has ever encountered. You are also the least helpful female I know. Do not even pretend to be afraid for your physical safety. If anyone should be cowering, it is me and Octavian. Are you certain you and Gory are not demonic spawn arisen from the underworld? I have never met two ladies more fascinated by blood and gore."

"What about me?" Marigold asked, a little indignant that she was not considered just as bloodthirsty. Wasn't she the one who had found that dragon-like skull? And traveled from Devonshire to London with a crateful of skulls and bones? Did everyone dismiss her as a little pet?

Julius's grin broadened. "You are a marchioness now and should not be consorting with the likes of these two ghouls."

Syd harrumphed.

Gory looked surprisingly hurt. "Is this what you think of me?"

Marigold patted her hand. "If the two of you were men, you would be hailed as great thinkers of our day. Your advancements in medicine and forensic knowledge would be hailed as brilliant. As a marchioness, I will do all in my power to see that you are recognized for your intelligence and ingenuity."

"Thank you, Marigold," Gory muttered, tossing a glower at Julius.

Syd smiled at her, too. "Yes, thank you. You are a worthy addition to our circle of friends."

"Oh, look! There's Leo," Gory said.

Marigold gasped. "Where? Oh, I see him."

She jumped out of the carriage and ran toward him.

By the sound of footsteps pounding behind her, she realized they had all leaped out after her. Julius meant to stop her. Syd and Gory meant to steal the chance to hunt for bloodstains.

Leo took one look at her and his expression turned savagely angry. "What are you doing here?"

Marigold immediately came to a stop. "We wanted to search for Syd's reticule."

"Her reticule? What in bloody blazes are you talking about?" The remark only served to make Leo angrier. "How in heaven's name did Syd's reticule happen to end up on this street?"

"Well…" Marigold swallowed hard. "Um…we were riding by, since this is directly on the route to our house, as you know…and…" She could not tell him Syd had tossed it out.

"And what, Marigold?"

"It somehow fell out of the carriage." Oh, how lame this excuse sounded even to her own ears.

"Amazing. And you think I am stupid enough to believe that fib?" He plunged his hand into a nearby hedgerow and plucked out Syd's reticule. "Go home, Marigold. Now."

"It is not a fib. I would never lie to you. One moment it was on her lap, and then it was flying through the air and landed on this street. As to precisely how such a thing happened, I cannot say."

"Cannot? Or will not tell me the truth?" His eyes were fiery embers as he handed the reticule to Syd. "We have already searched outdoors for possible bloodstains. It is one of the first things we did for fear we might lose the killer's tracks in the impending rain. This assumes he left any tracks for us to follow."

"Did he?" Marigold asked.

"No. There were none to be found. Denby might have struggled with his assailant, but he did not wound the man severely enough to make him bleed. Satisfied? This is what you were really hoping to find out, wasn't it?"

Marigold nodded. "Are you sure the villain did not leave any other evidence behind? A footprint in the soil? An item accidentally dropped? A piece of fabric caught on a bramble? Well, we are here now and can help you search more thoroughly. Where's the harm? We can work efficiently. Assign us tasks."

"I will do no such thing. All you have done is disturb the area of the crime and possibly trampled clues. You are not helping, but hindering. The magistrate has been notified. We are going to seal off the vicinity as soon as he arrives. He and his men will conduct a thorough search immediately thereafter. We will conduct another search come morning when the light is better and we might find something previously overlooked."

Marigold gritted her teeth, now irate herself. "But the rain, Leo. How will you get any of this done within the next few minutes?"

"Likely, we won't. It doesn't change a thing. You are not staying."

Leo was being quite impossible.

She glanced up and felt several droplets fall on her cheeks. It was drizzling lightly now. "Really, Leo. If we don't–"

"Marigold, enough. I will not have you meddling." Leo truly looked as though he was at the end of his tether. Anger, disgust, impatience, all registered on his face. "Never mind the damn rain. You have likely wiped away all evidence with your big feet stomping across the area."

"I do not have big feet."

He emitted a grunt of disgust. "Fine, your tiny feet then. Who knows what you have crushed beneath those dainty slippers of yours? And what of your friends? All five of you have been walking upon the crime scene. How am I to tell which boot marks belong to the assailant and which belong to Octavian or Julius? I know they were trying to be careful. But can the same be said of you, Syd, or Gory? Were you even looking where you stepped when you ran to me?"

No, she had not been looking.

She had seen her husband and thought only of rushing into his arms...arms he had not extended to her.

"Let's hope you have not obliterated anything vital."

Gory cleared her throat. "Despite what you think, we were careful where we stepped. Since I am here, would you let me look at the body?"

Leo did not hesitate for a moment before answering with a growled, "No."

"Because I could check under his fingernails. He might have scratched his assailant. And I can help determine the height of the assailant. Is the knife still in Lord Denby? One can tell by the angle it was plunged into him whether–"

"Not necessary. We have already made that determination." Leo's voice was still a harsh growl.

"And there is also the matter of the blood spatter. Surely, the killer must have gotten some blood on his clothing. How does one stab another through the heart and not get a drop on him? Is the scene very bloody?"

Leo just glared at Gory.

"Because if it wasn't, then I would question the lack of blood. He might have been stabbed to divert attention from the true means of murder. If there is no blood, then he was likely dead before the knife was plunged into him. Blood does not flow if one is already dead."

Leo now spared a glance at all of them. "Go home."

Marigold's heart felt bruised. "Is this all you have to say in response to Gory's comments? They are quite thoughtful and intelligent. You know she is an expert when it comes to matters of blood."

"So am I," he said, trying to hide the undercurrent of anguish in his tone. "I bled for four damn years."

Dear heaven.

How could she have been so stupid as to forget this and all the pain he had endured while imprisoned? He had not confided the precise details, but she had seen the scars on his back and been told enough to know his pain must have been horrific. Had he watched others being treated just as brutally? Heard their screams?

She put a hand to her stomach as the realization of his ordeal hit her hard and nauseated her.

She had cried over Leo's scars the first time he had taken off his shirt and turned his back to her. And yet, she had not even considered how agonizing all of this was for him. How could she treat him so cruelly? They had wanted to help but were only rubbing salt into the raw wound of his years of hurt.

"Sorry, Leo," Octavian said. "They outsmarted me. I should have anticipated their tricks and taken them back to Chipping Way using a longer route. Truly, I am sorry."

Leo nodded. "Just get them back to my house, will you?"

"At once." He and Julius herded them back inside the carriage.

As the carriage jerked to a start, Octavian began to lecture them. "Seriously, do you have any idea how difficult this has to be for Leo? And you barge in on him as though you are on a picnic. Gory, don't you dare look despondent over being denied the sight of a dead body."

Syd tipped her chin up to protest, but Marigold stopped her. "Octavian is right."

Syd regarded her quizzically. "He is?"

Marigold nodded.

Octavian leaned forward, his big, looming presence naturally intimidating even though he spoke gently to her and her friends.

His gaze rested particularly on Syd. "You and Gory are on the marriage mart. Lady Dayne and Lady Withnall are generously sponsoring your come-outs. Is this any way to repay their efforts? How about you concentrate on gaining the attention of a *living* body? Someone capable of breathing and speaking. And you, Marigold…"

Her eyes widened in surprise. "What about me?"

"You are newly married. Do you think Leo wishes to lose his wife within a week of the wedding?"

"It has been two weeks since we were wed. Is it not painfully obvious Leo is more interested in Lord Denby's cadaver than he is in me?"

"Ah, you believe he is already tired of you, so that makes it all right for you to run around London in the middle of the night?"

"I am hardly gallivanting since you are all with me. And we are riding through Mayfair, not some impoverished part of London filled with cutpurses and other manner of low criminals."

Julius sighed. "Marigold, can you not see that Leo loves you and wants to keep you safe from harm? What if the killer had been lurking close by and decided to shoot you on a lark? You gave him the perfect opportunity."

Octavian nodded. "You were fortunate the killer did not stay around."

Tears formed in Marigold's eyes.

Leo was her lion and he fiercely wanted to protect her.

But as to loving her?

If only he did.

She would give anything to hear those words from him. *I love you, Marigold.* Would he ever say them?

Nevertheless, she was determined to apologize to him for her actions tonight, and then she would tell him that she loved him. He needed to hear the words from her every day and know the depth of her affection even if it was not reciprocated. How dense she was, and so unappreciative of all his suffering.

The rain started in earnest as they turned onto Chipping Way.

Sterling opened the door the moment the Thorne carriage drew up in front of their home.

Marigold was surprised their gentle butler had not already retired to his bed. Well, she would have had to rouse him out of a sound sleep to open the door anyway. "Shall I wait up for Lord Muir, my lady?"

"No, Sterling. I'll do it. One of us ought to have our wits about us by the time his lordship returns. He may not be back at all today. He and the Duke of Edgeware are investigating a murder."

When Julius and Octavian frowned at her, she realized this ought to have remained confidential. "Oh, dear. Sterling, I spoke out of turn. Please do not say a word to anyone about this yet. The news will likely spread later today. But for now, no one is to hear about it. Not even our own staff. Please, promise me you will keep this to yourself."

"My lips are sealed, my lady."

"Thank you." Marigold then offered her friends refreshments. "Are you hungry? Thirsty?"

Sterling offered to prepare a tray for them before he retired to his quarters.

"Not necessary," Octavian said. "You had better get some rest, Sterling. There could be a lot happening tomorrow."

Gory nodded. "I think the laces of my gown are going to burst if I eat another bite."

Marigold noted her other friends were also patting their stomachs to signal they were full. "Never mind, Sterling. Good night."

He bowed to her. "And to you, m'lady."

Syd made herself comfortable on the settee now that they were the five of them alone. "Who do you think did in Lord Denby?"

"I don't know," Marigold said. "I'm just relieved it wasn't Leo. And before you toss me looks, let me tell you that there is not a chance Leo had a hand in this since he was with me all night."

"Are you sure?" Octavian asked gently, taking a seat at the opposite end of the settee. "Why don't you tell us what is going on?"

Marigold was too wound up to sit just yet, so she paced in front of the fireplace as she recounted everything she knew about Leo's captivity and the three men he suspected of setting him up.

"I know what you are thinking because I thought it myself. He was out of my sight for about ten minutes while he went outdoors to scout Lady Gaston's grounds. Mr. Barrow assured me it would have taken at least twenty minutes for anyone to get to Lord Denby's home and back."

"So, Leo is ruled out as a suspect?" Gory mused while comfortably settled in one of the large wing chairs beside the fireplace.

Marigold nodded.

Julius cleared his throat. "Is it possible he paid someone to do it? Marigold, don't bludgeon me for asking. After what you've told us, this has to be addressed. I'm not saying he did, just that it is most convenient of him to be in sight of a hundred guests while someone was doing Denby in. No one could ask for a better alibi."

She stopped pacing and turned to Julius. "Leo would never pay anyone to commit the foul deed. It is completely impossible because he is so obsessed with his need for revenge. In fact, he is not merely obsessed but *possessed* by it, body and soul. He would never pass off the chore to someone else."

Julius held out his hands in surrender. "I am convinced, Marigold. Sorry if I upset you by raising the possibility."

"No, you were right to question," Marigold said. "We have to be thorough in our examination of every possibility if we are to help Leo. By Mr. Barrow's description, it sounded as though Denby died quickly. That is another reason to rule Leo out from committing the crime. He would not have wished the man a quick death. Meeting face to face, wrapping his hands around Denby's throat and slowly watching him choke to death is what Leo would do."

Syd appeared startled. "But Leo is not a savage. How could you love him if he were?"

"In this, he is." Marigold's voice was ragged. "What does it say about me that I can still love him?"

"He hasn't actually committed a serious crime yet," Gory pointed out. "As for his confrontation with Beldon, it was Beldon who tried to stab Leo in the back."

Marigold nodded. "Well, Leo might have provoked him."

"Leo was morally in the right to rough up the man. Any husband has the right to warn another man to keep away from his wife," Octavian said. "Any of us would have responded the same way. Beldon is the cowardly cur who went after Leo while his back was turned. Perhaps he only meant to draw the weapon and wave it in front of his nose or nick his arm, but he had to know the consequences of drawing his weapon for whatever reason. He is fortunate I did not kill him myself. As for Leo, he did nothing out of line."

That her friends did not consider Leo depraved was a relief to Marigold. She wanted them to see his good qualities and understand the torment that drove an honorable man to seek vengeance. Of course, she was going to stop Leo from doing the wrong thing. Since Beldon had fled to the Continent and Denby was now dead, the likelihood of Leo doing something heinous had dramatically decreased.

However, she could not let down her guard since Leo's cousin had yet to be dealt with. The man was a dishonorable, scheming weasel, according to Leo.

Was it true?

Or merely Leo rushing to judgment and falsely accusing Lord Cummings?

"Leo means to exact justice...his form of justice," Marigold told her friends. "And as a caution to all of you, do not believe him if he appears calm when he returns. There is no telling what might set him off because he is taut as a bowstring. Whether he shows it or not, he is furious someone beat him to Denby."

"As I would be," Octavian muttered.

Julius grunted in agreement. "So would I, I suppose."

To everyone's surprise, Leo arrived home not an hour later.

Marigold tried not to assail him with questions, but she was desperate to learn what had happened. "Let me wash up and then I'll come down and properly greet you all."

She quickly excused herself and hurried upstairs with him.

"I don't need you fussing over me, Marigold." He sounded surprisingly surly. Well, he was having a hard night, made harder because of her thoughtless actions.

"I know, Leo. But I didn't want you to be alone." She poured fresh water from the ewer into the basin on his bureau while he shrugged out of his soiled jacket.

"I am not alone. Mallow is here with me."

Indeed, Mallow was in the room, nestled at the foot of Leo's bed. Usually, he would have rushed to Leo, jumping up and down to gain his attention. But even Mallow sensed something was seriously amiss and did not let out so much as a tiny bark.

Marigold was relieved because she did not want her pup distracting Leo. "Did you find out anything more?"

"Clues to the killer?" He shook his head as he plunged his hands into the clean water. It immediately turned red from the blood he washed off. "No."

He grabbed the soap and began to lather it on his hands.

Marigold's heart sank.

Was it possible she and her friends had obliterated vital evidence in their heedless rush to be included in the investigation? "I'm so sorry, Leo. Is it anything we did? How can we ever make it up to you?"

Since his hands were now fully soaped, he merely leaned over and surprised her by giving her a gentle kiss on the forehead. "It was nothing any of you did. Don't fret, Marigold."

How could she not?

She must have hurt him so badly by ignoring his wishes when he was only trying to keep her safe. "Even if the killer left no clues behind, will you tell us what you did find? Or can you not speak of this incident yet? Is it too hurtful for you?"

He cast her a wry smile as he dipped his hands in the water again, and then took the towel she handed him to dry himself off. "I have a very snoopy wife who will not give me a moment's peace until I tell her what I know."

Marigold shook her head. "Yes, I am a snoop. But I will understand if it is too difficult for you to speak of Denby."

He arched an eyebrow. "Since when have you been so understanding?"

The remark cut her to the quick.

She loved him. Hadn't she shown it in every way possible? Did he believe she always put her own interests ahead of his?

How could he not? Isn't this exactly what she had been doing tonight? She could have stopped Syd from tossing her reticule. She could have insisted they all remain inside their carriage.

She had behaved abominably.

Tears threatened to cloud her eyes.

Drat.

She was not going to cry.

"Leo, have I been unbearably horrid to you? Yes, I must have been. Why did you not tell me you were so unhappy in the marriage?"

His eyes widened and he tossed the towel onto the bureau. "Unhappy? Whatever gave you that idea?"

"Shall I start listing all the reasons? I am naive. I am spoiled. I am selfish. I am demanding. I meddle. I–"

He sighed and drew her into his arms. "Come here, sweetheart. I know I was harsh with you tonight."

"I am not blaming you. I was so stuck on what *I* wanted that I gave no thought to you. I should have been more considerate of your feelings instead of sticking my nose in your business and being relentless about it. I was selfish, insufferable, and thinking of my own desires. I am truly sorry, Leo. We all wanted to help you. I may have been useless, but Gory and Syd could have contributed. Their knowledge of medical anatomy is better than most experts and would have been of great assistance to you."

He stiffened. "Is this how I make you feel? Useless to me?"

She burrowed against his magnificently hard chest, emitting a shattered sigh as he wrapped his muscled arms around her. "Yes. You shut me out of everything. But as I said, I do not blame you. How can I be anything but useless when I seem to always be getting in the way?"

"Blessed saints, Marigold. You are a little miracle. You are my sunlight." He hugged her tightly to him. "You are the best thing in my life."

A life he meant to toss away for revenge, but she was not going to mention this now. It was enough that he wanted her. She doubted she was the best thing in his life, but hoped to become special to him one day, if only he would give her the chance. More than that, he needed to give *them* the chance to grow old together in their marriage.

There was so much she had yet to learn. She was trying her best to acquire a wisdom of the ages and become a person Leo would be proud to call his wife.

She was trying to improve for herself, as well. With or without him, she meant to make something of her life. However, she hoped these years would pass with him by her side. She could not imagine her future without him.

Oh, how dearly she needed him.

"Let's return to our guests." He took her hand and gave it an affectionate squeeze as he led her downstairs. Instead of immediately striding in, he paused at the door of the parlor to stare at their friends. "All right," he said, letting out a breath as he apparently made the decision to confide in them. "I will tell you all we discovered at Lord Denby's. I will also tell you how Denby and I are connected, although Marigold might have told you that already. Well, it doesn't matter now. Let me talk first and then you can ask your questions. Anyone care for a drink?"

Octavian tossed him a look. "Why? Do you think we'll need it?"

"It's up to you." Leo poured himself a brandy. "I surely do."

"What did you learn that has you so rattled, Leo?" Gory asked.

"Nothing," he said with a harshness aimed mostly at himself. "That's just the point. Entirely the point. Four years of surviving on dreams of retribution, and…"

"That pleasure was snatched from you?" Syd remarked, cautiously finishing his sentence.

Leo nodded. "I spent years thinking of this moment, planning it out. But nothing turned out as I expected. Not Denby. Not his home. Nor his servants."

Marigold was having trouble following along. "What did you find?"

He groaned. "I'm not even sure what I was looking at. None of it made any sense."

"Care to explain?" Octavian appeared just as uncertain as she was. What were they to make of Leo's words?

As for Leo, he had not poured much brandy into his glass. It was just enough to slake his thirst and nothing more since he needed to remain clearheaded. He stared into the glass a moment, then tossed its contents back in one gulp.

Setting his glass aside, he now turned to face them all. "Denby was a royal envoy, but what did any of us really know of him? He managed to climb high within the royal inner circle, but how? Who were his connections? Where did he go to school? Who was his family? Ian could tell me nothing, nor could Mr. Barrow. This man traveled in the loftiest circles, yet he is little more than a cipher to us all."

Marigold put a hand on his arm, feeling his muscles ripple with tension. "Surely someone has to know how he got his assignments."

"Yes, but who? This is yet another investigation to be started by Ian. Denby was reputed to be rich, having somehow made a fortune in profitable ventures starting with that Carpathian mining venture. That was four years ago…years that I was locked away and never thought to see the light of day. But we searched his home and there was not a single, blessed sign of wealth."

"How can that be?" Gory asked.

"I have no idea." He poured himself another drink. "None of us know what to make of it."

Marigold glanced at her friends. Syd and Gory were quite clever, and Gory in particular seemed to understand the mind of a killer. Could they help solve this mystery?

Well, there were obvious reasons why someone might lose their wealth. Did it not happen often enough that an earl or other nobleman lost their family fortune at the gaming tables? Or simply bad investments.

Leo sighed. "Seems to me, we are looking at something that goes far beyond a bloody Carpathian mining contract. We'll need to dig into every other diplomatic assignment and business dealing Denby was ever involved in. Ian and his agents in the Home Office had already started looking into this. But it has been weeks already and they have nothing to show for it."

"It takes time to gather evidence," Julius said.

Octavian nodded. "You think he was part of an organized ring of traitors? A group not interested in fomenting overthrow of the government, but merely to subvert their interests and divert the profits to themselves. It is not surprising Edgeware has been slow to unravel it. He would have to move carefully. There may be powerful people involved. Some very close to the Crown."

Marigold's mind was once again awhirl with questions. "Do you think Beldon was in any way involved? Could Denby and Beldon have been working together to get you out of the way?"

Leo cast her a wry smile. "My pet, I have no idea."

"Oh, Leo. Let's talk through the possibilities."

"Do you think I have not gone over this in my head for years?"

She nodded. "I'm sure you have. But after a while it all becomes caught in a rut, doesn't it? Like a carriage stuck in the mud and the wheels just keep turning and turning, and digging the carriage into a deeper mire."

Syd agreed. "Let us talk it out and see if we come up with something fresh. Marigold, you go first."

Marigold immediately agreed, for she was eager to do anything that might help Leo. "Here's what we know. Beldon has always been envious of Leo. Perhaps he was thinking to put him through a few hours or perhaps a few days of hurt, so he arranges a fake assault with Denby's assistance because Denby has the contacts already in place. Beldon may have wanted to make himself appear the hero in later rescuing Leo. But Denby had other ideas."

"Such as?" Julius asked.

"He wanted Leo out of the way far longer. Leo would have caught onto Denby's sabotaging the Carpathian mining negotiations, and because he is honest and loyal, he could not be bribed."

"So Denby ordered him imprisoned for all these years?" Syd mused.

"It may not have been intended to go on for that long. Once out of their control, anything could happen...and unfortunately, it did," Marigold said.

Leo shook his head. "After seeing the condition of his residence, I don't think Denby ever wielded that much influence."

Octavian stared at him. "Then who did?"

CHAPTER 12

"I DON'T KNOW," Leo remarked, absently stirring the amber liquid in his refilled glass before taking a healthy swallow. "Perhaps Beldon and Denby might have had power to exert by working together. But it sounds sick. Two devils colluding to get me out of the way. And then what? Betraying each other because they are running scared now that I am back in England?"

"Still makes no sense," Marigold said. "Beldon is reputedly on the Continent, so he is unlikely to have done in Denby. Although, I suppose he could have paid someone."

Leo frowned. "If there is a connection between the Beldon and Denby, I mean to find the solid proof of it."

Marigold nodded. "And we'll help."

Botheration.

He knew Marigold was eager to investigate with him, even though this was the last thing he wanted. Someone had killed Denby. Perhaps this same person wished to kill him. He did not want Marigold anywhere near him if an attempt was made on his life.

Neither Marigold or her friends seemed in the least concerned.

"Yes, Leo," Gory said. "You must let us help. And before you utter a protest, just stop this nonsense of protecting the *little* ladies. You know I am not delicate in the least."

"Nor am I," Syd added.

Marigold, who could not look fierce even if her life depended on it, cast him a determined frown. "Nor am I. And don't you dare snicker at me, Leo. I may be younger and have less experience than the rest of you, but I am not stupid."

Had he made her feel inferior? It was never his intention. But he was not surprised this was her conclusion since he was refusing to consummate their union and had shut her out of many parts of his life.

Of course, his reticence had made her feel as though their marriage was a sham even though it was quite precious to him. "Am I snickering? You are right. It is time I brought you all in, but not in any dangerous capacity. I could use your research talents. Nothing else."

Syd shot to her feet, then sighed and sat back down. "Well, it is better than nothing. Tell us more."

As they listened, he gave them a little of his history with Denby and spoke of the ambush in the Carpathian mountains. However, he glossed over his years in captivity, merely mentioning it in passing since there was nothing much to say about it other than to list the warring factions he believed had imprisoned him.

The mention of those warring factions was only relevant because the ladies might turn up something in Denby's past that linked him specifically to one of those factions. "I was handed off from one to another, but the prisons were pretty much the same." So were the beatings, but he was not going to mention those either because recounting the misery he had been put through would leave softhearted Marigold in tears again.

"But they kept you alive," Octavian said, musing aloud. "There must be some significance in that."

Leo nodded. "I often wondered at the reason. I still do not know why. There was never a ransom request, so they weren't looking to take my money or extort the Crown. So why not simply kill me and be done with it?"

"Someone wanted you alive," Marigold remarked. "That sounds like Beldon, right? He wanted you to suffer, but also wanted to keep you around so he could continue to play his envy games."

Leo stared into his glass. "But why keep me imprisoned for

four years if this was his plan?"

"Because he had lied himself into a corner," Marigold said, her lips delicately pursed as she gave her reasoning. "How could he come forward? It would mean revealing his betrayal. Yet, he must have had some hold over Denby. I don't know. This is all quite confusing. Denby was afraid of what you might learn about him if you were ever set free. So, he agreed to Beldon's demand to keep you alive, but would not allow you to be set free until enough time had passed to put some distance between those involved in your capture and then your eventual release."

"Let's concentrate on Denby for the moment since he is obviously a party of interest," Gory said. "Is it not troubling that he is so enigmatic to you and the Crown agents who pride themselves on knowing everything?"

"He even has Mr. Barrow stumped," Julius added, "and he is just as clever as any Crown agent."

Leo nodded. "Yes, I know. Everyone is puzzled. Ian has had his agents digging into Denby's past, as I mentioned."

Syd leaned forward in her seat. "But you still want our research skills?"

"Do you want us questioning his staff and neighbors?" Marigold glanced at her friends. "Surely, the Crown agents and Mr. Barrow would have questioned them already."

"I do not want you anywhere near his staff and neighbors. What I need you to do is discretely drop hints to the ladies in your social circles. Get them talking and see if anyone knows something about Denby or Beldon. Gossip, rumors, actual knowledge. Make note of all of it."

"We can do this," Marigold said. "Lady Withnall is London's most notorious gossip. She knows everyone's secrets, does she not?"

Syd agreed. "Yes, that is an excellent place to start. Denby seems to be the link to quite a bit of underhanded goings on. She must have heard something."

Leo liked the idea for several reasons.

Lady Withnall was an excellent resource and also knew how to be discreet. Most important, questioning her would distract

Marigold and her friends and keep them away from Denby's townhouse while it remained an active site of investigation.

The killer had run off after stabbing Denby, but who was to say he would not return to the scene of the crime to find out if they had hit upon any leads? Denby knew too much and this had gotten him killed.

If he had partners in these shady operations, and Leo was fairly certain the Carpathian mining venture was only one of many schemes, then this was an organized ring with several highly placed members. They had to be concerned Denby might talk if caught. But he might also have left behind incriminating documents that would expose them, so it was quite possible these villains would lurk near Denby's residence...or perhaps torch it.

Well, he was now getting ahead of himself.

Marigold seemed to be reading his thoughts. "Leo, we will do our best to stay out of your way, but you must promise to be careful. Your return to London obviously has important people scared. This must be why they killed Denby. They had to silence him before you could question him. It must have been *you* specifically the murderer was worried about. Why else wait until now to kill Denby if it did not involve you?"

Julius nodded. "That is a good point, Marigold."

"I will be careful," Leo promised. It was no sacrifice to give his word since he was always vigilant. Even while on his mission four years ago, he had suspected something was *off*. He'd meant to keep a close eye on Denby once they arrived at the negotiation table. But Denby must have sensed he was being watched and had to contain Leo. With him and Beldon in that delegation, and who knew what others were already in Denby's pocket or had been paid off, Leo was outnumbered and had no chance of escaping his fate.

But here in London, he had the backing of powerful friends.

Denby and Beldon must have panicked when they learned of his return, although it did not stop Beldon, the sick bastard, from pretending to court Marigold.

"All right," Leo said, his heart a little lighter as he shared his burden with Marigold and her friends. "Let's set out what we have before us. First, my capture and the fact I was not simply killed at the time. Also, the fact no one else in my entourage was taken. Beldon and Denby were in that entourage. The wounds they incurred were superficial and meant just for show."

Gory pursed her lips. "Whatever story they gave at the time to cover up what they had done will not hold up now that you are free and back in London."

"This is why they are all running scared," Leo said. "Second, no ransom request."

"Another oddity," Octavian murmured.

"Third, the need for a closer look at Denby. He was reputed to be wealthy, but his home is a townhouse in disrepair and he kept a skeleton staff of servants. He displayed no signs of wealth. How is it possible? A man of his stature? A royal envoy and he appears to have had not a shilling to his name?"

Marigold picked up the track of his thoughts. "He would be rich as Croesus if he possessed those Carpathian mining contracts, right? So, it is obvious he was merely working for others. Or he was the only one involved, but the Carpathians stopped paying him and now he is out of funds because of his spendthrift ways."

"Implausible," Gory said.

Marigold nodded. "I don't believe it either. So, are we all agreed? Denby was just a front man for other powerful individuals."

They all nodded.

Leo shrugged. "Ian will be looking into this financial aspect with the assistance of Mr. Barrow. They might call in Finn Brayden, too."

Marigold looked at him, surprised. "My cousin Belle's husband?"

"Yes, he's the best there is when it comes to financial matters. He'll know how to decipher Denby's records back these four years and earlier, if it becomes necessary. He will immediately spot anything amiss. It is my hope Denby's financial ledgers will lead us to those with ties to those mining contracts and other sabotaged Crown deals. As you said, Denby was merely a front man for someone far more powerful, someone directly in the royal inner circle. Denby could never have gotten in among them without proper introduction."

Octavian rose to pour himself a drink. "So, it could be that the funds were diverted straight into a secret account held by that powerful man and Denby was merely his lackey who only got the scraps."

"Just enough to make it appear he was wealthy?" Julius asked.

"It might have been more than scraps at first," Syd remarked, "but those payments may have dwindled as Denby became more of a liability than someone useful."

Marigold glanced at Leo. "I cannot believe he was bought off so cheaply when he was the one taking all the risk and knew all the parties involved."

"Promises may have been made to him," Leo said, "but what could he have done if those above him reneged on those promises? He stayed alive by keeping his mouth shut and accepting whatever they deigned to give him."

"I suppose he was in a bind," Octavian said. "He was in this conspiracy as deeply as those in charge. And he would have hanged along with them even if he were the one to turn on them and expose their crimes. Well, for purposes of our discussion, does it really matter what he did or did not do? Or whether he was well paid for his role or not?"

Leo shook his head. "Only to the extent it is easier to trace funds coming in and going out of his account. I don't know that it matters much how and where he spent his funds."

"It would help to form a more complete portrait of the man," Gory said. "Gambling debts? Blackmail? If his home was as shabby as you indicate, he certainly did not spend anything on himself."

"Let's set the reasons aside for the moment." Leo leaned a shoulder against the fireplace mantel, his gaze remaining on Marigold and her friends. "Finn will be able to tell us within a few days what came in and went out of Denby's account. He'll know if the man had any vices. He'll also be able to confirm whether Denby's betrayal of the Crown extended beyond this one negotiation."

"As you believe it did," Julius said.

"Yes, I think there is no doubt of it," Leo said. "People were bribed and strategically placed. My imprisonment was carefully set up. Denby could only have been a front man, for he was someone with no obvious connections, no friends or family to otherwise put him forward as a Crown envoy. Everything was too carefully crafted to be only a one-time affair."

"And what of Beldon?" Marigold asked. "Was he involved only the one time on your Carpathian mission or was he in it as deeply as Denby was?"

"I don't know and I don't care." Leo folded his arms across his chest, tensing as he always did at the mere mention of Beldon. "Even a one time involvement is enough to condemn him."

He thought Marigold might make some softhearted excuse concerning Beldon, but she merely nodded. "So that is two out of three of your suspects, Leo. How does Cummings fit into this equation?"

"If he fits in at all," Julius remarked.

"He must. I just haven't made the connection yet." Leo had always felt in his gut that his cousin had been involved.

Julius proceeded along that thought. "Is it possible the three of them were an integral part of a ring of elite thieves who regularly cheated the Crown?"

Octavian shook his head. "Denby was their man, the only one who was regularly sent off on these Crown missions. Or did Beldon also travel extensively?"

"No, Beldon only left England the once. This much we know for certain. Mr. Barrow confirmed it to me," Leo said.

"I've seen him around Town often enough these past few years," Julius added. "Never heard him talk of travels abroad."

"As to Cummings," Octavian continued, "does he often come to London?"

Leo shook his head. "No. I had Mr. Barrow look into that as well."

"So how were instructions sent to him?" Octavian asked. "I cannot imagine any of the conspirators being so foolish as to put anything in writing. Leo, do you know if your cousin regularly took trips outside of England?"

"According to Mr. Barrow, he did not." Leo sighed. "I don't think our talking it out is helping."

"Yes, we are back where we started," Gory said. "We'll ask the ladies in our circle of acquaintances what they know about Denby, Beldon, and Cummings. Starting with Lady Withnall, of course. She is our best resource. Whether the three of them were involved or not is significant only to Leo. What matters to England is that there may be someone quite high up in the ranks who is in charge of assigning these delegations for the purpose of cheating the Crown. This takes us straight to the top men in the Foreign Office."

Leo raked a hand through his hair. "This is likely why Ian has not acted on any evidence yet."

"And why he is making it appear as though he and his men have found nothing so far," Marigold added. "As for Cummings and Beldon...I do not know Cummings at all, but what I have seen of Beldon convinces me that neither one would ever be trusted with sensitive matters of sabotage by this high ranking villain. From the way Leo has described them both to me, they are unreliable and too loose-lipped."

"Beldon struck me as wily and conniving," Gory agreed. "Quite full of himself, too. I never liked him. Tell us more about your cousin, Leo."

"What is there to tell? The man is a complete dolt," Leo replied with a growl. "Ignorant, slothful, and a pompous fool."

Octavian grinned. "You like him, then."

Leo laughed, needing this bit of relief to ease his tension which was palpable enough to cut with a knife.

Marigold suddenly leaped out of her seat. "It is all starting to make sense to me now. I know this will sound a bit insane, but I think they were all involved in that Carpathian incident. Hear me out, Leo. Cummings wanted you dead so he could inherit your title."

Leo arched an eyebrow. "But I am not dead."

"Indeed, you are not," Marigold shot back with a grin. "Because something went wrong with his plan. I am glad we are talking this through. Here is what I think really happened, and what we have all been overlooking. Cummings approached Denby and paid him to have you murdered while you were on foreign soil. But Beldon was in the delegation and had already struck his foul bargain with Denby. Or maybe he struck it afterward. The point is, Beldon wanted you to remain alive so he could continue his sordid games. Denby either told him about Cummings, or Beldon caught on somehow."

Gory grunted. "What about Beldon's involvement in the mining negotiations? Was he involved in the sabotage of this deal?"

Marigold nodded. "Perhaps not directly involved, but he must have caught on to what Denby was doing. So he struck a bargain with Denby. His silence for Denby keeping Leo alive. Denby took Lord Cummings' payment, then arranged for Leo to be held in captivity and not killed."

"And Cummings could not say or do anything without implicating himself," Syd remarked.

Gory agreed. "So we have Cummings wishing Leo dead, paying his bribe, then unable to say anything when Leo survived for fear of implicating himself. Then, we have Beldon saving Leo's life...how ironic...because he needed him alive to fulfill his warped entertainment. He must have caught onto to Denby's plans of sabotaging the deal and promised to stay quiet about it so long as Denby went along with his plans for Leo."

Octavian groaned. "Is this not getting too complicated? What if we are completely wrong and there is no connection between any of these men?"

"Beldon and Denby are connected for certain," Julius said. "That is undeniable."

Marigold nodded. "There is a reason Leo keeps coming up with these three men as suspects. Beldon and Cummings might not have been involved in other dealings, but they all came together on this one mission for the specific purpose of harming Leo. Is it not easily confirmed by questioning Ian himself? Ian was one of the conservators placed in charge of the Muir holdings. Cummings would have had to approach Ian or perhaps he approached my cousin Rose's husband Julian who was also on that committee of conservators."

"And what would he have asked?" Gory mused.

Marigold already had the answers swirling in her head. "Well, first he would have sought to have Leo declared dead. When did he start muttering about it? What did he say? Anything that might have implicated him? Revealed something only someone involved in this villainy would know?"

Leo stared at his wife. "So you are on board now? You finally believe these three are traitorous wastrels?"

"Yes, but that does not mean I approve of your manner of justice."

"They are an unholy alliance," Leo said with a growl. "Cummings wanted me dead. Beldon wanted me harmed. And Denby did not give a rat's arse what happened to me, so long as he could sabotage the mining deal and not be caught." Leo raked a hand through his hair. "And you still think I should not kill them?"

"Well, Beldon has run off and Denby is dead," Gory pointed out. "His partners must have been furious when they realized he had taken bribes on the side. Who knows how else he was undermining them? I'm surprised they took this long to kill him."

Leo poured himself another drink. "I'm sure they considered it sooner. But he was the perfect front man for them. It would have been too much of a risk to bring in someone new. So they let him go with a mere warning never to divert from their plan again."

"Right," Octavian said. "They let the matter drop knowing Beldon and Cummings were not going to get in their way again. Those two had no interest in Crown affairs or how the lucrative deals were being purposely mishandled. They only wanted to hurt Leo."

"And now that Leo is back and turning over rocks to find those slimy snakes, the silent partners realized the time of reckoning had come." Syd smiled at him. "They got scared and killed Denby before he could turn on them. But we will help you dig up all the dirt necessary to break up their evil organization and convict them."

Gory nodded. "Beldon or Cummings must also remain suspects in Denby's murder. I know it is rumored Beldon fled to the Continent, but this needs to be confirmed. And Cummings, we know nothing about him. But if he paid to have Leo murdered, why not do the same with Denby? And why not come after Leo again?"

Julius rose and walked over to Leo's liquor cabinet. He motioned to the bottle of brandy. "May I, Leo?"

He nodded. "Help yourself."

"Seems to me," Julius said as he poured the drink into his glass, "if what Gory says is right, then anything beyond Leo's original mission and capture is best dealt with by the Duke of Edgeware and the Crown agents. With Denby dead and Beldon not likely to still be in England, we ought to be concentrating on Leo's cousin."

Syd nodded. "I agree. He must be out there, feeling desperate, and aren't desperate men always dangerous?"

"Minimal danger to Leo now that we are all going to be on the lookout for him," Julius said, taking a sip of his brandy.

"This does not mean any of us should let our guard down," Octavian said. "All of these villains are scared and desperate. Cummings is not the only one who might do something foolish and dangerous."

"Denby's partners will run," Marigold said. "They have nothing to gain by coming after Leo since he has no idea who they are. But Cummings gains everything if Leo is dead. He just has to do away with him cleverly and provide himself an unbreakable alibi."

"Nor can we ignore the danger to Marigold," Gory added. "If Cummings is afraid to challenge Leo, does it not make sense he will come after her? After all, she is his wife and he needs to stop her and Leo from producing offspring."

Leo stared at Marigold who was now blushing to the tips of her ears.

If only his idiot cousin knew Leo hadn't touched her in any way possible to yield offspring. Nor would Leo ever do so until this entire investigation was brought to a close.

Yes, he loved Marigold.

Dear heaven, he loved her.

But nothing had changed.

He still meant to ensure their marriage could be annulled.

No consummation.

Husband unhinged.

Annulment granted.

Marigold safely out of the way.

Julius returned to his seat, took a sip of his brandy, and then set his glass down and regarded Leo with a serious expression. "Your cousin's name has been brought up throughout our conversation. But we have yet to make note of something important. Do you have any idea where he is at this moment?"

CHAPTER 13

LEO DECIDED TO take Marigold with him when he met Ian at Denby's townhouse the following morning. Their friends had departed Chipping Way shortly before dawn and would return in the afternoon to catch up on whatever else Leo had learned. Syd and Gory were going to speak to Lady Withnall, but Leo had also written a note giving the pair permission to view Denby's body because they were going to break into the mortuary on their own, otherwise.

Also, he had to admit they did know their anatomy better than any medical men with years of experience in the field. He should not have been an arse about keeping them from the scene of the crime last night. He had only done so because he was worried the killer was still lurking close by and did not want to give him the opportunity to harm Marigold or her friends.

There was also a part of him that hoped the killer was close, because he sorely wanted to get his hands on him. Despite his outwardly calm demeanor, he was agitated and frustrated. He wanted the freedom to handle matters on his own and not have an audience following him around to comment on everything he did.

He especially did not want Marigold or her friends watching him as he killed a man.

Their carriage turned onto Denby's street. "Here we are, love. Stay close to me and do not question my instructions or I shall put you back in this carriage and send you home."

He knew he sounded surly.

Marigold was frowning at him again, obviously not pleased with his highhanded manner. He was terrible at taking orders, but his sweet wife was just as bad. These Farthingales raised their children to think for themselves, not merely obey an order because it had been given. They had been taught to question everything and stand up for themselves.

Had she not vowed in their marriage ceremony to honor and obey him?

Well, he was no paragon of a husband.

Nor was he in jolly humor at the moment because Ian was going to take full charge of this investigation and relegate him to taking orders. However, he swallowed his pride. He knew better than to defy to Ian. As a duke, he was higher in rank than Leo. More important, he was one of the smartest men working for the Crown and Leo was not going to do anything to undermine him, especially if men high in the Foreign Office were involved in treasonous endeavors.

To say anything would place Ian's life in danger, too.

In any event, Leo had given his oath not to interfere with the Crown investigation. He had promised to behave himself for thirty days and would hold to it. "Anything new?" he asked Ian, encountering him in the entry hall once he and Marigold had disembarked from their carriage and walked in.

Ian arched an eyebrow. "Good morning to you, too." He greeted Marigold cordially before responding to Leo's question. "Nothing yet, but it is only a matter of hours before Denby's organization starts to unravel. Finn Brayden is here. He's already dug up the name of a bank for us. Mr. Barrow is on his way there right now with two of his best men and a writ from the magistrate. They'll make certain no one at the bank attempts to destroy any ledgers. Finn will head over there as soon as he finishes going through Denby's accounts."

"That is excellent." Marigold was smiling as she turned to him. "Is it not excellent news, Leo?"

No.

He did not like being a mere bystander in this investigation.

However, he nodded. "Seems you have matters under

control."

"It is what I do, Leo. This is not a sport for any of us. You ought to know better than anyone. I need you to work with me, not grumble and resent me because I must have the lead here."

Marigold was nodding and casting Ian a charming smile. "We appreciate all you are doing."

Ian grinned. "We try our best. Leo, you don't look too pleased."

"Don't mind me. I'm just being an arse." He rubbed a hand across the back of his neck and sighed. "You're about to dismantle a serious threat to the Crown and catch some highly placed traitors. I know this is more important than my petty desire for revenge."

"Sticking your knife into someone you have adjudged to be guilty is not going to help anyone, least of all you, Leo. You'll have your revenge as we capture each conspirator and they stand trial."

"But you will have nothing on Cummings."

"Your little rat of a cousin? Yes, we will. If he paid Denby to kill you, then we will dig up the proof. A withdrawal from your cousin's account and a corresponding deposit shortly thereafter into Denby's account should be enough to start. As for the others, those who do not hang will rot in prison for the rest of their lives. Titles will be stripped, lands forfeited. The ones highest up in this organization will soon realize it is all coming apart."

Leo glanced at the stairs leading up to Denby's study and made a sound of disgust. "Brought down by Finn's accounting."

"Is this not better than having shots fired and innocent people getting hurt?" Marigold grumbled.

Ian glanced at Marigold as he spoke. "Finn is about to link these men to their treasonous activities. I stand ready with my Crown agents to bring them in. We intend to move fast and stop them before they flee England."

"We discussed the possibility of their fleeing last night with the Thorne brothers, and my friends, Syd and Gory," Marigold said. "Do you really think it will all fall apart so quickly for these villains?"

Ian nodded. "Yes, for certain. Now that we know which bank

they used to conduct their activities, Finn will find a name or series of names, or a pattern of deposits that can be traced to other accounts. It is just a matter of finding the accounts to match those transfers. Once we do, we'll have the direct link to Denby's cohorts."

Marigold listened attentively, no doubt thrilled to have any role in this investigation. Leo knew she viewed her primary role as his guardian. She meant to stay close to him and hold him on a tight leash. He supposed it was the only way she knew how to keep him out of trouble. "Is it possible they used other banks, as well?" she asked.

"Ian will have access to every bank in London," Leo replied. "He'll have his men on it as soon as Finn finds the links."

"Denby must have been up to his eyeballs in dirty dealings," Marigold remarked, leaving his side a moment to peer into the parlor and the dining room before returning to his side. "I still don't understand how he could wind up so impoverished. Well, he isn't quite destitute unless one judged him by *ton* standards. He kept a roof over his head and a small staff in his employ. His furniture is not fancy, but not everyone requires opulence. My friends, Syd and Gory, are going to question Lady Withnall. She knows everything about everyone."

Ian laughed. "You are right. The little termagant is downright scary sometimes. Shall we go up? Finn may have discovered something else for us by now. By the way, I have put Mr. Barrow's men to the task of checking around the gaming hells. He has a way of getting information out of everyone. The man is uncanny. I ought to recruit him as an agent."

Leo grinned. "He is good at what he does. I would not be surprised if Denby was a frequent visitor to those gambling dens, especially the copper hells."

"Copper hells?" Marigold regarded him quizzically.

"They are the less reputable gambling establishments," Leo explained. "Those who go there have their own vices and secrets, so they are not likely to gossip about Denby if they happened to see him there for fear they would be found out, as well."

Leo held Marigold's hand as they climbed the stairs and kept hold of it as they walked into the study. The murder had occurred here. He knew the body had already been moved but was not certain whether the blood had been cleaned up yet.

His instinct was to protect Marigold's delicate sensibilities. But the truth was, she could handle the gore. She was a tough, little thing. Not only were her friends veritable ghouls, but Marigold herself was used to studying desiccated bones. "I never thought Denby was particularly smart," he remarked. "It is easy to see how he can be left with almost nothing."

They greeted Finn, but did not want to distract him from his important work.

"Glad to be of help," Finn said. "Sitting behind a desk all day can be quite dull. Although I don't suppose I am doing anything different here. One desk is the same as another."

Marigold shook her head. "Oh, no. This is quite different. You are saving England."

Finn laughed. "I'll let Belle know you said so. She'll box my ears if I'm late getting home for supper."

"We three are married to Farthingale women," Ian remarked. "We may control the fate of England, but they control us. Do not fight it, Leo. You are as doomed as the rest of us. Marigold will have her way and keep you from implementing your revenge plan."

"Thank you, Ian." Marigold tipped her head up and smiled at him.

"Botheration," Leo muttered.

She stifled a grin. "Leo, you are grinding your teeth."

"Why should I not be angry? I don't care what Ian said. You are not to interfere."

"I am most definitely going to interfere. I am a Farthingale and proud of it. You are not an avenging angel, Leo. You do not have the right to exact death on those you believe plotted against you. That is for our courts to decide. Shall we move on and search for clues?"

He agreed because watching Finn sit behind a desk and unravel the entire treasonous organization was more than he could bear. "Ian, have you already searched the grounds this morning?"

"I had men go over it, but I would like you and Marigold to have a fresh look. Can't hurt to have more eyes on the task. Search inside the house afterward."

Leo resigned himself to the task.

He may have been sullen, but this was a vital part of any investigation. In truth, most investigations relied on diligently pouring over documents and searching homes. Speaking to potential witnesses. It was legwork and teamwork and careful review, not heated chases or shootouts with culprits. "Marigold is actually quite good at digging up buried things. I think she will be quite helpful. By the way, I've given Syd and Gory permission to examine Denby's body."

Ian laughed. "I was considering doing the same, but glad you were the one to authorize it. I would much rather have you facing the Duke of Wooton and explaining why you allowed women to meddle in an investigation of this importance."

"We are not meddling," Marigold insisted.

Ian raised his hands in mock surrender. "I am not the one who needs convincing. Dillie saved my life twice. You do not need to tell me what you are capable of accomplishing. Come back inside once you are finished and we'll plan our next steps."

Marigold took hold of Leo's arm as they walked downstairs.

He glanced at her hand as her small fingers curled around his forearm. "Keeping me tied to your apron strings? I am not going to run off and do something foolish."

"Well, it does not hurt to watch you closely. You are so wound up, Leo. You know you are. Everything bothers you, from Denby's death at someone else's hands, to Ian's control of the investigation. You even frowned at Finn who is doing nothing but going over ledgers."

"I know." He let out a breath in frustration. "What can I do? Beldon and Denby are out of my reach now."

"More important, England is safer because they are out of the way."

Ian came hurrying after them as they were about to walk out of the house. "I forgot to mention...we took Beldon into custody before his ship sailed for Calais."

Marigold gasped.

Leo was equally surprised. "You've held him all this time? Why? I did not think you knew about the incident between him and me in front of the Huntsford Academy. And why would you care about that?"

"I didn't really. But I reopened all the files on the Carpathian matter once you were freed, and did not like what I read. I've been at this long enough to sense when something does not smell right. His attacking you in front of Marigold gave me sufficient grounds to hold him. He will not be released any time soon. It is very possible he will be hanged for his role in your capture and the sabotage of those mining negotiations. I thought you ought to know."

Marigold nudged him.

Leo sighed. "Yes, good news. Beldon's a nasty one."

Ian nodded. "Why does he hate you so much, Leo?"

"I have no idea. Truly, he has envied me ever since we were in school together. My grades were better. I excelled in sports. But I never gloated over a win since it would have been poor sportsmanship. The young ladies seemed to prefer me over him. Nothing specific. As far as I know, I never stole a sweetheart from him. In truth, I would have purposely begged off even if I had liked the girl because it was the honorable thing to do."

He turned to Marigold and tucked a finger under her chin. "Although, had you been his sweetheart, I might not have been so honorable."

She cast him an impertinent grin. "Thank you, Leo."

He nodded and continued. "Beldon seems to have fed on this loathing over the years. Well, I don't suppose his reasons matter much now. As long as he is out of the way. My greatest worry has always been that he might harm Marigold."

"I have him securely locked away. That is not going to happen now."

Leo gave Marigold a light kiss on the forehead. "Our greatest concern now is to have your dragon exhibit finished in time for its grand opening."

Marigold studied him. "And finding your cousin, Cummings."

"I will take care of him." He'd spoken with too much vehemence judging by the way Marigold and Ian were now frowning at him.

With good cause, he supposed.

Having been deprived of Beldon and Denby, he mean to get his hands on Cummings before anyone else took care of him first.

Marigold continued to frown at him.

He arched an eyebrow. "What?"

"You may not care about saving our marriage, but I do."

"I will not have this discussion with you. I do not need you protecting me from myself."

"Enough, Leo," Ian said, sounding quite the duke in authority. "Are you going to search the grounds or not?"

"Are you going to pull rank on me and order me around? You are not my commanding officer."

"Actually, I am in command here, as you well know. I will kick you off this investigation if you don't behave. Your wife is welcome to stay, however. She has a much better attitude than you. Leo, stop looking at me as though you want to murder me. I seem to value your life more than you do. You are in a very dark place and must pull yourself out of it."

"Easier said than done," Leo grumbled.

"I know you are trying to put the past behind you, so don't let it swallow you up now. Keep moving forward. You would not have married Marigold if you truly wished to destroy yourself."

"He had to marry me," Marigold reminded him.

Ian cast her a gentle smile. "No, he did not have to kiss you and he did not have to marry you. But he did both anyway because he knows he needs you."

"No," she replied quietly. "I mostly get in his way."

Leo's heart tugged.

He had to stop behaving like an arse and make things right with Marigold. "Come on, love." He marched out of the house with Marigold by his side.

He also owed Ian an apology. He was one of Leo's best friends. In truth, he owed Ian everything. It was Ian who had managed his estate while he rotted away in a foreign prison. Ian and the other conservators serving with him who had done an excellent job of managing the assets and thwarting his cousin whenever the wretched cur attempted to have him declared dead.

It would take an entire lifetime to begin to pay this man back for all he had done on his behalf. He felt his throat constricting and his heart now began to pound.

Marigold remained by his side. "Leo, take a deep breath."

He curled his hands into fists to steady himself. "What if Ian never finds the proof? How long am I expected to *behave*?"

"Always, if this is what it takes for us to move forward and share a happy life. Between Ian, Finn, and Mr. Barrow, nothing will be missed. If your cousin is not implicated, then perhaps your instincts were wrong about him and he was never involved."

"He was. I know it to the depths of my soul. You believe it, too."

Marigold nodded but she still frowned at him. "You intend to disobey Ian's orders to stand down, don't you? Leo, do not be a fool and force Ian's hand. I could not bear to see you held on charges of murder. I never want to see you confined, not even within our marriage. It would destroy me if you did not want me as your wife, but I would let you go because I could never hurt you in this way."

Did she think he was in any way grumbling about her?

She was hope and light, a far better reward than he deserved.

That she cared for him and loved him was nothing short of a miracle. So, what was he doing? Why hold onto his rage when she was offering him peace and happiness?

He cupped her face in his hands and gave her a soft kiss on the lips, for the last thing he ever wished to do was beg out of their marriage. "Let's search the grounds, love."

They spent the next hour combing through the underbrush of Denby's overgrown garden. His assailant would have had to pass through here in order not to be seen on the street.

Leo's search uncovered nothing.

Marigold found a scrap of fabric, probably from a gentleman's jacket. She also found a button.

They turned the clues over to Ian, then took their time searching through the house. Since it had already been searched from cellar to attic by the magistrate's men and Crown agents, Leo did not expect to find anything.

Marigold sighed in disappointment, her frustration mirroring his. "Nothing."

They helped Ian question the housekeeper and cook. Those were also empty leads, although the housekeeper was able to give them a vague description of several men who had visited regularly. Nothing sufficiently precise to give them a solid lead. She did not even know their names. "It wasn't my duty to answer the door. These men did not leave calling cards."

"Did you overhear nothing?" Leo asked.

"Not a word, m'lord. It wasn't my business and I did not care."

This woman obviously resented Denby and cared more for her bottle of gin than knowing what he and his late-night visitors were up to. Had there been silver to steal, she would have taken it and run off at the first opportunity. Had she seen Denby stabbed, she would have gone through his pockets and taken any loose change before raising the alarm.

"I merely brought in refreshments before his guests arrived," she said rather defensively, "then he always dismissed me for the evening. Ask Greeves, if you don't believe me. Cook and I never got a good look at their faces. Greeves might have, though. As for last night, we did not know Lord Denby was expecting company."

They questioned Denby's cook next, but this also led to a dead end.

After spending what felt like wasted hours, he and Marigold bid farewell to Ian and Finn, then returned to Chipping Way to meet with the Thorne brothers and Marigold's friends.

Marigold sat with her lips pursed and staring out the carriage window, obviously lost in her thoughts as they rode along the congested streets. "Leo, how does a man live an entire life span without leaving behind a single clue as to his past? There was not a letter, nor inscription in a book, nor locket...not even a calling card to give us a hint of his life."

"Not even a Bible," Leo remarked, finding this quite telling since most people – even those with no religious scruples – would have had one passed down through their family line. "It is clear now that this man had no family or friends. This is what made him so perfect to be the man to front any scheme to defraud the Crown."

She sighed and nodded. "I hope my life never passes by so meaninglessly."

"You have already made your mark on the world with your discovery of that skull. Your name will survive in history."

She laughed. "Nonsense, I did nothing extraordinary. Someone else would have found that relic within a matter of days had I not already been digging at the spot. It was just luck that I happened there first."

"Not mere luck, Marigold. You have good instincts."

She cast him a wistful smile. "They were not of much use today."

"Nor were mine," he admitted. "You turned up a button and a scrap of fabric. It is more than I found. Those bits could turn out to be crucial in helping place someone at the scene if he was missing a button or had a torn jacket."

"You are thinking of your cousin, Cummings?"

"Why not?" They had been seated across from each other, but Marigold now scooted over to sit beside him. She nestled her sweet body against his. "Leo, do you think Syd and Gory found out anything worthwhile?

CHAPTER 14

TO LEO'S SURPRISE, Sterling had cakes, sandwiches, jams and creams enough for a party of ten set out for them in the parlor upon their return. It was all part of an elaborate afternoon tea, even though it was barely noon. Marigold's friends arrived close on their heels and Marigold bustled them all in to partake of the light repast. "You are just in time. I am sure you must be hungry."

Leo stayed back a moment as she led the others to the parlor. "That was most thoughtful of you, Sterling."

"Not at all, my lord. Lady Muir requested it before you and she left this morning."

"She did?"

"Yes, my lord. She knows how to be a good hostess."

Leo shook his head and grinned. "Stop giving me that I-told-you-so look, Sterling. I know I have married a treasure."

Of course, he should be telling this to Marigold and not his butler.

"She tries very hard to please you," his butler said with an air of fatherly protectiveness that seemed unwarranted to Leo since it should have been obvious to everyone how deeply in love he was with Marigold.

Leo was also quite aware of her affection for him. How could one overlook being greeted every morning with a kiss and an 'I love you, Leo' the moment one opened one's eyes?

Had he not told her these would be thirty days of bliss? Of course, he had also warned her that he would ruin their chance of a happy union because he meant to get his revenge on those who had put him through all those years of agony.

He dismissed Sterling, and then followed Marigold and her friends into the parlor in time to hear Syd say, "Gory is a marvel when it comes to dead bodies."

Julius groaned. "Dear heaven."

Octavian laughed.

Gory ignored everyone's comments and turned to Leo. "There was a considerable amount of blood spilled, but his body showed no signs of a struggle. Nothing beneath his nails. No bruising at his wrists or throat or on his arms. I gather you did not find so much as a bloody footprint or any palm prints other than Denby's either in his study or immediately outside of it when you searched again by the light of day."

Leo nodded. "Nowhere in the house, nor in the garden or along his street. This killer could have been a phantom, for all the clues he's left us."

"Well, that ought to be a clue in itself," Gory murmured. "He must have been trained in the art of murder. Obviously, we can rule out a crime committed in the heat of passion. This was planned down to the last detail. I would not be surprised if the servants were drugged to keep them from waking if Denby cried out. By the way, I believe Denby was drugged as well. You might want to have the contents of his wine bottle analyzed. I suspect laudanum was used on Denby and possibly on the entire staff to make certain no one interfered. This is why he did not show up for Lady Gaston's party. He must have been drinking in his study and already drugged by the time he ought to have left for her party."

"But that doesn't explain the Bow Street runner, Gibson, who Mr. Barrow had planted in the house," Julius said. "It did not sound as though Gibson was drugged."

"That is easy, he wasn't." Leo took an offered teacup from Marigold who was now serving him and her friends. "They had no idea Denby's butler was a Bow Street runner working an investigation. I'm sure Homer Barrow trained his men well. There would be no tippling while on duty. This is why Gibson was awake and found Denby immediately after the murder took place. He was downstairs, heard a thud, and ran up to look in on Denby."

"Just a thud? Did Denby never cry out?" Syd asked.

Leo shook his head. "Gibson claims he heard nothing. So, Gory's assessment is likely accurate. Denby was assuredly drugged. So was his staff. This was no doubt planned in order to give the killer time to search Denby's house and remove anything incriminating."

"But Gibson foiled that plan and so the killer had to make a hasty retreat," Octavian remarked.

"Gibson assured Ian he had locked every door and window downstairs, so we are fairly certain the intruder must have climbed up the trellis below Denby's study window. That window was open when Gibson rushed in. There was no sign of breakage, so it had likely been open when he climbed in. We searched the immediate area thoroughly and found nothing at all helpful. This man, whoever he was, moved with the stealth of a cat."

"I found that dark blue scrap of cloth near the garden wall," Marigold reminded him, and then turned to her friends. "I'm not sure if it is related to the crime. Anyway, it is so small a scrap, I don't know that it is possible to tell where it came from. Ian will hand it over to one of his investigators to see if he can match it to a particular item of clothing. And there was a button, too."

She shook her head and continued. "Denby lived his life in such a clandestine fashion, no one knew the first thing about him. Who would live like this?"

"Someone who exists in a lie and deals with people who are into bad things and do not want to be recognized," Octavian replied. "Were you able to speak to everyone on his staff?"

"There are only three in service," Leo said. "Two of them, the cook and housekeeper, were of no help. As Gory pointed out, they were drunk or possibly drugged. The third is the butler, a man by the name of Greeves. But Gibson took his place for the week, so he wasn't around to be questioned. Ian's men are tracking him down as we speak. He's the one most likely to have noticed something helpful. Recognized a face. Learned a name. Just one name is all we need to topple the entire organization."

Julius let out a soft whistle. "Then I hope Ian's investigators get to Denby's butler before others do."

"Did Denby keep an appointment book?" Octavian asked.

"It is likely, but we have not found it yet. Whoever killed Denby probably grabbed it off his desk. Thanks to Gibson's quick action, the killer did not have time to take any other incriminating ledgers. Finn Brayden was already working on those ledgers when Marigold and I arrived this morning. Now, your turn. Were you able to speak to Lady Withnall?"

"Yes," Syd said. "That woman is amazing. She knew very little about Denby other than to say she thought he was raised in Exeter. No family to speak of, although she did not think he had been raised an orphan. But he is not a young man, so it is likely his parents died years ago, possibly decades ago, and he was left pretty much to fend for himself. No siblings or other close relatives that she knew of."

Leo had stopped paying attention to Syd's report at the mention of where Denby had grown up. "Exeter?" he repeated, his heart quickening and his brain in such a rapid whirl, he thought it might explode. "Are you certain?"

Syd nodded.

He had been standing, but now took a seat beside Marigold for no other reason than he needed to be close to her, although he was not certain why. Nor could he explain the sudden need to hold her hand. He loved the way her delicate fingers rested in his palm. "There's his connection to my cousin, Cummings. He also grew up in Exeter."

Marigold frowned at him, but did not remove her hand from his. "Lady Withnall merely *thought* Denby had been raised there. That is hardly conclusive. How old is your cousin? He must be a few years younger than you, and you are not even thirty yet. How old was Denby? In his mid-forties?"

"Yes, but so is my cousin." Leo knew Marigold was awaiting an explanation of the Poole family tree. "Cummings' father and mine were brothers. Obviously, mine was the elder. A confirmed bachelor, or so everyone thought, until he met my mother and fell in love at first sight. Cummings was about to enter university when I happened along."

"He must have been shattered," Syd remarked. "All these years, thinking he would succeed your father as marquess, only to be suddenly denied what he had come to believe was his rightful inheritance."

Marigold turned to him, her shift so abrupt, she accidentally bumped the small table where she had set her teacup down. Her spoon clattered against the fragile, bone china. She took a moment to steady it before returning her attention to him. "We must report this to Ian right away. If anyone goes to Exeter, it ought to be one of his investigators."

"It ought to be me," Leo shot back gruffly.

She cast him a stubborn look and slipped her hand out of his. "Not on your life, Leo. That is a foolish idea. But rest assured, anywhere you go, I'll go."

"No, you won't. I forbid it."

She rolled her eyes. "I happen to be related to Exeter's current magistrate. Well, we are not exactly kin, but two of my Farthingale cousins, Willow and Camellia, are married to his cousins, Shayne and Lorcan Brayden. That is connection enough to make him a part of the Farthingale family. A word from me ought to be enough to have you barred from Exeter, if you mean to go there simply to kill your cousin."

Leo could not believe what he was hearing. "Lorcan Brayden is married to a Farthingale?"

She nodded. "Do you know him?"

"Yes." Lorcan was perhaps England's best Crown agent, but he was not going to mention it to everyone since Lorcan's effectiveness was due to people not knowing his true role for the Crown.

Marigold smiled. "Willow lives in Taunton with her husband, Shayne Brayden. He happens to be the Taunton magistrate. Their cousin, Rafe Quinton, is Exeter's–"

"Got it," he said, abruptly cutting her off. "No need to bother Ian. I'll ask Romulus *Brayden* to write me a letter of introduction."

"He won't if Violet tells him not to do it." Marigold cast him an irritatingly smug look. "You forget, she is also a *Farthingale*. We stick together."

"Gad, how many of you are there?" he remarked, not particularly concerned. No one was going to stop him, not even Exeter's magistrate. Quinton? Dare he ask if Rafe was related to Deklan Quinton? *Dear heaven.* It was Deklan who had found him and gotten him released from his hell hole. Lorcan was the best operative working in England, but Deklan worked the most dangerous foreign missions on behalf of the Crown.

Finally, he gave in and asked. "Is the Exeter magistrate related to Deklan Quinton, by any chance?"

Marigold nodded. "They are brothers, which also makes him a Brayden relation and therefore a Farthingale relation by marriage...even though they themselves are not married to Farthingales. Rafe is the eldest. And if you somehow wheedle Romulus into writing you a letter of introduction, have him include me because I am coming with you."

Blast.

Why did she have to be so stubborn?

He was not taking Marigold with him. "Have you forgotten about the opening of your Hall of Dragons exhibit? You cannot miss it. Aren't you supposed to give a lecture after the opening ceremony?"

"Yes." She stuck out her stubborn chin. "Have you forgotten that you are to have a ceremony, too? Some minor thing...oh, what is it again? Ah, yes. I remember. You are to be inducted as a Knight of the Thistle. Of course, this happens all the time. Oh, perhaps once in fifty or sixty years? Nothing important. The royal family and the entire House of Lords will not notice your absence, in the least."

His ceremony was a little over two weeks away. If he left now, he could easily make it to Exeter, deal with Cummings, and be back in time to receive the honor of a knighthood which was something he neither wanted nor particularly deserved.

He hadn't deserved that damn medal, either.

All he had done was be imprisoned for four years.

However, the opening of Marigold's dragon exhibit was next

week. He would not have time to ride to Exeter, deal with Cummings, and make it back for her special day. No, the timing was too close.

By the disapproving looks on the faces of her friends, it was obvious they all seemed to think the choice to make was obvious, namely that he should stay for Marigold's exhibit.

Well, none of them had endured beatings or that dark pit of madness.

"Let's calm down, shall we?" Gory said, clearing her throat. "Leo, I would like to make two observations. The first is that the Exeter connection is extremely feeble and you ought to have something more before you shoot a man down in cold blood. The second is that we need to return our attention to Denby. He is the link to everything. So, who killed him?"

Leo did not think he could listen to any more of this. "Unless it was my cousin, then the matter of Denby is no longer my concern. I know for a fact it could not be my cousin. Even in his prime, he was not nimble enough to climb up a trellis, kill a man, grab his diary, make his way back down the trellis, and disappear over a rear garden wall before Gibson got to the study, all of which he managed to do without leaving a trail of blood or footprints for us to follow."

"All right," Gory said. "So he paid someone to do it."

Leo shook his head. "Why? Because he was afraid Denby would come forward and accuse my cousin of killing me? My cousin had to know Denby was up to his eyeballs in far more sinister matters to worry about exposing him, especially since I am still alive."

"All right, so we are back to the basic premise," Julius said. "Cummings wants Leo dead in order to inherit. That is all we need to focus on. Either he is innocent and content to reside in Exeter, or he is guilty and Leo is in danger."

Leo sighed. "He is guilty. I haven't a doubt of it. Have I not been saying this all along? I am not getting the point of this discussion."

"If he is guilty, then I would think your cousin is in London at this moment plotting your demise," Gory said. "So, going to

Exeter makes no sense. I would hunt for him right here."

Marigold frowned at them all. "Why are you encouraging my husband? We ought to be making him see reason. He should not be hunting anyone down either here or in Exeter."

"Well, a man has to defend himself, Marigold. There is logic to what Gory says," Octavian remarked. "Kill two birds with one stone while he is hiding out in London. Yes, it is logical that your return and unexpected marriage makes him all the more desperate to be rid of you, Leo. That is more easily done directing his lackeys from here."

"Assuming he was ever involved in Leo's imprisonment or Denby's murder." Julius set aside his brandy.

"At last," Marigold said, smiling at Julius. "If your cousin wants you dead, then why kill Denby first?"

"I don't know and I don't care. He may have had nothing to do with Denby's demise and the timing was mere coincidence. I still need to find him before he finds me. Whether here or in Exeter does not matter. But I know he must be in Exeter since he is a coward who will not risk being seen in London. That puts him too close to the crime. Too many questions would be raised."

Marigold plunked herself back down beside him.

He knew he was upsetting her because he could feel her trembling beside him. She wanted him to let go of his quest for vengeance. How could he when he was so close to the end now?

Marigold's eyes revealed her heartbreak.

This was not easy for him, either.

"Leo, please. We need to discuss this with Ian and Homer Barrow. While Mr. Barrow is digging into Denby's past and his gaming hell connections, let him also ask about your cousin. In fact, let him expand his search to include houses of ill repute and every seedy, dockside inn or tavern. If your cousin is hiding out here in London, would he not be in one of those places?"

Leo raked a hand through his hair. "I'll speak to Mr. Barrow."

"And will you tell him to report his findings to Ian?"

"No. He is to report them to me."

"So you can get to him and dispatch him before Ian can stop you?" Marigold was now on her feet again with her hands curled into fists. "You really don't care about me, do you? Not me. Not our marriage. Not what might happen to you once they convict you of murder. Your rank affords you some privileges, so you will not be tossed into prison again. But do you really think you will ever be allowed to roam free?"

"I will if he takes aim at me first. I have every right to defend myself. Neither my peers nor any court will ever convict me."

Tears filled her eyes. "I see. It does not bother you that you might be goading an innocent man to his death? You have this all figured out, do you? Well, think about this…if you go after your cousin on this flimsy bit of evidence, then consider our marriage over."

She ran out of the parlor in tears.

Her friends were looking at him as though Marigold had a point.

Well, who cares what they think?

Let them all rot in a dark hole for four years and then pass judgment.

Octavian approached him. "You've convicted your cousin on the one fact tying him to Denby, that they were both raised in Exeter. It is a bustling thoroughfare, not some sleepy village. Thousands of people come and go through there on any given day. I understand how you are feeling and would probably feel the same as you were I in your position. I get it. But Marigold is right. You need more proof, Leo. You cannot kill a man simply because of where he lived."

"More important," Julius added, "you have the entire Home Office and the best Bow Street man and his team of runners working on this investigation. If there is even the whiff of a connection, they will haul your cousin in. You don't need to do anything more. They will see justice is done."

Now Gory came forward. "Stop thinking of revenge and start worrying about Marigold. Do you care anything for her? Because right now you are tearing her heart to pieces."

Since everyone else had given him a piece of their mind, Syd obviously decided not to be left out. "I will never forgive you if she is too heartbroken to attend the Hall of Dragons ceremony, not to mention give her lecture. This is her pride and joy. Would you be so cruel as to spoil it for her?"

As soon as he had shown her friends to the door, he went upstairs to look in on Marigold. Even though they always slept in the same bed, they had maintained their separate quarters for practical purposes. The door was always open between their chambers unless they were bathing or dressing. Not to hide from each other, but for the sake of modesty since she had a lady's maid and he had a valet always present at such times.

He found Marigold in her quarters, stretched out on her stomach and her face buried in her pillow as she cried her heart out. Mallow was beside her, whimpering as he curled up beside her.

He picked up Mallow, gave him a quick cuddle, then set him down on the floor. "Go to Sterling for a treat. There's a good boy."

Mallow stared up at him with big, sad eyes.

He sighed and knelt beside the dog. "It will be all right, Mallow. I'm not going to leave Marigold."

Apparently assuaged, he trotted off to find Sterling.

Leo closed the door behind him, and then stretched out on the bed beside Marigold. "Hush, sweetheart. Let me hold you in my arms."

"No. And if you dare call me *my pet*, I am going to hit you." She sniffled. "Well, I am not really going to hit you...just don't call me that anymore. I am your wife, not some little plaything brought here for your amusement."

"All right." Of all the woman in London, he had to fall in love with the one who had the softest heart.

He tucked his arm beneath her body and drew her up against him so that she now faced him and was nestled in his embrace. He'd heard an earful from her friends and did not wish to listen to more. Nor was he going to speak to her of this matter again.

This was no longer a matter of his getting revenge.

This was about protecting her.

Cummings wanted him dead, but he had military training and was a hard target to take down. If he were his cousin, he would be looking to get rid of Marigold. She was the easier target. Gentle, trusting, and completely untrained in the art of defense.

No matter what Marigold or her friends thought, there was no way Leo would allow Cummings to remain free to harm her. Perhaps Cummings had nothing to do with Denby's death, but this did not mean he or Marigold were safe.

"Sweetheart," he murmured, holding her close and caressing her until her tears subsided.

His shirt front was completely wet.

She was still sniffling as she now engaged him in conversation. "You have to tell Ian what we've learned and leave the matter of Cummings to him."

"Ian and his agents are too caught up in the larger investigation, one that is of far greater importance to the Crown. But I will ask for Mr. Barrow's help. If my cousin is hiding out in London, he will find him."

"And if he is found?"

"Does that not prove my cousin's guilt? Why would he come to London and hide out in some seedy, dockside inn if his motives were honorable? An innocent man would lease a respectable house in a respectable neighborhood and show his face around."

"And this is all the proof you need to kill him?"

His entire body tensed and his jaw ached from the strain of keeping his rage under control. It was not aimed at Marigold, of course. He would never harm her. "Marigold, this is no longer about me and him...this is about protecting you. Who do you think he will go after if he cannot get to me? I cannot risk your getting hurt."

"Oh, so you've put this on me now?"

"No, it is not on you. It is entirely on me to see that you remain safe."

"Don't kill him, Leo. You cannot hunt him down like a predatory lion searching for his next meal. I know I cannot stop you from looking for him, but this is where it has to end. If you find him, turn him over to Ian."

"What can Ian do if there is no evidence to link Cummings to any crime? He will have no choice but to release him."

"Perhaps it is enough to scare him into behaving. He'll know the Crown's eyes are on him. He would have to be a fool to ignore the risk."

"Greed has a way of skewing a man's thinking." He kissed her on the forehead. "Marigold, I need you to promise me one thing."

"Just one? Well, you can save your breath if you think I am ever going to be an obedient wife who will sit quietly by while her husband ruins his life."

"Oh, Lord. Why did I have to marry a Farthingale?" But his groaning laugh was affectionate and so was the kiss he gave her, a deep and heartfelt plunder of her lips.

He loved that she was always soft and giving with him.

Did she think he was not aching for this matter to resolve in the best way possible? But they would have no peace unless Cummings was dead or locked away in prison.

"I'm so proud of you, Marigold," he said, thinking of Syd's words as she departed. "Don't let your arse of a husband crush your dreams. No matter what happens in the coming days, promise me you'll attend the opening ceremony of your exhibit and give the best lecture anyone has *bloody* well ever heard. Promise me you won't give up on the things you are passionate about. Pursue them and do not listen to anyone who tells you it is not a fit endeavor for a woman."

He kissed her again. "You are my marchioness. You can do anything you put your heart to doing."

He sighed as she began to cry again. "Don't, sweetheart. No more tears, especially if they are for me. I'm not worth it. You, however, are the best thing ever to happen to me. Have I not said marrying you was bliss for me?"

She nodded. "For thirty days and our time is almost at an end. I cannot bear it, Leo."

He hoped they would make it to thirty years.

If only they could get beyond the Cummings obstacle.

As he held Marigold in his arms, he also made an important decision about their marriage. With Denby dead and Beldon in Ian's custody, held with enough evidence to convict him of attempting to murder a marquess, not to mention the evidence building of his involvement in a criminal organization that was about to come apart at the seams, the only threat remaining to Leo was Cummings.

It was a personal threat and nothing more, so there was no longer a reason to end his marriage to Marigold. In fact, there was every reason to further thwart Cummings by producing a son.

Gad, that sounded harsh.

He loved Marigold. Consummating their union was a way to strengthen their already strong bonds. Why not? He had never wanted to end their marriage, only meant to keep the possibility open for the sake of her safety.

He could handle Cummings. Yes, he wanted to kill his cousin just as much as the oaf wanted to do him in. But if required to save his marriage, Leo would put an army of Bow Street men on Cummings' tail for the rest of his days.

He could afford it.

Since Marigold appeared to be calmer now, he released her and rose from the bed. She sat up and stared at him, saying not a word.

He kissed her lightly on the lips. "I may not be back in time for supper. Don't wait for me."

"Where are you going?"

"To talk to Homer Barrow. That's all. I am not going to hunt anyone down. I am not going to kill anyone. If Cummings does not come after me, then I will not go after him. All right?"

Her dark curls bobbed as she nodded.

He reached over and brushed back a few wayward strands that had loosened from their pins. "See you tonight."

He strode out of the house with his shirt still wet from Marigold's tears, but he was not going anywhere that required him to look like a gentleman. Also, he needed the reminder of her tears to keep his ravaged soul civilized.

He had assured Marigold he would not do anything rash.

But it was a close thing.

What would he do if he encountered Cummings?

CHAPTER 15

MARIGOLD LAY ON her back with a moist handkerchief over her eyes to lessen the hideous redness brought on by her tears.

There would be no more spilled.

Nor would she chase after Leo and fall to her knees begging him to come home with her. Ian had warned him. Her friends had warned him. She had shed a lake full of tears warning and begging him to let the appropriate authorities deal with his cousin.

If all this had not stopped him, then nothing would.

After ten minutes of lying quietly with the handkerchief over her eyes, she sat up and set it aside. Her maid happened to walk in just then. "Help me, Jenny. I need to fix my hair. And have Sterling order the carriage brought around. Oh, my husband didn't take it, did he?"

"No, m'lady. He rode off on his horse."

"Good. I won't be gone long. If he returns before I do, just let him know that I've gone to the Huntsford Academy."

"All right, m'lady? But won't it be closing soon?"

"Yes, all the more reason for me to hurry. The new exhibit opens next week and I need to be certain all is proceeding according to schedule."

It was not really necessary for her to check up on the work since Mr. Smythe-Owens was quite capable and did not really require close supervision. But she had yet to write her speech for the opening ceremony or finish preparing her lecture notes.

Seeing the exhibit would help get her thoughts organized again, especially now that they had been completely jumbled.

Two footmen accompanied her, positioned at the rear of the carriage as they slowly wended their way along Regent Street toward the Huntsford Academy. She peered out the window, worried she would arrive after the place had closed and make this trip a waste of time. But she had felt the need to get out of the house.

To her relief, they reached their destination with twenty minutes to spare.

This would give her plenty of time to view the dragon exhibit, make her comments, and check out anything else that caught her eye. "Good afternoon, Mr. Smythe-Owens," she said with cheer, spotting the amiable curator as she entered the Hall of Dragons that was now emptying of visitors since it was nearing closing time. "I've come to see the progress. Do you have a few minutes for me?"

He cast her a genuine smile. "Yes, of course."

He called over two of his assistants and instructed them to supervise closing of the museum. "Check every nook and cranny. Make certain everyone leaves."

"Yes, Mr. Smythe-Owens," they said in unison and scurried to attend to the task.

The curator now gave his attention to her. "Lady Muir, I think you will be delighted with the work done so far. We used Miss Appleby's drawings as a guide to recreate the primordial atmosphere. It will thrill everyone who views the display."

Adela, before becoming Duchess of Huntsford, had formed an explorer's club when growing up in her Devonshire town of Dartmouth. Miss Appleby and a few other like-minded adventurers had joined, but their numbers never rose above ten. It was a very small but enthusiastic club. Marigold had gotten to know them quite well while working with Adela at the Devonshire dig.

The members of the Devonshire explorer's club devoted every free moment to hunting for relics among the seaside caves. Their hunts usually yielded little success until the day Adela discovered a group of previously unexplored caves hidden amid an overgrowth beside a cliff.

Miss Appleby was a talented artist and Marigold was eager to see the latest drawings she had sent. "Oh, my. These are stunning." Then she saw the display that was hidden behind a tall drape and cordoned off to keep visitors from wandering in while the work was ongoing.

It was as though she had walked into one of Miss Appleby's drawings.

She looked up to view the giant creature hovering above her, its wings spanning almost from wall to wall. The back wall had been painted to evoke the scene of an untrampled world, one filled with gray mist, lush vegetation, and ominous caves. The sun was a tiny golden ball tucked away in a corner and barely noticed amid the trees which were also a part of the painting and dominated the back wall.

Prominent was the large skull, for the flying creature had been displayed as though swooping down for a kill.

This was her skull.

She had found it.

Of course, it did not belong to her. However, she had pride of discovery.

She smiled at the curator. "It is magnificent. Thank you for doing an excellent job. One almost feels the creature is alive. I cannot wait for the opening ceremonies. What a day it shall be."

"We'll require additional guards on duty," he said, pursing his lips as he thought about the event. "The crowd will be large and there will be a rush to the Hall of Dragons. His Grace has engaged Mr. Barrow and his Bow Street runners. They seem to be very busy just now and I have not been able to get anyone's attention to review the security concerns. It has been days now and I've received no answer to my request for a meeting."

"Oh, I will see what I can do for you." She did not want to mention the Denby investigation. "As a matter of fact, I can stop by his office on my way home and leave word for him."

"That is most generous of you, Lady Muir."

"Not at all. I am so grateful for the beautiful work you've done.

Glad I can be of help in any way." It felt odd to be referred to as Lady Muir, but also quite nice.

Along with her title came deference and respect. Unearned, but why quibble when it served her purpose to be listened to and obeyed? This was all the more reason why she liked Mr. Smythe-Owens, for he had shown her this respect before her marriage when she was merely Miss Farthingale.

She left the Huntsford Academy feeling much better.

The museum had now emptied out and hers was the only carriage standing in front of the massive edifice. The two footmen immediately stood at alert, opening the door and putting down the steps as she approached. She addressed the driver before climbing in. "Collins, I need to stop by Mr. Barrow's office before we head home."

"As you wish, m'lady."

Mr. Barrow's place of business was not far from the Huntsford Academy and they reached it with minimal inconvenience despite the clog of pedestrians, carts, and carriages.

One of the footmen escorted her into the Bow Street office.

Leo had obviously given orders she was to be watched at all times. Not that she minded, for Leo would go wild if he thought she was unattended and easy prey for his cousin. She did not know if the man was in London or ever meant to do her harm, but why take chances?

A young clerk came forward to greet her. "May I help you, Lady Muir?"

He must have seen the crest on her carriage and known who she was. "Is Mr. Barrow here, by any chance?"

"No, my lady. I doubt he will be returning today. He's on an important assignment at the moment."

"Yes, I am aware. Is it possible to leave word for him? You see, the Huntsford Academy is featuring a new exhibit and we have scheduled extra surveillance since it will draw a large crowd on opening day. We have engaged Mr. Barrow and his runners for this event, but would like to meet with them beforehand so they might familiarize themselves with the place."

The young man's eyes lit up. "I have read about the Hall of

Dragons and how you discovered the skull of the giant beast that will go on display. How extraordinary! What a thrill it must have been for you."

Marigold could not help but smile. "It was one of the most important moments in my life…um, what is your name?"

"Wilbur Barrow, m'lady. Mr. Barrow is my uncle."

"A pleasure to meet you, Mr. Barrow. So you will relay my request to your uncle?"

He nodded enthusiastically. "Yes, indeed."

"Good, and let him know that if he cannot handle this assignment to please provide us the names of Bow Street runners he deems reliable."

"Oh, he will handle it," Wilbur assured her. "It is already on his schedule. His Grace, the Duke of Huntsford, would never leave such an important detail to the last minute. His brother, Captain Thorne, also stopped by earlier today to confirm arrangements. I shall tell you exactly what I told him. You are not to worry, the Barrows will be on the task." He lifted a letter off his desk. "Mr. Smythe-Owens has also contacted us. I will respond as soon as my uncle lets me know when he will be available for this walk-through of the museum."

"Thank you. You have put my mind at ease." She could see the young man was an amateur relic-hunting enthusiast, for his eyes had been shining since the first mention of the exhibit and were still shining. "You will all be on guard duties that opening day, but I shall deliver passes to you after the ceremony so that you and your families may enjoy a tour of the exhibition at your leisure at a later date."

He cast her a beaming smile. "That is most kind of you, Lady Muir."

"Well then, I look forward to seeing you in a week's time." She bid him good day and returned to her carriage. "Home, Collins."

"Aye, m'lady."

Marigold was pleased the trip had not been wasted. Seeing the exhibit come to life so beautifully had raised her spirits. Afterward, stopping by Homer Barrow's office and being assured he and his runners would be on the task had calmed her nerves.

As she ambled into the house, she was surprised to find Leo pacing like an angry lion in the entry hall. "Bloody hell, Marigold! Where have you been?"

Sterling was standing quietly by the door, his face ashen.

Dear heaven, Leo must have erupted like Pompeii's volcano to scare the man.

She calmly handed her reticule, hat, and gloves to their poor butler before turning to Leo. "I was at the Huntsford Academy inspecting the new display, as I'm sure Sterling told you. I took your carriage and had two footmen accompanying me at all times, just as you ordered. You won't let me leave the house without a battalion of guards to protect me. Unlike you, I am respectful of your wishes."

He emitted a low growl.

She ignored it. "The exhibit is coming along magnificently, by the way. I cannot wait for you to see it. I also stopped by Mr. Barrow's office to make certain he was still available for the opening day ceremonies. His nephew assured me that he and his men will be there. They are also going to tour the museum several days beforehand to familiarize themselves with the exhibits and the building. All is in order. How was your afternoon?"

He raked a hand through his hair. "Productive."

"Really?" Her eyes widened and she gasped. "Tell me everything that happened."

But as she was about to drag him by the arm into the parlor, she leaned forward and took a whiff of his jacket. "Did you roll around in the dirt? Well, the odor is something significantly more foul than dirt. We had better talk upstairs. Sterling, order a bath brought up for my husband."

"At once, my lady." He called over one of the footmen who had escorted her earlier and instructed him accordingly.

Marigold settled in one of the tufted chairs in Leo's bedchamber and began to ask her questions as he undressed. "What did you mean by productive? Oh, do stop seething and just tell me."

"I am not seething," he insisted as he removed his jacket, cravat, and waistcoat.

His valet rushed in, just in time to take the articles of clothing before Leo could toss them on the floor. The odor would have taken forever to get out of the carpet had he tossed them down.

"Take my shirt and trousers, too," he said, now stripping down to nothing.

Marigold blushed as he now strode around naked while awaiting his bath.

"You can avert your eyes if you do not care for what you see," he teased.

The tension eased out of her and she laughed. "Dear heaven, not on your life."

Her heart was pounding and her stomach was aflutter. She had never seen more beautifully formed muscles on anyone. "You know I love you," she said softly.

He grabbed a towel and wrapped it around his waist. "I know, sweetheart."

She sighed when he did not say it back to her, and tried to dismiss her hurt. "Is it just the Cummings situation that makes you unable to commit?"

He knelt beside her and cupped her face in his hands. "I am perfectly capable of committing to you and to our marriage. There was never a question. My concern has only ever been for you and how best to protect you."

"But things are now *productive*, so does this mean you are no longer in fear for my safety?" She inhaled sharply as she realized what this word meant. Oh, how could she be so thick? She shot to her feet. "Leo, did you kill your cousin?"

"No," he said with a grunt of disgust, rising along with her. "He is very much alive, as far as I know."

"Oh, thank goodness." She put a hand to her heart to stem its rapid beating. "Then what did you mean?"

"My cousin was in town but seems to have fled early this morning. He took a room above a rundown tavern by the wharves. Mr. Barrow thinks he had arranged to meet Denby or some mutual confederate of theirs last night, then must have panicked when he learned of Denby's death."

She nodded. "No doubt worried he would be next on the list."

"Bah! Not at all. It is just as likely he was the one who arranged Denby's death."

"That is implausible, Leo."

"Why? The confederate he met with last night could have been the assassin he'd hired to kill Denby. When the man reported the close call with Gibson, my cousin decided to leave London immediately and attend to my death another day. After all, he'd waited four years to do me in. What would a few more weeks matter?"

"I still say it makes no sense. What reason would he have for silencing Denby when their involvement was years ago and an insignificant hiccup in Denby's primary business?"

Leo began to pace across the carpet. "You are assuming my cousin was aware of what else Denby was doing. Likely, he was not. This makes his little arrangement to have me killed far more significant in his mind."

"Perhaps," she admitted, not having considered this possibility. "Do you think he knows Beldon is being held in custody?"

"I don't think so, but he'll learn of it soon enough."

"Leo, I am still not convinced about your cousin. Why wouldn't he come for you first?"

"He may have tried."

"And we were unaware?" She shook her head. "You notice everything."

He shrugged his massive shoulders, causing the butterflies in her stomach to flutter as they always did whenever she caught a glimpse of his body. "I like to think so, but none of us is infallible." He tossed her a casual smile that brought on more flutters.

She forced herself to concentrate on their discussion and not his finely sculpted form. "I cannot get past Denby's murder. Why him at all? Even if Denby realized your cousin was in London and trying to kill you, why would he care? And what reason would he have to report it to the authorities? Or even blackmail your cousin over it? Both of them participated and would be implicated."

"My cousin might not have planned to do anything to Denby,

at first. But things change. Perhaps he could not get close enough to me, so he modified his plan and sought to get rid of everyone who might implicate him. Is it so implausible? I returned in bad shape, love. It took several months for me to heal and restore my strength. I was in private care and constantly attended."

"So you were never left alone?"

He nodded. "Once I was better, I spent most of my time right here at home. A recluse, until a skull tore across my garden followed by the most beautiful young woman I had ever seen in my life."

She blushed.

"I was only just starting to move about in society when you came along and stole my heart."

"I believe what happened is you compromised me and then felt honor-bound to marry me." If only she had stolen his heart, she thought with much sadness. But he seemed content enough with her and was a truly good and kind husband to her, if one overlooked his bloodthirsty quest for vengeance.

"Oh, Marigold. You know me well enough by now. I *wanted* to marry you. No one needed to coerce me." He leaned over and kissed her on the forehead. "Wicked temptress. And now my cousin is frustrated because he still cannot get close enough to either of us. Between your exhibition and my being knighted, there are always people standing between him and us."

"Well, if he ordered Denby killed, then it was a monumentally bad idea. If this is true, Denby's fellow conspirators will now be out for his blood. So you see, Leo, you do not need to do anything. Those evil men will take care of your cousin for you. He's certainly stirred a hornet's nest."

"Right now those conspirators are all scrambling to save their own hides. They are not going to drop everything just to go off and silence my cousin who probably does not have a clue about their identities."

Marigold was relieved when the tub was rolled in and set on the tiles before the hearth. "Is there anything more you need of me, my lord?" Ethan asked, obviously not certain whether he should remain to assist him in bathing or leave the task to

Marigold.

Leo turned to her, his smile appealingly wicked. "Nothing more for the moment, Ethan. Just take care of my clothes. They definitely need airing. My boots need polishing, too."

"Very good, my lord."

He quietly left the bedchamber, closing the door behind him.

Leo now approached her, leaning in close as he placed his hands on either side of her chair to trap her in. "Where were we, love?"

Oh, what a body on this man.

Taut. Lean. Muscled.

Glorious.

She licked her lips. "Um, Cummings. But we really have no need to speak of him. We've said all that needs to be said."

Leo's every thought was of his cousin. He twisted his every action and skewed the significance of every clue so as to point to him as the culprit.

Marigold was relieved her husband had not done anything rash yet.

She just needed to keep him close for the next few days in order to give Ian, Homer Barrow, and Finn time to investigate and find the perpetrator.

She did not care if Cummings, some hired assassin of his, or Denby's cohorts had killed Denby. She just wanted Leo kept out of it for as long as possible.

"Marigold, do we have any plans tonight?" Leo asked, his voice a soft, seductive growl.

Her eyes widened, for the air suddenly felt charged between them. "No."

"No friends stopping by?"

She shook her head. "No."

"So it is just you and me?"

"Just the two of us, Leo."

He cast her a wicked smile. "Care to join me in the bath?"

CHAPTER 16

MARIGOLD WAS CERTAIN they would have water stains along the parlor ceiling come morning. She and Leo had displaced so much of the bath water, there was hardly any of it left in the tub. Waves had sloshed over the lip and onto the floor while they had engaged in what could only be described as a Roman orgy rather than an actual attempt to wash up.

However, they were both spotlessly clean.

Leo's marquess quarters were a sad, soggy disaster.

But it was all worth it, for something momentous had happened. She was now truly his wife in every respect. After their heated coupling, there was no possibility of annulment. In fact, it was quite possible she was carrying his child. She knew it was much too early to tell, but one could always hope. "Thank you, Leo."

He laughed and wrapped her in his arms as they now relaxed in her bed, their bodies tangled around each other. The door between their bedchambers remained closed while Ethan, several footmen, and every available maid worked to mop up the spill in his chamber and dry out as much as they could of the carpet and floorboards.

Leo gave her a gentle kiss on the lips. "It was time I made you mine, wasn't it?"

She nodded.

"It would have destroyed me ever to let you go, but I would have done it if this was the only way to protect you, Marigold. Is this not how love works? Sacrificing one's happiness for the good of the other?"

Her breath hitched. "Leo, are you saying you love me?"

He laughed again, his voice a deep, gentle rumble. "I was lost to you from the moment I set eyes on you diving from one flower bed to another while you chased Mallow and that skull around my garden. You were a glorious ray of sunshine spreading your light into my very dark heart. However, I would have planned on a longer courtship, and not actually courted you until matters between me and my cousin were resolved. Besides, you did not wish to marry before you were twenty."

He shifted so that she was now under him and his weight pressed lightly down on her. "Things did not go according to plan," he admitted with a rakish smile. "I couldn't keep my hands off you." He kissed her lightly on the lips and then turned serious. "I should have waited until the danger had passed. I'm sorry I brought you into this."

"It is done and there is no going back. I haven't regretted a moment," she said. "I love you so much, Leo. I just want to see you happy."

"I don't know that I am a cheerful soul, at heart. More of a grumpy bear, I suppose. Too arrogant and demanding. Not good at compromising. However, I like that you have the spine to stand up to me. You do it so gently, too. Firm in your resolve but never cruel. You are too good-natured ever to spew bile. And I am too besotted with you ever to hold my anger."

She sighed. "We just have to get past this Cummings business."

"We will, love."

By the undercurrent of steel in his tone, Marigold knew he was uncompromising on this point. He meant to go after his cousin and nothing she was going to say or do would change his mind.

Had any of her pleading gotten through to him?

She wasn't completely naive. Cummings was someone who needed to be watched closely. But if he had been in London and hired some killer to do Denby in, then Ian and his Crown agents would have him for murder since that hired man would not stay quiet and take the blame alone.

If it meant keeping Leo in her bed for the next few days to let the investigation run its course, then so be it. She and Leo were going to have a marathon bedroom romp. If the attention he lavished on her breasts was any indication, he would be receptive to the idea.

Therefore, it came as a complete surprise to her when she awoke the following morning to find Leo gone. Not merely from her bed. Gone from her bedchamber and gone from the house. She had just donned her robe and was about to ring for her maid when there came a knock at her door. She rushed to open it. "Oh, Jenny. I was just going to summon you."

"Oh, my lady," the girl appeared distressed as she handed Marigold a note. "Sterling is beside himself with worry."

"Sterling?" Her eyes widened. "Oh, no. What has Lord Muir done? Has he said something to Sterling or Ethan?"

Jenny was shaking her head every which way so that Marigold could not tell if she was replying with a yes or a no, or she simply did not know. "I'm sure this will explain it better, m'lady. He told Sterling to have us take particularly good care of you because you were going to be very angry with him and might never speak to him again."

Marigold's heart was in her throat as she unfolded the missive and read it.

I love you with all my heart, Marigold. You are my beautiful, shimmering light. I beg your forgiveness if my actions in any way dim this light that I cherish with all my heart and soul. But you must see that I am too broken ever to heal. If you choose never to forgive me and we must part, I will understand and respect your wishes. However, I must finish this quest, no matter the outcome. I know how hurt you will be when I am not with you for the unveiling of your new exhibit. Whether I am present or not, shine brightly, my love.

Ever yours,
Leo

Marigold sank onto her bed, utterly dejected and fighting to hold back tears. But after a moment, she regained her composure and had formed a plan. "Help me to dress, Jenny. But first have Sterling order the carriage brought around. I have errands to run."

"Yes, m'lady."

Marigold refused to shed a single tear for her impossibly stubborn husband. She was well beyond crying. Nor was she a weak, helpless lamb. If Leo was going to behave like a vengeful clot, then she was going to do her best to thwart him at every turn.

She could be just as stubborn as he was.

What was he thinking?

Cummings would be arrested within the next few days. Was there any doubt now that it was known he had been in London?

First, she had to speak to Ian and seek his help in stopping Leo, even if it meant confining Leo against his will. Leo had written about her never forgiving him. But the greater likelihood was that he would never forgive her once she put her plan into effect.

It did not matter.

She would deal with the consequences later.

One problem at a time.

Since she had no idea where Ian might be at the moment, she ordered Collins to drive her to his home. Dillie would know where her husband was, or at least would know how to send word to him. "To the Duke of Edgeware's residence," she said, scrambling into the carriage.

The two burly footmen Leo had hired to guard her were ever present and immediately took their positions at the rear of the carriage.

It was not long before they arrived at the magnificent Edgeware townhouse, one of the grandest residences in London. She hopped out and asked for Dillie as soon as the Edgeware butler opened the door.

To her relief, Dillie was home and came hurrying down the grand staircase to greet her. "Goodness, Marigold. You look frayed. What's wrong?"

"I need to find your husband right away. Do you know where he is?"

Her cousin shook her head. "Dear me, no. He never tells me anything. But I have nothing pressing to do today. The children are well taken care of. And for once, I am not hosting a tea or society meeting or preparing the house for some grand affair. I'll take you to his office."

"You needn't go to the trouble, Dillie."

"Nonsense, it is no trouble at all. Besides, I could do with an adventure." She studied Marigold. "And I think you could do with some supportive company. What has Leo done to send you off in frantic search of my husband?"

Marigold groaned.

"Never mind, you'll tell me on the way. Men are such clots. Even Ian is sometimes, but mostly he's wonderful. I'll take you to his office, but we'll use my carriage. Send your driver home."

Marigold placed a hand on her cousin's arm. "Dillie, this could be dangerous. I don't mind your joining me while we track down Ian. But that is all you must do. Will you promise me?"

Dillie frowned. "What is this about?"

"As you said, we'll talk on the way. Just keep in mind that you have children who need you, and a husband who will never get over losing you. So, I must be clear about this. You are to go home as soon as we locate Ian."

"Did Leo give you this same lecture? And did you listen to him? Save your breath, Marigold. However, neither of us will do anything stupid. Are we agreed on this?"

Marigold nodded.

"Good, come upstairs with me while I change out of my morning gown, and then let's find Ian. I hope he will be at the Home Office, safely seated behind his desk and not running off after dangerous scoundrels. Sometimes, I wish he was a lazy lump. But then, I don't suppose I would love him as much as I do. He's the wonderful fool who puts his life on the line for Crown and country every day. Fortunately, he knows what he is doing. But I will always worry about him."

"How can you not?" Marigold commented as Dillie now slipped on a gown suitable for going about London. "There are so many bad people out there who need to be stopped."

"Well," Dillie said while her maid quickly pinned up her hair, "whatever it is you must tell Ian…just report it to him and then we must keep out of his way and let him attend to the matter as he sees fit."

Dillie grabbed her gloves and reticule, took a moment to hug her children, and then led Marigold downstairs.

Since the Edgeware carriage was now being brought around, Marigold dismissed Collins and told him to return home. "Very well, m'lady."

However, her footmen refused to leave her. "Lord Muir will carve us into little pieces if we dare let you out of our sight," one of them said while the other nodded in agreement.

"All right. Problem easily solved." Dillie motioned to the two men. "One of you pile on beside my own footmen and the other hop up beside my driver."

Dillie then climbed into the impressive ducal carriage, and Marigold hopped in after her. Once they were settled, Dillie rapped twice on the roof and the carriage took off with a jerk.

"I still cannot believe I am a duchess." Dillie snorted as she settled comfortably against the elegant squabs. "I think my parents are still stunned any of their daughters found husbands, much less titled ones. You've done nicely for yourself, too. Marchioness of Muir."

Marigold sighed. "Oh, Dillie. I don't care about the title. I just don't want to be known as the *widowed* marchioness."

"Leo behaving that foolishly, is he?" Dillie patted her hand. "I fret about the dangers every day, but I can never let Ian know how much these risks he takes on behalf of the Crown affect me. He has enough of a burden on his shoulders."

"And I am about to pile another one on him."

"He will tell us if this is not something he can handle."

Ian's clerks came running out and immediately began fussing over them as Dillie's carriage drew up in front of the building that housed the Home Office. "His Grace is just finishing up a meeting and should be with you shortly. I'll settle you in his office. Would you care for a cup of tea, Your Grace? Or refreshments?" The senior clerk would not stop chattering and asking after their comfort as he led them into Ian's office.

"We are fine, Mr. Mercer," Dillie replied. "Thank you. Please do not let us put you out. I'm sure you must be very busy."

"It is no trouble at all. My pleasure, Your Grace." He glanced from Dillie to Marigold. "May I be so bold as to ask…I thought I knew all of your sisters."

Dillie laughed lightly. "We do look alike, don't we? Dark hair. Blue eyes. This is my cousin, Lady Muir."

His eyes rounded as though in recognition, but Marigold expected it was because Leo's name had come up often enough within the context of this latest investigation. However, she did not press Ian's clerk for information since he was not likely permitted to discuss anything of a sensitive nature with them.

They did not have long to wait before Ian hurried in.

She saw the soft smile he had for his wife, as though he wanted to wrap her in his arms and kiss her senseless. Of course, he would never do it in front of others. "What brings you here, love?" he asked Dillie, but his gaze kept darting to Marigold.

Obviously, he knew she had come to him because of Leo.

Marigold dispensed with the niceties since Ian had enough on his mind and did not need them taking up his valuable time with aimless chatter. "Leo's run off. Have you spoken to Mr. Barrow yet? Apparently, Leo and Mr. Barrow discovered Cummings was in London and possibly met with the man who killed Lord Denby. Leo now believes his cousin, and not Denby's cohorts, had Denby killed. That is quite a stretch, don't you think? My money is still on his cohorts. Not that Leo cares."

She took a deep breath and continued. "Not only that, but Lady Withnall thought Denby had been raised in Exeter which is where Cummings grew up. And they are of a similar age. Leo has now decided that Cummings must have been acquainted with Denby, and must have paid Denby to have him killed four years ago. But Beldon was with them on the Carpathian mission and stepped in to have him merely imprisoned instead because he wasn't through being envious of Leo or taunting him. Well, the long and short of it is, Leo is now chasing Cummings, who we believe has run back to Exeter. He must be stopped. I am referring to Leo, of course."

Dillie shook her head. "Did you understand any of what Marigold just said?"

He nodded. "All of it. I already have my best man on the task."

"You do? Is it Lorcan Brayden, by any chance?" Marigold asked.

Ian emitted a snort. "How do you...? Yes. I suppose I should not be surprised that you know of him since he is also married to a Farthingale. Dear heaven, what is England coming to? And just how many more of you are there?"

Dillie rose and kissed him on the cheek. "A few more. But you will send Lorcan after him, won't you?"

"I spoke to Mr. Barrow this morning. In fact, Lorcan is riding to Exeter at this very moment. Let's hope he catches up to Leo. I want Cummings brought back to London *alive* for questioning."

Marigold cast him a look of dismay. "Do you think Leo will respect your orders? Oh, goodness. What if he is obsessed enough to hurt Lorcan? I had better ride to Exeter and stop him."

"Absolutely not," Ian said in a voice of authority. "First of all, Leo will never harm Lorcan. Nor will he try to wrest Cummings away."

"How can you be sure?"

"Because Leo gave us his word. He granted us thirty days to conduct our investigation without his interference, and those days are not up yet." Ian's expression softened and he regarded her kindly. "Despite appearances, his sense of honor is stronger than his lust for revenge. It is, Marigold. I haven't a doubt."

Thank goodness.

For she had plenty of doubts.

Having relayed all the information she thought important, Marigold thanked Ian and rose. "We won't take up any more of your valuable time."

Ian smiled and came around his desk to kiss his wife. "What have you done with our little heathens?"

She laughed. "I left them unsupervised with hatchets and knives. What can happen?"

"Well, that's all right then." Now also laughing, he kissed her again. "See you at home, love." He then turned to Marigold. "Don't fret. Your husband has a level head."

"One would not think so by his actions," Marigold muttered.

"I've known him a long time," he said. "He irritates the hell out of me sometimes. But he will never do anything to jeopardize Lorcan's life or our investigation. He'll rant and rage, but when it comes down it, he will do what's right."

She nodded. "Thank you, Ian."

However, she would have described Leo as possessed and possibly crazed rather than merely irritating. Yet, Ian did know Leo very well, so she had to trust his judgement.

They returned to Dillie's carriage.

"Care to come home with me? Or do you have other plans for today? Other than tearing off after Leo, I mean," Dillie said.

"Would you be terribly offended if you just drop me off at home? I have yet to finish my lecture, and I have not prepared for our cousins meeting tomorrow. Since I am hosting, I had better make certain there is food in the house to feed you all. I have also asked my friends, Syd and Gory, to stop by afterward. I wanted to read them my speech for the Hall of Dragons exhibit opening."

"Oh, let them come earlier. We have nothing important to discuss among the cousins, anyway. Invite my mother and Lady Eloise, as well. I'm sure they'd love to hear it."

Marigold smiled. "Would you mind if I included Lady Withnall, too?"

Dillie laughed heartily. "Not at all. I adore her. She has been nothing but wonderful to me and Ian. Yes, please do. Oh, what fun. I am looking forward to learning about your dragons. The entire family will be attending the ceremony and lecture, too. But it is so much more interesting to have this first peek. Oh, this was a quick trip. We are on Chipping Way already. I wonder if my mother is at home? I might stop in for a quick cup of tea with her before returning to my children. I really have nothing more to do besides kiss them before they go in for their nap."

"Thank you for everything, Dillie." Marigold hugged her cousin and then scampered out of the carriage with the assistance of her attentive footmen. She thanked them, too, and then hurried inside.

Her first order of business was to sit with her cook and their newly hired housekeeper, another Mayhew relative by the name of Martha Mayhew. They reviewed what was to be served during tomorrow's cousins meeting. Afterward, Marigold went upstairs and finished a rough draft of her lecture. She would polish it after she heard her cousins' comments.

The morale of her staff perked up when they saw she was going on about her business in Leo's absence.

Inwardly, she was hurting terribly. However, it served no purpose to moan and despair.

Passing the night alone was hardest for her.

She and Leo had been married less than a month, and yet she could no longer remember a time when she had not been sharing a bed with him.

It seemed ridiculous that she should feel so empty without his big, warm body beside her.

The words he had written in his note whirled in her head as she lay in bed and stared into the darkness. *If you choose never to forgive me and we must part, I will understand and respect your wishes.*

Tears filled her eyes.

She never wanted to part from him.

Would he give her the choice?

Marigold woke early the next morning, washed, dressed, and then polished a few details of her speech. By noon, all was in readiness for her to receive her family and friends.

Dillie marched in early, which would have been considered a scandalous *faux pas* in ordinary circumstances. But they were family and any of her cousins were welcome to come by whenever they wished. "Have you heard anything from Leo?" she asked, breezing into the parlor where Marigold's staff had just finished setting out the tea, sandwiches, and cakes.

"Not a word. He is thinking only of revenge. I am inconsequential. Truly, Dillie. You needn't soothe me. I know his quest for vengeance matters more to him than I do."

Dillie frowned, but snapped her mouth shut.

"Hopefully, Lorcan will manage to pound sense into him. Leo

has to understand Cummings needs to be brought back to London alive. This investigation appears to be moving fast. Between Ian and Mr. Barrow, they have left no stone unturned. I only hope Leo..." The words suddenly caught in her throat. "...that he does not do anything stupid to interfere."

Dillie nodded. "Ian assured us Leo could be trusted. You must have faith."

"I do, just not in this." She sighed and shook her head. "No matter. We'll press on. Oh, I see Violet walking over."

Marigold loved having family close by. Having been raised in Lancashire, she felt as though she had missed out on so much. "Oh, and Daisy has just drawn up in her carriage."

Violet and Daisy entered arm in arm.

Now that the four of them were all standing together, Marigold thought it quite humorous they all looked so much alike. Dark hair and blue eyes. Of course, Violet had violet eyes, but who looked that closely? Mr. Mercer, Ian's senior clerk, would have had his head in a spin had he seen all four of them together.

Dillie was smirking at her and must have been thinking the same thing. "Oh, here come the blondes. About time you showed up, slow pokes," she called to Rose, Laurel, Honey, and Belle as they walked in.

Marigold grabbed Belle aside. "What has Finn told you?"

She rolled her eyes. "Greetings to you, too. And before you toss a thousand questions at me, I don't know anything yet. Finn has not been home in two days. I would blame Ian for keeping him chained to his desk, but this is all Finn's doing. He is thoroughly delighted to be on the task. I received one brief note asking for a change of clothes. I delivered them personally because...why not snoop? But he grabbed them out of my hands and rushed me out the door before I even had time to kiss him. What is he doing that is so fascinating?"

"It is a major Crown investigation," Marigold said. "I cannot reveal anything more."

"Well, it must be something enormously important," Belle remarked. "I could have been standing naked in front of Finn and he would not have cared a whit. Once it is over, I hope he will tell me what has his eyes sparkling as brightly as they were on our wedding night."

"Does Lorcan's sudden departure have anything to do with it?" Honey asked. "Cammy said she would be late today because he had to go out of town suddenly, and she was left having to run all the errands."

"Really, we cannot talk about it," Marigold insisted, turning to greet Syd and Gory. "Do not repeat anything of what has been going on," she quietly warned them.

The older ladies, Aunt Sophie, Lady Eloise, and Lady Withnall walked in next.

Her cousins ran to Lady Withnall and began tossing her questions. The little termagant rapped her cane on the floor for silence, then said, "I am not at liberty to discuss the matter. It is delicate and private."

But it was obvious everyone was bursting with curiosity.

"Do our husbands know?" Honey asked. "I vow, I will beat Wycke about the head if he's kept this from me."

"I'm sure Graelem doesn't," Laurel said. "He would have gone into hiding from me for fear I would get the details out of him."

Marigold breathed easier when they all finally settled in for tea and resorted to discussion of the usual *ton* gossip. Once the cousins were all chatting among themselves, she drew Syd and Gory aside. "Have you heard anything more?" she whispered.

"No," Gory said. "We were hoping you had some news."

Marigold shook her head. "Nothing. Well, the investigation seems to be moving along. Have you seen Octavian or Julius? Did they mention anything?"

"Haven't seen them today. We plan to head over to the Huntsford Academy tomorrow. Hopefully, we'll see them there."

"Excellent. I'll be going there as well. Just before everyone arrived, Mr. Barrow's nephew sent word that the Bow Street team will be meeting Mr. Smythe-Owens at five o'clock tomorrow afternoon to review security for the new exhibit's opening. I plan to join them."

"So will we," Syd said. "How about we get there at four o'clock and meet in the library?"

Marigold nodded. "Perfect."

Once they'd all had their fill of tea, sandwiches, and cakes, Marigold hurried upstairs to retrieve her speech. By the time she returned, the ladies had turned their chairs to face the hearth where Sterling had placed a small table to serve as a podium of a sort.

Marigold set down her papers, cleared her throat, then began to read her opening speech. When she finished, her cousins shot to their feet, cheering and clapping heartily. "Let's hope I get the same response from an impartial crowd this coming Friday," she said with a jaunty bow.

Eloise regarded her kindly. "You will."

Marigold then moved on to recite her lecture. "Well, I do not have the bone samples I was going to pass around the lecture hall. But just imagine what a giant tooth, or talon, or leg bone might look like."

She started her talk with an explanation of Adela's discovery of the caves, the wall drawings, a comparison to the Lyme Regis caves, and the results of their dig. She ended with a short discussion of what was in store for the future. "Well, that's it. I think I took up the entire hour. Is that too long? Were you bored? Confused? Inspired?"

Her Aunt Sophie rose and began to clap.

Next, her cousins shot to their feet and did the same.

Syd and Gory put their fingers to their lips and whistled.

Lady Withnall pounded her cane. "Well done, Marigold. You shall be a sensation."

Dillie's smile faltered.

Marigold knew what her cousin was thinking.

Yes, she would be a sensation and Leo would not be there to see it.

Where was Leo now?

Was he thinking of her at all?

CHAPTER 17

LEO WAS AN hour west of Salisbury when he suddenly tugged on the reins and drew Archimedes to a halt. He wasn't certain what made him pause, perhaps the brightness of the sun as its rays shone over the crest of a hill and turned everything golden. It might have been the sweep of orange wildflowers catching his eye in a nearby field. He had no idea what those flowers were precisely, only that marigolds were a similar reddish-orange color and he immediately thought of his wife.

"Marigold," he muttered, his voice aching as he spoke her name.

What was he doing?

Why could he not leave well enough alone?

He had promised to give Ian and the Crown agents thirty days to investigate without his interference. Now that he and Homer Barrow had discovered Cummings was in London...or had been until a day ago, what more did he need to do? Homer would have reported this finding to Ian yesterday, and Ian would immediately send one of his best agents to track down Cummings and return him to London for questioning.

Whether his greedy wastrel of a cousin would lie and slip his way out of any criminal charges, Leo did not know. Was it not enough for now that the oaf would be returned to London and held for questioning?

Did any of this matter if his relentless determination to seek revenge cost him Marigold? He shook his head and groaned.

236 | MEARA PLATT

"Archimedes, what have I done?"

His leaving Marigold days before she was to give her speech must have crushed her gentle heart. Her archeological findings meant the world to her. The skull she had unearthed in the Devonshire cave would now be the featured attraction in the Hall of Dragons. This new exhibit was going to be one of the most notable events of the Season.

Oh, he'd written her a letter meant to be supportive, for he was extremely proud of her accomplishment. But were not his actions more telling? By leaving, he was confirming her worst fears, that she was unimportant to him.

And yet, the opposite was true.

"Yes, I'm a fool."

Leo laughed as his stallion snorted and shook his head. "No comment required, Archimedes."

But even his horse understood that he was in the wrong.

Leo whirled him around and rode back toward London. This decision somehow unburdened his heart. Barring any catastrophic delays, he would make it back home in time to join Marigold at the Huntsford Academy for her big day.

He hoped she would forgive him.

He was a callous, inconsiderate dolt.

But Marigold was too softhearted to hold a grudge and would forgive him, no matter that he was undeserving.

Also, she loved him.

Beautiful souls like Marigold did not fall so easily out of love.

She had given him her heart and it was his for always...his to crush and break. Bollocks, he had to make things right.

Leo had been riding eastward for about two hours when he decided to stop at a nearby coaching inn to rest his mount and grab an ale for himself. He had just walked out of the stable when he recognized Lorcan Brayden striding toward him.

Lorcan grinned when he spotted Leo. "I'll be damned. I was hoping I would catch up to you before you reached Exeter. Seems I needn't have worried. What happened? Why are you here? I was sure you would be a half a day's ride ahead of me."

"I was. Come inside and I'll buy you a drink. Are you hungry?

I hear the food is excellent." He pointed toward an empty table at the back of the inn. "Let's sit there so we can talk without being disturbed. I suppose Ian's pretty much fed up with me. Did he give you orders to shoot me on sight?"

Lorcan chuckled as they walked to the table and shifted their chairs slightly to keep their backs to the wall. "No, he just told me to tie you up, stick a bag over your head, and toss you onto the next mail coach back to London. You are going back to London, aren't you?"

"Yes." He kept his eyes trained on the travelers coming and going from the busy establishment. "I give you my word."

"Good. I don't want any trouble when I bring your cousin in for questioning."

A maid brought over two tankards of ale.

Lorcan drank thirstily and then set the tankard down on the rough-hewn table. "I have my tracking dogs with me," he said, taking another swig of his ale. "They haven't picked up your cousin's scent at all."

Leo did not think this was surprising or of particular cause for concern. "He might have taken a longer route home for just this reason. He has to be worried Crown agents or Denby's cohorts are after him. Not to mention, he knows I am out for his blood."

"Maybe. Do you think he is clever enough to throw us all off the scent? I'm not sure. It seems to me, this is a man who is in over his head and has made mistakes. If he were running home, I think he would simply make a desperate, mad dash for it. My sense is that he might have left that pigsty of a tavern where he had been holing up, but he stayed somewhere else close by."

Leo frowned. "You think he never left London?"

Lorcan shrugged. "I'll continue to Exeter anyway. However, it is a good thing you are returning. If he is still in London, you don't want to leave Marigold unguarded."

"I have footmen with her everywhere she goes," Leo said, more to convince himself he hadn't been a fool. "And my Bow Street runner has assigned his men to watch who comes in and out of Chipping Way. They stand on guard around the clock."

Lorcan glanced into his now empty tankard of ale. "But it isn't the same as having you there, is it?"

"I know," Leo admitted. "That's why I'm heading back. Finally using common sense instead of allowing rage and anger to control me. But what about you? What will you do if my cousin is not in Exeter?"

"I almost prefer that he is not. Then I can search his home and anywhere else he might have hidden incriminating evidence without his interference or attempts to destroy that evidence."

Leo grunted. "He probably destroyed all traces years ago There'll be nothing left to find."

"Maybe, but I'll find it if there is. Rafe Quinton is my cousin and the magistrate there. He'll help me out."

Leo grinned. "I've heard about Rafe. Apparently, my wife is related to just about everyone in England, including this cousin of yours."

Lorcan laughed. "Same can be said of my wife. Lord save us, but these Farthingales are everywhere. I suppose this makes us family. *Blessed saints*. Ian, too. Anyway, Rafe will fill me in on all that is going on in his town. He'll know where I need to search and will issue whatever local warrants necessary." He patted his breast pocket. "This warrant issued by Ian ought to be enough to scare the blazes out of Cummings. Ian gave me a cursory briefing, but tell me everything that happened in the past, Leo. I know there is a whole history between you and your cousin."

As they awaited their meal, a hearty rabbit stew, Leo filled him in on all that had transpired four years ago and more recently. Lorcan may have learned much of it already from Ian, but it did not hurt to go over the details on the chance something had been overlooked.

Once they parted ways, Leo spurred his mount to a gallop. He was eager to reach London, but he still had a full day of riding tomorrow, as well as the rest of today.

The weather held up, allowing him to make excellent time.

He reached London at the twilight hour on the following day, pausing a moment on the outskirts to look at the shimmering rooftops and the murky Thames in the distance. Smoke spewed from chimney stacks and the city seemed to go on endlessly.

Somewhere within that sprawl, Cummings could be lurking and hatching new plans. "We're almost home, Archimedes. How are you holding up, old boy?"

Archimedes stamped his hoof on the ground, a signal he was eager to be back in his stall in the Chipping Way mews.

Leo was just as eager to be home and take Marigold in his arms. "All right. Let's go."

Sterling cried out in surprise when he opened the door and saw Leo standing on the other side of it. "My lord! Welcome home!"

"Good evening, Sterling." Leo strode in covered in dust and sporting a four day's growth of beard.

"Good gracious." His butler bowed and clasped his hands together in worry. "We did not expect you. I'll let your valet know you have returned."

"Just my valet? And how about my wife? Where is she? I think she would appreciate knowing I am here."

"Oh, yes. I have no doubt she would. But she's gone off to Lord Finchley's ball."

Leo frowned. "On her own?"

"No, my lord. The Duke of Huntsford and Duchess Adela escorted her. They only left twenty minutes ago. You might catch up to them if you…well, you cannot go as you are. You'll need a bath and formal attire."

"Indeed. Have the tub brought up to my quarters and let Ethan know I have returned." So much for expecting to find his wife tearfully wailing and moping around the house. He was spent after all those days of hard riding, but he bloody well was not about to let anyone dance with Marigold. Had she given the supper dance to another gentleman?

Well, he was not that much of an ape to call a man out for paying attention to his wife. If he did find her dancing in the arms of another man, he had no one to blame but himself. He was the one who had abandoned her. That she had not taken to her bed with an attack of the vapors served him right. Besides, he trusted Marigold. She did not have a faithless bone in her body. "Ah, Ethan. There you are."

"And ready to do battle," his valet said with a grin, holding up his shaving gear.

Indeed, Ethan was in his element, fussing over Leo's attire, preparing the bath and tossing in...were those fragrant oils? Dear heaven, what was he doing? He had no intention of smelling like a spring garden. "Where's the sandalwood?"

"That is next, my lord. First we must remove the stink of horse sweat off you."

He sighed. "All right. I'll leave you to it."

After all, he wanted Marigold clinging to his body and not pushing him away.

Next, Ethan shaved Leo's beginnings of a beard, a task Leo could have attended to himself. But Ethan was having none of it. Apparently, two weeks on the job as his valet was all the experience Ethan needed to take full command.

Leo had to admit the lad was good at his job. Not thirty minutes later, he was clean shaven, presentable, and ready to head out to Lord Finchley's ball.

His carriage awaited him out front, Collins perched atop. "Good evening, m'lord. Nice to have ye back with us."

He greeted the man and climbed in. "To Lord Finchley's."

It felt odd to sit alone, for Marigold had always been with him lately. He ran his hand along the worn leather, noting the scratches left by Marigold's crate of bones. Lord, he missed her. Well, they would ride home together.

After paying his respects to Lord Finchley and his wife, Leo slowly made his way through the crowd. Ladies in silk gowns and glittering jewels were everywhere to be seen. The men all wore their formal white tie and black tails, for this was one of the more elegant affairs of the Season. There was quite a din, so he did not know if anyone had heard Finchley's steward announce his name.

Several ladies cast him beckoning looks as he walked by.

He had eyes only for Marigold...or would have eyes only for her if he could ever find her amid the crush. Ethan had mentioned her gown was a silvery blue silk.

Bollocks.

Blue seemed to be a favorite of the ladies tonight. Well, it was a favorite for most affairs since golden candlelight seemed to bring out the shimmering beauty of the blue particularly well. He knew this because Ethan had thought it important to lecture him about it for a full five minutes as the lad shaved him.

What could he do but listen while Ethan had a razor at his throat?

Finchley's elegant ballroom was ablaze with candles, the tapers dripping wax as they sat poised in their holders in the crystal chandeliers.

The orchestra was playing a quadrille, and someone mentioned it was the first dance of the evening.

Had Marigold been claimed for this opening dance?

He tamped down the surge of jealousy.

Why should she not dance?

As he continued through the crowd, he spotted Ambrose, Duke of Huntsford, standing with his brothers, Octavian and Julius.

Octavian's eyes widened in surprise as he approached. "Well, I'll be damned. I never thought to see you here, Leo. But I sure am glad you are. Finally came to your senses, have you? What happened to bring you back to London? You could not have made it to Exeter and back in this short time."

"I didn't." He raked a hand through his slightly damp hair. "I got halfway there, decided I was an idiot, and turned back."

"Because of Marigold's exhibit opening?" Julius ventured.

Leo nodded.

Ambrose slapped him cordially on the back. "Good to see you again, Leo. Come with me and we'll find our wives. You haven't met Adela yet, have you? She and Marigold are as thick as thieves."

"I haven't had the pleasure, but Marigold raves about her. Your wife can do no wrong in Marigold's eyes. She must be quite the paragon."

"Well, she's certainly made my life interesting," Ambrose said with a chortle. "Come on, we'll find them in the wallflower corner. Some things never change, do they? I'm sure they're huddled with Syd and Gory discussing ancient bones and other dead things."

"Julius and I will join you," Octavian said. "They're to play a waltz next and I've promised Syd to claim a dance. Her father's been bringing some rather unsavory gentlemen around to their home lately and she's worried he intends to marry her off to one of them. He tried it last year. I'll be staying close to her all evening, ready to swoop in if one of those wretches tries anything with her."

"As for Gory..." Julius shook his head. "I have no idea what her uncle has in mind for her. Not that she needs protecting. She's more than capable of taking care of herself. Still, I think she appreciates it when we stay close."

The four of them cut a path through the crowd.

Leo had no idea how Marigold would respond to him, but he doubted she would make a scene. She was too much of a lady. His heart shot into his throat when he saw her with her three friends. They were huddled together, their attention on something Adela held in her hands.

It happened to be the fossilized toe of a creature of indeterminate origin.

"Bloody hell, Adela," Ambrose said with a moan. "Put that thing away."

The ladies finally looked up.

"Leo?" Marigold blinked twice, then emitted a soft cry and flew into his arms. "Am I dreaming? Are you really here?"

He wrapped his arms around her and kissed her hungrily on the lips, a kiss that lasted longer than was proper. But he did not care what anyone thought. She was his wife. How much of a scandal could that stir?

Idiot marquess besotted with his beautiful wife.

Marigold deserved nothing less.

Her skin was warm and fragrant, a mix of cinnamon and mint...or something that was as fresh as mint, and he could not help inhaling the intoxicating scent. "Yes, I'm back. Can you ever forgive me for leaving you the way I did?"

She nodded. "You came back to me. Thank you, Leo. I know how difficult it must have been for you. What happened?"

"I came to my senses, that's all. I'm so sorry I abandoned you.

Suddenly, getting to Cummings did not seem important. I realized I had to be here for you. He's still a danger, mind you. He needs to be dealt with."

She nodded. "Ian's sent Lorcan to bring him back for questioning."

"I know. I encountered Lorcan at a coaching inn as I was riding back home. He did not have to convince me to turn around, for I was already on my way home." That sounded nice, the mention of home. Marigold was this very thing for him. It wasn't the pretty townhouse on Chipping Way. What made it a home was Marigold living there with him.

That she appeared so willing to forgive him was a testament to the kindness in her heart. He silently promised himself never to hurt her like this again.

They now turned to their friends so that Ambrose could introduce him to Adela. She was an attractive, young woman with intelligent eyes. Ambrose seemed content in the marriage, an obvious love match. "I'm glad to finally meet you, Leo. Marigold has told me so much about you."

He winced. "Some of it good, I hope."

She nodded. "All of it. I assume you will be attending tomorrow's opening of our Hall of Dragons, and Marigold's lecture."

"Wouldn't miss it." He gave Marigold's hand a light squeeze.

They spoke a little longer, then Leo excused himself to go in search of Ian. "He isn't here," Marigold said. "He's in the midst of taking down Denby's cohorts. They've found the man who was paid to kill Denby and offered him leniency if he told them everything."

"They found him?"

She nodded. "Yes, and were able to match the scrap of fabric I found in Denby's garden to a tear in his coat. That button, too. So, with this man now talking, all is falling into place. Mr. Barrow is also contacting his sources and Finn is still digging through Denby's accounts to come up with more names. They now have half a dozen men in custody who are confessing their misdeeds and naming more names."

"This paid killer was reluctant, at first," Octavian said. "But as others were brought in, he realized he had better start cooperating."

"So, he spilled his guts?" Leo felt a wave of satisfaction wash over him, but also regret that he had not been there to assist. He had only himself to blame, for his stubborn determination to take down Cummings had blinded him to all else going on around him.

Octavian nodded. "Yes, apparently so. Seems the cur was willing to give up his own grandmother to save his hide."

"Does Ian have actual proof as to who paid him?" Leo tensed in anticipation of the answer.

Julius now joined in. "Denby's cohorts. Sorry, Leo. I know what you are thinking, but your cousin had no part in this particular plot."

"How can we be sure? Both he and my cousin were holed up in a seedy, dockside tavern then. Was it the same tavern? Could it be that much of a coincidence?"

Julius shrugged. "The killer is obviously a trained professional. Denby's cohorts might not be the only ones interested in retaining his services. I still believe Denby's murder and your cousin's presence is unrelated, but we don't have all the details yet. Mr. Barrow has been asking around. But I would guess your cousin was hiding out here and hoping to hire this man to kill you, then probably got scared off when Denby was murdered."

Perhaps, as Julius said, the timing of Cummings' presence in London and Denby's murder were mere coincidence, but Cummings could only have come here for one reason. The only question in Leo's mind was, did his cousin plan to go after him or Marigold? A knot formed in Leo's stomach as he digested the information given.

Probably him first, for the point was to kill him off and inherit the title.

Yes, Leo knew his cousin had come for him.

But if Cummings was not able to find him – since Leo had been dashing off to Exeter to track him down – then the cur's next target would have been Marigold. *Dear heaven.* He had put her in danger by his own rash action.

"Leo, you are tense again," Marigold murmured.

He released a breath. "They're playing a waltz next. Dance with me, love."

She smiled up at him. "I thought you would never ask."

He led her onto the dance floor, drawing her close as the waltz began. She leaned in and began to breathe him in. "Are you using a new cologne? The scent is divine."

He laughed. "Ethan saw fit to anoint me with fragrant oils. I gave him a hard time about it, but I see he was right. Stop sniffing me, Marigold."

"I can't help it. You are intoxicating."

He laughed. "You are quite delicious yourself."

He twirled her around the ballroom, following the circle of other dancers. While he loved holding his wife in his arms, he did not like that they were amid this ballroom crush. He wanted to forget about his cousin for tonight and simply enjoy the evening, but he found it impossible.

Had the wretched Cummings gotten in somehow? Was he here now and watching them?

Leo knew he would never shake this worry until Cummings was locked away or dead.

Marigold was studying him as his mind drifted.

"Sorry, love." He forced himself to concentrate on their dance. He was never one for light chatter, but he wanted Marigold to enjoy the evening even if he could not. "Has anyone claimed you for the supper dance?"

She looked up at him again with her big, gorgeous eyes. "You, I hope. There's no one else for me, Leo."

"I know. You're an angel. I'm the dolt in this marriage."

She grinned. "I shall remind you of this when I do something foolish and require your forgiveness."

He laughed again and guided her into another twirl. "You are letting me off too easy."

"No, Leo," she said, now turning serious. "I will not deny I was hurt, but I understood. You believe your cousin is a dangerous man. His actions are certainly suspicious. But the fact remains, Ian and his Crown agents have not been able to link him to any misdeeds yet."

"Marigold, don't start. Let's just enjoy the ball." He did not want to have this conversation with her in the middle of a dance floor.

"You have judged him guilty, Leo," she said, ignoring his request. "You are determined to impose your own justice, and you have no right."

He was not going to fight with Marigold tonight. In theory, she was right. England was a civilized land where rules prevailed and men received fair trials...for the most part. But in practicality, she could not be more wrong. She was in danger while that man remained free. "Love, I've had a long ride home, and you will have a busy day ahead of you tomorrow. Shall we make our excuses and leave early?"

She nodded.

They bid farewell to their host and friends, then returned home to find everyone on their staff awake, some walking the grounds and others walking down their street with lanterns held high.

"Something's wrong." Leo hopped out of the carriage but told Marigold to remain seated inside. "Sterling, what is going on?"

The butler cast him a pained look. "It is Mallow, my lord. We cannot find him."

Marigold scrambled down from the carriage. "How long has he been missing?"

"Could not be more than fifteen or twenty minutes, my lady. I let him out in the garden to do his necessaries, the same routine as always while I locked up the house. When I returned to fetch him, he was gone."

Leo glanced at Marigold whose expression had turned anguished.

He took her hand in his. "We'll find him, love. He probably broke out to chase after some pretty female. Go on up to bed. You have a big day tomorrow, and the streets are not safe at this late hour."

"Are you forbidding me to search?" She tipped her chin up in defiance, her eyes now ablaze in anger.

So much for their happy reunion.

"Search the house," he said, appreciating that Marigold needed to do something productive. "He might have run back inside and gotten himself locked in a cupboard or the cellar."

Her eyes narrowed, but she nodded because it was plausible the little scamp was trapped somewhere in the house.

Leo did not think Mallow had slipped back inside. Would he not have barked? Or scratched frantically and been heard? His mind was already tearing through the possibilities. The first was the most dire, that Cummings had taken Mallow. He did not want to think about what his sick-headed cousin might do to the helpless dog.

Nor did he want to think about Marigold's heartbreak if his fears proved true.

Mallow, use your wits. Come home.

Leo watched Marigold grab a lantern and hurry into the house to begin her search. Once she was inside, he turned to his butler and footmen. "Sterling, take a few men and search thoroughly through the shrubbery."

"Are we to tread in your garden beds, my lord? They will be damaged."

"Trample them, if you must." As sorely as his heart needed to look upon his pristine garden, his place of solace and tranquility, those flowers could be replaced.

Mallow could not.

The little spaniel was a member of their household and had a place in Marigold's heart. His, too.

But where were the Bow Street runners assigned to guard Chipping Way?

While his staff searched for Mallow, he conducted a private search for those men. He found one unconscious in the alleyway behind his garden wall and immediately called for help. To his relief, this runner seemed to be coming around by the time his footmen arrived. "I'll be all right, m'lord. Let me help in the search."

"You cannot stand on your own feet yet, Arthur." He turned to his men. "Carry him into the kitchen and have Cook put the kettle on for tea. If he needs to lie down, help him into one of our guest chambers. And tell Sterling to send for Dr. Farthingale."

"M'lord, what about Henry? Is he…?"

The runner was referring to his Bow Street colleague.

"I'm going to look for him now." He found the other runner a few streets away, stabbed and trying to stagger back to Chipping Way. Leo helped him to sit against a tree, for he looked as though he was about to lose consciousness. "Don't move, Henry." He needed to question the man before he passed out. "I'll summon help. Lie still. You're losing too much blood."

Leo withdrew his handkerchief and placed it against the wound which appeared to be a grazing slash along the man's side, too near his vitals organs to dismiss. "Hold the handkerchief there and press down."

"M'lord, I tried to follow the man. He was about yer size, but heavier than you. Looked to be in his forties. Dark hair. Clothes were decent, as though he'd fit in among the gentry. He took yer dog and ran this way. There was a carriage waiting for him on the corner. A hired hack. Tell Mr. Barrow. It was one of Ogilvie's hacks. Ogilvie will give us the name of all the drivers on duty tonight."

"That is very helpful. Sit quietly now. My men will get you into the house."

He tore back home, made certain Sterling had sent a footman to fetch George Farthingale, and then ordered several footmen to follow him. Before he could leave, Marigold hurried downstairs and called out to him. "Wait! What is going on?"

He quickly told her. "The Bow Street runners are both hurt. You'll need to take care of them until your uncle arrives to treat their injuries. One of them, Henry, is bleeding several streets away. He needs to be carried back here."

"I'll have rooms prepared for them."

"Thank you, love. Next, I'll fetch Mr. Barrow and we're going to wake this Ogilvie fellow. He must have a list of drivers who are working tonight."

She clasped her hands and nodded. "I won't delay you, Leo. Do whatever you must. I'll take care of the Bow Street men."

She began issuing instructions to their housekeeper and maids.

Leo took off with his footmen, relieved Marigold was not the helpless sort who would retire to her bedchamber and be of no use to anyone. These Farthingale women, even those as young as Marigold, were clever and competent.

He knew Marigold's heart had to be breaking over Mallow, but she would not let it show while she tended to those wounded men.

Since taking a carriage through the London streets in search of Homer Barrow would waste too much time, he ordered Archimedes saddled. As soon as he and his footmen had settled the Bow Street runners, Leo hurried to his chamber to change out of his formal attire. He could not walk through the roughest dockside neighborhoods wearing these clothes. Besides, they were stained with blood.

He washed the bloodstains off his hands, then quickly changed into more suitable attire. The sort one wore when skulking through the seedier parts of London at night. He was about to ride off when a lad who identified himself as Wilbur Barrow arrived. "M'lord! Wait!" he cried, breathless but trying to relay a message. "My uncle asked me to check on his men."

"Then you know both are hurt."

The lad nodded. "I saw your footmen carry Henry into your home. He said the scoundrel rode off in one of Mr. Ogilvie's hacks. I'll take you straight to Ogilvie's stables. He keeps a man on duty overnight and he'll have the list of drivers. But I'm not sure how we are to track them down or even know which one to look for."

"Let that be my worry. How did you get here?"

"I walked, m'lord."

Leo sighed and extended a hand. "Here, climb up behind me. There's no time to lose. Where are Ogilvie's stables?"

It took them about ten minutes to reach their destination. As it turned out, Ogilvie himself was on duty. "M'lord, I have ten hacks out this evening. It is nigh on impossible to tell which driver picked up your man. I promise to question them when they return, but that won't be for hours yet."

250 | MEARA PLATT

"Do they all drive around in the same area?"

"No, I have them spread out," he said, rubbing a plump hand along his prominent jowls.

"Where does each start off?"

"Well, each has an assigned street, but how will this help you? These are just starting points. Who knows where their fares will take them afterward?" The clock in Ogilvie's office chimed two o'clock. "These drivers have been picking up fares for hours now."

Leo shook his head. "I understand. Just give me the starting locations."

Ogilvie listed each driver and his designated area.

"Let's start with Abner Simmons," Leo said. "His route is closest to the docks. Does he check in with you at all throughout the evening?"

"No, m'lord. Not unless there's a problem with the horse or carriage. But Abner's been working a double shift so he may come back early. I cannot promise, but there's always a chance."

"Wilbur, go find your uncle. Tell him what has happened and have him and a few of his best men begin asking around the docks for anyone seen with a little spaniel. You are then to come back here and question each driver as they return. Especially look out for this Abner Simmons. But if any driver tells you he picked up a gent with a small dog, make a note of the driver's name, where he dropped off his fare, and get as good a description as possible of this gent. Write everything down. Do not think to keep it all in your head. I cannot risk mistakes."

Leo was also concerned that Mallow, being so little, could be hidden beneath his abductor's jacket so as not to be noticed. He hoped the resourceful pup would bark to attract attention. "There's a tavern called the Blind Bear near the dockside warehouses. Do you know it?"

"No, m'lord. But my uncle will." Leo gave the lad directions to the tavern because he wanted him to report there once he had gotten information from Ogilvie's drivers. "Now you know it, too. I'll be checking in at the Blind Bear every hour. Your uncle and you need to do the same. We cannot go off haphazardly on our own."

0000000000

"I understand, m'lord. We need to compare information. Narrow the search area. Approach this gent in teams, for he may be armed and dangerous. My uncle's been training me. This will be my first assignment."

Dear heaven.

Was he leading this innocent lad to the slaughter?

"Wilbur, you are not to make your way to the Blind Bear on your own. Have Mr. Ogilvie's driver, the one who picked up that fare, bring you there. He is to remain with you until I have had the chance to question him. Got it?"

"Yes, m'lord."

"Do not dismiss him for any reason. I do not care if he is exhausted."

The owner, Ogilvie, had been listening and sought to assure Leo, as well. "My drivers will take their orders from me. I'll make certain it is done."

Leo dug into his breast pocket. "Wilbur, when you get to the Blind Bear, buy Mr. Ogilvie's driver an ale and some food if he is hungry. For yourself, as well."

He then turned to Ogilvie and handed him enough to cover Wilbur's fare and more than a little extra for his cooperation.

"Very generous of you, m'lord." He smiled as he tucked the payment into his shirt pocket. "Come around any time you need assistance."

Leo now regained Wilbur's attention. "It is likely the scoundrel had the driver drop him off at a corner location. Wilbur," he said, looking Homer Barrow's nephew squarely in the eyes, "on the chance the driver saw him go into a tavern or a private house, just get the location and report it to me at the Blind Bear."

The boy's mouth drooped in disappointment.

Dear heaven, Leo did not want this untrained boy trying to be a hero. "Do not confront this man on your own. You will only put your life and that of an innocent driver at risk. Got it?"

The lad nodded, but there was a glint in his eyes that worried Leo. He understood how eager the lad was to prove himself. But Cummings had shown himself to be dangerous, not to mention twisted in the head. What reason did he have to steal Marigold's dog other than to torment her? Nor would he hesitate to kill Wilbur if he caught him snooping around.

"I'll need your promise," Leo insisted. "You are not to go anywhere near the fellow, only report his whereabouts to me or your uncle."

"I promise, m'lord," he said, impatient with Leo's persistence and obviously disappointed to be reined in.

It felt like forever, but took less than two hours before Wilbur and the driver, who was indeed this Abner Simmons, turned up at the Blind Bear. Homer Barrow and two of his best men had turned up only minutes earlier. Leo immediately questioned the driver. "M'lord, the man I picked up went into the White Rose tavern with the dog."

Leo also tried to make out Wilbur's scrawl on the notes he had taken down. Since none of the other drivers had reported picking up a fare with a dog, this was the obvious lead to be pursued.

"Did you notice anything else about the man, Mr. Simmons?"

"How do you mean, m'lord? Well, I did not get a very good look at him considering it was dark on the street, but he was not a young man, I can tell you that. As I told the lad, and he took down m'words...I'd guess him to be in his forties. On the portly side. Dark hair. Not pleasant. I'm sorry, m'lord, but I think he might have been hurting the dog to keep him quiet. The little tyke was whimpering and cried out a time or two."

Leo's heart tugged.

Marigold would be devastated to hear of this.

If there was any good to be gleaned from the fellow's report, it was that Mallow was still alive and had not been drugged. Hopefully, the little fellow would suffer only from bruising and nothing worse. "Stay with us, Mr. Simmons. We'll need you to identify the man once we capture him."

"Aye, m'lord. With pleasure. I don't take kindly to anyone so low as to steal a lady's dog."

Homer Barrow knew of the White Rose tavern. "It is a nasty place, my lord. However, the owner owes me a favor. Wilbur, wait with Mr. Simmons in his hack. That tavern is no proper place for a peach-faced lad."

Leo allowed Homer to take the lead when they reached the tavern. It was now after three o'clock in the morning. Despite being six of them together, Wilbur, Simmons, the three Bow Street men, and himself, they all kept their hands on their weapons and remained ever on the alert along these dark and eerily empty streets.

A lone thief was of no concern, but men operated in gangs around here.

Leo hoped he and his companions looked tough enough to be left alone.

When they reach the tavern, Leo reminded Wilbur to remain in the hack with Mr. Simmons while he and Homer Barrow went inside. Homer had positioned his two men by the back door on the chance Leo's cousin attempted to run.

The owner was a portly fellow with sharp eyes and a grizzled voice. He gazed at Leo warily, but seemed comfortable enough speaking to Homer. He told them where they would find the gent with the dog. "Upstairs. Third door on your right. This makes us square, Homer. I don't owe you no favors anymore."

"Until I do you another good turn and save your worthless hide," Homer replied.

They climbed the narrow stairs and made their way with stealth down a dark hallway that was hardly wide enough to walk down one at a time. As they approached the room in question, Leo heard Mallow's frantic barks and then a sharp yelp of pain. "Stupid dog! You're more trouble than you're worth. I ought to kill ye and be done with–"

Leo burst through the door, easily shattering the flimsy latch and old, rotting door. He'd drawn his pistol and Homer also had his drawn, both weapons trained on...who was this stranger? He was not Leo's cousin. "Touch that dog and I'll put a hole between your eyes."

Mallow, who was unbound, now leaped into Leo's arms and began to lick his face. "Are you hurt, little fellow?"

To Leo's relief, the spaniel only appeared frightened and perhaps a little sore. Otherwise, he did not look to be seriously injured. However, the scoundrel now cowering and begging Leo not to kill him was a thin, wiry man, a complete stranger who nowhere fit the description the hack driver had given them of Mallow's abductor.

Of course, Leo knew his cousin had been the culprit.

"Where is he?" Leo growled.

"I don't know who ye're talking about," the man said, sniveling as he lied through his teeth.

The man had shifty eyes. Leo knew all he would get out of him was lies, unless he put the pistol to the man's head. Which he now did. "I am of noble rank. I can splatter your brains against the wall and no one will convict me. What is it to be? Your life or that of the man who left you here to face my wrath?"

"Ye wouldn't kill me for innocently tending a man's dog, would ye? I swear to ye, m'lord. I had no idea it wasn't his. Take him, if ye say he's yours. I don't want no trouble."

"Tell me where the man went." He struck the cur lightly with the butt of his pistol when he began to make up an obvious cock-and-bull story. That shiftiness in his eyes gave him away and frustrated Leo as he was about to be lied to again.

"He said he had something important to do and would be back later. He ain't told me where he was going or what it was he had in mind to do. Just tend the dog, he says to me. Why would he tell me his plans? I'm only good fer mindin' his dog...and it wasn't even his. He wasn't comin' back, was he? Just left me here to take the blame. Double-crossing snake."

Leo still held his pistol to the man's forehead. "You have to the count of three to tell me where he is going. One...two..."

"Wait! Don't blow me brains out! It's all I know, I swear it on m'mother's grave. He was a gent and paid me to watch the dog. That's all. Ye can have what he gave me. I don't want the money."

"My lord," Homer said quietly, "go home to your wife. I'll take the man to the magistrate and have him held until we catch your cousin. This knave, if he wishes to escape hanging, might think harder and come up with some helpful information." He then turned to the sniveling weasel. "It is not enough to prove your innocence by identifying the gent as the thief who snatched the dog. He also attacked my runners. They will be able to identify him, too. So, if you want your freedom, think hard and come up with something helpful that we do not already know."

Leo kept his weapon trained on the man. "Call your men in, Mr. Barrow. I'll have the hack driver drop you off at the magistrate's office."

"No, m'lord. Let the driver take my nephew back to my office. There isn't room for me, this scurvy fellow, and all my men to fit. We'll make our own arrangements. But will you do me the favor of escorting Wilbur? He's young and a little too enthusiastic for his own good. I do not need him getting shot because he thinks to play the hero."

"Yes, no worries. It is right along my way home. I'll see him safely delivered." Leo had no idea how these Bow Street runners would get out of here, but they were resourceful and knew everyone. As for him, his Archimedes was a massive war horse and knew how to defend himself from attack.

"With your permission, my lord, I'd like to stop by your house afterward to check on my men. Would it be all right for me to stop in once I put this knave in the magistrate's hands?"

"Yes, of course."

He strode out of the establishment, no doubt catching the eye of several cutpurses who would just as soon cut him up as grab his coin purse. But his glower warned them off. It was a glower mixed with a tinge of madness, for this is what Leo was feeling. Anger. Frustration. Fatigue and exasperation. He was to the point of snapping.

His cousin was proving to be infuriatingly slippery.

He marched to the carriage, trying to calm himself down. "Wilbur, you are to come with me."

"Yes, m'lord." His eyes brightened until Leo told him he was merely to be dropped off at the Bow Street office.

"But surely, there is more to do!" the lad protested.

"Your uncle's needs you at his office to coordinate the day's assignments. This can only be left to someone he trusts."

Wilbur appeared crestfallen. "All I do is follow my uncle's orders."

"It is excellent training. Pay attention and you'll soon be as good at the job as he is." After making this quick stop, he watched Simmons drive the hack off to Ogilvie's stable, and then started for home.

Marigold would be worrying herself sick over Mallow.

The little pup was still trembling in his arms. He licked Leo's face while Leo petted him to calm him down.

As soon as he turned Archimedes onto Chipping Way, Mallow began to bark excitedly. At first, Leo thought the dog was rejoicing to be home. But he realized something was wrong when Mallow growled and leaped out of Leo's grasp. "What the...?"

He dismounted and ran after Mallow who was pattering down the cobblestones in a mad dash toward Number 5 Chipping Way, home of the elderly Lady Eloise Dayne.

Bollocks.

Marigold came running out of the house. "Leo, I–"

"Blessed saints! Get back inside. Now!"

She came to an abrupt halt, turned, and ran back in.

Leo was surprised she had obeyed him, but she must have heard the ferocity in his tone and dared not protest.

Bloody hell.

If Mallow was growling, it meant Cummings was here and had likely come for Marigold.

Had his cousin been watching their home and known he had left town? What he could not have realized until this moment was that he had returned. Nor had his cousin expected Marigold to attend Lord Finchley's ball without him. Fortunately, she chose not to stay home while her fool of a husband ran off to Exeter on a wild goose chase.

Had his cousin decided on a whim to take Mallow when he could not find Marigold at home? It seemed likely.

Sick bastard.

Leo hopped over Lady Eloise's high gate and followed the sound of Mallow's barking. The little imp had easily crawled beneath the gate and was now growling and baring his teeth at a shadow behind Eloise's prized lilac trees.

As Leo approached, a dim light suddenly filtered into the garden. Someone had lit a lamp in Eloise's parlor. *Blast.* Until this moment, the garden had been plunged in a moonless darkness, allowing Leo to approach the shadow without being seen. He now noticed the glint of steel in the man's hand and dove just as a shot rang out.

A burning sensation exploded in his left shoulder.

He was too riled to care and fired a shot in response. But he knew he had missed when Mallow, still barking, tore back onto the street.

Leo always carried two pistols as well as two knives. He now removed the second pistol from its sheath, warned Eloise's butler to get back inside when he opened the parlor doors leading onto her terrace to peer out, and then Leo took off after the prowler who could only be his cousin.

But getting shot had slowed him down more than he liked to admit. He was bleeding and his head was spinning, but he was not letting the bastard get away.

Eloise's gate was open by the time he reached it, and Mallow was already halfway down the street, growling at an escaping form.

The moon was hidden behind a blanket of clouds. If not for a lone lamp glowing at the end of the street, Leo would never have been able to make out the retreating form.

More lamps were now being lit among the Chipping Way townhouses, for the shots exchanged had awakened the neighbors who were now peering out their windows.

He hoped they would remain indoors to allow him a clean shot of the villain, but his heart sank when he saw two people emerge from his home. Sterling was holding a lantern while Marigold held a rifle that appeared to be twice her size. Did she know how to fire the weapon? She would break her shoulder from the force of the recoil if she did not hold it properly, assuming she got off a shot before Cummings shot her. "I told you to get back inside!"

"Get down, Leo!" she cried and raised the rifle.

Another shot split the air and someone shrieked in pain. It was a high-pitched shriek, and he could not tell whether it was a man or a woman's cry.

"Damn it, Marigold! Did you hurt yourself? Get back inside!"

258 I MEARA PLATT

"It wasn't me," she called back.

The man was still moving. In fact, now limping toward Marigold with pistol raised. Leo ran toward him, but he was too far away to tackle him. He raised his arm and aimed his pistol to take his shot. The pistol jammed. He tossed it aside and took out his knife. "Cummings! Here I am. Why don't you come after me?"

"With pleasure, Muir." His cousin turned and aimed his pistol at Leo, his face distorted with hatred.

Leo was about to hurl his knife straight into his cousin's heart, when another shot rang out. His cousin laughed as it appeared to miss him, but suddenly shrieked again and then dropped like a stone. His head hit the street with a sharp crack and then a splattering sound. Had the shot struck him, after all? Well, it did not matter since the fall had finished the job. His skull was split open and his brains now oozed onto the cobblestones.

Leo carefully approached the prone form and saw his neighbor, Romulus Brayden, also cautiously advancing. "I did not think your shot got him," Leo muttered, now leaning over his cousin's motionless body.

"It wasn't mine," Romulus said, "I only fired the first one that grazed his leg."

They both stared at Marigold as she ran forward dragging the heavy rifle. Sterling was at her heels, the lantern swaying back and forth in his hand. Her eyes looked wild in the golden light. She appeared horror-stricken and about to faint. "Did I kill him? Oh, Leo! Am I a murderess?"

"For defending yourself and your husband from a madman? No, love. No one would ever consider it murder."

"I only meant to distract him by shooting over his head." She seemed ready to toss up her accounts.

"You didn't aim high enough," Romulus muttered.

"You didn't do this," Leo said, grabbing her rifle and catching her in his arms just as her knees began to buckle. "Sweetheart, don't faint on me."

She let out a sob. "I didn't mean to kill him."

"Sterling, take this damn rifle." He then turned to Romulus. "Watch him carefully, he's dangerous and may be faking."

Romulus felt for a pulse, and then began to check his cousin's body for weapons. "No, Leo. He's dead as a doornail."

Marigold struggled to catch her breath. "Oh...I did kill him."

"As anyone else in their right mind would have done," Leo insisted. "But you didn't kill him."

Mallow was now leaping up and down beside them.

"I don't believe it." Romulus inhaled sharply and then looked up at them. "Marigold, it is as Leo said. You missed him completely. The only shot that hit its mark was mine, and I only got him in the leg. He must have tripped over a rock or something. The blow to the head when he fell is what killed him."

Leo began to laugh. "Yes, he tripped over something, all right."

Marigold frowned up at him. "What is so funny?"

"Gallows humor, love. What perfect irony." He kissed her on the nose. "You didn't kill him, Marigold. It was a fierce lion by the name of Mallow who tripped him up and brought him down. This is why the little fellow has been hopping up and down and barking at us. He's been trying to tell us he took care of my cousin. Well done, Mallow."

Marigold bent down to scoop the dog up in her arms. "My hero," she said, now snuggling him and cooing at him as though he were a newborn babe. "Did the bad man hurt you? My poor, brave boy. Who's going to get a bath and a treat? *You* are. Oh, yes, you are."

Leo stared down at his own grimy form. "How about me?"

He could also do with a treat, namely Marigold nakedly cuddling him. But he would not hold his breath for that to happen. Tonight, he would likely be left to his own bath and his own bed while Mallow grabbed all the attention.

Sighing, he took them both into his embrace. "Mallow has a little cut on his leg, but otherwise seems fine."

Sterling pointed toward the house. "Dr. Farthingale is still here tending to the Bow Street runners. They'll both live, thankfully. I think he ought to look after you and Mallow next, my lord."

"Yes, Leo. Have him tend to you both." Marigold put a hand on his arm to lead him inside and then emitted a soft cry. "You're bleeding! Why didn't you tell me?"

"It is nothing. Just a graze." He'd forgotten about his arm in the ensuing chaos.

By this time, everyone on Chipping Way was awake and out of their homes. They were a motley group, milling around in their nightclothes. Violet rushed out to Romulus to make certain he was unharmed. He rose to stand between his curious wife and Cummings' body. "The danger has passed, love." He gave her a kiss on the forehead. "Go back inside. Hyacinth might awaken."

Violet ran her hands over her husband's body to make certain he had come to no harm. "All right," she said, satisfied Romulus had not been shot. "Don't be long. Tell me everything when you return."

"I will, you snoopy Farthingale." He kissed her again and watched as she scooted back to their house. A moment later, she peered out of an upper floor window to watch as her husband once again knelt beside the body.

John and Sophie Farthingale, along with Pruitt, their butler, opened their gate and ventured onto the street. "What in blazes happened here?" John asked.

Leo wanted to go inside and leave the explanations until tomorrow. But he and Marigold would have no time tomorrow either…well, it was already tomorrow and the sun was now starting to rise. Their lanterns were no longer necessary as night now turned to grayish dawn. "Your brother is at my house, John. He's tending to some wounded Bow Street runners. We've had quite a bit of excitement at the house."

"But Marigold is fine?" Sophie asked.

Leo nodded.

"Thank goodness." John now arched an eyebrow. "Did this excitement have anything to do with Marigold?"

"Well, yes. In a way. All is well now," Leo assured him. "You may as well come inside and we'll fill you in on what has happened. I doubt anyone is going to get any sleep tonight."

"Does the invitation include us?" Lady Eloise asked, scurrying toward them with her faithful Watling beside her.

It was a veritable party on the street.

"Yes, why not? Although I doubt Lady Withnall will forgive

you for getting the gossip first," Leo teased.

They were all about to step inside Leo's house when Homer Barrow arrived with the two Bow Street men who had assisted him in capturing the churl holding Mallow at the White Rose tavern.

Not a minute later, the magistrate and several of his constables arrived.

Ian showed up on their heels. "You've been busy, Leo. I heard you were back. Before you ask who told me, I am not at liberty to reveal my sources." He glanced at Cummings' body still lying on the street at the spot where Mallow had taken him down. "What happened here?"

"This is what we would like to know," John Farthingale muttered.

"Leo did not kill him." Marigold stepped protectively in front of him, although he certainly did not need protecting now that Cummings was dead. In any event, he did not need his soft, but extremely stubborn wife, getting between him and danger. "Uncle George has opened an infirmary in our home, which is a good thing because Leo has been shot and Mallow has a cut on his leg."

She motioned for everyone to follow them in. "I'll have Cook put the kettle on for tea and set out some cakes for us. Please make yourselves comfortable in the parlor. We won't be long, but Uncle George must tend to Leo first."

She carried Mallow to the stairs and frowned at Leo when he did not immediately follow her.

"Right, I'm coming." He raked a hand across the nape of his neck. "Ian, do you mind waiting a few minutes for my report?"

"I don't think I have a choice. You had better listen to your wife. We'll be fine. We're all family anyway. I'll grab a glass of your finest brandy. John, care for one?"

"Why not?" he muttered. "Thank goodness we're running out of Farthingale nieces to sponsor."

Sophie laughed. "Oh, I'm sure we'll have more descend on us. Admit it, John. You would die of boredom, otherwise."

"My dear, I shall survive quite happily without crazed killers terrorizing our street. In fact, I long for the day when it shall be just the two of us in that big, sprawling house."

"Don't forget, we still have Hortensia."

John sighed. "Ah, yes. Ian, I'll need that drink."

As the others followed John into the parlor, Leo and Marigold went upstairs to Leo's bedchamber. Mallow was still curled in Marigold's arms, quite content to remain there all evening.

Ethan bustled in. "My lord, let me help you off with your clothes."

"Just my shirt, Ethan. No time for another bath this evening. Everyone's waiting downstairs for my report." Once his shirt was off, he sank onto the stool by his hearth with an aching groan. "Bring me fresh water and several cloths."

No metal had lodged in his shoulder, thankfully. It was just a graze, but that hot metal had done a job of tearing up his flesh. Marigold looked on, nibbling her lip as she fretted. "Leo, what can I do to help?"

"Nothing, love. Just stand beside me. I need to look at you and know you are all right."

She nodded. "I am fine."

Leo would have preferred Marigold's sweet hands on him, but she was still holding Mallow and he did not have the heart to deprive the little fellow of the comfort of her arms. When Ethan brought him the ewer now filled with clean water, Leo poured it into its accompanying basin, then took one of the cloths and stuck it in the water to thoroughly wet it. He then began to delicately wipe the blood away. "Ethan, fetch me a bottle of brandy. Not my best, this isn't for drinking."

"Right away, my lord." He ran downstairs, leaving Leo alone with Marigold once more.

"How are you holding up, love?" Now that he had removed his shirt, she was taking in his scarred back and bloodied shoulder. He feared her soft heart had reached the limit of what it could handle.

"Not very well, if you must know," she said with a shaky laugh. "I cannot bear to see you hurt."

"This looks worse than it is. My worry was for your injuries."

"Mine?" Her eyes rounded in surprise. "I wasn't hurt at all."

"You fired my rifle. That must have bruised your shoulder." He continued to wipe away the blood from his own shoulder as he spoke.

"Oh, that." She nodded. "A little bruise. I hardly feel it. Oh, Leo! He might have killed you tonight! The fiend, lurking around our home, hurting everyone who got in his way while hoping for a chance at you."

He stared at her. "Marigold, he did not know I had returned to London. He was coming for you."

Her face drained of color and she sank onto a chair beside him.

In all this time, had she not realized?

"He grabbed Mallow out of desperation because he could not find you at home."

"Leo, are you serious?"

He nodded. "Thank goodness you decided to attend Lord Finchley's ball. He must have assumed you would be a sweet, obedient wife and remain home while I was away. Marigold!" He dropped the wet cloth into the basin and leaped to his feet, wrapping an arm around her as she began to sway.

"Oh, Leo! What a disgusting creature! Is it a sin to kick a man when he is already dead?"

CHAPTER 18

MARIGOLD WATCHED QUIETLY as her Uncle George cleansed Leo's wound, applied several stitches that would now add another scar to his already scarred body, and then bandaged his shoulder. He quickly did the same to Mallow's leg, although the little spaniel did not require stitches. But her uncle cleansed and bandaged his leg just to be sure the cut would not get infected before it had time to properly heal. Mallow enjoyed exploring, and Marigold was never sure where he dug or what he dug up when left on his own in the garden. Oftentimes, he returned needing a bath before being permitted back into the house.

Leo donned the fresh shirt Ethan had left for him.

Marigold smothered her disappointment now that Leo's magnificent body was properly covered. His broad shoulders and taut muscles never failed to melt her insides. But he was paying no attention to her at the moment, for he was all business and needed to give Ian his report. "George, care to join us downstairs for refreshments and gossip?"

Marigold's uncle grinned. "No, you'll fill me in later. I need to stay close to those Bow Street runners. These next few hours are critical. But I will have a cup of tea and a sandwich, if you have some on hand."

Marigold nodded. "I'll have Martha bring up a tray for you at once. Fruit, cheese, bread, cakes, cold ham, and whatever else you'd like. I've had a bedchamber prepared for you, as well. Just tug on the bellpull if you require anything more."

"Thank you, Marigold." He put the roll of bandages back in his medical bag and then returned to his patients.

Ethan also excused himself to attend to the latest set of Leo's bloodied clothes.

Leo now rose to head downstairs, but Marigold held him back a moment. "Leo…"

He arched an eyebrow. "What is it, love?"

She shook her head. "I owe you an apology. How could I have been so heartlessly cruel to you?"

He put a finger to her lips. "No, sweetheart. You've kept me sane while I was on the brink of madness. But the ordeal is over now. I am avenged and ready to move on to enjoy the happy marriage you have offered me."

She cast him a soft smile despite her obvious turmoil. "All thirty days of it?"

"I think we've moved beyond that, haven't we?" His grin was equally affectionate. "Thirty *years* is more what I have in mind. Sixty years, if we are so fortunate. I don't ever want to be without you, Marigold."

"Good heavens. I am so in love with you, Leo. I don't think it is possible to love someone more fiercely than I love you. I want you to know how sorry I am that I ever berated you. Obviously, I was the fool and did not fully appreciate how badly you were hurting."

"You were my splendid angel when I had nothing left in me but that raging beast." He kissed her, a beautiful kiss that was soft and also passionate. "Now it is my turn to give you advice that you will likely ignore. However, you are to give your speech and then a lecture in a few hours, sweetheart. Everyone will understand if you retire to your bedchamber instead of joining us downstairs."

"And miss a word of what you have to say? I shall be drummed out of the Farthingale snooping society in disgrace," she teased. "Besides, they won't stay long and I couldn't fall asleep without you lying next to me. I couldn't, Leo."

"All right." He held out his hand and she eagerly took it.

Marigold walked downstairs with Leo and Mallow, her two

wounded warriors. As soon as Leo sat down, Mallow hopped onto his lap, curled into a tight ball, and promptly fell asleep.

Well, Leo was the little fellow's hero, too.

Listening to Leo's account of the evening, Marigold felt even more ashamed of herself for giving Leo a hard time about his cousin when the man was clearly every bit as wretched as Leo had claimed. She marveled that Leo had endured four years of a brutal imprisonment and still retained his humanity.

It spoke to the nobility of his soul.

She had experienced a few hours of agony over Mallow's abduction and wanted to take her fists to that dead man's body. How could she have been so glib? So righteous and imperious? And all the while, Leo had been in agonizing torment.

Despite everything, Leo had never turned his anger on her.

This also spoke to how fine a man he was.

She looked up at him, wishing she could tell him how much she admired and adored him. But he was now filling in Ian and the rest of his audience on all that had transpired. While he did so, she quietly went about pouring tea and serving refreshments to everyone in the room.

By the time Ian and the magistrate had finished questioning Leo, and the constables had carted the body away, the sun was coming up and birds were now twittering in the treetops. As for Mr. Barrow, he'd chosen to grab a few hours of sleep in another of their guest chambers in order to look in on his men.

By the time everyone else left to return to their homes, Marigold could hardly move her legs to make her way upstairs.

She had so much she wanted to say to Leo, but all thoughts fled when she entered their bedchamber. She did not remember slipping out of her gown, or climbing into bed, or setting her head upon her pillow. She was asleep on her feet and could remember nothing after she had entered her bedchamber, except for ogling Leo as he removed his shirt and then wrapped his arms around her as he led her to bed.

This was all she ever needed, to be in his arms.

Jenny woke her up what felt like five minutes later but had actually been four hours. "My lady, it is ten o'clock. You will never make it to the Huntsford Academy on time if you do not get up now."

"Let my husband go first." Marigold felt along her bed, but Leo was not there. She sat up, still groggy. "Where is he?"

"Checking on the injured Bow Street men. He's already washed and dressed, and has had his breakfast."

"Gad, that man is irritating. Must he be perfect in everything? He is the one who ought to be exhausted and yet he is awake and perky as a daisy."

Jenny giggled. "Well, he is not exactly perky. He is usually frowning and grumbling unless you are around. You are the one who makes him smile."

Marigold found this heartwarming. "I make him smile?"

Jenny nodded. "But he won't be smiling if he sees you still abed when there are a hundred people waiting for you to make your speech at the Huntsford Academy. Mr. Barrow has already headed over there. He wants his men in place well before the ceremonies start."

There was a knock at her door.

Marigold hoped it was Leo, but it turned out to be some of their staff bringing up the tub Jenny must have ordered for her. As soon as the others left, all save Jenny who had remained to assist her, she scampered out of bed, tossed off her nightclothes…who had changed her into those? Then she sank into the tub and scrubbed herself while Jenny washed her hair.

Once done, she donned her robe and sat on the window seat while brushing out her hair. Jenny had opened the window to allow in the fresh air and Marigold caught the scent of lilacs now in bloom. The sun was brightly shining and it promised to be a beautiful day.

The birds were still chirping in the trees.

Well, a lot had happened last night and even her feathered friends must have had something to say about Leo's horrid cousin and the manner in which he met his demise.

Her housekeeper knocked at her door and then quietly poked her head in. "My lady, I thought you might prefer to have your breakfast in your bedchamber this morning. I had Cook prepare something light since your stomach might be in a roil after last night's excitement. Not to mention today's opening ceremonies at the Huntsford Academy."

"Thank you, Martha." Her stomach was in a knot of anticipation, for she had never given a lecture before or even a short, introductory speech. She could not handle more than a cup of hot cocoa and a bland crumpet to tide her over.

Her hair was still damp, but Jenny styled it in an elegant, upward sweep that would frame her face softly once her hair dried.

For today's events, she donned a cream silk gown and a pale green pelisse with gold silk trim that went over the gown. The outfit was completed by a gold silk belt that wrapped around her body just below the bodice and tied at the front with an elegant, gold clasp. She donned pale green slippers and a jaunty hat that resembled a French beret with a pale green feather sticking out of it.

Leo strode in as she was about to go in search of him.

He folded his arms across his chest and leaned against the bedpost. "Love, you look beautiful."

She blushed. "You are looking quite handsome yourself."

Dear heaven, this wasn't the half of it. He looked magnificent, clad in dark jacket, buff trousers, shirt of crisp, white lawn, a silk cravat, and a waistcoat of forest green that matched the color of his eyes and seemed to enhance the beauty of them. "Leo, you do not even look tired. How do you manage it? Jenny made me lie back for a full ten minutes holding cucumber slices over my eyes to take away the purple circles under them."

He moved toward her now, wrapping his arms around her and nuzzling her neck. "That explains why you are so delicious."

She laughed. "Oh, you beast. You smell wonderful, too. I will never get out of this bedchamber if you don't stop tempting me. Did Ethan add fragrant oils to your bath again this morning?"

He groaned. "Yes, and do not encourage him. A man should not smell like a flower garden."

She brushed her hand along his cheek and the line of his jaw. "He did a nice job shaving you, too."

"I shaved myself. I am not completely helpless."

She rested her hand against his jaw. "No," she said in a ragged whisper, "you are quite amazing."

He kissed her lightly. "So are you, love. Are you ready? Our carriage is waiting out front."

She nodded. "How are the Bow Street runners doing? May I take a moment to look in on them? And Uncle George, is he still here?"

"George left an hour ago. The men are doing well and Martha is treating them like royalty."

"Good, they deserve to be. Mr. Barrow and his other men will be guarding the Huntsford exhibits. I hope all goes smoothly today."

"It will. Enjoy the day, Marigold. It is your time to sparkle." He kissed her again. "But you always do. You are my beautiful ray of sunshine."

After personally thanking each Bow Street runner and making certain they had been adequately fed and pampered, she went downstairs with Leo to fetch her notes and bone samples from his study. "Oh, I need another moment for Mallow before we go. Where is he? Keeping out of trouble, I hope."

"He's in the garden munching on a bone. Must be scraps from the kitchen." He opened the door to his study and stood aside as she entered. "I suppose Cook must have taken pity on him after his ordeal yesterday...or...blast! How did that little devil get in here?"

Marigold's papers and bone samples had been neatly stowed in a pouch atop his desk, but those bone samples were now strewn all over the floor. "Love, I'm so sorry."

Marigold was off in a shot after her spaniel. "Mallow! Bad dog! Oh, you are a very bad dog!"

Mallow's ears perked.

He leaped to his feet as she tore out of the house and ran toward him.

"Give me that bone, you little imp!" She ought to have been angry, but found herself laughing instead because Mallow was regarding her so innocently. Thank goodness he hadn't chewed her papers. The other bones could easily be put in order while on the carriage ride. She had plenty to pass around to show the audience. In true lion fashion, Mallow had grabbed the biggest one.

She hoped his little teeth had not done too much damage to what they believed was part of a leg bone from an ancient wolf.

Something about this scene felt familiar.

She glanced toward the study and realized Leo was watching her.

Her heart caught in her throat upon noticing his expression. It was as though the weight of the world had lifted off his shoulders.

There was pure happiness in his smile.

Of course, they had done this before. He had first met her while chasing Mallow around his garden. What was he thinking now?

CHAPTER 19

LEO LAUGHED WHILE watching from his study window as his wife chased her wayward dog around the garden. "Sterling, can you believe this?"

He and Sterling had quickly gathered Marigold's bones and put them back in numerical order. All save bone number 5 that Mallow had in his grip. They were now peering out the window, watching Marigold attempt to catch the nimble hound.

She was not doing too well.

"Mallow, you bad, bad dog!" she scolded as the little imp raced into the rhododendron. She was about to lunge in after him when Mallow darted out the other side, still dragging the bone.

"Shall I help her, my lord?" Sterling said, trying not to chuckle.

Marigold was also laughing and did not appear at all put out.

Leo's heart melted. "No, I'll go in a moment."

This is how he had first set eyes on Marigold. Best day of his life. Here they were a month later and he knew his life would be wonderful and ridiculous every day that she was with him.

"Sterling, I love that woman," Leo muttered.

"Your admission is wasted on me, my lord. I think perhaps you ought to be telling this to your wife."

"Indeed." Still laughing, Leo hurried out into the garden.

He had hired a renowned landscape designer to make his garden a place of peace and solace. But this chaos was so much better. He grabbed Marigold before she could dive into the forsythia. "You'll never get the pollen off your gown, love. I'll catch him."

"Oh, Leo. Is this not familiar?" She smiled up at him, her eyes sparkling and her smile pure sunlight.

"Yes, how can I ever forget the day you upended my life?" He kissed her on the cheek. "I fell in love with you as I watched you and Mallow destroy my flower beds." He released her to reach into a yew bush where Mallow had next chosen to hide. "Success!" He extracted one dog still holding onto a bone that was bigger than his little self.

"Drop it, Mallow," he said in a tone of authority.

The little spaniel let the bone fall to the ground.

"Good boy." Leo scratched him behind his ears while Sterling, who had run out after them with wet cloth in hand, wiped drool off the bone before handing it over to Marigold.

She was still casting Leo her sunshine smile that warmed the deepest recesses of his heart. "Shall we go, love?"

"Yes," she said with a nod, "we had better hurry or we'll be late."

Leo handed Mallow over to Martha who had run outside as well. "Take care of the little sultan."

She giggled and scurried inside with him.

Now ready to leave for the Huntsford Academy, Marigold settled beside Leo in the carriage, her body pressed to his as though they were sewn together. He expected she was still a bit shaken from last night's excitement. Not to mention, her big speech followed by her lecture was today.

He watched as she rifled through the pouch and counted the bones, settling the gnawed bone in its proper place. "I'm glad you are with me, Leo."

"So am I, love. You'll be amazing."

"The exhibit will be amazing. But I hope to instill wonder in the hearts of all who attend today."

He took her hand and gave it a light squeeze. "You certainly have captured my heart."

The line of museum visitors waiting to get in was already around the corner by the time he and Marigold arrived. He hurried her inside, relieved to see Homer Barrow and his runners already in place. The danger from Denby, Beldon, and Cummings had passed, but it was not so easy for him to relax while in a crowd.

Perhaps he never would.

The opening ceremony began. Huntsford gave his speech and then Adela had her turn. Marigold stepped up next. Her enthusiasm as she welcomed everyone to the new exhibit was infectious. She was ebullient and the crowd cheered wildly when she finished her address.

Perhaps he had cheered loudest.

Once the speeches were over, the exhibit opened and visitors were guided through the museum to the Hall of Dragons. Leo took a moment to check in with Homer Barrow. "M'lord, how are my men, Arthur and Henry?"

"Doing well. George Farthingale felt comfortable enough to leave their side. He'll return later. My housekeeper knows to summon him if there is any sudden change."

"It is very good of you to take them in and treat them as family. Not many would have been so generous."

Leo knew how petty and disdainful some in the Upper Crust could be. "They protected my wife, as I should have been doing instead of riding off to Exeter."

"But you rode back, my lord. Who knows what Lord Cummings might have done had you not been there to stop him? Does one no good to fret about what might have been or what should have been. All that counts is the present and what we make of it."

Leo watched as Marigold continued to charm everyone. As the hour approached for her lecture, he entered the lecture hall and took a seat beside Syd, Gory, and the Thorne brothers. "Marigold put her heart into preparing this talk," Gory whispered. "You will be impressed."

The hall was overflowing with those who wished to hear her speech. Marigold easily spotted him in the front row since those seats had been reserved for family. Her smile was wide and her eyes lit up. Worried he hadn't noticed her, she waved to him.

He smiled and winked, then blew her a kiss.

Moments later, the hall fell silent as Adela introduced Marigold. "Please join me in welcoming Lady Muir."

Marigold stepped up to the lectern. "Since the dawn of man..."

The hour flew by.

The crowd was enthralled by the bones she passed around. Someone remarked on the bite marks on bone number 5. Marigold cleared her throat. "Yes, well. Sometimes wild dogs get to them before we do."

Syd snorted. "Wild dogs? By the name of Mallow, by any chance?"

"It is within the realm of possibility," Leo remarked.

Everyone got to their feet and cheered when she finished her talk. She remained beside the lectern graciously answering questions.

Ambrose walked over to him. "Well? How does it feel to be married to London's sensation of the Season?"

"Feels good. I had no idea she was this knowledgeable about ancient artifacts." This gem had been sparkling before his very eyes, but he had been so caught up in his dark thoughts, he'd paid no attention to how much of a treasure she was. He must have hurt her feelings quite badly, so lost was he in thinking only of himself.

Yes, he had told her that he was proud of her and encouraged her to pursue her passion for archeology. But it was all superficial bluster because he was not really paying attention to all she was quietly accomplishing on her own.

He hoped his presence here today would make up for some of it. Marigold, with her sweet, kind heart had already forgiven him.

He knew he needed to do much more to earn that forgiveness.

"She fits right in with Adela, Syd, and Gory," Ambrose remarked. "They are very intelligent women. This is partly the reason I opened the Huntsford Academy. No one is shut out. All scholars are welcome."

"Is this your idea of recreating ancient Athens in England?"

Ambrose nodded. "Something like that. More in honor of my father. This was really his dream, but my brothers and I understood the importance of it and were determined to bring it to fruition. The Hall of Dragons is a spectacular success. We'll be adding to it, of course. But I'm also going to be opening a forensic laboratory. I'm thinking of asking Gory to be in charge of it. The girl is brilliant."

Leo arched an eyebrow. "That will cause an uprising among the scientific community, not to mention your wealthy donors. Will anyone use your services if they know a woman is in charge?"

"Perhaps not at first. But one must start somewhere, is that not so?"

Leo nodded.

"Just look at the enthusiastic responses Adela and Marigold have received with their presentations. The public does not care. It is only the so-called gatekeepers who are afraid of them and would rather stifle innovation than allow outsiders into their ranks. Others are kept out for the sole purpose of protecting their territory. It matters nothing to them that their ideas are often outdated and inflexible."

As the day drew to an end and the museum was now closing, Marigold sought Leo out. "There you are. I thought you might have gone home without me," she teased.

"Never, love." He kissed her on the forehead. "I heard your opening speech and then I was in the front row to hear your lecture. I had no idea you were an authority on ancient bones."

"I'm not really. Adela knows more than I do. And Gory and Syd certainly know more about anatomy than either of us. But this is the fun of our explorer's club. The ideas that flow are inspiring."

"Are husbands allowed?"

She nodded eagerly. "Yes, of course."

He caressed her cheek. "I listened as everyone raved about you. I even gave some young newspaper man an interview about you. He said his name was Hawkins and he identified himself as a reporter for one of the gossip rags. Ambrose assured me it was all right to talk to him, that the man had been with you on the Devonshire dig."

Marigold nodded. "I think he is sweet on Miss Appleby. She's the talented artist in our group who sent Mr. Smythe-Owens the sketches she copied off the cave walls. Mr. Hawkins is also an amateur archeologist and has joined our explorer's club. However, his gossip sheet assignments prevent him from attending most of our meetings. Leo, have you been inside the Hall of Dragons yet?"

"No." He raked a hand through his hair. "Some things are not so easily overcome. Dark room. No windows. Maybe next time."

"I understand."

But she looked disappointed. The skull was her treasured find. The display had stunned even the most jaded of museum patrons. Even the Duke of Wooton had come by, which was quite a coup since the man was never known to leave the Home Office. After viewing the exhibit, Wooton had come up to him and offered his congratulations. Of course, Leo had done nothing. The triumph belonged to Marigold and Adela. "I'm sorry, love. Truly."

She placed her arm in his. "Leo, you *never* have to apologize to me for this."

He frowned. "But it is something you cherish."

She looked up at him, his little ray of sunshine. "I cherish you more. Let's go home." Then she laughed. "I almost fainted when someone in the audience commented on Mallow's bite marks on that bone. Did you hear them?"

He chuckled, too. "Yes, love. You handled it beautifully."

She rolled her eyes. "Dear heaven. I was sure Adela and Ambrose would be furious, but they were remarkably understanding. I suppose it helped that my lecture was well received. An anonymous benefactor just pledged a tidy sum toward completion of the forensic laboratory. Of course, it could be a prank. But Ambrose will check it out."

They had just left the museum and were about to walk to their waiting carriage when Leo came to a sudden halt.

Marigold looked up at him. "What's wrong? Did you forget something?"

"Yes, we have to go back. Come with me." He led her to the Hall of Dragons which was now empty of visitors since the museum was closing. The only ones left in the place were Marigold's friends, Adela, Syd, and Gory, and Huntsford and his brothers, but they were all in Huntsford's office. Even the Bow

Street runners were gone, leaving just a few night guards on duty.

Marigold gasped when she realized what he meant to do. "Leo, it isn't necessary. You have nothing to prove to me."

"Think of it as something I need to prove to myself."

She nibbled her lip. "You are very thickheaded, aren't you?"

He laughed. "Yes. Take me through the exhibit, love."

"We'll need a lantern. Even though the Hall of Dragons is kept in darkness, the visitors would be falling all over each other if we did not have some light to guide them through here. Ah, Mr. Smythe-Owens has yet to put these away." She pointed to a table of lanterns beside the door to the exhibit.

Leo lit one and held it up as they entered the tomb-like hall. "It's very dark," he muttered.

"Yes, but it is no different than being out on a moonless night. It isn't the darkness that rattles you."

"One feels the air rushing about you when one is outdoors. One sees stars. And hears birds and crickets chirping. One can breathe." He coughed and his heart began to race. "Perhaps this wasn't the best idea."

"We are almost there, Leo. And I am with you. I won't let go of you. Hold the lantern up higher so the light shines toward the ceiling. Look. There's my dragon. Doesn't its skull look marvelous?"

The breath caught in his throat.

He had never seen any sight so wondrous. This flying creature's wings spanned the width of the hall and it appeared to come to life in the glow of firelight. Its eyes glistened like fiery rubies, and its jaws were open as though it was about to grab an unsuspecting prey in its jaws.

Leo stood in awe.

The torment of his years of captivity began to melt away. Perhaps he was meant to endure great hardship in order to appreciate the greater joy in marrying Marigold. What would have become of him had he never been held prisoner? He would have returned to London after the Carpathian mission and circulated among the *ton*, for certain.

Would he have married before ever meeting Marigold?

By returning to England after an uneventful trip, would Cummings, his ogre of a cousin, have succeeded in catching him unaware and killing him?

He shook out of those thoughts.

None of this mattered. Life had taken its course and he was married to Marigold, this amazing woman who dreamed of the impossible and brought it to life. And she was not yet twenty.

She smiled up at him, an angel in the glow of firelight. "Impressed?"

"Yes, immensely." The room no longer felt like a tomb because she was with him. His soul was beginning to shed its burden because everything felt possible with her by his side. He was far from cured. Indeed, he was not going to come in here ever again unless there was a dire need.

Perhaps someday he would just walk in on his own and not feel the walls close in on him. But he already knew he could do it with Marigold by his side.

He took in the mural drawing, this recreation of mist and foliage that made it appear as though one was walking through a jungle. There were smaller displays within the vast hall, but he did not think he would hold himself together long enough to view those beyond a cursory glance as he was passing by.

Perhaps he would summon the courage another day.

Marigold led him out, saying nothing as he handed her the lantern and then doubled over breathing hard. But it took only a few breaths for him to return to himself. "Let's go home, Marigold."

"Yes, I am exhausted. Adela and Ambrose are hosting a reception tonight. We had better nap if we are to make it through the evening. And do not think of getting amorous, Leo. We really need to sleep."

He chuckled. "As you wish."

"Because we have all week to catch up on...*you know*," she continued as he led her to their carriage and helped her in. "And Gory told me the most outrageous story. You will never believe it because it is so outrageous."

He climbed in after her and instructed Collins to drive them home. Only then did he turn to her, his eyebrows arched in curiosity as the carriage drew away. "What has Gory told you? I would not believe half her stories. She has quite the ghoulish imagination."

Marigold blushed and cleared her throat. "It is not about dead things. It is about indiscreet liaisons in *carriages*."

He laughed. "Sex in a carriage, Marigold? What would any of you know about that? But isn't that an interesting idea?"

"No," she cried, now aghast and her eyes round in surprise. "It is shocking and utterly impractical. What if one were to arrive at one's destination early and hadn't...*finished* yet?"

He laughed again and drew her onto his lap. "Yes, that would be awkward."

She nestled against him. "And what if one were caught by the footman as he opened the door to receive the surprise of his life?"

"I am sure any experienced footman will have seen far worse."

"Worse than a lady who had no time to fix her gown or hair? I shudder to think of the spillage. And what of the man caught with his breeches down around his ankles?"

"And his bare arse pasted to the leather seat bench. That would be extremely uncomfortable in the heat of summer. He'd have to peel his naked arse off the hot leather."

"Ugh, Leo! Not to mention, who would ever want to sit there knowing he'd...*ew*?"

"So does this mean we are never to engage in a naughty liaison in a carriage?" He kissed her lightly on the lips and then kissed her slender throat. "Because I think we would be clever enough to do it right. There's something to be said for the bouncing that goes on when one is–"

"Leo!"

"Never mind, sweetheart. Forget I said anything. It shall never be mentioned again. Nor shall I think of it on our next trip to Devonshire."

"You would join me in Devonshire?"

"Of course." He grinned wickedly. "I'll take you in my carriage. It is a very long ride. Plenty of time to indiscreetly–"

"Leo!" She playfully swatted his arm. "Do not tease me, you

wretched man."

"Wouldn't think of it, love." When they returned home, he helped her out of the carriage and then led her upstairs to their quarters. Ethan and Jenny awaited them, but Leo ordered them to leave and not return until it was time to prepare for the Huntsford soiree.

"We are dead on our feet after last night's excitement," Marigold explained, although no explanation was required. By the look on *his* face, neither Jenny nor Ethan believed she would get a wink of sleep.

They bowed, keeping their heads down to hide their smirks, no doubt.

Leo tried to keep his hands off Marigold because she was tired and so was he.

The struggle was useless.

Similarly, she tried to keep her hands off him.

They spent the next two hours nakedly pawing each other.

But the hour of sleep they did manage was enough to hold them through the soiree.

Leo kissed Marigold on the cheek when they arrived at the Huntsford residence and she went off with her friends. Gory had some odd looking dead thing to show the ladies.

Dear heaven.

He retired to the cards room with Huntsford, his brothers, and Eloise's grandsons, Graelem and Gabrield Dayne.

Graelem was married to Marigold's cousin Laurel, and had been married longest of all of them. They had all been drinking, and Graelem now decided to spout his words of husbandly wisdom. "Men and women do not speak the same language, my friends. This is the secret to a long and happy marriage. Learn to take the cues and disappear into your study whenever you hear your wife respond to you with the following words: *Fine. Nothing. Go ahead. Really? Whatever.*"

"Not that lecture again." Gabriel was grinning from ear to ear. "Graelem, you do realize you are drunk."

"Yes, completely potted," Graelem agreed, "but also very happily married. These rules apply no matter the condition of the husband. Whether drunk or sober, always remember these words and be immediately wary if you hear your wife utter them. Take the word *fine*. What does it mean when your wife tells you something is *fine*?"

"That all is well," Julius ventured, chortling as he shuffled the cards.

Graelem took a sip of his brandy and then set the glass down on the table with a *thunck*. "No, you poor, deluded bachelor. *Fine*, especially when used during an argument, means your wife has decided the argument is over. She knows she is right and you need to shut up now or you will end the night sleeping in the kennels with your hounds."

Leo and the Huntsford brothers chuckled.

Graelem had more to say. "And when she tells you *nothing* is troubling her? Run away as fast as your legs will carry you. It means something is bothering her and you need to be worried she is going to take it out on you. Because she will. I refer to the kennels and hounds again."

Octavian groaned. "Are you suggesting we do not marry?"

"Not at all. Best decision of my life was to marry Laurel. I knew it the moment I set eyes on her. She had just trampled me with her horse and broken my leg, but things improved after that first encounter."

Leo sat back and listened, not remembering when he had ever felt so at ease. From his vantage point, he had a view of the parlor and could see his wife, Syd, Gory, and Adela still huddled over something dead and ancient. Marigold's eyes were wide and her smile was brighter than the candles gleaming in the crystal chandeliers.

Julius still held the cards in his hands and had not bothered to deal them out yet. "Tell me more, Graelem."

"When you want to do something and she is not thrilled with your decision but tells you *go ahead*...this is not giving you permission. This is a dare. You are going to lose this dare. Do not proceed unless you have an inexplicable desire to sleep in the kennels with your hounds."

"Should we be writing this down?" Octavian muttered,

holding his side as he tried to squelch his laughter.

"No! Do not write this down. She will see it and you will be sorry. If you do write it down, you are to memorize it immediately and then burn it."

"Pray, do continue," Leo said, now curious to hear the rest of Graelem's wisdom. Not that he ever had a worry about Marigold. She was too sweet ever to take anything out on him. If anything, if she were unhappy about something, she was more likely to hold it in. But did it not help to understand the cues she was giving off when something was bothering her?

Graelem cleared his throat and continued. "When she tells you to do *whatever* you want, this is also not permission. This is similar to *fine*. If you do this, you will regret the consequences because she is thinking long and hard on how you will pay for this mistake. You will once again be sleeping in the kennels."

"With the hounds," Leo, Octavian, and Julius laughingly said in unison.

"And next we get to *really*," Ambrose said. "What does this signify? I only ask because Adela has said this to me a time or two when we disagree over something. Which we rarely do, but it does come up on rare occasion."

"Ah," Graelem said, grinning at Ambrose. "*Really* is her polite way of telling you that you are a complete and utter arse and she cannot believe you would ever say anything so stupid."

Ambrose's brothers burst out laughing.

"Oh, Lord!" Octavian was going to tumble from his chair with laughter. "I knew I liked Adela. What a genteel way to tell you to go shove it."

Since Graelem had no more words to offer up, they proceeded with their card game. They were all in their cups, although Leo was probably soberest of all because one could not shed the caution ingrained after years under threat of death in a single day.

Danger still lurked, did it not?

There was the matter of Denby's cohorts still to be resolved, although Ian, along with the Duke of Wooton and the Crown agents who served in the Home Office, had most of them in custody and were about to dig up the last of the worms who had infiltrated the Foreign Office.

The scandal would be explosive.

He set aside his brandy, deciding he had better stay sober until all the traitors were rounded up.

Yes, he was being overly cautious.

Cummings and Denby were dead.

Beldon would either be imprisoned for life or banished from England.

As for himself, Denby's cohorts were never concerned about him. He was incidental to their operations. Nor were they ever his primary concern. Not that any of it mattered now that they were all about to be brought down.

But those years had affected him in so many ways. He had forgotten how to shed his cares and simply enjoy himself. However, the evening passed pleasantly enough, and he was quite mellow in the carriage ride home. He relaxed against the squabs and took his sleepy wife in his arms as the carriage made its way along the London streets. "I love you, Marigold," he whispered with aching sincerity.

She was on the verge of falling asleep, but muttered a sweet response. "I love you, too. I love you so much, Leo. I would do anything for you."

Anything?

"Even have sex with me now in the carriage?"

She sprang up as though someone had lit a fire under her sweet derriere. She frowned at him, and kept frowning at him. "Really?"

Graelem's warnings came to mind. "Just teasing, love. Oh, ha, ha. Just a jest. Wouldn't think of it. I'd probably get sores on my arse from the scratched leather."

"Are you blaming me now for scuffing up your leather seats with the crate that contained my skull and bones?"

"What? No? Most of the scratches were already there."

Her chest puffed as she emitted a huff. "Most?"

Lord above.

Why had he started this conversation?

"No, none. I mean none of it is your fault. It is all mine." He sighed. "Marigold, go back to sleep."

She nestled back against him and yawned. "Honestly, Leo. You sound awfully muddled. Did you have too much to drink? Well, it was a very long day for both of us. But...*whatever*."

Bollocks.

Was it starting already?

Were they falling into old married habits?

He moaned.

Marigold began to giggle. "Graelem gave you his words-to-look-out-for speech, didn't he? Laurel said he would. Good grief, Leo. You should have seen the look on your face."

He stared at her and chuckled. "Wicked woman! You had me going."

But did this mean Marigold would consider an indiscreet liaison with him in a carriage? Or not?

He was afraid to ask.

Nor would he ever, since he had no intention of sleeping in the kennels with Mallow. Not that the dog actually slept in a kennel. The little beast slept at the foot of their bed or by their fireplace on a plump pillow made specially for him.

He had dogs at his country estate, but none were spoiled as Mallow was. Marigold adored her little spaniel and Leo adored Marigold, so he was not about to contradict her wishes. He watched her as her eyes fluttered shut once again, and she soon fell asleep against his chest.

The past few days of danger and excitement had finally caught up to her. She remained in a deep slumber and did not stir when their carriage drew up in front of their home. Rather than rouse her, Leo carried her inside and up the stairs to their bedchamber.

She was so exhausted, she did not even wake when he undressed her. Her maid, Jenny, had set out her nightclothes. Marigold muttered unintelligibly as he shifted her out of her clothes and then tried to ease the nightgown over her head.

When he was done, he stripped out of his own clothes, then took all into his bedchamber to be left for Ethan and Jenny to attend to in the morning. He returned to Marigold's bed, as he always did, for as much as she liked curling up against him, he liked it more and needed the comforting feel of her body burrowing into him.

He sank onto the bed beside her and took a moment to watch her innocent face that was so beautiful by candlelight.

He'd spent four years in darkness questioning his fate. Why me? What have I done to deserve such torment?

Now, looking upon this sparkling light that was Marigold, he also questioned his fate. Why me? What have I done to deserve such happiness?

CHAPTER 20

Chipping Way, London
Six Years Later

MARIGOLD STARED AT her husband as he prepared for today's investiture ceremony for their new king, William IV. Leo had been installed as a Knight of the Most Ancient and Most Noble Order of the Thistle six years ago, and he certainly looked the part of a valiant knight now. Big, brawny, and magnificent. A warrior capable of defending Crown and country, although most of those granted knighthood had no military background.

But Leo was born with a proud and valorous heart.

A warrior's heart.

When he stood in his knightly garb at times like these, she felt as though he had the reborn soul of an ancient Celtic king. Even the motto of this most noble Order of the Thistle described him to the last detail. *Nemo me impune lacessit.* No one provokes me with impunity.

She thought of Denby and Cummings, both long since dead, and Beldon who was imprisoned for life and would never be set free, for his dealings had gone beyond mere envy of Leo, as it turned out. Denby had dragged him into other Crown dealings. Not often, but it only took the once or twice to bring him down along with Denby's other cohorts. In paying Denby to arrange for Leo's capture, he had given Denby and the others involved in the scheme to cheat the Crown a blackmail hold over him. It could be said he had a hold on them, too. But apparently, these were not men to cross and Beldon feared for his life.

It was a bad business all around.

But justice had been served.

These men had provoked Leo and met their fate.

She shook out of the unpleasant thought as she watched Ethan assist Leo into his attire that befitted a royal courtier, for this is how he was garbed, in shirt, doublet, breeches, and silk hose.

Marigold watched in awe as Ethan placed the magnificent, velvet mantle denoting his status as a Knight of the Order of the Thistle around his broad shoulders. Over that splendid robe was placed the riband and star. The star was a jewel-inlaid brooch that had the order's motto inscribed: *Nemo me impune lacessit.*

Marigold could not help but smile.

Leo looked so fierce and serious, yet she and Mallow ran roughshod over him, and he never once complained. She and Mallow had a propensity for leaving bones all over the house, she with her ancient relics, and Mallow with his leftover scraps from the kitchen.

She suspected Leo loved all of it, especially their little girls who thought of Leo as their moon and stars.

Tears formed in her eyes as the jeweled collar was placed over his head to rest upon his shoulders.

Here stands a knight.

Indeed, she could see Leo among King Arthur and his Knights of the Round Table.

"Are you ready, Sir Leonides?"

He arched his eyebrows. "Must we go? You know how I hate these formal affairs."

"You'll survive it, my brave and gallant hero. It is not every day England receives a new king." She had also taken care in choosing her attire, although it was much simpler for her. She only had to look smart by society's standards and not put on any elaborate renaissance gown.

The investiture of King William IV was to take place before hundreds of lords and ladies, with a good representation of her own family in attendance since many of her cousins had married into the nobility, including herself.

Who would have expected any such thing while growing up in Little Mutton?

When they arrived at Westminster Abbey, Leo was escorted into a chamber behind the nave while she was led to the pews. To her delight, Dillie and Adela were seated beside her, for their husbands were dukes of the highest rank, only the royal family being superior to them. Their husbands would be in the procession that included Knights of the various Orders, bishops, chancellors, highest ranking peers, not to mention the king, queen, and royal princes.

After the ceremony was over, it was time to welcome the new king.

Marigold smiled and bowed, and thoroughly enjoyed the reception that followed. She met crowned heads of state, princes royal, and even bowed before their newly invested king. But the moments she loved best were the precious few she had with Leo who was in demand and being pulled every which way. But he always spared a moment to touch her hand lightly or cast her a private smile.

He approached her now, his eyes alight and his smile enchantingly wicked. "Love," he whispered, putting his mouth to her ear just as she took a sip of a most delicious India tea, "I think this momentous occasion calls for a special celebration, just you and me. Sex. Carriage. Meet you outside in five minutes."

She choked on the tea and had a fit of coughing as it swallowed down the wrong way.

It had become a private jest between them. After two children and possibly a third on the way that Leo did not even know about yet because she had only begun to suspect the possibility a few days ago, they had certainly not done *it* in a carriage. Nor would they ever, if she had her way.

The very idea.

He would never be able to lace her back up properly or put her hair back in order, so everyone would know at once what they had done.

He knew the suggestion riled her.

Not that she was unreceptive to his advances, but their activities were confined to the bedchamber, and one naughty incident in Leo's library against his bookshelves that had led nine months later to Gwendolyn, their first child.

Others looked on in concern as she tried to recover her composure.

"Lady Muir will be fine in a moment," Leo said with a straight face, taking the cup from her hands before its contents spilled onto the exquisite, emerald silk gown designed for her by London's most sought after modiste just for this occasion. "She is a bit overwhelmed by all the pomp and splendor."

"Really, Leo?" she whispered after recovering from a coughing spurt he obviously found hilarious. *"Really?"*

The man was obviously bored and needed to be taken home before he caused more mischief.

He leaned in close again, his lips softly brushing against her ear, the light touch sending tingles shooting through her. "Sorry, love. Forgive your arse of a husband? I couldn't resist. I love you to pieces. I love you with all my heart and soul, and every breath in my body. But you are so deliciously prim and sweet, I couldn't resist."

She supposed she could forgive him.

After all, he loved her.

Her life was heaven because of it.

He was still leaning close, his breath warm against her neck and sending more tingles through her. "Lord, Marigold," he said with a groaning chuckle, "stop looking at me in that stern schoolmistress way. You know it drives me wild, and then I am going to kiss you senseless in front of everyone."

"I wasn't thinking of scolding you. I was thinking of something else."

He drew back to study her face, and then arched an eyebrow. "What were you thinking about? Not your skulls again."

"No, not skulls or bones, although it is in a way related." She smiled at him and began to tear up with the happiness of it.

He lowered his gaze to her bosom that had grown a little

larger, then her belly that had also seemed to be growing as had her appetite, then back up to her face. His eyes widened and he sucked in a breath. "Marigold...?"

The next words strangled in his throat and she saw everything he was feeling expressed in his usually stoic face. He was laid open, raw and exposed. No mask or facade to hide behind. No polite smile and distance kept. He was her lion at his most primal, and now he had not only her and their two girls, but another little cub on the way.

Perhaps this one would be a boy.

She could not think of anything more wonderful than a tiny Leo wreaking havoc in their household.

Discreetly, he took her hand in his. "Have I mentioned that I love you? Have I mentioned that you are the sun and the earth and the moon to me? Toss in all the stars in heaven, as well." He laughed as he raked a hand through his hair, and then began to look around. "You shouldn't be standing. Not in your delicate condition."

She wanted to throttle him because he was now going to guard her more closely than the king's guards watched over the Crown jewels. But she also wanted to throw her arms around him and kiss him. "Leo, I am feeling fine."

He would not stop staring at her. "I need to take you home."

"Really?"

He grinned. "Don't give me that *really, Leo, you are such an idiot* expression. It is not a stupid comment and I am not an arse for worrying about you while you are in a delicate condition."

"You are not taking me home. We are not permitted to leave until the king retires. Do not even think about it."

The reception finally ended in the early evening and they returned home to one of the sweetest sights Marigold had ever beheld. Their daughters were already in their nightgowns and slippers, freshly scrubbed and readied for bed, their damp hair neatly done up in braids. But they must have escaped their nanny, for they were chasing after Mallow who was tearing about the garden and darting in and out of the shrubbery.

Gwennie and Theodora giggled as Mallow darted into another

bush and then out of it only to start running circles around them, all while carrying… "Oh, Leo! The little scamp has stolen one of my new slippers! I haven't even worn them yet."

She tore into the garden. "Oh, Mallow! Bad dog! Give me that!"

Leo strolled out leisurely after her, grinning like a hyena as she chased after the little bandit, and holding her back when she attempted to dive in after him. "Marigold! Your condition."

"You might help," she grumbled.

"All right, love." He winked at the girls, and then called out in his most authoritative voice, "Mallow, come here!"

Mallow immediately trotted over to Leo and sat in front of him, tail wagging.

Leo bent on his haunches and gave him a few scratches behind the ears. "There's a good fellow. Drop the slipper."

Mallow dropped the slipper.

Marigold rolled her eyes.

Leo laughed.

Their housekeeper ran out to take Mallow back inside, and Jenny rushed out along with her to reclaim the stolen slipper.

Leo now turned to their girls who were looking up at him with their big, blue eyes, uncertain as to their fate. He jested that they were his little Marigolds because of their blue eyes and dark hair. Well, they did resemble her. And since Leo loved her, he simply melted over the girls. "Did you miss us, my darlings? Come give your Papa a kiss."

They rushed into his arms. "Papa! Papa! We are ever so sorry for Mama's ruined slipper. We didn't mean to let Mallow get at it. But they were so pretty and we wanted to try them on," Gwennie said.

"I'm sure your mama will forgive you. Accidents happen. Where is Nanny Welburne?"

Gwennie blushed. "We didn't mean it."

Leo arched an eyebrow. "What else didn't you mean to do? Besides letting Mallow at your mama's slippers."

"We spilled our milk," Theodora said, her big eyes tearing up as she regarded her father with trepidation.

"We spilled it on Nanny Welburne's gown," Gwennnie

clarified, her eyes also big as full moons and turning moist. "She had to change out of it and we promised to be good until she came back."

Leo tried to look severe, but Marigold noticed his lips twitching and knew he was never going to discipline the girls. "But instead of staying put in your room, you tiptoed into our bedchamber and tried on Mama's slippers?"

The girls nodded.

"They are ever so pretty," Gwennie said.

"Like fairy slippers," Theodora added.

"Then Mallow ran off with Mama's slipper and we wanted to get it back for her," Gwennie continued to explain, bringing their adventure full circle.

"You meant well, didn't you, my angels?" Leo said, excusing their misdeeds.

Good grief, the man was soft as pudding.

Marigold did not have the heart to discipline them, either. In truth, they were sweet girls and rarely misbehaved.

She looked on as they now showered kisses all over Leo's face.

That night, he showered kisses all over her face as she nestled in his arms. "How far along do you think you are, love?"

They were settled comfortably in bed. "It's too soon to tell, Leo. It may yet be a false alarm. I've missed one month of my courses and the second is late, but quite a bit has been going on in our lives. Anything could have thrown off my schedule."

He kissed her on the forehead. "Just slow down a little until we are sure."

"I will try, but Adela is preparing several new exhibits for the museum, a children's maze that will take them on different adventures depending on which direction they turn while finding their way through it. We are also designing a cave with drawings on the wall to replicate the feeling of walking back in time. Is it not fascinating?"

"Yes, love."

"Then we'll be hosting the explorer's club next Thursday in our home, and after that my cousins meeting is held here next Monday." She let out a breath. "But I will be careful not to overdo it, Leo."

She smiled as he drew her closer.

And sighed as he wrapped his arms completely around her.

"Are you happy, Leo?"

"Happy as a lark, Marigold." He kissed her again. "I have you, my ray of sunshine. Love you, sweetheart."

They fell asleep to the rhythmic chirrs of the night, the windows open to allow in a soft breeze, and the drapes left aside to allow in the morning light. Marigold did not think Leo would ever fully rid himself of the darkness that had gripped his soul in those terrible years.

Often, he would reach out to her in sleep, needing to hold onto her.

He called her his ray of sunshine.

She was going to give him all the sunlight her heart could provide. "Sweet dreams, Leo."

THE END

Dear Reader

Thank you for reading *Marigold and the Marquess*. Leo, the brooding, rather grumpy, handsome as sin marquess, had to fall head over heels in love with Marigold Farthingale, that little ray of sunshine. I hope you have been enjoying the latest in the Farthingale series, including *The Viscount And The Vicar's Daughter* and *A Duke For Adela*. Coming up next are the romances for Adela and Marigold's friends, Lady Sydney Harcourt and Lady Gregoria Easton. They'll find their matches with the Duke of Hunstford's (Adela's husband) brothers, Octavian Thorne (that big, hunky ox), and Julius Thorne, their very capable and confident younger brother.

I welcome you to all the stories (including several novellas) in the FARTHINGALE SERIES, and if you are in need of even more Farthingales, then please try my Book of Love series where you will meet a host of Farthingale cousins, all of them sweet and innocent young ladies who cannot seem to keep out of trouble. In fact, they attract trouble wherever they turn, especially when it involves some very steamy, alpha heroes and that mysterious, red-leather bound Book of Love. Next release in the Farthingale Series is *The Make-Believe Marriage* because Lady Sydney Harcourt and the Duke of Huntsford's brother, Captain Octavian Thorne, are going to have to do some quick thinking to keep her conniving father from selling her off in marriage to one of his creditors in settlement of a large debt. What are the chances Syd will fall in love with that big ox of a Thorne? Hint: I'd say they were pretty good. As for Julius and Gory? Our Regency goth debutante is going to turn to Julius for help when someone murders her odious uncle and she is worried that she might be accused, or worse, that she might be the next victim on the list.

Keep reading to enjoy the first chapter of *The Make-Believe Marriage*, and don't forget to grab your free Farthingale novella after the sneak peek.

SNEAK PEEK:
THE MAKE-BELIEVE
MARRIAGE
CHAPTER 1

London, England
September 1825

CAPTAIN OCTAVIAN THORNE'S head was pounding as he lay prone on the damp grass while trying to restore his senses after falling off the roof of Sir Henry Maxwell's townhouse in London's elegant Mayfair. It was dark, well after midnight on this rainy night, and he had taken the plunge while trying to stop Lady Sydney Harcourt from breaking into Sir Henry's bedchamber to steal her father's debt vouchers. Syd, who was fast becoming the bane of his existence, was now by his side, her bosom grazing his chest as she leaned over him to run her hands along his big, brutish body. "Leave me alone, Syd."

"Don't move, you big ox. I'm just making certain you haven't broken any bones. I did not mean to push you off the roof. I thought you were one of Sir Henry's men trying to stop me. You might have said something before I shoved you. What are you doing here?"

"Me? What in blazes are you doing here?"

"Trying to find my father's vowels and destroy them. Don't move yet," she said with urgency when he attempted to sit up. "Please, Octavian. You might have broken bones."

"And you might have been caught by Sir Henry," he grumbled back, angry enough to throttle her. "What do you think he would have done to you if he had found you skulking in his bedchamber?"

"Nothing I care to think about," she admitted, placing a soft hand upon his neck to run her fingers lightly across the nape before sliding her hands down his chest and leaving a fiery trail wherever she touched. "I saw him go out earlier. I knew he would not be home. Nor is he likely to return for at least another hour. He frequents those debauched gentlemen's clubs. Look at you, what a mess you are. You ought to know better than to climb onto those rain-slicked tiles."

"Stop lecturing me and stop touching me. I came here to rescue you. Sir Henry does not keep his business papers in his bedchamber, something I could have told you if you had bothered to ask me."

"He doesn't? How do you know this?"

"I have my sources," he shot back, his irritation growing along with his discomfort. He was wet, bruised, and still on fire because Syd's body was still practically atop his and she would not take her hands off him.

"Is the Admiralty investigating him?"

"None of your business."

She said nothing more as she cupped one of his hands in hers and ordered him to wriggle his fingers. "Good, they're all moving." She then ordered him to do the same with the other.

"I haven't broken any bones." He had merely fallen off the low roof and landed in dense shrubbery before rolling onto the wet grass. It had been raining until half an hour ago which was why both he and Syd were soaking wet. As for his injuries, they were minor. Only a small bump to his head acquired when his skull came in contact with a protruding tree branch.

"Octvian, do you think you can walk? Let me try to find us a hack and–"

"No, my carriage is around the corner. You're coming with me to the Thorne residence. I dare not deliver you back home. If you are desperate enough to sneak into Sir Henry's home, this can only mean your father intends to do something foolish involving you." He inhaled sharply, feeling a twinge to his ribs that he ignored since any bruises incurred would fade within a day or two. "Syd, is he threatening to betroth you to Sir Henry? Why did you not come to me as soon as you learned of his plan?"

She gently brushed a stray lock of hair off his brow. "You are a good friend, Octavian. How can I toss you into my father's messes? As for your question, the answer is no. There is no betrothal planned."

"No betrothal?" There was something in the tone of Syd's voice that had Octavian sitting up and grasping her hand. "Is he going to marry you off straight away then? No betrothal contract or banns read? Tell me the truth, Syd. Is this what he plans to do to save his own hide?"

She finally broke down and allowed her tears to fall. "Tomorrow is the big horse auction at Tattersalls, so Sir Henry will be attending that all day. I'm to marry him the day after tomorrow unless I can get my hands on my father's vowels and destroy them. The wedding is to take place at St. Andrew's Church. The plan is for Sir Henry to purchase the license, my father consents, and the ceremony occurs straight afterward. No more than ten minutes, start to finish. Everything a girl dreams of."

Octavian caressed her cheek. Sir Henry Maxwell, the lecherous old goat, had already buried two young wives. He had no intention of allowing Syd to be the third ill-fated wife, although why he should bother was beyond him. He had survived major battles with less injuries than incurred while rescuing this hazardous hoyden from her numerous scrapes. "So, he has no license yet?"

"None yet." She shook her head. "But what does it matter? He and my father have it all arranged. And I cannot find some hapless clot to marry me because I am not yet of age and need my father's consent."

"Hapless clot?" Octavian could not believe what he was about to offer. Syd was the most infuriating young woman it was ever his misfortune to know, but he had somehow taken her under his wing and sworn he would always protect her.

Yes, he had merely sworn this to himself and never actually made that vow to Syd. However, a vow was a vow. It made no difference who knew of it. She was in trouble and he was determined to save her. One thing for certain, life would never be dull with her. He rolled to his feet with care and drew her up along with him. "Come, you little nuisance. We had better leave before we're spotted."

He gave her no chance to protest, quietly lifting her over Sir Henry's gate and climbing over it next. He caught hold of her hand again, refusing to let go of her until they were safely back at his residence because he did not trust her to stay put.

To his surprise, she did not try to fight him. Instead, she cried fresh tears the moment they were safely in his carriage and underway, making rapid time as the conveyance clattered through the London streets that were empty at this late hour.

Seeing her so beaten down was far worse than seeing her angry.

Octavian drew her close and wrapped his arm around her shoulders, wishing she would get that blaze in her eyes and rail at him again.

Seeing her scared and vulnerable completely destroyed him.

The rain had renewed by the time they reached the Thorne townhouse he shared with his brothers. Ambrose, who was the eldest of the Thornes, was Duke of Huntsford and owned the house. He and their youngest brother, Julius, both of them bachelors and not often in London other than on business, shared the home with Ambrose. That would soon have to change since Ambrose was married to Adela, one of Syd's best friends, and they were busy starting a family.

But for now, they were one big, happy family residing together.

Octavian was the only Thorne in London at the moment. Ambrose and Adela were in Devonshire excavating more fossils while Julius was in York attending to family business matters. Octavian was due to travel north to Glasgow and Greenock on behalf of the Royal Navy at the end of the week, an assignment he could not refuse while still actively commissioned.

An idea sprang to mind, but he was not going to discuss it with Syd until they had changed out of their wet clothes and got warm liquids into them.

He took her straight inside as soon as the carriage drew up to the Thorne front gate. "Thank you, Hastings," he said to the driver. "I'll have no further need of the carriage tonight."

"Very good, Captain," the man replied with a nod, obviously relieved to be getting out of the rain himself.

Syd said nothing as they walked inside, but held him back when he was about to lead her upstairs. Her eyes widened in surprise. Well, not surprise so much as shock and horror once the import of what being alone with him meant. "Octavian, do you expect me to spend the night here with you? I–"

"Not another word, Syd. What difference does it make? The best thing that could happen is for word of your indiscretion to get out causing Sir Henry to refuse to marry you."

She did not appear to like the idea at all. "But then he will hurt my father."

"Your father is a little weasel who will manage to slip out of his punishment somehow." Octavian tried to suppress his anger but could not and it resounded in his voice. "Besides, it might do him some good to get knocked about."

"Octavian!"

"The man obviously needs sense pounded into him. Why are you so considerate of him when he never spared a thought for you or your mother? He's burned away the Harcourt assets at the gaming tables or on fanciful business schemes, and does not give a fig about having you bear the punishment for his actions."

Since he was still holding onto Syd's hand, he felt the ripples of shame flow through her. "Sorry, Syd. Falling off a roof in the pouring rain tends to put me in bad humor."

"My father is an awful scoundrel," she said with aching sadness. "I cannot blame you for despising him. But he has been a loving father to me. He does not mean to do the things he does. He keeps thinking his luck will turn with the next roll of the dice or the next ridiculous business venture."

"That does not excuse him." He led her upstairs to his bedchamber and lit a fire in the hearth. The wood had already been stacked neatly in the grate, so it took him little time to get a healthy blaze going. While it was not a cold night, dampness filled the air and Syd was shivering.

He raked a hand through his hair.

What was he to do with her?

She was desperate for help and too ashamed ever to ask for it. Her heart was so battered, she did not even comment when he strode to her side and removed her coat and cap.

Octavian studied her by the golden firelight that illuminated his bedchamber.

She had donned boys clothes that were a few sizes to big for her. Cap, shirt and jacket, breeches, and sturdy boots. Tendrils of wet hair were pasted to her cheeks, and her glorious mass of ginger-blonde hair was barely held up by the few pins that had not yet fallen out.

She was soaked, bedraggled, and looked achingly beautiful.

"I'll fetch you a nightgown and robe from Adela's armoire," he said with a rasp to his voice. "Dry yourself off as best as you can. I won't be gone long."

"Do you expect me to sleep in here?" Her eyes, as she now gazed at him, were an ensorcelling green, as translucent as the crystal lochs one encountered in the Scottish Highlands. They were also filled with pain and humiliation.

"Yes. But we are not going to share the bed, if this is what has you concerned. I am not going to touch you, Syd. You have my word of honor. Let me get those dry garments for you and we'll figure out the rest of it once we have both dried off."

He left before she could object.

It took only a moment for Octavian to dig through Adela's things and pull out a sturdy, cotton nightgown and light woolen robe. He would leave Syd to go through the rest of Adela's belongings tomorrow and pull out whatever gowns and unmentionables she needed for their journey.

What else could he do but take her to Scotland with him? It was the only way to keep her out of Sir Henry's clutches. He had planned to leave at the end of the week, but there was nothing to stop him from leaving tomorrow instead.

All he needed to do was keep weapons out of Syd's reach when he told her what he intended to do. No discussion. She was coming with him.

And he was going to marry her.

"Oh, you're back already." Syd had done little more than pull out the pins in her hair by the time he returned to his bedchamber. It was a large, well-appointed room with a big, canopied bed, a desk, several comfortable chairs, a thick, oriental rug, and an ornate Chinese screen that he had received as a gift from the Admiralty along with a recent promotion.

Syd could easily change behind the screen.

"Here, Syd. Take off your clothes and put these on. I'll turn around while you do."

Octavian could not see over the screen since it was taller than even his impressive height, but wanted to give her that extra margin of comfort and turn away. Besides, he needed to get out of his own sopping wet clothes.

She hesitated, but nodded and dipped behind the screen.

He tossed a towel over it. "Use this to dry yourself off."

"Stop giving me orders, Octavian. I know what to do."

"That's what I'm afraid of," he muttered under his breath, sincerely concerned about her state of mind. Lady Sydney Harcourt, albeit his dream woman – Lord, help him, what a disaster – was just as often the bane of his existence. Stubborn. Reckless. Too smart for her own good.

Too soft for her own good.

Unless he stopped her, she was going to sacrifice herself to save her undeserving father, the Earl of Harcourt, and Octavian had no intention of allowing this to happen. He tried to keep his heart from exploding within his chest as she tossed over each item she had been wearing until she had nothing left to toss and was now naked behind the screen.

Lord, help him.

His heart was not the only body part he could not seem to control.

He had just flung off his jacket, waistcoat, and shirt when she tipped her head around the screen and huffed. "It is not your place to rescue me from my father's mistakes."

He turned fully to face her and strode closer, wanting to grab her by the shoulders and shake sense into her. But he dared not touch her in his current state of arousal. How did this girl manage to turn him upside down? Most times, he did not even like her. "It is not your place to sacrifice yourself on the funeral pyre he created. I don't care what devil's pact your father signed onto. Sir Henry is a blood-sucking leech and you are not going to marry him."

Syd reached out and smacked him on the shoulder. "Octavian! You haven't the right to tell me what to do."

He had every right because he was going to marry her whether she liked it or not. By heaven, he was going to protect her even if it killed him, which it probably would because this girl did not know how to stay out of trouble.

Since she was frowning at him, he suspected she was not going to be happy with his edict. Not that he cared. Someone had to inject sense into this situation.

Not that he was sensible in the least just now.

In leaning over to swat him, Syd had unwittingly given him a glimpse of a bare breast peeking out from under her tumble of hair. He took a step back before he knocked the screen aside and tossed her naked onto his bed.

"I am not discussing this with you," he said with a growl and strode to the fireplace to stare into the flames while struggling to cool the heat pulsing through his loins. After a moment, he spoke again. "You are coming to Scotland with me. Your father will have no obligation to Sir Henry once his vowels are paid, is that right?"

"Yes." Syd fumbled behind the screen to don her borrowed nightgown and robe. "Why are you asking me this? Octavian, do not be so foolish as to consider paying off Sir Henry."

He had stripped out of all but his wet breeches, and thought it safest to keep them on for now. He needed that cold water at his loins because he refused to embarrass himself in front of Syd. She did not love him. He did not love her…that is, what he felt could not possibly be love since half the time he wanted to throttle her.

And yet, he responded to her like a bull in heat. "How great is the debt?"

It could not have been too extravagant since her father had cleared all his past debts only last year after sacrificing his niece to his then largest creditor, a surly but otherwise honest Scot. By chance, the pair fell in love.

Syd would have no such luck.

Sir Henry was repulsive in every way.

Yes, the better plan was to grab Syd and haul her off to safety, her father be damned. Afterward, they would work out the details of a debt repayment and agree to some sort of betrothal arrangement or marriage settlement. Yes, it had to be a marriage settlement. He did not want Syd continuing to be at risk because she was merely betrothed to him. Her father would never honor that betrothal, nor even suffer a pang of conscience before stealing Syd and marrying her off to that repugnant oaf, Sir Henry, or another of his creditors. "We can marry in Scotland without your father's consent."

"I am going to beat you about the head if repeat that suggestion. You must let me go to Sir Henry," Syd said, her voice tight with despair. "*Please.* My father's debt to him exceeds five thousand pounds. I cannot ask you to pay off such a vast sum. So you see, his life is at risk unless my marriage to Sir Henry goes through."

"And what of your life? Save your breath, Syd. I am not allowing him to sell you into bondage for his mistakes. You are not a commodity to be traded in this fashion."

"I know you mean well, but–"

"Be quiet." Octavian knew he could be a rude arse at times, but did this occasion not warrant it? "You are not talking your way out of this."

"And what exactly is *this*? What gives you the right to interfere?" She was standing beside him now, clad in a nightgown buttoned up to her throat and a soft pink robe.

She gazed up at him with her luminescent green eyes. "Octavian," she whispered brokenly and put a hand on his shoulder. "What about your life? Your happiness?"

How could he ever be happy if she was miserable? "We'll work out the terms of our arrangement, I promise. Something to suit us both. I could not live with myself if ever you were hurt."

She pressed her lips to his shoulder. "Why do you have to be so nice to me, you big ox? I have been nothing but trouble for you."

Yes, all she said was true. Why he should bother with her at all was beyond him.

As the son of a duke, and now brother to the current Duke of Huntsford, in addition to being a Royal Navy captain wealthy in his own right, he was used to women fluttering around him, willing to hop into bed with him at his mere nod.

They were easy women.

Uncomplicated.

Demanding nothing of him beyond the pleasure of his body.

So why was he determined to marry Syd, this hoyden who would make it her life's ambition to irritate and rile him?

He saw her shiver lightly as he stared at her.

The girl was scared, but too proud ever to admit it.

So typical of her.

"Gad, you are an idiot," she whispered.

He laughed. "I know."

"Octavian, are you serious about marrying me?"

"Yes, Syd." He stared once more into the flames, afraid to look at her achingly beautiful face for fear he might decide he actually loved her. He wanted affection left out of their union entirely. Syd was already too hard to handle. She would be impossible if she sensed how deeply he cared for her.

Her father needed to suffer a little for his callous behavior and Sir Henry needed to find himself another wife...one who was *not* Syd. In truth, he was doing both men a favor. First, teaching her father there were dire consequences to his foolhardy actions. Second, relieving Sir Henry of the misery Syd would put him through.

This girl was simply not biddable.

"Octavian, if you are going to be stubborn about taking me to Scotland, then you had better know everything. My father has gambled through my dowry and the trust funds my grandmother left me. I went to the bank yesterday and…" Her voice hitched. "The account has been closed. The manager advised me the last of the funds were withdrawn last week. I don't even have the means to run away with you."

"Oh, Syd," he said with a wrenching groan. "You are under my protection now and not going to pay for anything."

"But I would bring nothing into our marriage." She appeared sincerely distressed by something that truly meant nothing to him.

His brother had impressive wealth as Duke of Huntsford, but Octavian had acquired his own fortune on the high seas and never required his brother's largesse to survive in the style to which he had become accustomed. "I don't need your dowry. The decision to marry you has nothing to do with any fortune you might bring with you."

"Which is none."

He wiped a tear off her cheek.

Oh, Lord.

This girl was too proud for her own good.

"We'll figure this out," he said, hoping to console her. He could not bear to see her cry. "I promise you, Syd. You know I would never hurt you."

"I know." She buried her face in her hands. "Oh, why do you insist on saving me? I had numbed myself to the misery of marrying Sir Henry. I was ready."

"You will never be ready for what Sir Henry has in mind for you. Get some sleep now. We have a long journey ahead of us."

She looked up at him. "A fake betrothal might work. Then you would not have to give up your happiness for me."

"A fake betrothal will never work. Your father would never honor it, even if he were inclined to give his consent, which he is not."

"A fake marriage it is then," she said with a nod. "Thank you. I will try to be as unobtrusive as possible."

He suppressed a burst of laughter.

Syd did not know the meaning of unobtrusive.

"I'm not sure how one fakes a marriage," she mused. "Once vows are exchanged, the marriage is presumed done. Once it is consummated, there is no turning back."

She paused to reflect on this a moment longer, then her eyes widened. "Oh, I see. We do not consummate it. Is this what you have in mind? That is an excellent idea. You give me the protection of your name in marriage, but we can always undo it at a later date if it proves necessary. I will turn twenty-one in nine months time. Then I will be free of my father's control…and you have only to say the word to be free of me. I will grant you the annulment if you wish it. I expect such a thing is easily accomplished in Scotland since they are quite lax about this sort of thing, right? Quick ceremony. No bother about being of age. Quietly undone within the year. Thank you, Octavian. Yes, I will marry you. I wish we were on the road already. Nine months," she repeated softly. "I don't even have nine minutes to spare."

"We'll leave tomorrow morning and stop off at Gretna Green before making our way to the Greenock shipyards." He had won this round, but why did he feel like the loser? It would not be a true marriage. She would leave him in nine months time. Would they lead separate lives all the while?

"How are we to travel north?" she asked, now smiling as they made their plans.

"In one of the Huntsford carriages. Do you think I travel by mail coach?"

She gave a soft trill of laughter. "No, I don't suppose you do." But her mirth quickly faded. "Octavian…"

"What, Syd?"

She clasped her hands in front of her and would not look him in the eye as she spoke. "What *arrangements* are we to have on the way up?"

Bed. Naked. Wild, wanton sex.

But that was just his aching loins having a say, and the last thing Syd needed to hear. "The thing of it is," he said, trying to sound logical so as not to scare her off, "I cannot leave you in a room on your own. Your father and Sir Henry will quickly figure out you have run off and might pick up our trail. It is safest if we share a room. I can make a pallet for myself on the floor wherever we stay. In any event, no reputable inn will allow an unmarried lady as young and pretty as you to sign in on her own. You'll have to pretend to be my wife, just for the week it takes us to cross into Scotland. We'll travel fast. Marry the moment we cross the border. Then you will be my wife in truth."

She stared up at him with those ensorcelling eyes of hers. "So, just to be clear...in that time, what will you expect of me?"

"On the trip to Scotland? Nothing of *that* sort, Syd. I will not touch you without your willingness. But what I will expect is for you to behave, to actually look like a newlywed in love, to not run off on your own as though you answer to nobody, or punch some poor wretch because he uttered a remark not to your liking. Can you do this?"

"Of course, I can. Do you have so little faith in me?"

"I have every faith you are going to make me regret this undertaking."

"Octavian!"

He ignored her indignant huff.

There was more to discuss, but he was tired and still a bit achy from that fall. He wanted to check out the lump on his head which was merely the size of a tiny goose egg and had not broken skin, but one could not be too careful about such things. Then he wanted to sleep. There would be time tomorrow to think about their marriage plans. She believed an unconsummated marriage was something easy to annul. In truth, it was not. There needed to be more grounds than the bride remained a virgin.

Both of them would have to come to terms with this being a permanent marriage if an annulment was impossible. Divorce was out of the question for him. He had a career in the Royal Navy. He would soon be made an Admiral of the Fleet.

All would be lost if they divorced.

Even a quiet annulment might ruin his standing.

"Syd, if the fake marriage cannot be undone, can you be my wife in truth?"

She looked up at him again. "Share your bed? Bear your children? Is this what you are demanding?"

"I am only trying to think of all possibilities."

"I see. It is not an easy answer, but something we must consider before taking another step. I have never even kissed you."

"That is something easily remedied."

"I suppose." She nodded, reaching out and lightly running her finger across his lips. "In truth, I have never kissed anyone before."

This was not surprising, for Syd, as beautiful as she was, tended to scare off men. She was very smart. In fact, he considered her brilliant. Easily smarter than him when it came to book knowledge. "Then I'll be gentle."

Her eyes grew wide again. "You will?"

Octavian nodded. "I will always be gentle with you. You need never worry that I will hurt you."

"It never crossed my mind. Truly, Octavian. I know you are big and can appear quite daunting when you scowl, which you seem to do a lot around me. But I have always trusted you. You are the most honorable man I know. Well, same can be said for your brothers. Your father raised excellent sons."

He breathed a sigh of relief, for was this not a major step toward a good marriage? They had no chance at a decent union if there was no trust between them. It also helped if the wife was not deathly afraid of the husband.

He did not think Syd was afraid of anything.

Well, having to marry Sir Henry Maxwell had her gravely concerned.

Octavian tipped her chin up so that their gazes met. "I am going to kiss you now, Syd. All right?"

She nodded.

"Close your eyes and put all thoughts out of your head. Kisses are about pleasure. No ploys or stratagems required."

"I will try. But I am very tense right now. Not merely because I am about to be kissed by you, which is an unexpected turn of events, but a welcome one, if I am to be truthful about it. But I have so much on my mind, and now I have to worry about letting you down."

"You will not let me down." He took her hands and placed them lightly on his shoulders.

"How can I not? I am a novice at this and...oh, you've wrapped your arms around me."

"Keep yours on my shoulders. Close your eyes and stop talking."

"Well, that is not very romantic of you."

"Sorry. I do not want you talking yourself into a state of fretting. Kisses are about feelings, Syd. How does it feel for you to be in my arms?"

"Unexpected, actually." She reached up and nuzzled his neck. "Is that bergamot?"

He nodded.

"The scent is nice on you. Your skin is warm. Your body is surprisingly nice. Well, not very surprising. It's just...you have no shirt on and I am touching your skin. I've seen naked cadavers, of course. But this is not at all the same thing. Would we do this in the marriage?"

"What? Me holding you in my arms? If you like."

"Octavian, you are being remarkably cooperative."

He stifled his laughter, knowing she was already tense and would run off at his slightest misstep. "It is what husbands and wives do in a good marriage."

She nestled against his chest. "My parents have a horrible marriage. The only thing I learned from them was never to do what they did. Please don't be angry with me if I make mistakes. Starting with kisses. My parents never kiss each other."

"Then this is important, Syd. If you don't like my kisses, we had better rethink the situation."

"I'll consider it carefully. I promise."

This is what he liked about Syd, her natural honesty.

She was not a schemer or a manipulator. You always got the truth from her. Perhaps this is why he felt confident she would give him an honest answer about their kiss, even if it did set her plans back to square one.

She tilted her head up to give him unimpeded access to her lips.

He closed his mouth over hers, pressing down gently at first, and then sinking his mouth deeper onto hers until he felt her fingers curl upon his shoulders and heard a soft moan escape her lips.

He held her in his arms as though she were delicate and precious, which she was...although perhaps not really delicate. He liked that she was brave and spirited, and especially liked that she was now kissing him back with innocent ardor.

Blessed saints!

What was he doing?

Had this kiss just sealed his fate?

He ended the kiss and awaited her response.

She stared at him for the longest time, then burst into tears.

This is why Syd was the most frustrating young woman it was ever his misfortune to know. Could she not even test out a kiss without twisting his heart in knots? "Syd, stop crying. Are you going to marry me or not?"

GET THE MAKE-BELIEVE MARRIAGE NOW!

Interested in learning more about the Farthingale series? Join me on Facebook! Additionally, we'll be giving away lots of Farthingale swag and prizes during the launches. If you would like to join the fun, you can subscribe to my newsletter and also connect with me on Twitter. You can find links to do all of this at my website: mearaplatt.com.

If you enjoyed this book, I would really appreciate it if you could post a review on the site where you purchased it. Also feel free to write one on Goodreads or other reader sites that you peruse. Even a few sentences on what you thought about the book would be most helpful! If you do leave a review, send me a message on Facebook because I would love to thank you personally. Please also consider telling your friends about the FARTHINGALE SERIES and recommending it to your book clubs.

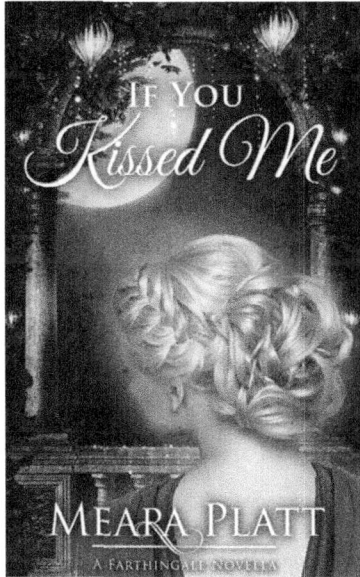

Sign up for Meara Platt's newsletter
and you'll receive a free, exclusive copy
of her Farthingale novella,
If You Kissed Me.

Visit her website
to grab your free copy:
mearaplatt.com

●

ALSO BY MEARA PLATT

The Touch of Love
The Taste of Love
The Song of Love
The Scent of Love
The Kiss of Love
The Chance of Love
The Gift of Love
The Heart of Love
The Hope of Love (novella)
The Promise of Love
The Wonder of Love
The Journey of Love
The Treasure of Love
The Dance of Love
The Miracle of Love
The Dream of Love (novella)
The Remembrance of Love (novella)

BOOK OF LOVE CONNECTED NOVELLAS
All I Want For Christmas (novella)
Tempting Taffy (novella)

DARK GARDENS SERIES
Garden of Shadows
Garden of Light
Garden of Dragons
Garden of Destiny
Garden of Angels

THE BRAYDENS
A Match Made In Duty
Earl of Westcliff
Fortune's Dragon

ABOUT THE AUTHOR

Meara Platt is an award winning, USA TODAY bestselling author and an Amazon UK All-Star. Her favorite place in all the world is England's Lake District, which may not come as a surprise since many of her stories are set in that idyllic landscape, including her paranormal romance Dark Gardens series. Learn more about the Dark Gardens and Meara's lighthearted and humorous Regency romances in her Farthingale series and Book of Love series, or her warmhearted Regency romances in her Braydens series or Moonstone Landing series by visiting her website at www.mearaplatt.com.

Printed in Great Britain
by Amazon